# BENSON AT SIXTY

**Also by Michael Carson:**

*Sucking Sherbet Lemons*

*Friends and Infidels*

*Coming Up Roses*

*Stripping Penguins Bare*

*Yanking Up the Yo-Yo*

*Serving Suggestions* (short stories)

*Demolishing Babel*

*The Knight of the Flaming Heart*

*Dying in Style*

*Hubbies*

*Previously Loved* (an exhibition and catalogue)

*The Rule of Twelfths* (short stories)

# BENSON AT SIXTY

## MICHAEL CARSON

For Peter and Diane Clee ... and their Family

# Sonnet 30

When to the sessions of sweet silent thought
I summon up remembrance of things past,
I sigh the lack of many a thing I sought,
And with old woes new wail my dear time's waste:
Then can I drown an eye, unused to flow,
For precious friends hid in death's dateless night,
And weep afresh love's long since cancell'd woe,
And moan the expense of many a vanish'd sight:
Then can I grieve at grievances foregone,
And heavily from woe to woe tell o'er
The sad account of fore-bemoaned moan,
Which I new pay as if not paid before.
But if the while I think on thee, dear friend,
All losses are restored and sorrows end.

– William Shakespeare

# PART 1

# Q.A.

# 1

His trusty backpack over his shoulder, Benson walked from the station through the park. As he walked, listening to *The Coffee Cantata* on his MP3 player, he kept a weather eye out for druggies, and rough boys and girls from Sir William Grout's Media City Academy, while at the same time trying to stop his ear-buds from dropping out.

The ear-buds were irritating Benson. They had come with the bottom-of-the-range MP3 player and were worked into the cord that he was supposed to place around his neck in order to allow the little player to sway on his front like some medal of modernity. Problem was, no matter how he fiddled and twisted them into his ear canal, the ear-buds fled from him.

Should he take the MP3 player back to Asda and inform some hapless associate that there was no such thing as progress? Or soldier on and see if his ears would get the message and somehow exercise muscles not exercised before to hold the earbuds inside his portals? It might just happen, of course. But if Benson's experience of life was anything to go by, it probably wouldn't.

What would he say to the lady at Asda's help desk? He could not find any fault in the little player, a minor miracle in its way. It weighed hardly anything, and he could not get his head around the way it stored so much. No, it was the mode of delivery that did not suit him. Did he have freaky ears? Once upon a time he'd thought they stuck out, but he'd forgotten about all that for many a long year. He had not heard people complaining about ear-buds falling out. He'd seen kids barrelling along on bicycles – on the pavement, of course – with them sticking in their ears as if held tight by superglue. Even the queer little jumps the kids made atop their queer little bikes would not shift them. It was the Devil's own job to find earphones with bands that crowned the head and fixed themselves upon the ear. They were certainly never offered as part of the MP3 package.

Were they designed for Chinese ears – and Chinese ears alone? Did the manufacturers not think to collar a few expatriate English teachers and explore the terrain of the western ear canal in all its variety and wonder? Had Asda bought a consignment from China that didn't suit the Western market?

Perhaps he'd arrive at the help desk and the lady would say: 'Don't tell me! It's the ear-buds, isn't it, love? I wish I had a pound for every customer who's had to bring them back because of that. A real design fault. Pity. Nice little player otherwise, and designed with an eye to the customer-on-a-budget. Did you try them in the wind, by any chance? A lot of customers say they just fly out of the ear in the least bit of wind. Is that *The Coffee Cantata* you've uploaded – or should I say downloaded? I thought so. And it's the Fischer-Dieskau isn't it? Hard to find, but well worth the search. Never been bettered.'

Benson sometimes tried making his black woolly cap – bought at Gap in a sale so deep that the purchase had made him feel cheap at checkout – fit over the ear-buds and anchor them into his ear canal. This worked after a fashion, but the weather was not cold enough to justify a hat, so he sweated as he listened to Bach, which was really not the object of the exercise.

What would Johann Sebastian Bach, mighty Bach, Shakespeare reborn for music, with his output of a dozen kids and music filling 170 compact discs ... what would The Man make of this MP3 player? Benson had heard they stole quality from sound to compress it and fit more on. Was there advance or retreat for civilisation in his little gizmo? He'd have to consider that further. It definitely shut out the Babel of Birkenhead – at least when the wind dropped. But in that shut-out sound was life. So was it just another isolating device, one more thing to distract, keep people away from the richness of a billion God-given present moments? Anyway, one thing was for sure – maybe – Johann Sebastian would not have been able to avail himself of an MP3 player, not with all those kids, demanding patrons, those choirs and orchestras and mighty German organs to see too.

Benson turned off the MP3 player, surrendering to the hubbub of the real world, as opposed to that of his own mind, and let the buds fall from his head and hang down below his chest, a bit like his chests were starting to do.

What was he doing here?

He hadn't walked up this road since 1965.

St Bede's was still going. He knew from *Friends Reunited* – a site he tiptoed around anonymously – that it was. But the Brothers had taken a back seat. The MP3 player of the school still pushed out education in Catholic Surround Sound, but the means of communication, the ear-buds of The Lord that had made such an indelible impression on Benson, had largely fallen by the wayside.

Benson came to the roundabout thinking of change, decay, transmutation and disappointment. Up the hill stood the gates of St Bede's. All I need to do is knock at the door and ask for Brother Hooper. Then I'll tell him that

I am Martin Benson, make my apologies for the past, and wish him a happy retirement. Then off to Littlewoods' closing-down sale for a suit. What could be simpler?

Well, a lot could be simpler. Like spreading an MP3 player with peanut butter and Marmite, popping the confection into his mouth like a savoury Mars Bar. And swallowing. That would be easier. Still, Rob says that it has to be done. If I am to be well-adjusted and stay sober, I've got to clean my side of the street.

Benson stopped, contemplating the hill up to St Bede's. *My side of the street.* Don't make me laugh! What about *his* side of the street?

But that was no good. Rob had nodded sagely – he was a master at nodding sagely – and said that Brother Hooper's side of the street was Brother Hooper's own concern. It was clear that Benson had been haunted by his old headmaster for the forty years since leaving St Bede's. The steps that Benson was taking demanded that he surrender not only to his addiction to alcohol, but to all the character traits that had caused him to drink so obsessively. Resentments, Rob asserted, were the number one cause of alchies slipping, and Benson's resentments against the Brothers in general and Brother Hooper in particular were holding back his recovery. Time to bite the bullet and lance the malignant pustule – first boiling the lance – and walk away with a spirited spring in his step to become the New and Improved, Sober Martin Benson.

'But what if he gives me a hard time?' he'd said to Rob, like a runt squaddie pleading with a steely sergeant major to be excused P.T.

'Not your concern. Ninety-nine per cent of what happens is not your business, Martin.'

'But what if he won't accept my apology?'

'Not your concern. You're doing this for your own peace of mind.'

'But what if he runs to the drawer and brings out his big black strap?'

'Make an excuse and leave ... this isn't about pleasure.'

'But what if...'

The conversation had gone on and on. Every time Benson encountered Rob – several times a day, seeing that they lived together – he was asked if he had done the deed. Benson shook his head like a naughty boy who'd not done his homework. Rob, unimpressed, said, 'You do want to keep your sobriety, don't you? You do want to be happy? You've got to root out all the things in your life which made you drink.'

Benson had nodded. 'OK-OK, I'll do it.'

Rob said he'd heard that before. He did not want to see Benson again until he had done the deed. They would stay in their respective parts of the house. Neither did he want any of Benson's succinct textings, long phone calls or companionable walks on sandbanks. Only with amends made to Brother Hooper would he be allowed back to Rob's scrawny bosom, to bask in the wan sunlight of his friend's approval. But it was all so hard! Why was everything so *fucking hard*?

Benson looked at St Bede's grand gates, grand as any stately home's. Across the gravel path was the front door of the Brothers' House. Inside would be Brother Hooper, greatly changed, doubtless ekeing out his retirement in the big house and surrounded by big books full of great ideas, or, rather, Great Ideas, and praying for the souls of all those gone-before or gone-over-the-wall or closed souls in open prisons, Brothers.

'This is a moment of decision,' Benson told himself. He looked up at the sky, his favourite bit of Merseyside, for a sign. But, apart from a gas-guzzling EasyJet making its approach to John Lennon Airport through the murk of grey, there were none that struck him as in any way definite.

'Above us only sky' was John Lennon Airport's motto. Benson shook his head at the line. It was obvious even to the dimmest gink that there was far more above us than sky. There was The Unknown for a start and Lennon, with his Maharishi and psychedelic advantages over ordinary mortals, should have known that better than most. But John Lennon couldn't resist rhyming 'try' and 'sky'. Probably wrote it in some purple haze with Yoko slicing the sushi in the their posh kitchen looking out over Central Park, little knowing that long after what he was to know of his story had ended, some grey committee in Liverpool Council would sit around some overpriced table and brainstorm his name and unimaginative line onto Speke Airport. 'Good for business,' they'd say. The bottom line. The world was always bouncing along the bottom line, or so it often seemed to Benson.

Mind you, Wirral Council could be just as bad. They placed the little aspirational tag, 'Wirral has heard the cry of The Earth', on all their wheely bins into which the populace consigned old computers, tins, plastics, rubble and, in certain notorious cases, body parts. They called Wirral 'Eurowirral,' then stopped. They...

*Accept the things you cannot change...* He heard Rob say it. Clear as anything. A sign?

He projected himself forward into the next five minutes. He heard his feet crunch the gravel. The ring of the bell, the barking of the white Pyrennean mountain dog the

8

Brothers had doted on (no, he'd have been dead for forty years). The grand vestibule, the turning staircase, a whiff of cabbage and incense as the door opened. A lower, stale stench: the sweat of middle-aged male virgins. A stench which, now a phantom in his nostrils, filled him with old stale fears, only cured in the old stale days by communion of bottle-neck with gullet.

'Yes?'

'I don't know if you remember me.'

'I remember you. You're Martin Benson who left the Brothers under a cloud and came back here to screw as much education as you could out of us. Glad to see you've kept the weight off. Mind you, obesity's all the rage these days. What can I do for you?

'Er...' *Clean your side of the street!*

'Out with it, man!'

'Er...' *You a man or a mouse, or wa?*

'Married, are you?'

'Er...' *Fuckin' gerron with i'!*

'Grandchildren by now, I suppose? Good Catholics all. Mind you, no Bensons at St Bede's. I'd've remembered. Too thick are they? Isn't the new pope a fine man?'

'I've come to ... to...'

Littlewoods' closing-down sale sirened. They might run out. I'll come back later. He put the earphones back in and switched on to switch off both present and past.

He made a resolute left turn towards the town centre.

# 2

The salesman in Littlewoods headed straight for Benson. Benson could see it happening. He tried to move on ... away from the four or five suits remaining with their big red price stickers on them, price after price crossed out and lowered to the £19.99 that had started his pulse racing ... to Underwear. But the man followed. Lord, Benson thought, he must be desperate. I'm usually invisible in shops. I have to throw a tantrum to get help – not that Rob allows me tantrums these days.

The odd bits of unloved underwear gave Benson no protection. The salesman still had him in his sights. He backed into a rail of dressing-gowns. One slipped off its metal hanger and swooned on to the parquet floor. Benson trod on it, an old-fashioned woollen one with a muted tartan pattern. It brought Dad to mind. He looked down at it. *Shop-soiled*, he thought. A bit like me.

'A sad day,' the salesman said.

Benson was startled. Momentarily he wondered if the man was privy to his forlorn performance outside St Bede's. Or had something shocking happened in the great world between the end of the nine o' clock news and now? Another 9-11, perhaps, or the Queen finally keeling over? Benson couldn't help but feel a little sorry for the salesman. He looked a bit long-in-the-tooth to be on his feet all day. Pity about the weakish chin. A strong chin with a bit of jut made it harder for its double to really take hold and hang down unflatteringly. It wasn't that the man was fat. Maybe he was on statins and had gone soft. Statins caused muscle to waste. Benson blamed his bingo wings on statins. But to end up hang-dog and desperate in a hang-dog and desperate closing-down sale! How old was he? Fifty-five? Sixty? Same as me, give or take. And, if I'm honest, pretty much in the same leaky boat. *Should not have got old without being wise.* 'A bit,' Benson said.

'Really deep cuts. Most extreme cuts. Cuts to the bone. Nay, cut clean to and through the marrow.'

The penny dropped, but the tinkles as it danced on the parquet echoed Benson's failed mission of the day.

And Life? Where had all that gone to? And that nice parquet? When the shop shut, what would happen to that perfectly serviceable flooring? Would it serve for whatever Littlewoods morphed into after closure? A Pound Shop? A Primark? A Drop-In Centre for the council? Or would it be ripped up, wheely-binned, buried or burned? And what would happen to the salesman?

'You require a suit, sir?' the sad salesman asked.

'Yes, I do. I have been told that a man my age should have a suit. Tell you the truth, I don't wear suits when I can help it.'

'You distrust any enterprise that requires new clothes, do you, sir?' the sad salesman said, managing a sad smile.

Henry David Thoreau! Odd to hear him quoted in a dying Littlewoods' branch. A bit like coming upon Maria Callas singing for spare change in the Lime Street subway tunnel.

Benson couldn't resist. He picked up the intellectual baton, and ran with it, across the finishing line of the Sad Aphorism race (Over-Fifties Only).

'Most men live lives of quiet desperation,' Benson said.

'Very true,' the sad salesman said, with a wide smile

that brushed his sadness away. 'I used to be a teacher, but I retired hurt.'

'I know what you mean. Do – did – you enjoy working here?'

'You know, I did – do. You meet people – like your good self – and every day's a bit different. Also, you can leave it all behind when the shop shuts.'

'That's nice. More than nice. Essential. I was a teacher,' Benson said, and he thought, *If I'd stuck to it, I could be here now, one deep straight furrow to look back on with sweet satisfaction, and a pension in prospect...*

'Really? Where?'

'Abroad,' Benson said. 'I started teaching kids – in Liverpool. Wayne Rooney's alma mater actually. But I couldn't take it. Felt like a kid myself. When the kids headed for me along the corridor like Mogul Hordes, I just panicked. So I got out of that and started teaching English as a foreign language.'

'There's a lot of it about. Where did you go?'

'Saudi Arabia, Oman, Iran, Sumatra, Borneo, Nigeria, Ghana, Colchester...'

'Not much call for suits, then.'

'Suits,' Benson said. 'Ah, yes. I'd forgotten them. Mind you, even *that* teaching didn't really suit me. I never found anything that quite suited me.' What was he doing, waxing all confessional in the closing-down Littlewoods? Well, why not? Why the fuck not? It was bred in the bone. In the marrow. Suited him. Always had. Only trouble was, he could never quite tell the whole truth about the past. He was still a bred-in-the-bone liar while in confessional mode.

'Retired now, are you?'

'Semi. I burn words and pictures on wood. It's called 'pyrography'.'

'And is there much call for it?'

'There wasn't at first, but there's a growing interest. Sometimes I can't keep up with the demand.'

The salesman seemed pleased. 'Can't keep up with the demand. I quite envy you, sir.' He glanced around at what remained of the shop. 'Would that we were similarly placed.'

'I offer a variety of items. What I do is this: I buy breadboards, wooden spoons, mallets ... from cheap shops, and add value.'

'And what do you write on them?'

'I like to write poems. I'm fond of poetry, and pyrographing poems helps get them into my head.'

'Mmm...'

'But my biggest selling items assert "Souvenir of..." followed by the holiday destination. I can burn them in no time, but they don't give me much in the way of satisfaction. I also do sayings: "Live and Let Live", "Live For Today" ... that sort of thing. And a popular one is, "Have I turned the gas off?" I've been told by people who have given them to the elderly that they're a life-saver.'

'What do you write on mallets?'

*'If I had a hammer, I'd hammer in the morning. I'd hammer in the evening, All over this land. I'd hammer out justice. I'd hammer out a warning. I'd hammer out the love between my brothers and my sisters all over this land.'*

'Trini Lopez,' said the salesman.

'Peter, Paul and Mary,' said Benson.

'So your work is useful as well as artistic?'

Benson thought about that. 'I like to think so,' he said, as though he were being grilled by Mark Lawson.

The salesman looked around. 'It's fascinating,' he said

– and Benson believed he was speaking the truth. 'But I'd better get back to the vexed question at hand.'

'Suppose so.'

The salesman rooted through the rail of suits at speed.

'I also pyrograph on pieces of driftwood,' Benson said.

The salesman took out a suit, appraised it and replaced it. 'Do you use a poker?' he asked, returning to rooting.

'Sometimes. But the poker is difficult to control (*You can say that again!*). I have a range of pyrography pens. You plug them into the mains. The nibs are made of wire. Different thicknesses. I make them myself. I also use the sun and a magnifying glass when I can. That needs a very steady hand.'

'But most ecological and environmentally friendly, sir!'

'Yes, I suppose it is. I hadn't thought of that. Perhaps I should put "Sun burnt" on the back. And "No electricity was used in the manufacture of this quality product".'

'Maybe you should,' the salesman said, and let out an exclamation of satisfaction.

He held out a black suit with an unusual blue stripe. He turned from looking at the suit to appraising Benson. 'This is a nice one. Not sure the trousers will fit, but they might. What do you think? This would suit a wedding or a funeral.'

'That's handy. I want one that'll see me out.'

'You shouldn't talk like that.' And the salesman gave way to a little shiver that was both sad ... and camp.

'S'pose not.'

'Not married yourself, sir?'

'No. How about you?'

'Was. You know.'

Benson didn't. He nodded sagely, like a man of the world. 'I'll try that suit,' he said.

'The fitting room's this way, sir,' the salesman said. 'I'll bring my tape measure.'

'Call me Martin,' Benson said.

# 3

Benson left the stripped and expiring cadaver of Littlewoods with a spring in his step, a suit in a big Littlewoods bag scrunching his left leg, where tottered the shadow of tumescence – and the sad salesman's telephone number. His name was Len and he was free most evenings, he told Benson, as he pressed the tape measure with great conviction against the no-man's-land between scrotum and arsehole and, pushing hard, announced, 'Thirty inches. In old money.'

'I'm usually twenty-nine,' Benson said.

'You dress on the right.'

'Er ... do I? Normally I think I stick out slightly in the middle.'

'You are a card.'

'Am I?'

Benson stopped and transferred the suit to his knapsack. He wondered as he did so if he ought. The suit might crinkle. And the bag might crinkle too. The bag might be worth storing under his mattress in a pristine condition. With Littlewoods no more he might be able to produce the bag in twenty years' time – if he was spared that long – and evoke cries of tearful sentimentality from the populace. They'd gather round him and offer big bucks or, if he ever got the hang of eBay – he could buy there but couldn't master sell – he'd be able to sell it there.

He put the earphones into his ears and switched the

player on. The MP3, as was its bottom-of-the-range custom, went back to the start of *The Coffee Cantata*. He pushed the slide a few times and found *Missa Luba*.

The buds stayed put. They stayed put in spite of a wind blowing over Birkenhead town centre from the north, in spite of the loud drums and the voices of his old friends, the African children. The voices told him to retrace his steps, scrunch the gravel, ring the doorbell and do the necessary with Brother Hooper.

But *Missa Luba* had told him all sorts of things in the half-century since he had first heard it while sitting round Novvy's Black Box stereo with the other novices. The music had beckoned him to search out the poor and share their fate; to embrace joy of life and warmer climes and people. He had never tired of the piece, but never quite managed to obey its simple message. His original EP had been lost in Aberystwyth; the LP bought in Times Square (that had included *Missa Criolla*) had been scratched into oblivion. For years Benson lived on his memories of the piece until Amazon flowed into his life and promised a CD. Then, after days of difficulty, he had converted the CD to MP3 and inserted it into his new purchase.

Funny how the music of his teens stayed with him. He had overlaid that basic stock of *War Requiem* and *Missa Luba* and *Matthew Passion* and *Hary Janos* and *Rite of Spring* and Percy French and *West Side Story* and *Carousel* and *Elizabeth Schwartzkopf Sings Songs You Love* and Jimmy Crumit and Joan Baez and Bob Dylan's first eight L.P.s, and everything by Leonard Cohen, with everything by Mahler and Bach and Wagner and Schutz and Springsteen and Armstrong and Roberta Flack and Peter Gabriel and Schubert and Um Kalthoum and Fairuz and Ravi Shankar and Stevie Wonder and Richard Thompson and *Billy Budd* and *Peter Grimes* and *Death In Venice* and Skip James and Blind Willie Johnson and John Prine. But those first things, bought and played into scratched-to-death black halos, were the ones which still fully tumesced his flaccid heart.

Though Benson had only a passing knowledge of Youth Culture – overheard on pavements as it squirted like piss from passing cars; viewed with open-mouthed horror as he flicked Freeview channels – he wanted to tell Youth that it ought to be stocking the nests of its never-more-open-than-now brain and heart with quality stuff. Were they all going to end up at sixty with 'Fuck your bitch' echoing again and again in its myriad crass computations where Benson had the *Missa Luba*? But he pulled back. *You can't look at me and not see yourself.* That's what Stevie Wonder sang on his new CD. It was exactly what Rob told him as well. When Benson went on and on about the state of things, Rob looked bored and said, 'But look where your ideas have got you? Fuckin' well Live and Let Live.'

Yes, but...

*Missa Luba* was working now! He passed Marriot's Motorcycles and ogled the bikes. So closely did he ogle them that his nose hit the pristine plate glass, leaving an unsightly grease mark. Should he go in? No. If he went in he'd have to interrupt *Missa Luba* and maybe face Mr Marriot's ire about the grease mark. Anyway, *Missa Luba* was directing his feet back to Brother Hooper. If I get there before the end of the 'Agnus Dei' I'll do it. It will have been *meant*. He dawdled. The piece finished just after he passed Birkenhead museum, which wasn't a patch on Liverpool's and belonged in a museum. That's clever, he thought. Did I think that up? 'Birkenhead museum belongs in a museum.' No, probably not.

But the urge to get the deed done had not gone. He flicked the slide back and after some interference from *The Coffee Cantata*, Benson managed to find the start of *Missa Luba* again. This time it would be *really* meant if he could make it to the gate before it finished.

On *Desert Island Discs* Ken Livingstone had chosen *Missa Luba* for one of his eight. A man of great taste and discernment. But Ken said after Sue had played the piece – the 'Sanctus' – that probably all the singers were dead, killed by the ravages in the Congo since independence from Belgium. No, surely not! Benson'd thought, stopping what he was doing (making an All-bran loaf). But why not? He'd seen people casually killed. He knew a bit about killing and chaos. Benson listened the harder.

Pasolini had used *Missa Luba* in his film of *The Gospel According to Matthew*. Pasolini's films were the visual equivalent of his teenage music obsessions. He never tired of rewatching Pasolini. Was that because of *Missa Luba*? No, it was much more than that. But *Missa Luba* was a symptom. The 'Sanctus' had been used in Lindsay Anderson's *If*, but he did not chase up copies of *If* or the rest of Anderson's output. I could be the only person in the world listening to *Missa Luba* at this precise moment, Benson thought. He often thought such thoughts. He had thought this while watching the BBC production of *Cymbeline* the previous night on his DVD player.

Brother Hooper had told Benson to read a Shakespeare play every week for the rest of his life. He had not, though he had gone to see Shakespeare whenever he could – not often. But was it having Brother Hooper on his mind now, and for some decades, that had caused him to accept the offer of *The Complete Plays of Shakespeare* from the BBC Shop (at some considerable saving) reasoning that it would be the only way to really absorb The Bard before the grim reaper took him to the winnowing barn? It wouldn't do to arrive in heaven – if heaven was his destination – meet the Bard and not be able to say he'd seen and absorbed all his oeuvre, would it?

Benson arrived at the gate of St Bede's just as the 'Sanctus' was finishing. By some strange grace, he did not hesitate. He scrunched across the gravel, frowned at the weeds – seeing them as a mirror of his beboozed, bamboozled soul – and rang the bell.

# 4

'How long is it?' Brother Hooper asked.

'Over forty years.'

'Strange.'

Benson shifted in the easy chair uneasily. He nodded, but could not think of anything to say. Brother Hooper was looking at him. His bottom lip cradled his upper lip as if he were about to cry, while the rest of his face – all point and overhang – stressed the total impossibility of such a melting. A long silence followed.

It was uncomfortable at first. Benson frantically delved about for something to say. A few wise aphorisms bubbled up, but they would not have cut the mustard. Brother Hooper did not seem to be uncomfortable. He hardly seemed to be 'Brother Hooper' in fact. It was daft for Benson to think that the door would be answered by the Brother Hooper of forty years ago. The man who had been his headmaster had lived more years since Benson had last seen him than he had lived before. Of course he was different.

This was the room in which Brother Kay – the vocations Brother – had looked at Benson with excited – and exciting – appraisal and pronounced that Benson had a vocation from God to be a Brother. The room had been richly Victorian then. But, like Benson and Brother Hooper, it had not been spared forty years. A stick-figure crucifix in steel hung where the highly realistic and bloody one

21

had been. Pine tongue-and-groove aged by tobacco and time and the breath from rosary recitations and parental complaints and Brothers announcing that they planned to leave ... covered the walls and ceiling. The easy chairs were institutional Ercol, ready at any moment to be moved about to form the shape for meetings and staff conferences and sad little partings and reunions – like the one about to take place. It was a utilitarian room. No longer the Brothers' Parlour, the place where the congregation came to unwind, drink a dram and bitch about such as Benson, well out of earshot of the chalky world.

And what about him? If Brother Hooper had changed, what about Benson?

He did not want to go down his side of that street.

Brother Hooper was still regarding Benson. His expression had not altered. Rob could be like that. Rob was great at silence, generally when Benson had said something that hinted at some tip-of-the-tongue trickle of honesty, but did not complete the declaration. What would Rob say now, if he were sitting here? *Fuckin' well get on with it!* That's what Rob would say.

'I came to apologise,' Benson said.

'Did you? What for?'

It was Benson's turn to cradle his lip. 'I have gossiped shamefully about the bad treatment I got from you – forgetting all the good things you gave me.'

'There's been a lot of that about. Apology accepted. I apologise to you for the mistakes we made. We were, I suppose, of the times. Times have changed.'

'Oh. Er...'

Brother Hooper asked Benson if he'd like a sherry. Benson declined, and Brother Hooper poured himself a glass. He was still as tall and angular as ever. What was different? The face was lined, but he had no double chin, and his neck was in better shape than Benson's. He sat back down and took a sip. Then he looked at his watch. No glasses! He wasn't wearing glasses! Had he had that pricey Russian op? Surely not. Contact lenses? Probably, but a bit vain. A miracle?

'Have I come at a busy time?' Benson asked.

'I am retired,' Brother Hooper said. 'But I find it wise to observe routines. I fulfil the role of caretaker at St Bede's. I pick up crisp packets, rub off graffiti written on toilet walls that impugn the integrity of various members of staff. I brush leaves, and mow lawns. And I consider my life, just as you seem to have been doing. You know what they say, don't you?'

'The unconsidered life is not worth living.'

'Precisely, though I prefer, "un*examined*".'

'Mind you,' Benson said, as he had often said before, 'the over-examined life is not worth living either.'

'I wouldn't know. I don't think I've reached that stage yet.'

'Er...' Was that a put-down? Was Brother Hooper saying that he, Benson, was boasting of the extent of his self-examination? 'I was joking,' Benson lied.

Brother Hooper nodded. 'Did you recognise me when I came to the door?'

'After a moment, yes. There haven't been many days since I left St Bede's when I haven't thought of you.'

'I could be flattered, I suppose. But, like much of education, our teachers are so memorable because constant repetition of the same faces and foibles lodge them firmly in the brain. You saw me every day for several very impressionable years. Not surprising that you remembered me. I remember most of my own teachers. And they, were they living, would remember theirs – and so back in a seamless classroom tree to the very start of things. I did not remember you, however. Not at once.'

Benson could not resist a feeling of great disappointment that he had not been the object of Brother Hooper's obsessive thoughts and resentments over the last four decades. But that was part of his own self-obsession. It did not take a genius to do the sum of how many boys went through a teacher's career compared to the number of teachers through a boy's.

'You never joined St Bede's Old Boys?'

'I didn't feel I'd be welcome.' And as he said it, Benson realised for the first time in his life the deep structure of Old Boys. It came as quite a fright. That's what I am! An old boy, a child who's grown old, a lost baby soul in an old body. *Here's one for the lost soul, Benson!* Who'd said that? No more than the truth. So why had it taken him all this time to understand it? Cocks coming at him from the past ... through holes in walls, over sand dunes and rainforest tracks, at the front door of foreign flats, in blacked-out public toilets, from the glimmering pixels of the internet and the black-and-white photos in library books. Here's one for the lost soul, Benson!

Brother Hooper sighed. 'I suppose you weren't alone in that,' he said at last. 'Only a tiny percentage of Old Bedeians joined back then. I'm at a loss to know what happened to them – even to some of the most memorable ones. Of course, *Friends Reunited* has unblocked a lot of lost souls. I do find that website fascinating. I wish more would include photographs, however.'

And Brother Hooper looked at his watch again.

'I'm taking up your time. Perhaps I should go?'

'On no account,' Brother Hooper said. 'True I do have

24

some duties, but they're mainly of the crisp-wrapper-picking sort. I like to go and pick them up during playtime, so that the guilty can see what trouble they put an old man to. Not that it stops them, but it's good for my humility. Though I'm replete with mixed motives whenever I make a stab at virtue.'

'I know what you mean,' Benson said. 'I do know what you mean.'

'So,' Brother Hooper said, 'what have you been up to all these years?'

Benson took a deep breath and told his story.

# 5

'Goodness,' Brother Hooper said. 'You've certainly moved around.'

'That's the one constant,' Benson said enigmatically.

'Where were you happiest?'

Benson thought about that. He could always deflect the question with another question re. the nature of happiness. His view on the subject these days was largely inspired by Rob, and backed up by books at bedtime he nodded off to: namely that happiness was something which can only exist in the present moment. No matter what the circumstances, one has the gift of happiness if only one looks for it. Why? Benson wasn't sure. The funny thing was that, despite everything, when he yanked himself for a second into the present moment to ask himself if he was happy, the answer came back in the affirmative.

Still, he decided to look back at his travels and said, 'I was happiest in Iran. The second time.'

'Iran. When were you there?'

'October 1977 to February 1979.'

'And why do you choose that time? Wasn't there a revolution around then? You were expelled by the revolution, weren't you?'

'Yes.' And he wondered if that was why he chose it. He had come alive holed up in his Ahwaz flat with curfew from dusk to dawn and the sound of gunfire. He'd felt like a good person, sheltering his stone-throwing students from the Army when they knocked at his door. He'd only appreciated the danger when, back in Britain, he watched the media view of events and wondered how he could have hung on for so long. But, of course, he'd had Emerson for company through the bad last days in Tehran when it became clear that the game was up and they had to wait in a flat without electricity or heat for a hen's tooth of a plane ticket out to reach them.

'I loved the job, the people, the feel of the place,' he said.

'What was it about the place?'

Lots of sex: the masseur at the Sa'adi Bath-house, the old fellow on the bridge over the Zayandeh who flashed, and became a regular. Just thinking of him now stirred Benson. But, for Brother Hooper's benefit, Benson skirted all that and spoke of the blue-tiled domes surrounded by palm trees in a vast mustard sand and ashen-rock landscape. The emptiness and silence. The stars so dense they veiled the sky like a golden hijab. The beauty of Islamic calls to prayer and swooping swifts at sunset. The local crafts, the carpets.

'But what made the second time better than the first?'

Lots of sex: the masseur at the Al Bustan Bath-house, the activity by the Karun river ... 'I was in Isfahan the first time. The most beautiful city in Iran – and possibly the whole world. But it was full of foreigners. Ahwaz, though it was a pretty humdrum city, was friendlier, because the people were not under siege from multinationals.'

That was true. Not completely true, but true as far as it went. The answer also opened up one of Benson's pet theories about the whole falling-out between Iran and the West since 1979, and the dire happenings of the present. He was about to launch into all that when...

'Am I what you expected?' Brother Hooper asked.

'I wasn't sure what to expect. I think I gave you a lot of grief.'

'Not as far as I can remember.' Brother Hooper noted Benson's surprise. 'In my book, 'grief' was the given, I suppose. I was a young man – comparatively – when you were at St Bede's. Full of myself, a headmaster at thirty. To tell you the truth, I look back at that time as the best of times. The worst of times has been since then.'

'What happened?'

Brother Hooper looked around, at the Brothers' parlour, at the view of the garden, at Benson. 'I lost a lot of friends, for a start,' he said at last. 'Brother O'Toole died, Brother Wood went off to be a priest, was ordained and worked for a year or two in Shrewsbury, then just upped and left. I could go on, but you probably know most of it. The Brothers shrank and have almost disappeared as a congregation.'

Benson nodded, but did not ask why. After all, he thought he knew why. The talk of cruelty, the sexual scandals, the coming of consumerism and the placing of things spiritual on the back burner – with the gas, as if in strict adherence to his pyrographic admonition – turned off. He only had to look at his own life: the ideals that had ended in the mud. The search for 'Dearest Him', then, 'Dearest Him' proving illusive, turning to the darkness of parks and his endless ability to rationalise away the ideals he had been brought up with. The world made it easy, and the Church was right in a way: World, Flesh and Devil managed very efficiently this downward trajectory. After all, what was each individual Brother but another flawed fellow like himself? If he had been hurt by them, then it stood to reason that they had been hurt by him.

If he had been tempted by lust, then so had they. If he
... How would he have managed had he stayed in the
Congregation and gone from school to school? He'd have
taken on the mores of the Brothers about him ... the
strap would have become a part of him. And lusts? Would
he have been able to keep his hands to himself? He'd
not often had an itch that had gone unscratched. Though
there was no temptation towards abusing kids, if there
had been, and if he had been driven potty with the
frustration of being unhappy in just such a parlour as
this, would he have been able to restrain himself? Possibly
not. Not if his past record was anything to go by. He
congratulated himself – then switched the congratulations
to the nebulous Higher Power whose only concrete definiton
was that He/She/It was NOT Benson – and realised that
all trace of anger at Catholicism had slipped away. A
miracle. In a way.

'What was Saudi Arabia like?'

'Calvin's Geneva with shops,' Benson said. It was a
response he'd practised over the years. He was fond of
remembering a flight between Dhahran and Shiraz he'd
taken during Ramadhan 1970. After six months' teaching
in Saudi Arabia he'd been ready for a change. He took
off after the frisking and gun-toting of Dhahran airport
and, after a half-hour flight, landed in Shiraz. There were
smiles and welcomes at the airport. An old taxi took him
to his hotel, and he passed by parks and blue-tiled mosques
and rose bushes growing on the verges. People were
making things, selling things. There was a hubbub and
colour to everything. Carpets hung from balconies. They
even covered the roads, happy to be ridden over (it
tightened the weave apparently). By sunset he had met a
group of students anxious to speak English with him and

was writing down the words of the song from Zeffirelli's *Romeo and Juliet*, which they all wanted to consign to memory. He walked with them to the tombs of the poets Hafiz and Sa'adi, and told them horror stories of life in Saudi Arabia. He still had their addresses in an address book that was falling apart. But he did not write. A side of him thought a stamp with the Queen on would get them into trouble. Another side couldn't be arsed to make the effort.

Benson told Brother Hooper most of it, and Brother Hooper kept looking at his watch. 'But,' Benson said, 'those students in Iran I let down as well.'

'How so?'

'When I went to work in Iran, I didn't keep in touch with those first friends who had made me fall in love with their country. I dropped them. Then, after the revolution, one of them wrote a letter which, after many adventures, found me. He wanted help to leave Iran. I did not reply. I rationalised that a letter from a westerner would be intercepted and would get him into trouble. But the real reason was – I don't know – a kind of laziness of the heart. Of course, I was drinking heavily then.'

'Were you?'

'Yes. I'm gay as well.'

'I really must get on,' Brother Hooper said.

Benson got up, wondering if Brother Hooper had taken in his last observation, which he felt to be gutsy in the extreme. 'I've taken up a lot of time.'

'We must continue this conversation – if you've the stomach for it. Perhaps you can tell me about some of the boys – men – from your year.'

'I've lost touch with pretty much everyone.'

Brother Hooper nodded, and stood up. He conducted

Benson to the front door, thanked him again for coming, and repeated his invitation.

The door shut behind him.

# 6

Rob was fiddling with his motorbike when Benson opened the street door and entered the garden of his house.

'You're home early,' Benson said.

Rob grunted.

'I've been to see Brother Hooper.'

'About fuckin' time,' Rob said. 'Did he take you over his knee?'

'No. We had a really good chat.'

'And you're feeling better, are you?'

'Yes.'

'Told you.'

Rob smiled at Benson. Benson beamed back. Benson's smile wiped the smile of Rob's face. This often happened. Nothing to worry about.

'You're home early,' Benson said again, though he did not remember saying it the first time.

'The last on the list didn't show up.'

'How many have you passed today?'

'Two.'

'How many tests did you do?'

'Seven.'

'What did they fail on?'

'The usual,' Rob said. 'Just weren't ready.' Rob wiped his hands on a pair of Benson's old St Michael underpants. These Benson had consigned to the ragbag for low dusting. Try as he might, he could not get Rob to use the correct bag of rags for the correct task. He kept all his tools in pristine order and condition, but had these odd blanks. *Just weren't ready.* Benson nodded to himself. Rob had failed Benson twice, only passing him – with some reluctance – on the third occasion. His heart went out to the five disappointed motorcyclists. Mind you, it was for their own good. 'Cup of tea?'

'Yeah,' Rob said.

'Inside or out?'

'I'll come in. Give me a tick to clear the tools and put the bike away.'

'Your place or mine?'

'Ours,' Rob said.


Benson trotted inside, a spring in his step. To have Rob back all friendly and loving with him was a great relief. Not that 'loving' in Rob's terms was characterised by moonlight and roses. No, that was not Rob's style at all. Tough Love was more than a mere quality or strategy in Rob's book; it was, quite simply, his credo and, even deeper than that, the vital ingredient at the marrow of the man. He lived by it, both with regards to himself and all the people he came into contact with: neophyte motor-cycle riders, fellows in QA (Queer Alchies), his grown-up children and his best friend and partner, Martin Benson. He had failed those five people for their motorbike tests because it was the right thing to do. He had exiled Benson from his bed because Benson had made a mountain out of the molehill of setting matters to rights with Brother Hooper. It was for Benson's own good. Benson knew it was, and was grateful for it most of the time. He liked the trouser-press element of the relationship, partly because it made such a change to him and his lifelong sloppiness, partly because it could be intensely erotic.

'I bought a suit.'

Rob was massaging his hands with Swarfega. He pushed past Benson, rubbing against his bottom with his slim front as he went. 'Littlewoods?'

'Yes. I was really scraping the bottom of the barrel.'

'Buy anything else?'

'No.'

'Good.'

Benson poured the strong brew of tea. To suit Rob he had to put five Typhoo bags in a pot, and leave it for five minutes. Anything less than that and Rob would say it wasn't tea at all. *Call that tea?* Yes, it was good that he hadn't bought anything else. Rob was convinced that Benson bought stuff to fill himself up in the same way that he had used alcohol. Not that the stuff he bought ever worked like alcohol had, but as he bought it and carried it home he always thought it might.

Very early in the game, Rob had sussed out this side of him and, being Rob, had honed in on it on a daily basis.

'Done any work today?' Rob asked.

'I finished the consignment for Muriel.'

'We could take it to her on Saturday. You can take me on yours, if you like.'

'Can I?' Benson was cheered. This was really a breakthrough. Normally, he and Rob took both bikes – he his little red Honda CG 125 – Rob his own BMW. Rob followed, like the riding examiner he was, while Benson rode in front, doing his best to get everything right.

34

It occurred to Benson sometimes that he spent a great deal of his life doing his damnedest to please Rob. Still, why not? Pleasing Rob both pleased Benson, and helped him keep to the extreme straight-and-narrow that Rob was nurturing in him on a daily basis. Anyway, it wasn't a one-way-street. Rob in his turn was buddied by Jack, who rode a Harley, had ridden the Harley he owned clean across America before shipping it from New Jersey to Liverpool, and risked his life every year in the Isle of Man – and him heeling seventy – but always managed to come back unscathed. Rob had a relationship with Jack which mirrored Benson's relationship with Rob. Rob often gave Jack 'a seeing-to' when they went off on retreat. It was a charitable act, he said, seeing as Bill wasn't up to it, and nobody else seemed inclined.

And Jack in his turn lived with Bill, who had started a gym back in the mists of antiquity. He had been sober for forty years and, Jack said, had taught Jack everything he knew about sobriety and keeping sober and living in the day. Who Bill relied on for honest and tough love, Benson did not know. But there would be someone.

But the main thing was that it worked. He was happier than he had ever been. He loved the idea that these men passed on the message of QA to one another. He had found at long last, and after many wanderings, blind alleys and shallow scratchings on the world's surface, a way to live.

Many years before Benson had decided to stop drinking, a couple of gay alcoholics had decided to start their own meetings for other gays. They followed the Twelve Steps of Alcoholics Anonymous, were members of that fellowship, but had decided that it made more sense for gay alcoholics to have meetings for their own kind, to take gay sponsors and work through their problems – many of which had to do with sexuality anyway – away from the larger world of alcoholics. Many still went to 'straight' meetings – Benson and Rob did themselves – but it was those QA meetings that they really found useful, and were able to identify with most. After all, at straight AA meetings a lot of the matters brought up in 'shares' were not anything to do with them. And at the straight meetings, when gay people tried to share their concerns, they lost the rest of the group. Most of all, in conventional AA it was recommended that alcoholic men had a man as his sponsor – the person who helped him through the program of recovery and practice/ascension of those twelve steep steps – and women had women. But for the gay alcoholic, this did not fully fit the bill either.

Rob had discovered Benson on the promenade one summer night five years before. Benson had gone to the prom to see what he could pick up, but had been so drunk that he'd passed out on the dog-dirty cruising spot. Rob fell over him.

Benson didn't remember too much about that night. But he must have let Rob frog-march him home and put him to bed. He'd left Benson his number, saying that he'd come round and see him again when he was in better shape. Benson had thought Rob had sex in mind, which he had, but not until he had told Benson about his own experiences with booze.

For many years, Benson had woken up badly hung over, resolved that that day he would not drink. And drunk. This was a daily thing. Six hours of generally solitary drinking, a dram taken to bed, and those wretched hangovers and mad resolutions. When he rang Rob the next evening he was still feeling queasy and readying himself for some hair-of-the-dog. But Rob had arrived, ordered strong tea – like today – and told him his own story.

'You'd gone there looking for a man, hadn't you?' Rob had started off.

'Er...'

'Yes or no?'

'Yes.'

'Usually do it when you're pissed, do you?'

'Yes.'

'Reckon drinking's a problem?'

'How do you mean?'

'How do I fucking mean? Is it costing you more than money?'

Benson thought. 'Yes, but I don't know what to do about it.'

'I used to drink. Of course, everyone did round our way. I was born on Cleveland Street. Pub on every corner. I got an apprenticeship at Laird's in the sixties, and drank pints with me mates. Had to drink pints or they wouldn't have been mates. It went on like that until I was drinking in the morning to face work. I drank to go on dates. I was drunk when I got married. Drunk when I first had sex. But not for years did I question any of it. Only when the wife walked out on me and took the kids did I think I might have been drinking more than anyone else. Then I get laid-off at Laird's. Well, what do you do when you've got some spare redundancy and time on your hands? See to the kids, get them well kitted out? No, piss it up against the wall. Alcohol took me wife and kids, lost me the council flat I'd got, made me unemployable. And I still didn't get that there was a problem. I took to drinking sherry in Victoria Park. One night I was out for the count

37

on a bench and some yobs came along and thought it would be a lark to beat up a drunk. That got me into the hospital with multiple fractures and internal bleeding. And you know wha'? As soon as I came to I was trying to get anyone who came near the bed to go and buy me a bottle. Mad or wha'?

'Anyroad, a man came around and spoke to me just like I'm speaking to you. He said there was a way out. I wouldn't ever have to drink again, if I followed certain steps. Fancy coming to a meeting with me, do you?'

He had and he hadn't, but did.

'Wrap up warm,' Rob said. 'It's a cold old place, the meeting-hall. And I'll take you there on the bike.'

# 7

PC Pat Bakewell and WPC Sandra Horner sat in their unobtrusive neighbourhood watch van in a quiet and leafy street a mile from Benson's house. PC Bakewell surveyed the tree-lined avenue and the rows of solid semis sitting in a sober and orderly line behind them.

'Could've had one of them,' PC Bakewell said. 'If...'

'Cost an arm and a leg,' WPC Horner said.

'Do now. Didn't then.'

'Who'd've thought it?'

'Wha'?' PC Bakewell scratched his nose, giving it a surreptitious pick as he did so.

'Thought that they'd get so pricey. Round here,' WPC Horner said.

'They weren't pricey then, Sandra. But the wife wouldn't.'

WPC Horner bristled. 'Hasn't she got a name, then?'

PC Bakewell felt a bristle of fear and anger. That was two bristles. He knew that they were two. His counsellor had told him they were two. It was Flight versus Fight, or vice versa, the counsellor had said. He breathed deeply. 'Laura wanted a house near her mum.'

'That's better,' WPC Horner said.

PC Bakewell felt just one bristle now. He was still angry, but the fear had gone. Was that good? Well, it had to be better. Stood to reason. 'You don't know her mum.'

'I do, actually,' WPC Horner said. Then she stabbed, 'Lovely woman.'

PC Bakewell ignored the pain – and the tremor of 'fight', of the stab wound. 'Where you know 'er from?'

'Circle dancing,' WPC Horner said.

PC Bakewell nodded to himself. Typical. Circle Dancing at the Social Services hall on a Tuesday night. The Wife went with her mother. Off they clopped, like Guy Fawkes and the boyos, for a spot of plotting.

Three kids passed. Bakewell and Horner watched. Baseball caps backwards on shaven heads, warm-up suits, trainers, looks-that-killed. They took in the slogan on the Police van: 'We're watching you, mate!' They stopped. PC Bakewell felt his heart rate rocket. He reached down and rotated the scanning knob. The surveillance camera turned to the kids, looked down from its great height. The kids watched it. The camera stopped, eye-balling the kids. One stuck out his tongue, jerked up the hood of his jacket. The others barged him forward, then they too raised their hoods to cover features, grasped their groins and jittered about. Much barging and many biffs. They skulked off.

'Nowhere's safe these days,' PC Bakewell said.

'We're here,' WPC Horner said, righteously.

'Yeah, I know, Sandra, but we can't be everywhere.'

'Fortunately,' WPC Horner said.

PC Bakewell was about to protest for the sake of protesting. But he knew that WPC Horner had spoken no more than the truth. If you wanted to see out thirty years and retire fit and viable to get value out of the pension, you had to be in the right place at the right time. You had to avoid those situations that you could not change but which could change you with a stab in the back, a shotgun that could turn you into a colander, a syringe that could jab you with the slowest of deaths.

You had to be circumspect. True there was a duty of care, whatever that meant when it was at home. But you had to be three wise monkeys as well, when the circumstances were right. At last PC Bakewell said, 'Me mum says she wishes we were like those big Irish bobbies.'

'What big Irish bobbies?'

'The big Irish bobbies who'd take scallies down an entry and administer justice with a big pair of fives. It was cheap, easy and it kept crime off the streets, me mum says.'

WPC Horner was thinking of something cutting to say to this when the rock came through the toughened glass windscreen and landed with some considerable force in her lap, along with thousands of little glass jewel shards of windscreen. She cried out.

'You OK?' PC Bakewell asked.

WPC Horner moaned. 'No, I'm not fuckin' well OK. OK? Get me to E.R,' she said.

As PC Bakewell manfully punched out the rest of the shattered windscreen – keeping the running away and advancing kids well in sight – then gunned the vehicle away, WPC Horner balmed the pain with thoughts of time off. There might be a medal in it, too. There might be medical retirement. There might be an end to the fear, the loose bowels, the feeling of impending doom which dealing with the public, day in, day out, gave her. Why hadn't she followed Jeanette to Canada? Jeanette was operating a bookshop and lobster bar on the Bay of Fundy and had a lovely girlfriend called Carol. That could have been WPC Horner if she had only had the guts. Instead. Instead...

WPC Horner's thigh throbbed on, telling her that maybe, just maybe, a limp caused by a scally lob might be the making of her. Anyway, assuming they could tidy her up and let her out, she'd go to a meeting tonight. A meeting might fix her.

PC Bakewell radioed in the incident. The switchboard told him to go straight to the hospital, where the staff would be notified of their arrival. He gunned the van towards Clatterbridge hospital at a speed that made the sensitive surveillance equipment on its roof whistle and whine out its impotence.

# 8

'Shall I try on the suit?' Benson asked Rob after the tea.
'Go on then.'

Benson took the suit upstairs to his room. As generally
happened, the trip from kitchen to room played his life
back to him in a minute: the Indonesian wooden statues,
the Persian and Afghan rugs, the collection of hubble-
bubble pipes, the painting on glass of The Death of Ali,
the Persian miniatures, the Tuareg swordsticks, the coolie
hats, the Bedouin hangings, the Pasolini film posters, the
bookcases stuffed with travel guides and language courses,
the pieces of poetry burnt into driftwood, the framed
maps, the batiks, the pottery... He knew where everything
had been bought, could remember chapter and verse of
negotiations, where each had hung or sat in the flat or
bungalow or hut of some foreign outpost, how each had
been shipped and after many adventures come to this
white house at the top of New Brighton.

When Benson bought the house in the late nineties he'd
had plans of turning it into a Bed and Breakfast. The thought
still came to mind, but he quickly banished it when he
considered how the arrival of strangers would disrupt the
peace he had found with Rob and the group of friends who
had come into his life. Added to that was the fact that
neither Benson nor Rob were particularly practical. The
house was old and it would take big bucks and months of
work to bring up to scratch. And neither wanted it up to

scratch. If it were fit for visitors, Benson would have to exile his trophies to one of the box rooms, and Rob's motorbikes and parts would end up in the shed.

Then, of course, with guests meandering round the house he and Rob would have to regularise their sexual activity. As things stood, their intimacies took place anywhere in the house, or in the private garden ... wherever the feeling came over them. It was usually Rob who took the initiative, coming at Benson from behind, fumbling him open like a thirsty drinker wrestling with the seal on a bottle of Scotch, and taking him there and then. The kitchen was a favourite spot. Benson had spent a great deal of time over the years lying face down on the old pine table while Rob had his way with him from the standing position. It was one of Rob's little kinks and it dovetailed nicely with one of Benson's. He never tired of the frantic acts of sex, which might occur while he was doing some low dusting – seldom, it has to be said, despite his vast collection of dusters – or was bent over the balcony looking out to sea.

After all, that had been his sexual life. Fumbling acts of guilt-ridden sex at the back of the prom, a prom he could see from his bedroom window, had been the start of it, etching titanium braille into his brain from an early age. Perhaps, looking back, he had been abused by the men who picked him up, led him off to the darkness behind walls and groynes and did him; but if that was so, he had been the instigator. He would not let them go until they had pleasured him. He pursued them, rather than the other way round.

It had, he thought, been a substitute until he could find Dearest Him and make swooning silk-sheet love in a carpeted room – a room rather like his bedroom with its four-poster and view of sea and deep jig-saw of old rugs. But that had not been on offer or, if on offer, not something he particularly wanted. Was that true, though? A side of him had wanted it. He had met many men in his younger days who offered him more, even offered the great inconvenience of turning their own lives upside down in order to be with him, and love him. But they had been tried, and then told, 'Let's just be friends.' After all, how could a friend fulfil the trashy part of him that craved anonymous, dangerous, seedy sex?

Well, Rob could. Partly this was because Rob knew everything about him. He concealed nothing from him and, if he did, sure as eggs were eggs, Rob would loosen his grip on the secret – *You're as sick as your secrets* – and tell him what was what. So it suited Benson to be taken just when he least expected it. The house at the top of New Brighton played host to their coupling and, just as the objects awoke the chapter and verse of his past, so the kitchen table, damp basement, rose arbour, back stairs, front stairs, attic, pantry, hall – upstairs and downstairs, shower room, garage, leather sofa in the TV room, Ercol rocker in the morning room – pricked memories of their love-making. It was as if the whole world of furtive and erotic escapades had been boiled down to one rich concentrate, in a white jam-pan of a house with a sea view.

And, in retrospect, Benson could vividly recall most of the anonymous sex he'd had over the years. In the lean days after he had come back to his home town he used his memories to fire himself up. When he got sober he tried to recall all the sexual episodes he had experienced in an erotic life that went back more than forty years. This he did, delighting in the return of memory after decades of befuddlement; determined to lay himself open and take an inventory of his unexamined life. It had gone something like this:

1950s

1. Bruno and Eric in the garage.
2. Man in toilet
3. Bruno under the gun emplacements at the back of the prom

1960s

4. Andy, the man from the library
5. Clitherow at the orgy
6. Dr Leptos at Aber
7. Farmer
8. Eisa
9. Eddy in New York
10. Carlton in New York
11. Man in Vondel Park, Amsterdam
12. Henry in DOK
13. Three Dutchmen in Thermos 2
14. Man in toilet (Delft)
15. Moroccan on ferry to Harwich
16. Moroccan in London
17. Henry in San Francisco
18. Five men in Dave's Baths, San Francisco

1970s

19. Saudi Guard (grey beret)
20. Saudi taxi driver
21. Saudi Guard (red beret!)
22. The Pink Panther
23. Drunk Sudanese at Dhahran airport
24. Shia houseboy
25. Two Saudi taxi-drivers
26. Three policeman (Riyadh flat)

27. Visitor (Riyadh flat)
28. Electricity meter reader (Riyadh flat)
29. Man who stole my Habit Rouge (Riyadh flat)
30. Prince Abdul Wahhab bin Abdul Kadir (Palace)
31. Black servants of Prince Abdul Wahhab (Palace)
32. Two men by thirty-three arch bridge, Isfahan, Iran
33. Elderly flasher on waste ground by Zayandeh river, Isfahan
34. Masseur at Al Saadi Bathhouse, Isfahan
35. Masseur at Al Bustan Bathhouse, Ahwaz
36. Policeman in Friday mosque basement, Isfahan
37. Metal engraver in metal engraving workshop, Isfahan Bazaar
38. Two carpet salesmen, Isfahan Bazaar
39. Bill in San Francisco
40. Two actors (from The Cricketers) London
41. Man in Victoria Bus Station, London
42. Kermit in Nassau
43. Rob in Nassau
44. Man in churchyard, Nassau
45. Two black Alabaman tourists in Nassau
46. Churchill in Nassau
47. Two men on beach, Paradise Island
48. Jim from Philadelphia in London
49. Amos from Baron's Court (!) Poppers
50. LeRoy from Black Mikado (Brixton)
51. Oscar from Earls Court
52. Abdullah (Palestinian) Sur, Oman
53. Saeed (Beni Bu Ali Tribe) Al Wa'afi, Oman
54. Sa'ad (Egyptian) Sur, Oman
55. Ali (Omani) Muscat, Oman (stole a case of beer)
56. Othman (British Council spy) Muttrah, Oman

1980s
57. Laurence, San Bruno California
58. Carl, San Francisco
59. Many men is Dave's Baths, Man's Country
60. Edwin, New York (died of AIDS)
61. Paul (Colchester)
62. Tim (Iran and Colchester)
63. Fadl (Saudi Arabia)
64. Taxi – driver (Saudi Arabia)

1990s
65. Tom (New York, Santa Fe, Buenos Aires, London)
66. Peter (Irish poet)

2000s
67. Sundry men on the prom (Say, ten)
68. Rob (New Brighton)
69. Jack and Bill (for charity)

*Something like that.* The list was no more than a ball-park figure. Some of the encounters had stuck in his memory; some been washed out by the brown-out of booze.

Of course, it was impossible to know whether his mad actions had made him incapable of sustaining humdrum sexual relations, or whether the need to flit from prickly flycatcher flower to flower was bred in his gay bones. Benson tended to the former view. But while tending to the former view, he had also tended to blame Catholicism, the times and the Law for the way things had turned out. Mind you, it was not that there weren't lots of people warning him to straighten up and fly right. Trouble was, growing up with the illegalities of the situation, the guilt that every gay of his age had to a greater or lesser extent had been raped by, wasn't it bound to happen that 'gay' became 'queer', just as 'straight' became twisted, with the passing of time and the loading down of the head, heart and trigger fist with the wilder varieties of erotic imagery?

Benson climbed into the suit pants, and caught sight of a photo of his granddad on the wall. He had come from Ireland, married Benson's grandmother and never looked back, or to the side. At least that was what Benson gathered. It seemed to him to have been an admirable life. What would he think?

'Well, probably he knows,' Benson thought. The notion did not scare him or fill him full of embarrassment. His secrets were out and he was grateful for that. Mind you...

He put on the jacket, then opened the wardrobe to see himself in the full-length mirror.

The mirror took in the bedroom as it swung open. He saw the sea, the point where Mersey turned to Irish Sea and the Belfast boat heading out. It was a pivotal point, and a pivotal part of his decision to buy this white confection of a too-big house at the top of the town. The mirror turned, taking in the charity-shop furniture – furniture held little interest past the practical for either Benson or Rob – and, finally, with a creak, the mirror turned its long narrow eye to Benson in his new Littlewoods' suit.

Benson appraised himself. Not bad. A shirt and tie would look smarter. Still, not a bad fit. Jacket a tad short? No, don't think so. Pants a bit long? With some shoes on ... black? Brown? The overhang would be eaten up. A sock down the pants on the big day? No. Socks down the pants are infantile. I'm trying to grow up, godamnit!

He turned his attention from the suit to the face. He looked tired. Not that he was tired, but he looked it. No double chin in this generous mirror, but one appeared in his bathroom mirror. But then he was looking down. And the light was all wrong. A real liar, that light in the bathroom.

'What you want for tea?'

'Coming...' Benson said. He made for the stairs. *What you want for tea?* That was a joke, Benson thought. Rob was simply asking what Benson was going to cook.

'What do you think of it?'

Rob looked at the suit. 'How much?'

'Nineteen ninety-five.'

'It's fine. Do for anything,' Rob said. 'Now what about tea?'

'Coming up,' Benson said. He started provocatively chopping onions at the pine table.

# 9

Jack aborted – not for the first time – the plans Rob had proposed to Benson the night before. No longer were Rob and Benson to ride together on the little Honda to deliver the consignment of pyrographed products to the souvenir shop in Loggerheads, bonding publicly together, spooned and exposed, the passing cars and their occupants with no inkling of the deep structure playing out between the two men on the little motorbike.

Foiled again! Jack was stealing his friend away for some QA shindig on the Llyn peninsula. They'd ride out on separate bikes, the clever intercom between them communicating private thoughts.

Benson, though miffed, knew that nothing should be allowed to get between a man and his sobriety. Jack, as Rob's buddy, was his spiritual adviser and had advised Rob that the QA shindig on the Llyn would help Rob's sobriety no end, even though he had not announced his intentions to Rob until the last minute, the news reaching Benson in the dying seconds of that last minute.

There was nothing else he could do but take it on the chin. This he managed, consoling himself that Rob had made progress by his *willingness* to ride on the back of the bike, while Benson drove. This was a step forward in Benson's book, an acknowledgement that Rob thought Benson was – despite his inability to perform the 'lifesaver' glance-back prior to manoeuvring on every occasion – deemed sufficiently competent to have his expert significant other on the back. Not that Rob have been 'on the back' in a literal sense; a great big parcel composed of pyrographed wooden articles enjoying that risky perch, hanging over the blurred tarmac, encondomed in a plastic sheet, steadied by stern elastic straps.

So Benson spent Friday packing his parcel for Loggerheads. He was able to give it more space and bubble-wrap than would have been the case if Rob had occupied his pillion seat. Now, it would just be Benson and the parcel for the bike to worry about.

When finished, he wrapped the box in the stout piece of black polythene and took it down to his bike, which lived – knowing its place – in the far corner of Rob's garage. He placed it, straddling pillion seat and carrier and carefully attached it with the red elastic ropes – the exact red of the Honda. He then mimicked every sort of wind buffet by barging the confection from all angles, pronouncing Honda and parcel Rob-and-Welsh-traffic-cop-approved, then returning to his workroom to plot product development.

While rummaging in a bargain bin at a Birkenhead pound shop, Benson had come upon boxes of rubber stamps. Thinking on his feet, knowing he would buy them despite the fact that he'd come to the shop on the lookout for pine breadboards, spoons, and rolling pins, Benson bought the rubber stamps because they were too cheap to leave lonely and unloved in the unlovely shop. He pounced, and took them to the checkout – along with his planned booty of pine items itching for a good burn – where it was his turn to feel cheap, as he handed over a tenner for the lot.

To the right of checkout were yellow bottles of room

odoriser – or, rather, 'room odoriser': butyl nitrate, poppers, sex-enhancing muscle relaxant. It was called 'Nuts and Bolts' and was being offered for sale at one pound and ninety-nine. The sight of the bottle excited him. Just like that. As the woman made change and conversation, her customer was back in seedy situations – his heart thumping fit to burst; his lust rampaging and his muscles relaxing to allow anything to happen.

He was a few yards back outside the shop and down the road before he came to himself. 'Phew,' he said out loud.

When he got home, he found that he had brought a treasure trove of really quite good designs to his pyrographic lair. There was a galleon under full sail, a transatlantic liner, a slogan which asserted, Be The Change You Want To See in the World – Mahatma Ghandi, a Chinese landscape, TWO lighthouses, a rhinoceros, a trio of Indians dancing, a dove. There were plenty of others, too, but they were a bit childish, and not worthy of a burn.

Most of the really good pyrographers could burn pictures onto wood. They had – Benson reckoned – the same beauty as wood engravings. Benson had tried to draw a mouse eating an acorn using his hot pen, but he didn't have the knack. He'd ruined lots of wood trying, mind, and returned reluctantly to writing beautiful sentences in his best italic script – a skill given him half a century ago by Novvy at the monastery.

The rubber stamps allowed him a way round this lack in the drawing department. He would attempt to use them like traces. He'd got prizes for tracing at school. He'd really shone, and enjoyed the whole process. Proceeding around – say – North and South America with his pencil taking in every delta, estuary and peninsula, making sure the tracing paper stayed smoothly in place, the pencil communicating the whole truth of the shape, his tongue sticking erect from his mouth, seeing the bays, peninsulas and capes as if he was there in real life, consumed him, body and soul. When finished, he admired it as Mum admired a hanky well-ironed as it steamed on the ironing-board. He'd turn his trace over and scribble until the pencil was as blunt as a tongue, sharpen it, scribble, and, the back of the trace as communicative as carbon paper, transfer his trace to his exercise book.

It had been a lot of work. Mind you, the repetition etched the shape of North and South America (or a million other images) deep into his brain. But these days, carbon paper was really hard to find. Anyway, if he were going to make a profit, time was of the essence. And that was where the rubber stamps came in so useful.

The black ink would be blotted out by the burn going over them, the finished article looking as if it had been created directly from his head and via the red hot nib to the wood.

That was the idea anyway.

He sanded a breadboard and wrote down a poem in pencil. The spacing came naturally. In the early days he had had to rule lines that he first measured in order to fill the planned space, but he had not given up writing it all down in pencil. He then soaked the lighthouse rubber stamp in the black ink block, blotted it lightly on a piece of newspaper and carefully placed it at the bottom of the board, in the centre.

Very nice, he thought and, plugging in his pen, lost himself in the woodsmoke of creation. When Benson came to – for that is how it always felt after a session with his art – a handsome and unusual breadboard had awoken like Sleeping Beauty from the forlorn orphan of the pound shop. He, Benson, had given it uniqueness and – hopefully – turned a pound to five ninety-nine. Wholesale.

He looked at the clock. The whole procedure had taken an hour. Not even approaching minimum wage. Still, he'd take it to Muriel in Loggerheads, present it to her as a gift, and see what came of it.

The thing was that while at work on his pyrography he was locked into the present. Practically every self-help spiritual book he read reminded Benson that The Present Moment was the one he should inhabit. It was, a variety of authors of every belief, culture and tribe, agreed, all that we had. The past was a done deal, couldn't be changed and ought not, on any account, to be lived in. The future, while it might need a modicum of planning, was basically a fiction over which poor old human beings had little in the way of control. Remembering that Death – the leveller, the bringer of peace, the thief in the night, the undertaker's dream and his customer's nightmare – would, despite the ministrations of NHS Direct, acupuncture, millions of repetitions of pious mantras, rigorous performance of the Twelve-Step programme, thousands of shares in British Aerospace and at QA, things left undone that ached to be done, places not visited, friends not made, beds and underpants not changed ... come. Plan for the future all you liked, it was still only a fiction.

So what?

So don't live in the fiction of future.

He had cut out of a newspaper a quote by Dennis Potter, whose plays had convinced him – for a while –

55

that television wasn't all bad: *The only thing you know for sure is the present tense and that nowness becomes so vivid to me that I'm almost serene. I can celebrate life. Below my window in Ross now the blossom is out. It's a plum tree, it looks like apple blossom but it's white, and, looking at it through the window when I'm writing, it is the whitest, frothiest, blossomest blossom that there ever could be.*

Potter had been dying of cancer when he spoke those words. He was viewing spring for the last time. Benson longed for moments of Pure Present. Sometimes his pyrography gave it to him. He was absorbed by it. Sometimes.

But most of the time Benson lived in past and future, unless – as he was doing now – he drew back, emptied his mind and existed without thought in the moment that was presenting itself to him. But after another drawing of lines on breadboard, copying down of poem in pencil, he was back to composing the future: how he'd manage this big house as time passed, what Rob was up to, why things had not worked out differently in the past, and how his abiding lack of interest in interest, Tessas and High Yield savings accounts, his overall total fecklessness, would impact his future.

Not that it mattered in the big picture. The big picture was a blank, a swirling mist of mystery. Benson looked up. 'Mist,' he said. 'Story', he continued. 'Missed Story. Mist Story,' he concluded. That was the mythical moment: a mist story.

The voice of Rob came to him. *Get your sad arse to a meeting. Sharpish.* Yes, but … Rob had gone straight from work to burn rubber on Welsh roads with Jack. They would probably stay the night at the bikers' B&B that smelled of old dinners and socks. They might even get up to some rumpy-pumpy – Jack's term for what they did together after long sessions of meditation, sitting at the damp edges of Celtic wells.

Benson did not mind Rob and Jack having the odd fling. Jack's partner Bill was, to say the least, not in the first flush. Rob said he was far too spiritual to be interested in sex, and, as if that weren't enough, he had a dicky prostate. Benson had been included on a number of occasions and, after the initial embarrassment of it all, found it quite rich and meaningful. Their Higher Power smiled down on them, three lowly recovering gay drunks engaged on a queer sort of spiritual path. Anyway, sex, Benson told himself, was a form of praise. He was in thrall to men's dicks – always had been. They were, as far as he was concerned, the pinnacle of creation. Why not bow down and worship them in whatever ways his mind and heart dictated? For was not that worship also prayerful acknowledgement of the Higher Power, who had spun them into existence?

Anyway, Benson occasionally had a fling. Not often. No one tended to ask. But so long as he was upfront with Rob – who did not seem to have a jealous bone in his body – it was fine.

Rob and Jack were two heavy bookends that contained and sandwiched Benson. They were really alike, Rob and Jack. Both had been married in the dim and distant past. Both had grown-up kids. Just as no one contradicted Rob when he said, 'I'm afraid I can't pass you. You're just not ready' so no one – well not Benson at any rate – demurred when Jack announced that there had to be a sudden change of plans. What was it that made both men so commanding? What was it in Benson that could no more have argued the toss and walked away than he could fly?

It wasn't as if he was completely wet and supine. He had done things which would make your average Merseyside resident gasp. That year in an asbestos bungalow with no electricity and green water in Oman, though the thought of it still sent shivers through him, he had survived. Neither had he been afraid during the Iranian Revolution. He'd ventured out in the midst of the mayhem to buy his bread and cheese, his fags, yoghurt and milk. In Kano, when that 'false messiah' was killing everyone in the Old City, Benson had carried on regardless in the centre of that old city trying to give Hausa-speaking businessmen the basics of Business English. And that was drawing a veil over his flat overlooking 'Chop Square' in Riyadh. He'd also given corrupt and inefficient bosses a piece of his mind on more than one occasion – albeit when he'd been given his ticket out and had the visa on his passport stamped – so why be so powerless and 'wet' before Jack and his best friend? Why could he not have asserted, 'Ted and I have other plans'?

It was no good saying that both Rob and Jack had something about them that 'demanded respect', though both did. There was something close to Benson's core that asserted their right to be obeyed. What was it? *God*, said Benson on the hill, *grant me the serenity to accept the things I cannot change; the courage to change the things I can and the wisdom to know the difference.* But, Lord! There were years of struggle in those twenty-seven short words.

Still, a meeting was what he needed, and wanted. Meetings he went to without Rob gave him a certain freedom. Perhaps meetings without Benson in attendance gave Rob a bit of freedom too. Who knew? Though honesty was demanded from him in all his affairs, it was especially demanded from meetings. But with Rob in attendance Benson censored himself. He didn't quite know why. It was all part of the conundrum. Best not think about it.

Smoke filled the room, forming a slow-sway hammock under the light. Tea dropped off the fictional plate that was future, to be replaced by thoughts of playing *Tristan and Isolde* (the Furtwangler version) at high volume while he padded round the empty house, showered, changed, watched Channel Four News and got ready to go and lay out his worries on the table.

# 10

The meeting of QA on a Friday took place at an old Unitarian church hall on Malcolm Lowry Street a few hundred steps from Benson's house. It was not in the main room – a bleak place, sixty-four magnolia-painted bricks in height with strip lighting that did people's heads in, and cobwebs dating back to The War. No, the gay meeting was in a small room that had a rectangular table and twelve chairs. Any more in attendance and it was necessary to bring in chairs from the big hall and a shocking jam resulted. Still, the meeting was seldom full on a Friday.

You could never tell, though. A big football match on the television might have been expected to reduce attendance, but never did at QA. But Saturday night meetings had been blighted by two shows on the television that sounded a bit like *Opportunity Knocks* and *Come Dancing*, but which Benson had never seen. Anyway, it wasn't his business whether people chose some television show over the benefits of a meeting ... mind you, it was a bit odd. First things first, and all that...

Benson got to the door of the hall. A pink triangle had been stuck to it with BluTack. He gave it his 'that has nothing to do with me' look as he passed it in case somebody on the lookout for scandal should see him going in. Then he went in, thinking how 'Old Benson' he was to have given the notice such a look. *Don't worry what other people think of you; worry about what you think of other people.* On the next door was the notice which told him Health-and-safety Allan had beaten him to it.

## QA can accept no responsibility for loss, damage or personal injury due to whatever cause while visiting these rooms

There'd been a bit of murmuring when the notice went up. It seemed to go against the spirit of the fellowship in some fellows' opinion. Nothing happened in this world, after all, without the Higher Power allowing it. Still, Health-and-safety Allan couldn't help himself. He had his own particular cross of powerlessness. A Health and Safety Officer of no mean, though very *mean*, reputation, he had diverted his obsession and compulsion from alcohol to enforcement of all things healthy and safe into the rooms of QA. Mind you, this had not always been the case. When drinking, Health-and-safety Allan had been extremely lax. Then his job at the council had just been a way to pocket money for drink. He'd drunk before work, during work and after. He went into blackouts, awaking befuddled and befouled in police cells. There wasn't much time in between his drink-obsessed leisure activities for enforcing Health and Safety. QA had made a new man of him, or, rather, breathed life and sobriety, vim and scrupulous attention to all things healthy and safe, into the old one.

Since becoming sober, Health-and-safety Allan was the scourge of everyone in the County Borough who lived in the same present moment. One might think that the dead escaped his ministrations but, according to Health-and-safety

Allan, even they could still decimate the living with their unsteady gravestones and the rotting foundations of weeping angels, broken columns and cockeyed obelisks. A visit to the local cemetery showed forth his stalwart energy and attention to duty of care. Gravestones had been laid safely on the safely-horizontal ground by the hundreds. Laid down, flat as the dead, statues of the Sacred Heart, angels, infants – the cement crevices in the robes filling up with rainwater and reduced to serving as birdbaths for sparrows. Stark Health and Safety notices detailed dire penalties unless prompt action be taken forthwith by survivors of the deceased (or 'relevant co-owners' as Allan put it).

'Hello, Allan,' Benson said cheerily.

'Watch your step on that lino,' Allan said.

Benson looked at the curling grey lino tile, about to trip him up, and nodded. 'Are you well?'

Allan said he was fine, and went out to the kitchen, leaving Benson to read the slogans on the wall.

Benson liked AA slogans, but at QA you got slogans not seen at the 'normal' meetings.

GIVE A SUCKER AN EVEN BREAK was Benson's favourite.

GLITTER AND LET GLITTER was another.

SHINE! (A GOOD SHINE TAKES ELBOW GREASE!) was still another.

SEE TO THE INNER MAN AND THE OUTER MAN WILL SEE TO HIMSELF, while not a favourite, often gave him pause. He paused.

Health-and-safety Allan returned with the pump Thermos of ready-milked tea. This surprised Benson, as Health-and-safety Allan had said something once that had stuck with Benson, and a lot of the time not a lot that Allan said did stick: 'You know pump Thermoses are the ideal lodging place for legionnaires' disease,' Allan had said as someone was trying to pump the dregs out of the battered Thermos which had done the meeting sterling service over the years.

'Are you the tea-maker tonight?'

Allan looked at his watch. 'One minute to go. Looks like it, don't it?'

'It does a bit.' Benson pumped himself a cup of tea. 'You know what you said about legionnaires' disease?'

But Allan stepped in. 'Don't worry about this pump Thermos. It spends the rest of the week completely immersed in a washing-up bowl of strong bleach.' He consulted his watch, and said, 'Time to open the meeting. Will you do the Chair for me, Martin?'

'I'd be glad to,' Benson said, thinking he'd just chat frankly with Health-and-safety Allan. But then Deirdre came in – in company with her partner, Wayne. Deirdre was Head of Sales at Cottage Garage in Meols. QA had helped her through her sex-change – Benson knew a lot more than he had wanted to about that particular procedure. In the months leading up to it, and the years following it, Deirdre's shares (pre-op) had gone on at some length about what he was in for, what had driven him to it, how dreadful he felt to be seen as a man ... and (after the op) the incredible benefits accruing to the gender shift. Being trapped in a man's body, Deirdre reckoned, had been at the nub of his alcoholism. He'd drunk away twenty years. He'd married Charlotte (his wife, who though divorced now and living with a golf professional was still his best friend) and drunk away the years of his three kids' growing (he still loved the bones of them and had made his amends to them, and they were really supportive) but all that was in the past and he was as happy as anything to have met his partner, Wayne.

Wayne didn't say much at meetings. It was mainly through Deirdre's shares that insights were granted into aspects of Wayne's character – all flattering. Wayne was Deirdre's 'Rock'. He worked in the offices of a large container-shipping company – something to do with Logistics – though for years he had sailed the seven seas as an engineer on a succession of container ships. Benson wasn't sure whether QA was the place for Wayne. Not that it was any of his business. But sometimes he wondered whether Wayne could find identification with the shares of gay alchies. He had, undoubtedly, embraced aspects of the queer vocation by teaming up with a former man. That former man, however, had had the central aspect of gay attraction (in Benson's book) struck off and consigned to the furnace that billowed smoke day and night all over Wirral. And was Deirdre's NHS-provided new equipment up to the job, or was it like their dentures? Still, it was first and foremost what Rob always said, *Ninety-nine per cent of what happens around you, Martin, is not your business.* So, using those tools to detach himself, he tried not to question too deeply.

He was, however, curious about how Wayne and Deirdre got on between the sheets. Whenever pictures arose in his head, he tried to banish them, and replace them with something more lofty. But it was a struggle, especially as he found Wayne with his fine fit body (and him past fifty!) and his becomingly-bald head and strong features, an attractive proposition. Not that he stood a chance. Wayne only ever had eyes for Deirdre.

Benson decided to get the meeting going by talking about fear in general and his own in particular. Normally, he said, his own fear involved embarrassment. He was scared not of the big things, the rational things, like being beaten up, or getting a life-threatening disease, but of being made to feel small. He knew how much that sort of fear was linked to pride but it was embarrassment that always bumped into him. Still, he wasn't unique. Soldiers, for example. Were they really courageous when they marched stalwart into battle, or were they running towards the enemy because they were afraid of being embarrassed in front of their mates as they ran away? What the world called 'cowardice' might, like many of the things the world took as true, be false. For 'cowardice' had its courageous side, because it exposed the 'coward' to endless embarrassment – perhaps even worse than facing the enemy. Anyway, as far as he could see in examining his life since putting down the drink, most so-called vices, and ditto for virtues, were awash with their opposites.

Health-and-safety Allan shuffled, and took a moody gulp from his tea. Benson decided to give an example in order to clear up any confusion:

'For example, when I look back at my 'love life', so called, I'm reminded that mostly I had to be drunk to go out looking for sex. I couldn't manage to face the embarrassment of exposing myself sober. Drink was a tool, and it worked. It loosened my inhibitions. It made embarrassment disappear.'

'I think of my time working overseas, mainly, but it could apply to cruising on the promenade. I was brought to these rooms by a gay fellow who stumbled over me on the prom, and stopped to help. Sometimes I wish that this had happened years, decades, before. For thirty years or so I woke up in beds, or in the desert or bath houses or back room of some bar wondering what had happened, how I'd come to be there ... even wondering sometimes what country I was in. I'm lucky to be alive, not only

65

because of the drink but because of the places and situations the drink took me to.

'Since coming to QA I've managed to stop drinking a day at a time. I hardly think about it. But I think about the other stuff: the fear, pride, the habits of the heart, that made me such a prime candidate for alcoholism and caused me to waste so many of the opportunities that life offered me. I've done my best to clean house, to make amends for things left undone that I should have done; things done that I should not have done. To examine my life ...'

At this point the door of the meeting room opened again with a creak. Benson remembered that he'd forgotten the WD40 he'd been vowing to bring for ages, once again. In hobbled Busy Sandra on a Zimmer frame with three wheels, brakes and a plastic basket on the front. Benson got up to hold the door open for her, and to move chairs about so that Sandra could have easy access to the table.

'Welcome, Sandra,' Health-and-safety Allan said.

Benson could see that Allan was dying to ask Busy Sandra about her Zimmer. Well, he couldn't. He'd just have to postpone gratification. It would all come out in the fullness of time.

'Martin is doing the Chair,' Health-and-safety Allan said.

'I've almost finished,' Benson said, furiously changing course, like a Mirror dinghy in the river with a supertanker bearing down on it. 'I was just going to mention this week. Rob has gone off with Jack for a retreat on The Llyn. I was working on my pyrography, when I had a jolt of fear about the future. (To Sandra: 'I was talking about Fear before') but tomorrow is tomorrow. With the tools I have learnt here, I'll be able to face it. Back to work I went and without trying I was focussed on burning every word perfectly. When I do my pyrography that often happens – I find myself totally absorbed in the work. If I don't inhabit the present moment, the burn will be too deep, or too shallow; I'll make a spelling error, ruin a whole morning's work – it's impossible to erase a mistake when it's burnt on. You could say that my alcoholism was a disease that had burned itself into me. It took my youthful idealism; it made it possible for me to put aside any notions I had of right and wrong and of the implications of my actions. I loved booze, because it made it easy for a few hours each day to live in the wasps' nest of my head. I paid for it, mind. Hangovers and a day jaundiced by the poisons that alcohol exacts in return for its high. These days, I'm doing my best – with the help of my Higher Power ... *and all of you who listen to me and confide in me are part of my Higher Power* – to amend my life. I do this by following the suggestions made, by putting my stuff on the table, by being aware of what is happening when it is happening, by realising how powerless I am when left to myself. I bugger things up many times every day. I'm no saint. The point is that I am on the road, and busy trudging towards a happy destiny. I hope as many as want to will share with me tonight. Thanks very much for listening to me.'

'The meeting's open,' Health-and-safety Allan said.

'My name's Sandra. I'm a gay alcoholic. Sorry I was late. Spent the last two hours in Casualty being checked out. I'm in pain. Fancy a drink to help me put up with it, but I'm not going to have a drink today. Fear's a funny thing. Usually I don't think I'm a frightened sort, but maybe in my job. I'm a police officer...' (everyone in QA knew that ... hence the name) '...and probably I've got used to it. Earlier on today – only about three hours ago – myself and a colleague were on surveillance duties in the town when these scallies passed by. We thought little of it, just beamed the camera in their direction. Then a brick came through the windscreen and landed on my knee. The docs at the hospital think I've cracked a bone. Got to go back in the morning for more X-rays. But you know how I feel? Fucking great. That's how...'

Sandra went on and on about the fear she had not been acknowledging all those years while serving the public. Every day as she put on her uniform there was the fear. It stood behind her whispering the awful possibilities into her ear ... (Benson nodded in agreement) It never stopped. Usually it was manageable, but how much better would it be to be just slightly pissed? The edge would be taken away. But that was no longer an option. Drink had led her to some terrible places. Her partner had walked out on her, though there were signs she might come back now that she had a year's sobriety under her belt. So she could readily identify with Martin's feelings. 'Thank you,' she concluded.

Benson would dearly have liked to come in again. But this was not part of the ethos of QA. A share was a share. A conversation was a conversation.

Health-and-safety Allan introduced himself, and commenced his share. Benson felt he could have done Allan's share for him. It tended to run along the same polished rails that reached back into the past of his drinking, trundled over the points of realisation that he'd had enough, then came slowly and serenely to a halt at the station of sobriety and the window boxes and cheerfully-painted Victorian woodwork of day-to-day time put in sober, vigilant and fully aware of Health and Safety.

So Benson took the time to wonder why Busy Sandra

was called 'Busy'. Of course he knew that 'the Busies' was a nickname for the police-force. What puzzled him was why that name had stuck to the police in general, and Sandra in particular. Was it meant ironically? There was never a policeman around when you needed one. But they insisted on racing through the town – and the road abutting Benson's house – at unsafe speeds with sirens blaring. To Benson's way of thinking, that was just showing off, and the best way there was to warn thieves and bullies of their presence so they'd have plenty of time to make off and save the Busies the business of all that paperwork and untidiness in the cells. And what had Busy Sandra been doing sitting in the car and swivelling surveillance cameras when a good face-to-face piece of human interaction might have done the trick, while sparing her damage to her knee?

Benson tried to stop thinking such negative thoughts. Slowly, reluctantly, they swivelled away from the Busies and honed in on Health-and-safety Allan. He had heard that Health and Safety Allan was spectacularly well-built. 'His lash goes on and on,' was what Mechanic Gerard had said. Mechanic Gerard no longer came to meetings and rumour had it that he was back to occasional bouts of binge-drinking, selling back copies of *The Big Issue* outside Somerfield's to feed his habit (made extra pricy by much sniffing of cocaine because doing so kept him awake to drink more, this in spite of having a perfectly good job as a car mechanic for the Kia garage). 'He hadn't had enough,' Rob had said. 'He'll be back when he's had enough.'

'What happens if he doesn't?' Benson had asked.

Rob shrugged, 'He'll die.'

Well, he'd had enough of Health-and-safety Allan, Benson

MICHAEL CARSON

thought. Mechanic Gerard told Benson he'd always been
partial to a well-built man, but Allan's endowment went
beyond the realms of the possible. 'All you can do, Martin,
is give it a hug, and weep,' he'd said. 'Sad in a way. It's
everything I fantasise about but when you're up against
it in the flesh and fantasy becomes reality, it's a huge
turn-off.'

Benson, being Benson, could not believe it would be
such a turn-off. But he closed his mind to the possibility
of having a go. It would not be seemly. Then he thought
of the Poppers at checkout in the Pound Shop. Then he
was in San Francisco bath houses...

'It's huge. It might be possible with a bit of help ...
But.'

But, as Health-and-safety Allan went on – and it never
ceased to amaze Benson how small meetings could expand
in the length of shares to fill the available time slot,
rather like gas in a bell jar – he allowed himself to wonder
how 'prodigious' prodigious might be. It was curiosity,
pure and simple. But when had his sexuality been more
than curiosity? From those meetings of The Rude Club
in pre-pubescent antiquity, curiosity had been what drove
him on. Anyway, anything prodigious was attached to
Health-and-safety Allan. That ought to stop curiosity straight
off. He could also, were he to succumb to Allan – not
that he'd been asked – only imagine the declarations and
provisos he'd have to sign before they got down to the
business of the night...

...*The provider of this service declares that he is free from
all sexual diseases ... see attached signed and certified copy
from the Wirral Health and Safety Authority and the Council's
Agents for testing, HIV/HEP.1, 2, 3. He also wishes to state
that those who perform sexual acts with the aforementioned*

70

*owner of prodigious endowments should be aware of the risks involved; consider – after due inspection and measurement of endowments, both length, girth and circumference – whether on previous occasions he has managed to accommodate comfortably and without physical or emotional damage, harm or mishap, a similar set to the prodigious endowment under discussion (noted and logged in the Health and Safety directorate No 169690/ BC49383LF...)*

Allan was going on about the fine line between the things that could be changed, and the things that could not. Benson should have been listening. The topic was highly relevant to him at the moment. But his thoughts were wandering at an uncontrollable rate. Perhaps if Allan'd shave his head, instead of combing the sidelines of his scant thatch over the pitch of his bald dome he'd be more attractive. Change his glasses? Not wear a tie? Discard his cardigan with those two bulging pockets containing water-free washing gel, a Swiss army knife, some Elastoplasts, and a little ball of red elastic bands (picked up from the street but disinfected prior to use)?

And thus poor Benson continued. He was only shaken from his most unspiritual reveries by Allan saying thanks, which had to mean that Deirdre had nothing to add.

Benson popped a pound in a polystyrene cup and Sandra did likewise. Then they watched as Allan pushed a fiver in. After The Serenity Prayer, Busy Sandra said she'd better get home.

'Yes, of course, I can drive!' she asserted – a tad huffily – to Benson's enquiry. Benson forgave her almost immediately, with only a split-second of brief-flowering resentment in between. Busy Sandra was in pain, after all. He bade her goodbye. Then Allan and Benson returned to the room to clear up. The meeting had lasted an hour.

'Where was everyone?' Benson asked Health-and-safety Allan. 'Friday night's usually fairly busy.'

Allan shrugged, and stacked the chairs. 'That's how it is, Martin,' he said.

Of course, Benson knew that. That was obvious. Two sides rose up, however. First, it was a cliché. Second: it went so clearly contrary to the way Health-and-safety Allan arranged his life. He never looked at dog-dirt on the pavement and asserted that that was how it was. No, he got onto the blower with the Community Patrol and recommended surveillance. Benson gathered together the five used mugs and took them to the kitchen. Allan followed him in and supervised as he washed the mugs. It made him nervous. Allan didn't say anything. He stood behind Benson with the Thermos cradled against his chest, but at any moment, Benson thought, he'd mention water temperature, rinsing, and the danger lurking in apparently clean surfaces.

But Benson managed to wash, rinse, and dry (with a pristine Allan-endorsed tea-towel) without anything being said. He must be coming on.

'A lot not here tonight,' Benson said.

'They're all in Wales,' Allan said. 'There's a big gathering there.'

'Yes. That's where Rob is. With Jack.'

Benson wiped down the stainless steel draining board with a throw-away antiseptic cloth Allan always supplied.

Allan nodded. Then he opened a brand-new antibacterial wipe and went over all the bits that Benson had gone over, while Benson stood, like Patience on a monument thinking uncharitable thoughts, saying nothing.

'Just to be on the safe side,' Allan said. He gave the meeting-room one last look, then closed the door, and locked it.

They stood outside on the cold early-spring street. 'Fancy coming to mine for a coffee?' Allan said.

'That would be really nice,' Benson said, feeling himself rise up; then put himself down with the rest of him.

# 11

Benson arrived at Loggerheads at 11 the next day, proud of himself. Despite a beastly side wind that buffeted the little bike, Benson and his parcel, he had managed to make it in under an hour. And he had not broken the strict Welsh speed limit once. Rob, and his Higher Power, he reckoned, would be proud of him.

Mind you, he'd been sorely tempted to speed up while on the road to Queensferry. A police car appeared in his rear-view mirrors – kept impeccably clear and exactly placed for maximum rear vision (though not forgetting the eternally invisible blind spot, which required Benson's second-nature lifesaver glance to make sure doom was not heading up in that sneaky way doom did) – and had followed him closely. So close was the police vehicle that if Benson had needed to brake suddenly there was little chance of it being able to stop without giving his rear a biff. He wondered what the policemen inside could be laughing about, for that's what they were doing. It was no laughing matter. He gave a nudge to the rear brake, enough to set the brake light on, but not enough to slow him. This had no effect.

Fortunately, Rob's advice on such a situation came to mind, 'Don't be intimidated.' He carried on as he was. There was nothing else to do anyway. The cars were passing him in the other lanes – breaking the speed limit with impunity. He wondered then if the police were interested in the box on the back. It hadn't shifted, had it? He felt behind him, but all seemed in order. He crossed the Queensferry bridge over the Dee. His geography teacher had told him that the Dee had been straightened. It pushed up to Chester straight as a stick. This had caused the silting up of the estuary and made the Dee hopeless for shipping.

The police car put on its lights and started its siren. It came out from behind Benson and roared off after some car. *Which* car it was hard to decide. Any one of them could have been the gleam in their hawk-eyes. Stood to reason. If he was riding on the speed limit, all the others were breaking it. The police were a law unto themselves.

A brief feeling of resentful pique that he had not after all been the centre of the police-car's attention nudged into him, through him – and with the aid of a QA slogan ('Accept the things you cannot change') out the other side. Since getting sober he'd longed to be breathalised. His brush with the busies was over. No chance of showing his virtue at the side of the road. Time to get back to enjoying the ride.


The cowbell, hanging from the ceiling at just the right level to crash against the top of the door, crashed against the top of the door. Benson staggered into Muriel's souvenir and trinkets shop, and closed the door behind him with much tenor tinkling. Muriel appeared through a bead curtain, stubbing a fag out with one hand while fanning smoke from the vicinity of her mouth with the other.

'Bona to vada your eek, Martin,' Muriel said in a camp-follower Kenneth Williams voice.

Benson wished Muriel would drop all that. But he knew from past experience it was hopeless. He smiled at her. 'Here I am,' he said. 'Are you well, Muriel?'

'Can't complain,' Muriel replied. 'How's my favourite queer pyrographer?'

'Fine, thanks. A bit cold from the wind, but I got here in one piece. As you see.'

'Where's Rob?'

'He's off on the Llyn with Jack.'

'And he didn't take you?'

'Rob's a law unto himself.'

'That Rob! It's the little ones you've got to watch! Like your leather jacket!' Muriel said, coming up and giving the jacket a feel, then pinching Benson's cold right cheek.

'I got it from Help The Aged,' Benson said. 'The Neston branch. Guess how much?'

Muriel approached and felt the black leather. 'Twenty?'

'Nine ninety-five.'

'That's good. It's from British Home Stores. They don't come cheap.'

Benson was shocked twice. Was Muriel being ironic? British Home Stores *was* rather cheap – well, affordable. And, though he knew the jacket was from British Home Stores – it said it on an inside label– he couldn't figure out how Muriel knew. He had rather hoped people would think it was from John Lewis. 'You are clever!' he said.

'It's written on the studs,' Muriel said.

Benson looked. 'So it is.'

'Still, you can't go wrong for 9.95. Did it keep the wind off?'

'Pretty much. I've got my thermals on underneath, though.'

'You ARE camp,' Muriel said and she disappeared to make him a mug of coffee.

Benson did not feel he was camp, at least not in the matter of wearing thermals on a motorbike in March. Muriel was the only one who ever said it to him. What was so camp about hi-tech black thermals – not cheap – that swanked about the effectiveness of their wick system, whatever that was? He did not take offence, though. For a start, Muriel was fair. She gave him a decent price for his work. Mind you, her mark-up was high, but somehow she managed to shift it. Anyway, Muriel had a sad past. Much could be forgiven her.

She was from New Brighton originally, Benson had learned, from Rob – who'd known Muriel during his heterosexual period. She'd married a sea captain who went off for long voyages to the Far East. They hadn't had any children, but they doted on one another. Leastways that was what Muriel said. Then on one voyage, while the ship was berthed in Kuching on the island of Borneo, her hubby had gone ashore and not returned.

Time passed. Muriel went out to Kuching to search. She found no trace of her husband. She returned home, waited a year, and sold up in New Brighton, buying a bungalow in Loggerheads, and turned a double garage into Muriel's Souvenirs.

Benson opened the parcel, and waited for Muriel. He looked around. As he surveyed the contents of the packed shop he could surmise why his work shifted. They were just about the only items he had noticed that were approximately local, and the only items that also had a use. The Welsh dragons, the toys and novelties, all came from China. And not for the first time Benson wondered what the people made of this bizarre stuff bound for

Loggerheads as it flashed through their poor, ill-paid hands.

'I've done something a bit different,' Benson said. 'I've brought you a sample.'

'Have you indeed?'

'Yes...' He delved among the entissued wooden spoons, and produced his new work on the breadboard.

Now Finale to the Shore
Now finale to the shore,
Now, land and life finale and farewell,
Now Voyager depart, (much, much for thee is yet in
    store,)
Often enough hast thou adventur'd o'er the seas,
Cautiously cruising, studying the charts,
Duly again to port and hawser's tie returning;
But now obey thy cherish'd secret wish,
Embrace thy friends, leave all in order,
To port and hawser's tie no more returning,
Depart upon thy endless cruise old Sailor.

Walt Whitman

'All that writing. Must have taken you ages!' Muriel said.

Benson hummed and hawed. 'It's something of a departure. I wonder if people will appreciate poetry?'

Muriel read the poem, and started to cry.

'What's the matter, Muriel?'

'It's so sad,' Muriel said. She searched for a tissue and blew her nose. 'Lovely work.'

Benson had known the poem was sad, but thought the lighthouses underneath might perk it up. Then he wondered if maybe Muriel was thinking of her husband. He could not say anything because Muriel did not know he knew, at least he didn't think so. And he hadn't given Muriel's husband a thought as he did it. It was by Walt Whitman. He'd read it out at funerals. It meant a lot to him. 'I can do happy ones, too,' Benson said, by way of dispensing consolation.

Muriel was looking hard at the breadboard. 'I think we're onto something, Martin,' she said.

'How do you mean?'

'What I mean is that poems are powerful. You saw how that one got to me. If it got to me it will get to other people as well. The point is to make them *appropriate* to all life's situations ... especially those situations where they think nothing's too expensive .'

'What sort of situations?'

'Weddings. Funerals. How about a personal message to lay on a gravestone or on one of those wayside shrines people are getting fond of?'

'*Because I could not stop for Death, he kindly stopped for me?*' Benson quoted.

Muriel frowned. 'Not sure about that. Makes Death sound like a bus.'

'I'd not thought of that. I thought it meant that the poet – speaking with irony – is saying that she was far too busy to pause in her busy life to consider Death ... but Death had other ideas, and stopped all her business for her.'

'How does it go on?'

'*The carriage held but just ourselves and immortality.*'

'There you are!' Muriel said. 'Death is riding the carriage!' She thought. 'No, don't think that's it. Not very sentimental, is it?'

'Isn't that a good thing?'

'Well, it might be a good thing. Don't know. But it's *definitely* not a good thing in the knick-knack business. And don't you forget it.'

'I'll put my thinking cap on.'

'Good. Think wedding. Think funeral. Think birth. All those big events make people carefree about dosh, and willing to spend a bob or three if the right sentiment strikes them.'

Benson watched as Muriel picked up the breadboard and turned it over and over. 'These easy to source?' It was a different Muriel now. A friendly dragon in the den of her emporium.

'Yes,' Benson said.

'And not too pricey?'

'A quid.'

'From the Neston Help the Aged?'

'No. The Liscard Pound Shop.'

'The lighthouses are good. Lighthouses are a seller. People like lighthouses. Know any poems about lighthouses?'

'Not offhand, but I can look.'

That's it, Martin. Give it some thought. How long did this take you?'

'About an hour.'

'Quite a time, then. Still, if people want them they'll pay for them. Drink your coffee.'

Benson did so.

'I've got a cheque for you,' Muriel said. 'Don't forget it.'

'I'll use it to invest in some breadboards.'

'Good idea. But keep up production on the usual. People who don't want anything usually leave with a wooden spoon, just to salve their conscience. I'll be in touch. It's been good to vada your jolly old eek.'

Benson left Muriel's shop with a light heart. As he rode
the Honda along the road back to Queensferry towards
the motorway up Wirral, he wondered about Muriel. She'd
started with her usual camp, then morphed into weeping
and with hardly a pause for breath turned into thrusting
souvenir shop owner with her eye on the bottom line.
Then back to the old camp. Which one was Muriel, he
wondered? He knew so little about her. How did she fill
her time in that bungalow next to the shop? Did she
have a sex life? Women friends? Still, she'd been a good
friend to him and Rob. And she liked his work, which
was great.

Seeing a sign for Holywell, Benson decided to drop in
on St Winefride.

The souvenir shop there was full of Catholic piety items.
He paid his entrance fee and dallied about taking everything
in. Some things never changed. Catholic devotional
requisites – like Catholicism – did not change much.
Thousands of holy pictures of every saint you could think
of – St Martin de Porres was there in his Dominican
habit and his dog playing around his ankles as he gave
Benson a straight look while cradling a crucifix. Trouble
was, St Martin in the holy picture wasn't black enough
for Benson's taste. It wasn't as if there were that many
black saints. Might as well make them black, one would
think, and not merely tanned. He passed along to the
statuary. St Martin managed to eyeball him out of the
crowd there as well. He was black. Very black. But you
seldom saw a black man that black. Anyway, it was a dull
matt black. No, not right either. St Martin was next to
St Maria Goretti, and St Therese of Lisieux was nudging

him from the rear. St Therese's relics had made a grand tour and brought out the trippers in their millions. At the time Benson had wondered about finding some pithy quotation from St Therese and pyrographing it onto a useful kitchen item. After all, she was patron of housewives. Her spiritual path had – as far as he could remember – involved doing the dishes and using the labour as a prayer that would be zapped up to heaven and there exploded by Divine Love and zapped back – greatly increased in potency, to grace somebody who was having a bad time on earth.

It was a lovely idea. It had fired him up as a kid and he still felt moved by it as he looked at St Therese – and him nudging sixty. Belief in such a thing obviously still moved believers. He was no longer of their ilk, though he sometimes wished he was.

Through the gardens leading to St Winefride's Well strolled Benson. The medieval building around the well had escaped, because of its remoteness, the vandals of the reformation. But it had not escaped a mauling from visitors, who had inked their names on the walls. Some had carved the time-blackened sandstone. Some of the older ones were quite beautiful and precise, done by professionals. But there was no denying that it was time for Welsh Heritage to come in and give the place a good going-over.

The well itself thrilled him with the strength of its flow. This was where the head of St Winefride bounced as it made its way from Winefride's neck down the hill below Holywell (which hadn't been called that then, of course). Winefride had been a teenage virgin and some scally chieftain had taken a fancy to her. When she refused his attentions he took his sword out and cut her head off.

Luckily for Winefride, St Beuno, Bishop of North Wales, was in the vicinity and, with a prayer, placed her head back onto her shoulders. This postponed Winefride's canonisation and much cake, jelly and pop rejoicing in Paradise. She went into a convent and died many decades later in the odour of sanctity.

So, for more than a thousand years, the memory of St Winefride had lived on. Charabancs of trippers – though not that day – came to pay their respects. Gerard Manley Hopkins, who had been based at St Beuno's monastery nearby when he wrote *The Wreck of the Deutschland*, had written a poem about her. Benson did not know, but suspected – and the suspicion gave him a deal of satisfaction – that St Winefride would be remembered long after the works and pomps of The Spice Girls or That's-All-There-Is Dawkins had been forgotten.

He reached down and took a sip of the water. He lit candles for Muriel, Rob, Jack and Health-and-safety-Allan. Then he went back to the shop, where he indulged himself by buying four copies of 'The Serenity Prayer'. They came in their own plastic wallets with the prayer on one side and Durer's *Praying Hands* on the other.


On the way home, he wondered where he stood on religion. Fellows at QA believed that a Higher Power had stopped them drinking and was helping them to stay stopped and learn self-knowledge. There were Catholics, Muslims, atheists in QA. But each one had a different view of a Higher Power. They were united only in the fact that this He, She or It had intervened to help them.

Trouble was that no Higher Power had intervened to stop terrorist atrocities, devastating earthquakes or the disappearance of Muriel's hubby. So why would he intervene for the likes of fallen Benson? While muttering in front of one of the endless programmes on Darwin the BBC threw at a patient populace – who were probably watching something else anyway – Benson felt that Evolution was no problem at all for believers. The Brothers at St Bede's had taught Evolution. They had simply said that it all started with The Prime Mover. He had set the whole thing going and then left it alone. What had followed over countless years were miracles of wonder and adaptation. Benson was lifted to exaltation in front of those David Attenborough vignettes of plant, animal and human behaviour which cried out that cups be handed out, Nobel Prizes awarded on a daily basis, to whatever was behind them. Whatever that was, they clarioned forth its intelligence. They sang Mysterious Hidden Genius. But Benson was no scientist, nor ever likely to be with his total inability to even pass an 'O' level in any branch. But he stood by mystery. Until the scientists could explain Creation in a manner he could understand, the Scientific Priesthood would remain an alien heretical sect who had got somewhat ahead of themselves, and ignored the main experience of the Common Man – intimations, feelings and emotions. He preferred to follow the injunction of Maria Von Trapp: *Nothing comes from nothing; Nothing ever could.* That would do for the time being.

Poems! Benson thought, as he approached New Brighton. I must find poems.

# 12

Rob had left his intercom off. Jack used it for chatting. That was fine sometimes. Chatting with Jack was one of the things Rob liked doing the best. But now, on the ride through Snowdonia (up the Conway valley to Betws-y-coed, past the Swallow Falls, to Snowdon, along to Porthmadog and the decommissioned nuclear plant of Trawsfynydd, to Bala), he wanted to concentrate on the road and the fields, corries, mountains and sky. He wanted his every turn of the wheels, gear change, touch on brakes, twist of acceleration, to be perfect. Rob craved one hundred per cent of Present Moment.

Riding his motorbike – at work and for pleasure – was what Rob liked best. And not just the riding: everything to do with the means of transport that gave him his income – maintenance, clothing, skilful riding, his vulnerable companions on the road – were the closest to prayer and the oneness with life that he had managed to achieve. And those actions were always bound up with living completely in the moment, putting his mind to the best use, which was: to live fully and spontaneously in the slippery present, savouring the myriad impressions that passed through his eyes, hands, feet – his whole body – as black tyres and finely tuned engine murmured like a monk along the ribbon of endless road.

So nothing could be allowed to intrude that might shatter total concentration. Martin, when he'd explained his feelings to him, had gone off and pyrographed. *Concentration is the Key to Power* on a paddle-shaped piece of old pine he had retrieved from the river. It sat on Rob's workbench in the garage. How was Martin doing? He'd be in the middle of his trip to Muriel's in Loggerheads. For a moment Rob imagined himself inside Martin's mind. What was he thinking? Sure as eggs were eggs, he *was* thinking. Trouble was, he used his mind to concoct all sorts of daft scenarios. A great rationaliser, Martin was. And what were rationalisations but perverting reality so that it suited you?

It was a tough slog to change the habits of a lifetime, but that was Rob's never-ending journey, and he hoped it would be Martin's. To see the self clear, to own up to it and use the mind as an efficient tool rather than an unhappy crone frantic and fearful in the corner, recounting tales from the past seen through the steam of sentiment or self-justification ... spinning his own future – and everyone else's – into a never-ending what-if of queer fiction.

Living in the present, Rob was certain, was the antidote he, Martin, and the rest of the human race needed to take in order to escape the tyranny of past and future. Martin knew that, but he didn't yet quite realise it. Rob felt that; sometimes, he realised it. There were signs, after all. Small shoots of hope sprang up: an inability to sit through news bulletins and pretty much anything on the television; he'd stopped taking a daily newspaper, favouring books and Martin's music – which was now becoming his own – wafting through the house.

He slid the bike into Betws-y-coed, watching for shadows and feet between the parked traffic on the main street that might turn substantial as his bike closed in. He eased the bike down to twenty, anticipated the family on the pavement walking out into the road with their baby buggy in the lead, and followed a route a foot to the left of the intermittent yellow lines. Sure enough, out the buggy came. Rob slowed down and let them across. Only when they were safely on the pavement again did he nudge the bike to the crown of the empty road. Here I am, he thought. Here I am.

There was no sign of Jack. Nothing new in that; Jack didn't like to breathe his exhaust. They'd arranged to meet in the car park at Swallow Falls. He signalled at the sign to the Falls, slid the bike onto its stand and rolled himself a small cigarette. He'd given up, got Martin to give up too – a day at a time – but these post-ride indulgences did not count. He watched the blue smoke rocking in the clean air, the breeze playing with it, deciding it was bored with the task, whisking it out of his sight into invisibility.

Rob could hear the Falls, like white noise in the distance. Cars passed, and drowned the sound out, but the tyre sound was watery too, like the sea heard late at night from home. He listened for the unmistakable sound of Jack's Triumph, but the traffic sounds had dispersed and the Falls were back. Rob stood, swaying slightly, tiny creaks coming to him from the joints of his leathers, thoughts leaking into his head that took attention from the Falls and the silence behind them. But those thoughts he acknowledged and patted gently on their way.

He felt a breeze coming from behind him. He heard it nudge through the branches of pines, swaying them across the valley of the youthful Conwy. The river grew up quickly past Betws where the land flattened and greened into pasture and campsites, in no time at all sighing to reach its goal between the arches of its Telford bridge next to King Edward the Confessor's castle, into the harbour of Conwy and out to sea. From there it would be able to look back on the way it had come.

The breeze stopped, Falls sounds returned, followed by a stronger nudge of wind, almost a gust, that caused Rob to shuffle his left foot to keep himself steady. Then he heard again the baritone beat of Jack's bike. Should they go to see the Swallow Falls together? He quite fancied it. You had to pay, but it might be worth it. You had to pay for everything.

Rob and Jack stood alone watching the churning water. Jack had bought his flask of sweet coffee the landlady had made up for them. It had two cups in its cap: the outer one larger, which Jack always took for himself; the smaller one nestling within, for Rob.

'I've some news,' Jack said, looking out and down.

'Oh, yes? Good, I hope?'

'Bill and me are going to tie the knot.'

'Tie the knot?'

'We're going for the civil partnership.'

'You never are!'

Rob turned to Jack then. Jack didn't say anything, just smiled. 'And Bill was wondering if maybe you and Martin would fancy joining us.'

'How do you mean?'

'The four of us can commit at the same time.'

'Commit?'

'You are being thick,' Jack said. 'What I mean is: we've come this far. Far enough to be pretty comfortable with who we are – after all those years of trying to be what we weren't. We've both got what you might call 'stable' relationships. Not that we're monogamous or anything – thanks for last night, by the way.'

'No problem.'

'Me and Bill don't get much past cuddles these days. He's not up to it.'

'No.' That was true enough. Bill had been through illness after illness. He kept bouncing back, but each bounce had less life in it than the previous ones. 'But you know me. I'm a bit uncomfortable with the idea of 'marriage' and 'husband' and 'wife'. All that stuff.'

'I know you are. But doesn't civil partnership skirt around all that?'

'I don't know. Then there's Martin. He'd probably think I wanted to make sure I got the house. God knows, I've got nothing to leave to him if I shuffle off first. But he's got that great big house.'

'Is that what you think Martin would think?'

'I don't *know*. But it's a fair bet, isn't it?'

'Have you *asked* Martin what he'd think?'

'No.'

'No. So your thinking about what Martin would think about the house is just based on nothing in particular, is it?'

'I suppose it's what *I'd* think in that situation.'

'Righto. So you put *your* miserliness into Martin's character and take it as sorted, do you?'

Rob kicked at the gravel, looked out at the tonnes of snow-melt water making for the sea. 'We haven't talked about that sort of thing.'

'But you're paying the outgoings, and you're still paying alimony to Yvette.'

'Not much. Not since she married again. The kids are working. Most of the time.'

'I'm just asking you to think about it. We'll be going ahead anyway. I was just thinking it would be nice if we could do the deed together. This is adult stuff we're talking about here, Rob. Do you love Martin?'

'Yes.'

'Why?'

'Apart from the sex?'

'Yes. I know about the sex.'

'He's easy to be around. I'm not. He can read me like a book and puts up with a lot. He's generous. Hopeless with money, of course. And he loves me. And loving me he makes me think a bit about what makes me loveable.'

'Do you tell him you love him?'

'Not in so many words, no.'

'But you're sure you do?'

'Yes.' Rob, stopped, bunched his lips to the left side.

'You always do that.'

'Wha'?'

Jack pointed. 'Tha'! It puts ten years on you. And I know you well enough to know what it means.'

'I was a lousy husband, but I wasn't a bad dad, was I?' Rob paused, watched Jack assent, albeit reluctantly. Not a fulsome assent. Jack didn't do 'fulsome'. 'Well – and I've told you this before – it's the fatherly bit that Martin brings out in me. Rich, that, considering he's three years older than me. I told him the other day that he should buy himself a suit. He was wearing that cowboy wool coat AND a red hoody. I said that a man should have a suit. So off he goes and buys a suit. And on the same day he goes and makes amends to his old headmaster – though he'd been putting it off for yonks. He respects me.'

'And you like to be respected, don't you?'

'Too right I do.'

'Do you respect Martin?'

'Yes.'

'How?'

'He knows a lot I don't. History, Geography. I've caught a lot off him. Music. The odd poem and book. It was Martin who got me to read *Zen and the Art of Motorcycle Maintenance*. Been out years and years, but I'd never heard of it. But it could have been written with just me in mind.'

'You really ought to talk more. Don't you think so? About the two of you.'

'I'm not good at all that.'

'And never will be until you try. It's fear we're talking about.'

'It's fear we're *always* talking about.'

'Of course, it is. Shall we finish the rest of the coffee?'

'OK,' Rob said. He watched Jack pour, took the cup and blew on the coffee. The steam blew about and was gone.

Bill handed Rob a piece of paper from his bag. 'Have a read of this.'


**Benefits and Rights**

In comparison with a civil marriage, civil partnerships will have the following equal rights, and responsibilities:

- Benefits that are income-related will be considered in regards to joint treatment
- Tax, including inheritance tax
- Benefits from state pensions will also become a joint treatment

- The duty of providing maintenance to your partner and any children of either party
- Each party of the union will become a parental figure and thus become responsible for any children either person may have
- Inheritance in regards to an agreement of tenancy
- Domestic violence protection
- Access to compensation of fatal accidents
- Success to rights of tenancy
- The registration of civil partnership will have merit for the purposes of immigration
- Hospital-visiting rights as next of kin
- Like traditional marriages, those that are involved in a civil partnership are exempt from being required to testify in court against one another
- Each partner has the responsibility to be assessed for child support, in the same manner as that of civil marriages
- Treatment comparable to that of a civil marriage in regards to life assurance
- Benefits that arise from Pensions and Employment

'I'll think about it,' Rob said. 'Congratulations, by the way.'

Jack smiled, looked at his watch. 'Time to get on,' he said.

## 13

It was wonderful to be home, gunning the tired Honda up the path to his house, unlocking the garage door and wheeling it back to the corner where it belonged. He watched it affectionately, heard the tick of its cooling engine, wished it were animate so he could feed it. Instead, he took a rag from the rag box and dusted the Honda down.

When the bike was pristine, he stood up and was taken by surprise at the luminosity of Rob's reflective motorcycling clothes. For a moment he had thought Rob was there, but Rob wasn't there. Rob was in Wales. He gazed at Rob's clothes hanging on coat hangers from the rafters of the old garage. He smiled, thinking of Rob doing everything right and proper on Welsh roads.

Benson stripped down and padded into the bathroom. He turned on the shower, waited a decent interval, then stepped under the just-right stream. He was warming up nicely when he heard the telephone ring. He considered his situation, then decided to let the answerphone kick in. One thing at a time. One day at a time...

Not a bad day, he thought. Not a bad day at all. A bit on the cold side for such a trip, but such a joy to be free as a bird on the bike! Of course, all that cold had made him want to go, so he'd stopped at a camping equipment and garden centre on the Wirral side of the Dee for a mooch round mallets in the shop, a coffee and a piss. He found mallets with a really nice grain, and cheaper than B & Q. He bagged four. He drank down a coffee, then went to the outside toilet marked 'Gentlemen'. (The word always made him think of Cardinal Newman). A man had come in, and looked at him frankly. Maybe it was the leather jacket. The man went into the lock-up, and Benson followed – worried about Wirral tent fanciers, but unable to spurn the man who was obviously desperate for relief ... It was a kindness. The least he could do.

But that was in the past now. He found himself becoming hard. Was the man becoming hard at the thought of him? Or was he in the shower scrubbing away like mad, his wife shouting up the stairs that his tea was getting cold? For a long moment he let his Imperial Leathered loofah encourage his tumescence. He thought about the man again ... then he thought about Health-and-safety Allan, who would definitely not have approved. Then he thought about his Higher Power. Did his Higher Power approve? Or had he come round to Benson's point of view? Then, following the logic of his squirrelly brain, he was back to Health-and-safety Allan.

When he'd got back to Allan's place, chatted, drunk the coffee, Benson had told Health-and-safety Allan that he ought to be going. Allan asked him if he really had to; that he had something to show to Benson if Benson wanted ... and he sort of knew that Benson might.

'What could that be, Allan?' Benson asked, all rampant and mock-innocent. It was a daft question. Allan knew him well enough from shares at meetings to realise what might float Benson's boat. And Benson knew he knew, and Allan knew that Benson knew he knew.

'You've heard about me, haven't you?'

'How do you mean?' And as he spoke the question, he knew that his old dishonesty was back and playing its old games. If he were an honest person, he would say, 'Yes. I've heard you've got the biggest dick between here and Timbuktu.' And he might add, 'I'd have stripped down to receive your cornucopia yonks ago if it wasn't for the fact that you haven't asked.' But, Benson saw, for the umpteenth time, that he was a long way from being an honest person.

' "How do you mean?" she says!' Health-and-safety Allan said. 'Go on, Martin. Have a look. I like people having a look. You don't have to *do* anything.'

'Are you *sure* I won't have to do anything, Allan?' Benson asked, his mouth all dry, and his erection screaming 'let me out!' against his rumpled, in-need-of-a-good-hot-wash cavalry twill.

'Positive,' asserted Health-and-safety Allan. 'I've done a risk assessment of just such a situation as this. It would be unsafe to make physical contact due to the fact that I don't have any condoms in the house. This is not a slip-of-the-mind on my part, but a conscious and considered decision to avoid things getting out of hand. I understand my endowment enough to know that any actions on its part demand full consent – and careful risk assessment – by any prospective recipient.' Allan thought, then added, 'Still, hands don't count – I've plenty of hand sanitiser – and what's a wank between friends?'

Benson was falling, falling. Again. 'Righto, Allan. But what we do here – and I'm still not sure – let it stay here. OK?'

'You don't even have to ask,' Allan said. 'Right. Are you ready?'

Benson nodded, and watched Allan recheck the curtains, the locks on front door, then return and give his place a quick just-to-make-sure glance. They were definitely – very definitely – two consenting adults in private.

'I'll take everything off, shall I?' Allan asked.

Again, Benson nodded.

Health-and-Safety-Allan undid the laces on his Hush Puppies. He removed them and placed them just right under an upright chair. Then he took off his socks – a white pair with the Scottish flag on them. He folded each in turn then placed them inside the shoes. His tie followed, folded and placed on the back of the chair. He undid the buttons of his white shirt – bottom to top. He removed this and placed it across the back of the chair. His vest followed. He stood stripped to the waist in front of Benson.

Benson was not greatly taken by Allan's slimness, nor his lack of muscle. He was flat as a plank from scrawny neck to belly button. His disrobing had also unsettled his precarious comb-over. You could count his ribs without any fear of making a mistake. Not even a paunch. A paunch could be quite nice. Just skin that had never seen the sun – probably for reasons of health and safety.

Allan smiled at Benson. 'Now for the best bit,' he said.

Well, thought Benson as Allan unzipped at a sudden breakneck speed, that's really not for Allan to decide. It's somewhat immodest of him to place himself in my shoes and assume that I will find what is to come in any way 'the best', though when . . .'

But thought failed Benson when Allan emerged from his underpants, bent to take them past his feet and stood naked in front of him. His jaw dropped. He concentrated on the priapic apparition in front of him. Never! Not in

Kano! Not in the Bahamas! Not in the States! Not anywhere had he ever seen anything like it.

'You shared that you were a 'size queen,' Allan said understandingly, 'What do you make of that?'

Benson just sat. Something strange was happening. Allan's penis had come into focus in all its glory. But when Allan spoke it had gone blurred, and Allan seemed to be standing behind the blur, all too untidily human and detached from the monstrous appendage on the front of him. Allan's body was nothing to write home about, nor even send a postcard, while what waved in front of him was something that deserved a whole body of literature. But...

'It's really lovely,' Benson said, as if enthusing over a homemade scone.

'Glad you like it,' Health-and-safety Allan said, putting on an American drawl.

There he goes again, Benson thought as the penis went out of focus and in came Allan. It was as if Jeremy Paxman had morphed into Kirsty Wark mid-Newsnight, leaving Benson with nothing else to do but switch off and go to bed.

Allan just stood there. He seemed quite happy, as if having someone to admire him was doing the job. Benson admired, but, while admiring, his thoughts were racing. He was considering the whole weirdness of sexual attraction. Was he gay in the way most men were gay? Sometimes he thought not. Sometimes he had the distinct impression that he had come to this by comparing. His comparison sites predated the internet and were as old as the hills: pictures in library books, African documentaries on the telly, men seen furtively in cottages. What else was he doing if not comparing endowments? Had the penis always been the centre of his erotic urges? Or had wanking and watching etched erotic braille into his brain? Had all that seeking about for sight of them (what one did with them apart from squeeze had come later) turned him into a homo? If he'd kept up practising on busts and vaginas would they have become objects of desire? Hard to tell. Hard to tell what was what. *And me pushing SIXTY! No! It's impossible! When I'm sixty I'll be grown up!*

But Allan – deeply into the present moment of display, a sparrow with a peacock plumage – what was his turn-on? Did his magic member rule him as Benson's ruled Benson? Was it like a compass point – or a rampant windsock in Allan's case – ordering the lacklustre body to which it had found itself attached to go whither it demanded, be the destinations ever-so-absurd ... like the present one?

'Thank you very much,' Benson said at last. 'You're beautiful.'

'No. Thank *you* very much. Does a fellow good to get it all out.' He paused, hoping for something more. But Benson held back, feeling mean and trying to gather together *a bit late* the sharp-edged shards of his fidelity to Rob. Allan put on his underpants. 'These are specially made for me,' Allan said with pride. 'They hold me in.'

'Like a Wonderbra?'

'No, not really. My underpants are designed to conceal rather than enhance. I don't want to frighten the horses.'

'No, of course not.'

The underpants went back over the apparition – and Benson was left imagining the fitting process at the engineering workshop at Underwear for the Over-endowed ... *We hold it in check until you want to let it all hang out.* Still, they were providing a useful service. The health-

and-safety implications for the borough council would be considerable were Health-and-safety Allan's endowment to be perceived looming through cloth by every Tom, Dick and Harriet ...

Benson got out of the shower and put on his towelling dressing gown. He padded into his bedroom and had lain down for a nap before he remembered the phone call. He picked up and listened to the one new message:

'Martin, it's Allan. I've been arrested. Can't tell you any more than that. Could you come to Manor Road police station and vouch for me? Ask the desk officer for WPC Horner. Please come.'

Benson didn't think. He got up off the bed and climbed into his clothes. He backed his old Metro out. Ten minutes later – keeping to the speed limit – he arrived at the police station. Of course, there was nowhere to park. Typical. The police didn't exactly encourage drop-in callers.

At last he found a place, though he was facing the wrong way. He locked the car and approached the front entrance at speed. For a moment he felt like a solicitor about urgent business for a client. He stopped himself. No, I'm not that. I am a fellow of Allan. I'm simply doing for him what he would do for me. I am not scared or embarrassed – well, I am – but it is something I must do.

Rob, he knew, would be proud of him. This thought gave him the courage he needed to take the steps up to the Cop Shop two at a time. He did not allow the hesitation of the daft automatic doors to faze him. In he went, like Gary Cooper into a saloon at five to high noon.

# 14

WPC Horner, as luck would have it, turned out to be Busy Sandra. She was standing gamely, surrounded by the open and supportive prison of her Zimmer, and talking to the officer behind the desk. She gave Benson a stern look which he at once interpreted as denoting that he was to keep quiet about knowing her. So, for form's sake, he asked the officer for WPC Horner, and he thumbed in Sandra's direction.

'I got a call from a friend of mine, Allan.'

'Surname?' asked WPC Horner.

'Mine? Benson.'

'No. Allan. What's his surname?'

'I don't know that, I'm afraid.'

'But this 'Allan' asked you to come even though you don't know him well enough to know his last name?' And Busy Sandra winked quietly.

'Yes. I know him very well, but we don't use surnames.' Benson was looking severely at WPC Horner, whose surname he had not known himself until it was thumbed his way. What was going on? Perhaps WPC Horner was doing all this for the benefit of her colleague. Anonymity had its drawbacks. Obituaries could pass by fellows from QA who were likely to want to attend their funerals. The bush telegraph usually made up for the lack, but not in the case of Dogma Dominic, who was known in his obituary as Father D. O'Sullivan of St Fintan's. That had fooled everyone.

'Come this way, Mr Benson.'

Benson followed Busy Sandra along a couple of corridors, and into a cubby-hole office. Two chairs, a table and an elderly computer took up most of the space.

'Have a seat, Mr Benson.'

'Is Allan all right?' Benson asked.

'He's all right. He's scared to death, but he's all right. You men! I just don't understand you at all.'

There did not seem to be any answer to that. Benson kept quiet.

'Between you and me, Allan has been caught in the promenade public toilets – along with about a hundred others. He's admitted to his offences – we caught him at it three times. On camera. But he won't accept a caution. And, if he doesn't accept a caution, he'll go to court. And, if found guilty – which he will be – well, his name could be in the local rag and he might have trouble keeping his job.'

'What did Allan do?'

'Well, he didn't get down to business. Not like most of the others. He flashed himself about the place. Lots wanted to ...' Busy Sandra winced '... to get more intimate, but he shied away. He just seemed to be there to show off – and I must say he has plenty to show. A lot of the officers who've seen the footage – and 'footage' is a pretty accurate description for what Allan has to flash – were quite upset by the sight. You men and your toys!'

'So what can I do?'

'You can persuade Allan to accept a caution. And then – once he's done that – you can take him home.'

'And you're sure it's the best thing to do? I mean, if it's a public toilet, it's sort of a given that you show yourself to a certain extent, isn't it?' Benson asked with a fair amount of faux naivety.

'Granted, but I doubt urination requires walking purposefully up and down the establishment shaking it about. Or am I somewhat naive about the mores of male public lavatories?'

Benson shook his head. 'So you had cameras in the toilet, did you?'

'One at head level; one at groin level. For six months.'

*There but for the grace of God,* thought Benson. 'That's a long time.'

'The problem has been going on for a long time. The neighbours are up in arms.'

Benson nodded to indicate how sad and pathetic other people's lives could be. Then he remembered his own. *You can't look at me and not see yourself ...* 'I'd better see him. Where is he?'

'In the cells. If you stay here, I'll bring him. You can talk to him.'

Busy Sandra opened the door. 'Try and get him to accept the caution, Martin.'

'Righto,' Benson said. 'But how are you, Sandra? I mean, in yourself?'

Sandra came up close to Benson and whispered, 'In pain. Underpaid. Overworked.'

Benson nodded sympathetically, though he could have argued over the finer points – mainly the one springing from 'underpaid'. He fielded Health-and-safety Allan's objections to accepting a caution rather well, he thought. Allan was in a state – as who wouldn't be? He couldn't think in his usual dogged fashion. Benson had to say again and again that it would prevent the whole thing getting out if he accepted a caution; he would be less likely to lose his post as king of health and safety; his colleagues were less likely to learn that anything untoward had happened. On the other hand – were he to go to court and be found guilty, which seemed highly likely – then the press, to quote Busy Sandra's weighty words, 'would have a field day.'

The main sticking point was that Allan kept asserting he hadn't 'done' anything. He hadn't actually touched anyone, and no one had touched him. He hadn't allowed it. For Health and Safety reasons.

'Yes, but according to Busy Sandra, you flashed it about.'

'But...'

'Did you or didn't you?'

'Yes.'

'Yes. And they've got you on camera. Maybe if you had got down to business they wouldn't be letting you off with a caution.'

'I've never been caught before.'

'They've never been so sneaky before. In the old days it used to be a siren or a blue light flashing, and that gave us time to do a runner.'

'But not any more.'

'No. Not any more.'


Allan accepted a caution. An hour later, Benson was leading him past the station sergeant. 'Nighty-night, Errol Flynn,' the man said.

Benson unlocked the passenger door of the car. Allan got in, and Benson pulled the seat-belt across his narrow chest for him. 'Safety first!' he told Allan, but Allan looked terminally glum.

'Can I come and stay with you and Rob?' Allan asked. 'I don't think I could stand being by myself tonight. I think I'd be a risk to myself. The thoughts keep going round and round.' He paused. 'I could drink on this.'

All sorts of thoughts bubbled in Benson's head as he hesitated – whether Rob would approve, the state of the sheets in the spare room, the distraction from poem-finding-and-burning, the temptation of Allan's presence, catering, ... but it all came together like a balloon – inflated itself past bursting with the mention of drink, and popped out as 'Course you can, Allan. What are mates for?'

'Thanks, Martin,' Allan said.

# 15

'Tea? Coffee? Something cold?' Benson asked, after he'd sat Allan down in the kitchen.

Allan consented to a tea and Benson, happy to have something to do that did not involve making conversation, something giving him time to think his own thoughts, to develop Allan-suiting strategies, bustled about making it. He checked the mugs to see they were pristine, and found to his great surprise that one was. He delved into the sugar bowl for lumps, smelled the milk jug for freshness, banged about in biscuit tins for some that had not gone soft, all the time whistling to himself.

'What I don't get is how we didn't have any advanced warning of police surveillance,' Allan said.

'Have you in the past?'

'Yes. There's generally a memo goes about: requests from the police to the cleansing department re. keys or opening and closing hours. That sort of thing.'

'But they've never used cameras before, have they?' Benson asked, alarmed, wondering if he was on film and being crowed about at this moment in some pornographic basement room at the cop shop.

'Not to my knowledge. But when you think about it, they'd have had to have council cooperation to install them. They'd be wireless, of course, but it wouldn't be an easy job to place them where no one would spot them.'

'I wouldn't dwell on it if I were you, Allan,' Benson

said, as he himself dwelled on it while throwing tea bags into the pot.'

'S'pose not.'

'Mind you, in my day some observant queen would have spotted things like that in no time at all. Quick jab with a nail file and back to business. People don't use their powers of observation like they used to,' Benson said, stirring the pot.

'It's the married ones I feel sorry for,' Allan said.

'How do you mean?'

'It's mainly married men that cottage these days.'

'I've often wondered,' Benson said, 'but how can you be so sure?'

'I'm sure.'

'Well, it would certainly explain them not being brought up to take surveillance seriously,' Benson said. 'I mean, have you ever been into a lock-up without checking for holes?'

'No.'

'Me neither.'

Benson, behind his tray, approached Allan, hoping for a happier apparition. He'd thought in his innocence that their easy conversation about cottaging mores would have perked him up. He was wrong.

'Er...'

'What?'

'Well, look at it this way, Allan. You obviously impressed that desk sergeant!'

'He was out of line. Way out of line. Errol Flynn indeed! Call that a compliment? I don't call that a compliment.'

'But it showed he'd been impressed.'

'Can't you just see them viewing the footage and having their mates in for a good laugh! Remember that case where someone in the surveillance room made a DVD and started selling it on eBay?'

'No. What happened?'

'He got the sack. But the tapes turned up on the internet for the whole world to gawk at.'

'It's a Trojan Horse, the internet,' Benson opined.

Allan nodded. Benson had the distinct impression that he hadn't taken in the full implications of his profound statement. Had he asked him why he thought the internet a Trojan Horse, Benson would have gone on about it being an exact parallel to the Greek myth. Without a by-your-leave, it had set itself up like a gift-horse – in the centre of people's houses. And we saw it as a gift, while really it was the ultimate intelligence-gathering tool, putting bad ideas into the heads of otherwise good people, giving messes of pottage, stealing intimacies, peddling distraction… And while he was on the subject…

'I shouldn't't've accepted a caution,' Allan said. 'I should have got a solicitor in to advise me.'

'But Busy Sandra said it was for the best. She wouldn't try to make things worse for you.'

'They could put me on the Sex Offenders' Register. Then the next time I have an Enhanced Disclosure it'll show up.'

'You're letting your imagination run away with you,' Benson said. 'Haven't you learnt anything at QA? Today is all we have. Anyway, Sandra would have said. She's got your interest at heart. You're OK now, aren't you – tea all right, is it?'

Allan nodded morosely.

'Good. So why fill your head with stinking thinking re the future? We can use our minds, Allan, as tools to get ourselves through each Present Moment. We can use it to sort out past mistakes and increase our chances of not repeating them in future. But we must try to resist the temptation to use our minds to invent horror films in the future. The future is unknown. If we live well in the present, the future will take care of itself.'

'But you're always thinking about the future, and worrying. I've heard you going on about getting old and sick and poor.'

Benson had been well aware of his own failings in the future department. But being hopeless at living in the present shouldn't stop him from reminding a poor flailing soul like Allan of what the failed preacher deemed to be true, should it? He wasn't a hypocrite, was he?

He admitted to Allan his failings in that department. 'But the point is, when I start getting all neurotic about what might happen in the future, I am becoming *aware* of what I'm doing. And you know what I'm doing, Allan? I'll tell you what I'm doing. I am learning more and more about myself and what makes me operate. A growing awareness of my tendency to fret is the best way to neutralise the behaviour because I don't mistake it for ... for ... what *will* be.'

'But I've got a lot to be worried about...'

'Maybe you have. Maybe you haven't. Whichever it is, it is beyond your power to control. So what is the next step, Allan? What's the ultimate tool in your toolbox?'

'I should hand it over to my Higher Power,' Allan said, without enthusiasm.

'Got it in one.'

Allan held his mug out for a refill. Benson chose to take this as a positive move on his part. But then Allan undid the impression by saying he'd better go and consult his solicitor. He might have options.

'If it'll help, do that,' Benson said. 'But they'll be closed tomorrow. Get some sleep. Rob will be back tomorrow. We can have a good talk with him. He's good on all this sort of thing. A bit of a rock is Rob.'

Benson sat Allan down in front of the TV and switched on. He went from channel to channel looking for something good. 'Hopeless!' he said.

'There's nothing on these days,' Allan said.

'Fancy a DVD?'

'Not much.'

'What do you fancy?'

'A cuddle,' Allan said.

'Come over here, then,' Benson said.

Allan scrunched up, close to Benson, and lay his head on his chest.

Benson looked down, then he wrapped his arms around Allan's head and squeezed him to him. *Amazing!* he thought. *I can fit my two hands completely around his skull. But all that activity inside! All those thoughts and emotions colliding with the brick walls or super-highways of habit! All those stone tablet dogmas, those route maps around the town, his wardrobe, the cutlery and crockery cabinets of home and the motorways of Britain! All that knowledge.* He crooked his head down and kissed Allan's bald spot, moved his right arm to pat his back. Once there, the hand moved around and around that back. He patted it like a mother burps a baby. He joined it with the other hand and squeezed Allan hard again. There was nothing to him. Such a small space he took up. Were he to die now and disappear, the settee would be back to itself with a brush of a hand. The problems would be forgotten. What would remain?

But the thought came round to himself. From where Benson sat on his interior-sprung throne framing Allan, the world would sit and frame him likewise. Like Harry Lime on the Big Wheel in Vienna we could look down on the dots and not worry what became of them. So very small after all. But before all he was human. He had to make the leap, to appreciate the wonderful chaos residing in each head, to forgive the clumsy failures of perception, the conflicts brought on by past experiences. The whole hugeness of the human undertaking. For it was as much himself as the other...

*No man is an island!* I'll pyrograph that. It's true. Every word. His hands ached to get his fire-pen into action on the project, but instead, he stayed where he was. Allan started to snore quietly. Benson dared not move a muscle. He stayed where he was and sought to dredge the poem – in his head still, courtesy of dear, dead Brother O' Toole, back to the desktop of his brain:

> No man is an island,
> Entire of itself.
> Each is a piece of the continent,
> A part of the main.
> If a clod be washed away by the sea,
> Europe is the less.
> As well as if a promontory were.
> As well as if a manner of thine own
> Or of thine friend's were.
> Each man's death diminishes me,
> For I am involved in mankind.
> Therefore, send not to know
> For whom the bell tolls,
> It tolls for thee.

Allan stopped snoring. A weak sun was setting out to the west. Benson watched the tangerine-skin shadow reach the skirting board by the window. In winter it never managed to shine on that north-facing window and the light – even though it exposed an area of window sill and dado rail in dire need of a duster – also told him that the world was turning towards spring.

Allan stretched, and shifted to a sitting position.

'You OK, Allan?'

'Yes, thanks.'

'Good,' Benson said.

# 16

The next morning, Benson tiptoed around the house, not wanting to wake Allan. He began pyrographing Shakespeare's Sonnet 130 onto the head of one of his new mallets, while sitting in his comfy easychair – bought at the hospice shop and covered in a bedouin weaving that always brought Juma'a to mind.

It was nice thinking of Juma'a, but when the wire nib of Benson's fire-pen heated, he had to give all his attention to what he was about to do. Was the mallet made of beech or maple? Not sure. He reduced the heat of the nib. Too hot, and the nib would make a thick burn – a thickness that would dictate the size of his characters. The sonnet had fourteen lines, packed tight with words and, while he knew that it would probably overflow the circular head of the mallet, finishing up trickling down the shaft, he was determined to make his burn suit the wood ... But, if the nib was too cool it would mean going over each letter twice or even three times before the black tattoo covered the wood. This could produce poor results. Then, of course, there was the vexed topic of what would happen when the fire nib went over the grain. Pine exploded and sparked lightning when so violated. All that aside, the right temperature and one fluent movement generally managed to shape a letter perfectly. The art was in finding that temperature. The craft to keep it pleasing.

His heart was thumping. Postponing the first burn to

allow himself to settle, he looked out of the window at the sea. A ferry boat – probably from Dublin – was heading into the estuary. The sea was calm, and he imagined people on the deck looking up at his house and envying him his view. But he dismissed that thought as vain, instead wishing them a safe landing and a happy onward drive to their ultimate destinations.

Turning back to the mallet, thinking how lovely it was merely as a plain piece of worked wood, thanking the anonymous man in Hull or Hong Kong who had prepared it for shipping out to the world, its surface already pyrographed by the lines and mottles that God had put there to signal its age, how like a picture in-the-round of sky and stratocumulus clouds the picture was. He held back the fire again, calling on his Higher Power to muse Sonnet 30 on to his creation, and thinking, *Am I A Lion or A Mouse?*, he struck.

The *W* appeared black and nicely italicised. He'd never quite 'got' italic writing – always thought because he was a left-hander and the nibs were never made for such as himself – but there it was scored into the surface with a red-hot nib that was about right. A tad cooler might still manage a clearer, cleaner cut, but there was no swelling of the line, no forest-fire-in-nanosphere conflagration out of his control. Relieved and inspired, he ventured: *When to the sessions of sweet silent thought.* Yes, that's good, he thought. He sought about in his rattan satchel, purchased in Kota Kinabalu, and got out his tape measure – a miracle in itself that it had managed to stay where he'd put it, as so little did – and measured the circumference of the mallet-head. Seven and a half inches, he thought. Longer than it looks. He contemplated the mallet-head and it too brought Juma'a to mind, and Emmanuel and

Wayne. Then he thought of Allan. He placed them all gently out of mind and pulled himself back from the brink of distraction to the present moment of creation. He measured the height of the line he had written, taking the capital *W* as his marker. No vertical stroke on *l, t, h, b, d,* k, *no dot of* i *or* j, *must venture higher than the pinnacle of the capital. Then, just as long as he managed to keep the hanging tails of* g, j, p, y, *and* q *from hanging too far down (Allan!), each line would take up a quarter-inch, with a one-eighth allowed for space between.*

All this mathematical computation brought Sister de Pazzi to mind. She'd banged in all those simple fractions, and they'd stayed. He'd not thought of her in years, decades – though Sister de Pazzi had called them 'deckets'. She'd called joined-up writing 'double writing'. Nobody knew what double writing was unless they'd had an Irish nun as a teacher. But, like Brother Hooper (I really must go and see him again!) and all his other teachers – well *nearly* all of them – they had given him skills he used every day. So why did he not think of them, and bless them, every day? He consoled himself that Brother O' Toole had come back, memorialised by the poems the Brother had forced him to learn by heart – and much else. He looked out to sea, and blessed them all. He thought of the hundreds of English language students he'd taught. Did they think of him? Then he thought of all the countries he'd worked in that were closed to him. Had he contributed to that? Was there some Step Work there? Probably, but not just at the moment.

Back to work, he told himself sternly. *I summon up remembrance of things past*, I suppose that is what I'm doing now. I suppose it's what I do an awful lot of the time. Funny – funny how the little book had opened at this page. People in QA told him there was no such thing as coincidence. But was this a coincidence, or was it just that Shakespeare spoke to every human – even him. *Everyman,* he thought. Good play that. Used to be done a lot. They named the theatre in Liverpool after it. Quite right, too. He'd seen it done in modern dress on the BBC. But not for ages. Not for ages. Probably too Catholic.

He measured, thought of Juma'a again, and found all was fitting. Mind you, there were some really long lines heading up along the way. *Watch yourself, mate!* Odd that. Every line was made up of ten syllables. Trouble was, the lines with lots of one-syllable words took up more than their fair share, due to the luggage of space they parked down between them. Still, line three's pretty easy. It's a cinch, that what it is … but I mustn't start getting proud of myself. Pride and falls. He'd have to go easy. Pride and falls. *I sigh the lack of many a thing I sought* Benson studied the line. Eleven syllables! Still that was the surface structure. The meaning hit him. People had died. People who had been his buttress. Now they had flown off but flew about him. He lived with many ghosts. He saw himself in hospices, visiting and trying to cheer. *There's a cure just round the corner. I read this piece in The Guardian.* There's a fellow who says that tea tree oil boosts the immune system. *It hadn't worked. He'd paid twenty pounds for a phial of it to add to Emerson's bathwater. The smell of it still reminded him of hoists and hospitals and morphine pumps and false dawns.*

*And with old woes new wail my dear time's waste;* Yes, that was true, all right. He did that all the time. He'd spat it all out in the general confession that had been his Step Five, but that didn't mean it was all done and dusted. 'We shall not regret the past nor wish to shut the door on it...' Well, no he didn't. Not usually. But, like recovery from his obsession for alcohol, it was a daily reprieve. To regret the past – Should have, could have, might have, if only I had/hadn't – the saddest words in English. Ways of expressing regret. But, mottled within the negatives, were flecks of pure gold, meetings along the Road of Regret which turned it into the Road Worth Taking. He couldn't regret all those countries he had worked in, all those students he had taught, all those people ... could he? *Then can I drown an eye, unused to flow,* and an opportunistic curl of smoke passed into his eye and smarted. He passed his right hand over it and continued burning. *For precious friends hid in death's dateless night* Oscar, Gerry, David, Tony, Don, Nabil, John, Frank, Michael, Carlton, Peter, Derek, Walt, Emerson ... and all those game Iranian trainee-helicopter pilots in his classes who soaked up English like a sponge and did Tom Jones impersonations and wanted to visit America and never thought that helicopters would ever be used in war. He had always thought there would never be war again; that all those Bell 205s, 206s and Cobras were parked on the Isfahan airstrip as a status symbol for the oil-rich, status-starved Shah to flash; to show Carter he was an ally by keeping Bell in business and allowing engineers relieved of duty in mad Vietnam to make a buck and decorate mobile homes in Texas with Qom silk rugs. But that wasn't what had happened. He had run off on Lufthansa, watched the return of Khomeini, the flight of the Shah, the sabre-rattling and hostage-taking, the war breaking out between Iran and Iraq: Mr Molaie, Mr Shadab, Mr Tabrizi, Mr Khuzestani, Mr Boviezadeh ... where were they? Where? Had they survived? 'English is the passport to the world,' he'd said. And he thought he had spoken true. But for those students it had also been the passport to helicopter-flying and to frontline duties in a war that incinerated millions. And he – Benson – had played his part.

He paused and brought as many faces as he could to his mind. They had meant a lot to him, those students, at least he'd thought so. Remembering them told him he had been a good teacher. The vocabulary and structure he had placed on their tongues and lips had been on their tongues and lips as they operated those helicopters to fight and die for their land. How many had survived? Benson looked out at the empty sheet of sea.

*And weep afresh love's long-since-cancelled woe* ... Well, he was doing that. No more than the truth. Face it. *And moan the expense of many a vanish'd sight* ... Benson stopped. He ran a hand over what had been achieved. Expense? He was paying the price now. He had rationalised his way through life. That is what I've done. I twisted the truth to suit my own ends. My head full of sixties' protest songs and news stories from Selma and Saigon did not get in the way of me leaving the pittance at the British Council and teaching the military. I went against what I believed. *'We will not regret the past, nor wish to shut the door on it.'* No, I'm not there yet. Maybe because I haven't made amends. But how do I make amends for this sort of thing? How?

He shook himself, thought how he'd have to have a good talk with Rob, and turned back to the sonnet: *Then can I grieve at grievances foregone* Ah, Shakespeare! Maybe I should take him as my Higher Power. He says it all. He can see through me. Just a grammar school education too! Left at fourteen! Did all this just flow, like a river in spate? He'd read somewhere that Shakespeare was a 'natural' whereas Milton had to pray for the descent of the muse, and labour over every line. Shakespeare was dead at my age. Maybe it would be easier if I just shuffled off. Maybe it's all absurd anyway. Maybe it's about right for me to close the curtains on this messy life and make room for the rising generation? *And heavily from woe to woe tell o'er The sad account of fore-bemoaned moan, Which I new pay as if not paid before...* But maybe Shakespeare had experienced all this as well. Is there consolation there? A lovely word, Consolation. Consolation prizes were all I ever got from stalls at the funfair. Maybe fond memories are my consolation prize for missing the star prize of integrity.

> *But if the while I think on thee, dear friend,*
> *All losses are restored and sorrows end.*

Benson surveyed his work. He had managed to make the whole poem fit the mallet! The friend for whom the sonnet was written has power over the poet: the power to lance the boil of all that comes back to haunt him from a life replete with lacks, woes, time's waste, dead friends, love lost, vanished sights, grievances, resentments. He thought of Rob. Yes, he's the one all right. The real thing.

He stood up, placed the mallet on the table and went off in search of Allan, hoping Rob would come back soon.

# 17

There was a bump in the white winter-weight duvet. Benson gave it a prod. When this produced an angsty moan, he blunted the sharp gesture by turning it into a gentle shake of the bump. Allan moaned again.

'You're not still in bed, are you, Allan?' Benson asked, like an exasperated mother choosing to ignore the bleeding obvious in an effort to register total incredulity bordering on disgust marbled through and through with despair.

A muffled affirmation.

'Have you been there *all day*?'

Another muffled affirmation.

'Aren't you feeling well?'

No response at first, then the bump started to move and Allan emerged, uncombed and very unhappy. 'I'm sorry, Martin. I didn't sleep at all last night. My brain was racing. I was scared out of my wits – still am. How am I going to face life after what happened?'

This seemed a bit thick after all the TLC Benson reckoned he had given Allan. 'Look, Allan,' Benson said. 'Nothing much happened. You flashed your bits in the cottage and were unfortunate enough to get photographed by those fucking busies who should be busy with more important stuff. You accepted a caution and now all you've got to do is keep out of trouble and ... and walk tall.'

'But what if it gets out? What if Environmental Health finds out? What if...'

'Cross that bridge when and if you come to it,' Benson said – amazed at his own sageness in matters to do with others.

'But I'm a Health and Safety officer!' Health-and-safety Allan said. 'If they name and shame me, I could be sacked. We've got to be beyond reproach. I have to go into houses and businesses where there are kiddies present. If I fail my Criminal Records Bureau Enhanced Disclosure – or if the Bureau rats on me over this – then I won't be able to do my job. And Health and Safety is my life!'

Having made that portentous and despairingly desperate assertion, Health-and-safety Allan sought to dive under the duvet again.

Benson watched, wondering how he could be of assistance. For all he knew, Allan was right. Maybe he would fail the Enhanced Disclosure. Benson had never needed one. You could pyrograph with a list of convictions as long as your arm. But he might have failed it, if the prying cameras had been installed – and there had been anyone in the place but himself – on the one occasion he had 'done the cottage' on the prom for old times' sake. As it was, he had just stood there, whistling *We Kiss In A Shadow*, and left after giving himself a good shake. *Too old for this lark*. Then he remembered the garden centre episode, and blushed inwardly.

Why, he wondered, as he watched the lump in the duvet turn more and more foetal in contour, do the police waste police time with this sort of nonsense? Doubtless the neighbours had complained. Well, he had complained about kids behaving badly *in his garden* and no one had shown up. He had complained about the vehicles belonging to Stoneacre Garage – parked where residents might like to park outside their own houses – having no road tax discs. Nothing. He had complained when dogs sowed the pavement close to his property with turds that a human would have been proud of – real three-flushers some of them... Nothing. No explanation about why nothing had been done. And yet they go to the trouble of installing cameras in a cottage and using their scarce resources to mount surveillance for SIX MONTHS! They did not stop all the heteros from doing their advanced courting sessions in their cars, sometimes on the roofs of cars. They did not stop the scandalous occurrences of dogging (the direct opposite of discreet cottaging) that he – Benson – had witnessed taking place in the sandhills. They did not stop anything that needed stopping. Rather they went about looking busy with their wretched sirens and their 'I rule the world' ways. Arrogant bastards! Big over-paid bullies!

Benson shushed his 'Me' side and let his sage 'I' side take the helm, and return his fragile craft to its QA-preferred default position: 'There's a meeting tonight,' Benson told the lump. No response. 'I'll go with you, if you like.' Still no response. 'You really should get yourself to a meeting.'

'But...'

'No buts,' Benson said, sounding like Rob, and knowing he sounded like Rob. 'Meetings are essential on occasions like this. You've got to get things into perspective.'

Allan's head emerged.

Benson shook his head, smiled down at Allan magnanimously. 'If I had a dick like yours, Allan, I'd never put it away.'

'It's my cross,' Allan said. 'Why can't I just be normal, like you?'

Benson elbowed that disparaging remark about his endowment to the sidelines. 'Nothing happens in this world without a reason behind it,' Benson said. 'You have received a great gift from your Higher Power. You and I know that we have been given a gift for seeing the glory of creation in the male human body. We don't know why we are attracted to other men's members when we have a perfectly serviceable one conveniently placed about our persons. It's a mystery – and I confess it can be a bit of a cross at times. But yours – and I hope I am not embarrassing you by pointing it out ... but I feel you need your endowment pointed out and celebrated – it's truly remarkable. Every sight of it, even recalling it in a place of tranquillity – during our meditations, say – can engorge us with gratitude for the unutterable beneficence, and randomness, of The Higher Power's ineffable handiwork.'

Benson stopped, wondering if there was a book in it. Perhaps a book on the magnificence of the male genitalia might be the Magnum Opus of my mature years! Writing a book would be wonderful, much better than pyrographing 'Souvenir of Loggerheads' on suitable softwoods. It would be the ultimate coffee-table book. Perhaps it should come with its own built-in and beautifully pyrographed-by-the-author coffee table. That could be a selling-point. And think how entertained Benson would be by the production of such a tome, which was bound to become the last word on the human penis. What should he call it? *The Human Penis in Art and Photograpy – A History*? *The Great Secret Exposed*? *Penis*? *Penis!*? Still, he mustn't get bogged down in all that. It might sell a million. Women might buy it too!

Health-and-safety Allan seemed unconvinced. 'All my life it's brought me nothing but trouble! And now this! You know what I'd like to do with it, Martin?'

'What?'

'Have it off.'

'You're talking complete rubbish, Allan! What a slap in the face that would be for your Higher Power! He chooses you as the recipient of the pinnacle of his creation, and you ungratefully want to throw it all away. When did you last do a Gratitude List? Because, Allan, I'd say your magnificent endowment should come in right behind your greatest gift...'

'And what's that?' Allan asked.

'You know. I shouldn't have to tell you that.'

'My Advanced City and Guilds in Health and Safety?'

'No, compared to your number one, the Advanced what-you-said is a paltry thing, Allan.'

But Allan could not get what Benson was driving at.

So Benson told him. 'Your *sobriety*, Allan. Your daily reprieve from Alcoholism. And, if you'll excuse me for saying so, Allan, that is the *sine qua non* for the rest of the list which, I trust, will cover many pages. But Number 2 – in this alchie's humble opinion – would be your gorgeous cock.'

Allan nodded, though not as enthusiastically as Benson would have liked. Now was probably not the time for Benson to broach what he wanted to broach, namely, if Allan would consent to pose for full-page glossy photographs to be given pride of place in his upcoming book, whose name had still to be decided. 'Your Health and Safety went to the wall when you were a piss artist, didn't it, Allan? Your dick was only good for pissing up against the wall, or in your bed. Didn't you once mention that you'd pissed in the wardrobe as a matter of routine when pissed?'

'You didn't tell anyone, did you?'

'No, of course I didn't!' Benson replied passionately. 'But it's not something a fellow forgets.'

Allan nodded morosely.

'All I'm saying is that you've got a lot to be grateful for. We all have. So have you done a gratitude list recently?'

'Not recently.'

'Well, you damned well ought to. I do them quite frequently – whenever I'm down in the dumps I do one. And if I did one for you, I know what Number 1 would be on my list ... above Rob, the house, three square meals, my health, a daily bowel movement ... and that's my sobriety. I know I'm repeating myself but I think you need the facts drummed in, Allan. I really do.'

'But you've got Rob. Who do I have, in spite of my big dick?'

'Ummm...' Benson began. It was true that Health-and-safety Allan, though he succeeded in keeping the citizenry informed of, and often enough barricaded away from, places of ill-health and hazard, had not managed to find himself a partner. Benson felt that – apart from Allan being Allan – even the most enthusiastic and willing of his conquests would, when push came to shove, be at a loss to know what to do with him. It was not as if Allan insisted or anything. He knew well enough that from the point of view of Health and Safety his own endowment needed stern warning signs – probably backed up by hazard lights in the vicinity. What could anyone do but put their arms around it in a loving manner ... and weep? That might be OK for some, for a time or two. But to have such limitations placed on one's sexual expression for much longer than that? Well, no.

But Benson did not feel he could be honest about that. Allan would know it all better than he did. Instead, he coaxed Allan out of bed with the promise of a long hot shower and a fluffy towel dressing gown for after. And, if he was very good, some hot chocolate.

\* \* \*

'That's a slippery surface if ever I saw one,' Allan said as he undressed. 'Don't you have a bath mat with suction cups on the back. They don't cost much.'

'We had one, but it perished. Got mouldy on the back and fell apart.'

'A dilute solution of bleach and water in an old spray bottle will stop that from happening,' Allan said. 'You don't have to buy those expensive products.'

'Do you think you'll manage? There is a grasp-rail. That was there when I bought the house, but I suppose it'll come in useful for me soon.'

Allan thought about that. 'A grab-rail AND a mat are a simple combination for saving people no end of serious, even life-threatening, injuries,' Allan said, and he removed his underpants.

Benson turned away, but not fast enough. When he did so, he was left with the impression on his retina, busy burning into his brain, of Allan's wonderful dick. 'Well you just be careful, Allan. Press the bell if you need me. That was kindly left us when the previous occupant went to the Seaview Home. He only lasted a week there.'

And he evacuated the bathroom.

Downstairs, he opened the freezer. He stood in front of the frozen cornucopia, seeing Allan's dick. He was brought to himself by the sound of a motorcycle heading up the driveway.

'Oh, God!' Benson prayed. 'What do I do now?'

And God, who looked a bit like the rider of the motorcycle, replied, 'Be yourself. Be honest.'

Rob came in, taking off his yellow luminous jacket. He had his leathers on underneath. 'You're back,' Benson said.

'Yeah,' Rob said. 'Give us a kiss.'

Benson did so.

'You're hard,' Rob said.

'Am I?

'You are. Very.'

'Did you have a good time?'

'A very good time. Jack's great company. We sorted a lot out.'

'That's good,' Benson said. 'I suppose you're hungry. You always come back from trips hungry.'

'Yeah. Hungry as fuck. But I'm chilled as fuck too. Fancy a bath. You can join me, if you like. You seem to need a good seeing-to.'

'Ummm,' Benson said. 'However, there is a bit of a problem...'

And, sitting Rob down, he told him everything – well nearly everything – that had happened since he'd been away.

# 18

By the time Benson concluded his tale, while at the same time making Rob a strong mug of tea, Allan had vacated the bathroom – leaving it pristine – and gone back to his room. Rob stripped off for his bath. Benson did the same, and in no time at all (the time it took to sprinkle some Radox into the steaming water and jiggle the green powder about and pronounce the water 'Just Right') Rob had mounted him like some scrawny mountain goat and was seeing to him most satisfactorily.

'You been playing about with Allan, haven't you? Have you?'

'A bit, yes,' Benson gasped, like a kid in confession.

'Good, was it?'

'We didn't *do* anything.'

'A likely story. Come on, out with it.'

'I *admired* it.'

'First, you admired it. But that wouldn't be enough for you. Come on, what else?'

Benson would have turned to face Rob and deal with the accusation eyeball to eyeball, but he was in no position so to do. Instead he felt the joyous feel of Rob's swinging scrotum tickling him from behind like a weighted powder-puff. He loved that. Always had. 'I ... I ... I ...' he said instead.

'It's all about you, isn't it? All. About. You. You need your ego deflating good and proper. That's what you need. That's What You Need.'

'Yes.'

'I didn't hear you.'

'Yes.'

'Did you let Allan into you?'

'You've got to be joking! Have you *seen* Allan?'

'You're a bit on the slack side. You *did*, didn't you?'

Benson tensed himself. 'OK. I did. I took him like sweeties. We did it all over the place.'

'On the motorbike?'

'Yes.'

'On the kitchen table?'

'Yes.'

'On me mam's sewing table?'

'No.'

'No?'

'All right. Yes.'

'Yes! Thought so. What am I going to do with you?'

'Just what you're doing.'

Rob accelerated. 'Like this?'

'Yes. Yes.'

Rob changed his angle of attack. 'Like this?'

'Yes. Yes.'

And Rob was silent, then. He always went silent then. Then he was against him, spooning into him. He gasped and lay still, while Benson supported himself with both hands firmly splayed on the bottom of the full bath.

Rob released himself and, without a word, got into the bath. His cock lolled among bubbles and green water. Like Ophelia, Benson thought. Benson scrubbed it down and then leaned deep into the bath – like a medieval pilgrim into the well of St Winefride, and partook. Then he scrubbed Rob's back, offered to wash his hair – an offer Rob declined with a grunt.

'I only looked at it,' Benson said.

'I believe you.'

'What about you and Jack?'

'A bit of a cuddle. I wanked him off. Took ages.'

'That was nice of you.'

'I owe 'im,' Rob said.

'So what do you think I should say to Allan?'

'Sounds to me like you've said all you can say. Tell him he can stay here for as long as he likes. He needs company, and he might go to pieces and drink if he's alone. If you ask me, a few days with nothing happening to get him into trouble should bring him back to the land of the living.'

'You don't think anything could happen, do you?'

'Hard to say. I'm not sure he should have accepted a caution. I'd like to know exactly what he signed. They can put you straight onto the Sex Offenders' Register. And that might mean trouble.'

'But Busy Sandra said it would be all right.'

Rob hurumphed, got out of the bath and Benson happily set about drying him with a fluffy white towel from top to toe. 'I love you, Rob.'

'So you should,' Rob said. 'You're not so bad yourself. On a good day.'

That was about as good as it got. The heterosexual side of Rob, the butch, cloth-cap side, couldn't do more than that. It was as far out of his comfort zone as he was prepared to venture.

'You know what I fancy right now?' Rob said.

'Surely not...'

Rob bothered Benson's mock-shocked rejoinder out of the way. 'Two big doorsteps of buttered toast, and a pot of strong tea.'

'Brown?'

'White.'

'Brown is better for you.'

'White makes better toast. We'll eat it at the kitchen table. I've got a couple of things to talk to you about.'

'Righto. I took the consignment to Muriel, by the way. She wants me to do poems for her.'

'What sort of poems?'

'Poems that suit weddings, funerals and car accidents.'

'Is there money in it?'

'Not sure. They'll take time. 'Souvenir of Loggerheads' I can dash off in five minutes, but a poem takes time.'

'Maybe you should get a proper job.'

'Not teaching.'

'No. I think we decided when you tried supply that you weren't suited to it. Remember how you were?'

'Yes.'

They tiptoed downstairs, hoping Allan would give them a bit of time together. *A proper job.* What could he *do?* Greeter at Asda? Salesman at B & Q? He'd wondered about being a home-carer. After all, he'd liked that job when he was a student in New York. He'd felt useful, needed, satisfied. But would he be up for all the lifting, now?

He needed to do something.


'Jack and Bill are going to tie the knot,' Rob said.

'That's nice,' Benson said, buttering Rob's toast.

'I haven't finished yet...'

'Sorry.'

'...Rob wants you and me to join them.'

'I must have been psychic when I bought that suit,'

Benson said, thinking of the sad salesman, and how he hadn't called. He ought to call to see if he'd managed to fix himself up with another job.

'To join them at the ceremony.'

'Best Man? Usher? I can do that, but you'd better be Best Man.'

'They want us to join them in a civil partnership. A double partnership.'

'Do they?' Benson asked. 'And what did you say?'

'I said I'd ask you.'

'Ask me what?'

Rob reached across and grabbed the buttered toast, though Benson still had some more butter on his knife to spread on it. He looked at the knife, wondering what it all meant. Is Rob proposing?

'What did I just say?'

'Well, you said that Jack and Bill wanted us to join them in a civil partnership. Do you want to?'

Rob squirmed. 'Do you?'

'Are you proposing?'

'Well, we might as well.'

'"Might as well!"' How do you mean, 'might as well'?'

'We're neither of us getting any younger...'

'No, but...'

'And we've settled down...'

'Yes, but...'

'And you said you loved me before...'

'And it's no more than the truth, but...'

'But what?'

'But...' Benson had a sudden flash of the obvious. Why all these buts? Why after all his time with Rob did he not see that any proposal, if proposal there was to be, would be couched in any other than the way Rob was expressing it? Here he was – on the cusp of his seventh decade – and the man he loved was trying to blurt out the fact that his love was reciprocated and would be appropriately celebrated and he could count on him until Death did them part. 'I'll give it some thought,' Benson said.

'Butter that other piece of toast, would you?'

A moment's let-down. Why no bended knee? 'Coming up!' Benson said, happy to know the bit of butter still on the end of his knife might not go to waste.

# 19

Health-and-safety Allan put in an appearance a few minutes later. Benson was pleased by the interruption, as Rob was going on about finances and the long-term and proper jobs. Allan had obviously gone to some trouble to look tidy: he had shaved – probably with one of Benson's ten-for-a-quid disposables from The Pound Shop. Tell-tale nick marks gave him – and the cheap razor – away. He'd dowsed himself with Benson's precious Caron pour un Homme, though there was some ancient but serviceable Old Spice standing hopeful but neglected next to it. He'd combed his comb-over fairly becomingly over his pate, though, and, best of all, was no longer looking terminally depressed … more resignedly damaged, like someone who has received news of a serious illness while at the same time being told that the prognosis for recovery was pretty good.

Benson was dragooned into making two further rounds of white toast, to which he added baked beans and baby spinach straight from the bag. Allan sat down at the table opposite Rob. Benson joined them, but got a look from Rob that spoke of one-to-one discussions imminent between him and Allan to which Benson might be better absenting himself.

'I think I'll go for a walk,' Benson said, '…unless I'm needed.'

'Don't talk to any strange men,' Rob said. 'See you at the meeting?'

'Righto.'

He put on his Woolrich coat, which always brought cold films – especially *McCabe and Mrs Miller* and *The Shipping News* to mind. It had, over a sage green background, horizontal stripes of muted yellow, red and blue. He'd bought it at a sale in a shop in Upstate New York ages ago and fancied it was the only one of its kind on Merseyside.

He set off into the encircling gloom.

Funny how things work out, he thought. There was all that past, all those penetrations, all the shallow scratches he'd made on the world's surface and many men's backs, all those countries, all those chances for a makeover of his old self in new places. All those moves. At QA they called these 'Geographicals'. It was a common tactic of the alcoholic type to think that a move would make all the difference. Relationships? Resentments? Recidivism? Recursion? Shake the dust from your feet! Pick up your passport! Un-nail your boots from the kitchen floor! Piss on your own front door! Farewell, suckers! You won't see me again in a hurry! See how *that* makes you feel! And off he'd popped. How many fridges had he bought and sold since he started moving about? A dozen, probably. And in all those countries he'd bought craft and music players and bedding and then sold them – or given them away – when he moved huffily on.

And those poor things lugged back, stored in Dad's shed, then moved to the cottage, flat, house he had bought, slowly but surely had weighed him down like an anchor holds a boat in place. They showed him where he had been, though a trip around the ethnic knick-knacks department of TK Maxx managed that just as well these days...

Most people – people such as lived in the houses he was passing, people living behind the same windows, drawing the same curtains morning and night, day after day, as children were born and hairlines receded and proper jobs rolled out behind them along with the steady rails of pension plans and experiences and a few thousand fridge-loads of food from Sainsbury and such, and tens of sets of sheets, and Christmases breaking the bank, and kids growing up, breaking hearts and banks again, changing and worrying their mums and dads sick prior to going their own way – they had lived lives that were in the main orderly. *From a disorderly passion for knowledge ... O Lord, deliver us!*

He had drifted, looking for Dearest Him or a good fucking, for the country that would welcome him as Aqaba had welcomed Lawrence of Arabia, for *something* that home was incapable of bestowing. He had never understood how they could have settled for that one deep furrow. He simply did not feel how the whole world turned. He had always known that it *did*, but all that passed him by on the other side.

Yet here he was! (He stopped, looked at the blank sky, and asserted: *Here I am!*) Here he was, a recovering drunk, and Rob had literally fallen over him a scant mile from where he had been born and borne him off to a world of slogans and ego deflation and spirituality that he would have scoffed at before he needed them like a drowning man needs a lifebelt. A Day At A Time. Live and Let Live. Move A Muscle; Change a Thought. Give a Sucker an Even Break. Most Men Can Be As Happy As They Make Up Their Minds To Be. And all this in his hometown, which had changed in so many ways. He had returned to a place – what had brought him back? What? Might

135

as well ask what brought house martins, swallows and swifts back – a place that had changed. Changed utterly.

He was walking around and around an oval. In the centre a stand of trees and grass. Daffodils were blooming – a carpet of them, seen dimly now in the red-to-yellow light of waking street lamps. Facing this area of green, its stern railings denying access to the owners of the houses all around it, the spacious semis stared at the stand of noble trees. They had not changed one iota. It was a quiet place to live, ideal for bringing up a family. Cars lined the road in front of the houses, but there was no way out except by the way you came in. For pedestrians it was different: two wide footpaths with bollards to keep tempted cars out, allowed access to the street where St Peter and Paul's church was ... while the other connected with streets leading into the body of the town, and to the one where he had grown up, where had been sired so many of the thoughts and attitudes, the fears and obsessions, that still accompanied him through his life half an odd century later. Here it all looked the same.

But that was an illusion. The doors of St Peter and Paul's had been locked shut for over three years. The congregation could neither fill it, nor pay for its maintenance. The priests had fled to more manageable churches – the R.C.s sharing one with the Church of England half a mile away, a building Benson had never entered. Funny how things changed. The mantra of the old. The mantra of the world. As a child he had been forbidden to enter Church of England churches. It had been a sin. Now the Mass was offered there, along with Anglican services, because times had changed. The marble columns and statuary of St Peter and Paul's snoozed unseen, uncared-for, unremembered by all but a few of the dying generations who wanted their church back.

And from his ignored grave in the cemetery half a mile away, Father Mullins – who had built St Peter and Paul's – returned to dust, his bones crumbling into the soil, along with the relics of his triumphalist dreams. He had been spared the slow decay of his great beacon of a parish church, built with the devout coppers of day-trippers during the Depression, decorated by successful Catholic building contractors and shipping magnates and shop-owners and faithful policemen like his dad. If Father Mullins could see what had happened, and maybe he could, then he would, doubtless, be thinking similar thoughts to Benson. Live long enough, die long enough, and the world became more and more peculiar. Long before one had a chance to become a ghost oneself, the world had performed its own geographicals – international, national, local, intimate – becoming a ghost landscape that both mirrored and prefigured one's own ghosthood. Nothing more true.

And people died. They jumped from the scale of living to that of death. Benson had watched them do it. Death had brought him back to church for the time it took to bury a loved one and he'd been amazed by the turn-out for his dad's funeral. He'd met faces he remembered but could not name. They'd come up to him to tell him of his dad's caring ways, his fidelity to the parish and to anyone who needed his assistance. By chance, he'd been home when his dad had died while delivering a mattress for the Saint Vincent de Paul. He'd survived his second wife, whom he'd nursed faithfully for a decade while cancers swelled and shrivelled, until the last one grew, and grew until it killed her. No, the scales were more like a park see-saw – not that they had see-saws any more. Gone the way of jerkers, that rough boys jerked too high, while Benson held on tight and prayed to the unknown patron saint of risky playground rides that it wouldn't end in blood. Benson saw himself increasingly alone on one end, up in the air and waiting for the crash downwards while the growing number of the dead seated in a grounded and stoic line on the other end, gazed up at him, held him frightened and aloft in the unlikely state called *living*. But the more dead there were, the more he was deprived of those old friends, the more the temptation came to slide from the see to the saw. His own death – which he thought about quite often these days – might be a friend. He would take him by the hand and lead his out of this peculiar world into somewhere that finally made sense.

He did one more circuit around the oval, then took the footpath leading towards his childhood home.

# 20

Whoever owned his home now was doing well. A four-by-four snoozed next to a small white BMW in the drive. The garden Mum had been so proud of had been rooted out and paved to accommodate the second car. The garage had been turned into a room, and another room built on top. Where the roof had been hung four windows, one dormer, three Velux. Benson's bedroom was still there, though the window was PVC double glazed, venetian blinds replacing the curtains.

For a moment he was tempted to knock at the front door that snoozed behind a spanking-new airtight porch. He could introduce himself as a curious former resident. He might inform the surprised but delighted new residents of the history of the house.

No, I don't think so, he told himself.

He fled the old cul-de-sac, his heart breaking with the weight of it.


What had started the drinking? It had been pretty measured at first; only becoming obsessive when he discovered how much easier social – and intimate – situations were with a skinful under his belt to stop him rattling. Drink had made all sorts of madness possible; it stopped thought; blurred his self-consciousness; helped him live in the exciting present. All the disciplines Rob was guiding him towards to make him integrate with the world, and with himself, to become a man of integrity, drink had granted instant access. He felt totally 'himself' whenever he drank, free to cruise with fluency, to make love with due diligence and to be myopic to the absurdity of so much of his behaviour. Not to see that he was forever diving head first into the shallow end. It was absurd – when viewed through the clear glass window of sobriety – to offer himself for a taxi rank full of bored Arab taxi-drivers ... but he'd done it under the influence of Saudi Sedeeki liquor and gone back for more most late Thursday nights, always primed with the illegal gut-rot stuff. 'Sedeeki' was Arabic for 'my friend'.

He walked, excited in spite of himself by the memory of a thirty-year-dead erotic memory. And there were more where they came from. They tumbled through his head one after another, those times of sluttery-under-the-influence, Benson as sexual outlaw, swanking about his conquests: *I don't know what came over me.*

But did he have one friend left to show for all that tomfoolery in Saudi Arabia and Iran and Elsewhere? No. Not a one. Lost, unwritten to, or dead. He could not think of any trade who had even treated him with respect – not that respect had been on the top of the shopping list. They had used him. What had they made of him? This foreigner who took them like sweeties and who didn't ask for anything back ... not a kiss, a touch, a mote of conventional satisfaction? What, indeed?

Sometimes he thought he possessed secret knowledge. These days when he heard baying mullahs and malignant radicals expounding on the evils of the West versus the purity of Saudi and Iranian youth, he would recall those experiences. Sometimes he and his expatriate chums (for men with tastes similar to his were Legion) would discuss the whole phenomenon. Their sex lives depended on the strictures of Islam for their fulfilment, though few had come to the region with such a picture of what the sex would consist. It was all going to be swaying palm trees and romance, rather than what it was: a grope and being taken against a wall, in the back of a taxi or in desert scrub, followed by post-ejaculatory contempt. A few souls sensed what was afoot for their hearts and turned away sad. But after a few tries the indifference of his tricks to all except the active satisfaction of their lusts, and an end to that day's itch, became not only expected, but desired. It fitted in somehow. It felt like pleasure and sin and penance and a numbing of need all in one neat stab.

Jumbo jets had spoilt things. The pure Saudi youth – and old leches – had been able to jet off to Bangkok for a bit of what they fancied. Women were imported as nannies and cleaners, and these also served to slake the frustration of sex-starved males. It was all getting a bit frayed even before AIDS entered the equation.

Benson had just finished a six-month stint in San Francisco writing a language course when he heard about something that stopped him in his tracks. Something was killing Homosexuals, Haitians and Haemophiliacs. That something was given the name GRID (Gay Related Immune Deficiency) at first, but soon turned into AIDS.

Having been something of a notorious figure around the gay bath houses of San Francisco and Oakland, Benson was one of the first in line for an AIDS test when they were offered.

Though he kept putting the thought aside as Old Benson whenever he caught himself thinking it, he was convinced that if anyone deserved AIDS, he did. It did not take

fulminating chiefs of police or kick-a-fellow-when-he's-down
Tories to tell him that. No, it came from much farther
back. The past he had buried deep under a pile of old
fridges, bedding, craft, experiences, and vistas. Catholicism
had got him off on the wrong foot, but had, like a
program running in conflict to the one on his active
desktop, stopped everything dead in a crisis. And here it
was.

The test came back negative, but AIDS acted as a
bromide to shrivel the tumescent sex life he'd enjoyed
just a year before. To bang in the point that the wide
world of sex had been banged shut in his face, he took
a job at an English Language School in Colchester, bought
a railway cottage on the Clacton Road, and rode the six
miles to work on a bicycle.

But AIDS came to Benson. It came over the airwaves,
through the mail as friends fell ill: friends who'd had to
flee Saudi Arabia – where HIV infection meant gaol. Some
came to visit, and stayed with him in the cottage. It came
to him from all directions, testing him, making him examine
his life and what he had made of it. As the scratchy rhetoric
from politicians and religious groups – many of whom saw
the illness that had caught up on them unawares as a
punishment from 'God' – it made him think of where he
belonged. He journeyed to London to join marches. At the
assembly points he surveyed the variety of gay human life
and generally tagged along with women wheeling prams
behind the banner of 'Lesbian Ratepayers' as he felt he
belonged there better than anywhere else.

But sex stopped dead in its tracks. He was becoming
a celibate, living on alcohol, his memories and a wank
when he was in any state for one. But he did not feel
any the less homosexual. He tried his hand at writing,

even managed to get a short story on the radio that pretty much encapsulated how he felt:

A Reuters report from the University of Tel Aviv's Genetic Labs. 17 October 1988:

> The removal of eggs from would-be but infertile mothers for transplantation into their own mothers has become a routine procedure here in Tel Aviv. The time has come when mothers can look forward to having the grandchildren they so yearn for. Worry, doubt and disappointment are being spliced away.

A conversation between Mrs Wright and Mrs Dainty on the top deck of a number 23 bus passing the National Gallery. Saturday, 9 pm, 18th of October 1998:

*(They glare at two men across the aisle)*

Mrs Wright:   It's disgusting, those two men.

Mrs Dainty:   Don't worry, love. They're a vanishing breed. By the time we're getting our pension, they'll be a thing of the past. The Appliance of Science.

From a radio phone-in programme. Christmas Eve 1999:

Listener:   And stealing a perfectly good word like 'gay'! Such an apt little word for denoting all the really nice things in life. The sooner we can have it back the better.

From a by-line in page 17 of *The Daily Express*, July 17th, 2000:

*The gang of youths then attacked a Mr Alfred Slade. Mr Slade is 34, unmarried, and a male nurse. He was brought for treatment at the casualty department of Kings Cross Hospital where he had been on duty until half an hour before the attack. The police are making enquiries.*

From *L'Osservatore Romano*, the newspaper of Vatican City, 15 August 2015:

*His Holiness Pope N'Baki the first has announced a postponement of the eagerly-awaited encyclical Noli Me Tangere (Don't Touch)*

October 30th, 2021. Graffiti painted in six-foot-high letters along the south wall of the Thames Embankment (opposite the Houses of Parliament) but not big enough for most of the members dining within to read and understand:

**If Michelangelo had been heterosexual, he'd have painted the ceiling of the Sistine Chapel in Magnolia Gloss.**

A confidential memo from the Pentagon Scientific Grants Committee (PESCIGCO) to the Quaker Hospital Pennsylvania: 6 November 2034.

*Following budget cuts, all grants for gene research are to be discontinued with immediate effect.*

4th July 2038. From a questionnaire given routinely to expectant mothers by NHS maternity hospitals and midwives:

**Our citizen gene selection programme can now assist you in having a healthier, happier baby. Tick the attributes you wish to erase:**

**MALE** ___
**FEMALE**___ *Tick one only*
*TENDENCY TO BALDNESS* ___
*TENDENCY TO SEXUAL DEVIANCE* ___
*TENDENCY TO MULTIPLE SCLEROSIS* ___
*TENDENCY TO SICKLE-CELL ANAEMIA* ___
*TENDENCY TO LACK OF DRIVE* ___
*TENDENCY TO LEFT-HANDEDNESS* ___
*TENDENCY TO A SENSE OF HUMOUR* ___

(Peaceable) march through Heartsease, Pennsylvania by white-coated men and women:

*'SAVE OUR RESEARCH! SAVE OUR WORLD!*

From *Hansard* 12 March 2050:

I would draw the honourable member's attention to the green paper, *Let's Cut It Out and Race Ahead*. We as a nation are already in the vanguard for widening the choices in gene selection. Downs Syndrome has been eradicated. The party opposite seem cast into the depths of despond that the people are so happy.

It is also so typical of the right honourable gentlemen to whitter on about the high-spirited antics of the men in our armed services. Thank God for their aggression, say I! Without their spunk, what would keep our country great I'd like to know? So what if they sow a few wild oats in the member's constituency, josh with a few mamby-pambies? It's a price well worth paying. They have a right to a couple of pints of a Saturday. And let the party opposite not forget: that we can refine and domesticate the results of wild oats in the twenty-first century.

From *L'Osservatore Romano* (the Vatican newspaper) 1st May 2069:

*Pope Shane the First has announced a further postponement of the long-awaited encyclical, 'Noli Me Tangere' (Don't Touch).*

From a Worldwide Rupert Virtual Reality programme (Extra superwide 3D / Sensual Overload + / Rose-Scented):

<u>Mrs Boddington:</u>   *A long time ago, it was. But I remember it as if it was yesterday. My little brother – Rob his name was – he was the last Downs Syndrome baby to pass away. Back in 2030 that was. I know I shouldn't say this. I'm the age for the Portillo Exit Hospital, but I don't care. Rob was the sweetest man. Everybody loved him. The gentlest creature in the world, he was. He*

146

*taught me so much about what people could be. He was too sweet for this world if you get me. But he would have fitted in just right in a world that was halfways decent. I suppose you could say he looked funny. But he had a good heart, and that was rare even then. It was a crime what they did and...*

From *The Sun* 'cost a Bomb' 3D eye-implant sensory newspaper (with extra Page 3), just below an account of the forced entry of Mrs Boddington into the Blatch Exit Hospital:

*Why do we choose to be bald? The lack of decent hairdressers has been blamed for the new fashion of baldness in women*

From *L'Osservatore Romano* 20 September 2077:

*Pope Heidi the First has annouced a further postponement to the encyclical, 'Don't Touch'. Pope Heidi is to be married to His Eminence Cardinal Hok Kim Bang in the newly-painted Sistine Chapel. The bride will wear a magnolia wedding dress which exactly matches the Sistine Chapel ceiling. The princes of the church will be flown in from all over the world to toast the happy couple.*

A conversation outside the Baroness Blatch Basic Media Studies School in Highbury, Islington, overheard by a remote mike of the citizen's charter intelligence-gathering unit, 16 September 2079:

| First Mother: | Look at those teachers! Bang on the dot of four and they're off. |
| Second Mother: | Got to pick up their own kids, I expect. Can't be too careful. Not these days. |
| First Mother: | Remember Mr Harrison? He worked all the hours God sent. |
| Second Mum: | But he was a bachelor, you know. Had more time for the kids. |
| First Mum: | Not like today. |

From a BBC to Brain Radio news bulletin, 20 September 2079 from the fourth and fifth world war front:

*I think you can virtually feel my despair as I watch the massed wounded of United Nation troops unministered to by any nursing personnel. For the last three decades UN officials tell me it has been impossible to find any male nurses. Soldiers prefer a cyanide capsule to...*

A meeting of S.A.G.E. – Seniors Against Gay Ennui – held in a rusting container near the ruins of Canary Wharf, 13th November 2080:

*Brother and Sister. We three are the last of us. Scientists and Society have sucked our kind off of God's Palette and out of the world with their little pipettes. In a while, they will see us no longer. They did not appreciate our virtues.*

148

*Our contributions to every aspect of society were overlooked, downgraded. They mocked us at football matches, beat us in the street, then spliced us off the human gene-pool. But we were people who could have told them about a gentler blending of gender. We understood the underdog because we knew how it felt. But we were a people poor at war. The things we did not understand ... the rape, pillage, the macho strutting ... are all that is left. Still, let's all join hands and sing 'Somewhere Over the Rainbow'. After that, we'll dance till we drop.*

From *Hansard*, 29 May 2086:

*I know one can't get good help these days – for one's first home, let alone one's second. Butlers are an extinct species, as I for one have reason to know. But I would ask my honourable friends opposite, whether they were responsible for the appalling lack of hygiene in the DIY kitchens of the House? We on this side of the House are well-known for our scrupulous housekeeping. But when it falls to The Party opposite to do the washing up or the ironing of table linen or the repainting of the Chamber, a bloody cock-up ensues. Gold leaf all over the Members' benches...*

Bulletin from the Presteigne Medical Centre, Powys, Mid-Wales. 23 September 2098:

While Doctor Lewis and Dr Powell-Jones were working on the genetic material of a patient, they discovered the gene they are sure is the cause of aggression in the human male. They did this by process of

149

elimination: it was the only one it could be; the only gene that has not yielded up its secret. They have called it after the patient they were working on at the time: Sergeant Albert ('Bruiser') Thomas of the fifteenth Powys Light Laser Bike Brigade.

From *The Church Times*, 25 September 2098:

The Archbishop of Canterbury asserted today – in the strongest terms – that the arguments concerning the rights and wrongs of gene therapy had many rights and wrongs in them.

Note pinned to the door of the Presteigne Medical Centre, 28 September 2098:

THIS CENTRE IS CLOSED WITH IMMEDIATE EFFECT. PATIENTS IN NEED OF MEDICAL ATTENTION SHOULD PRESENT THEMSELVES TO THE BOTTOMLEY EXIT HOSPITAL BUILTH WELLS AT THEIR EARLIEST CONVENIENCE.

From *L'Osservatore Romano*, 21 December 2099:

Just in time for the new century, the Sistine Chapel ceiling has just received a fresh coat of paint. The well-loved magnolia has been replaced by a silky white paint with just a hint of lemon. The publication of the eagerly-awaited encyclical, Noli Me Tangere (Don't Touch), has once again been postponed. Her Holiness,

Pope Heidi, has announced the birth of her thirteenth child, a son, to be named 'Jude'.

### The End

He'd sent off another, but it came back. *The End.*

Why am I thinking all this stuff? Typical of me. *We shall not regret the past nor wish to shut the door on it.* Rob has proposed to me. I should be thinking of that. I should be waltzing like Shirley Jones – or was it Mitzi Gaynor? – in love with a wonderful guy!

He looked at his watch. Half an hour until the meeting. You, my friend, need a meeting. He made his way home and at the front gate, collided with Rob and Allan on their way out. If Rob had been anyone else, Benson would have rushed up to him and hugged and kissed him as his saviour. But Rob was Rob. He contented himself by linking arms with Rob, who surprisingly did not shrug him off.

'Remember I mentioned a proper job?' Rob asked.

'Yes?'

'Well, Jack was on the blower while you were out. There might be one going.'

'What?'

'Can you swim?'

151

# 21

'I've never been on the sick since I was sober. That's four years,' Health-and-safety Allan told Benson he'd told the doctor. Turning up bright and early at the surgery, noting that the brass plate could do with some Brasso, the garden a lot of attention, the path-flags pulled up to smooth out the patient-and-wheelchair-tipping scarps and dips to health-and-safety-preferred 'true'. The doctor searched about to download a letter, and half an hour later, Allan was back with his hosts.

Benson had delivered the note to the relevant council office because Allan couldn't face doing it. He also carried an envelope containing a list of explanation and instructions re. the priority cases on his schedule which could not be ignored in his absence. All had been informed of the tragic lack of Allan by nine, and Benson returned in plenty of time to make the stressed-out man a hearty breakfast, prior to waving him off for a visit to his solicitor, Castle and Castle, the ones Benson had used when he bought the house, but had vowed he wouldn't have in again.

'He's back to his old self,' Benson told Rob as Rob was about to set off for work. 'I'm tired already.'

And that was when Rob had added lubricant to the sticky mechanism that had grated in Benson's brain since first being brought up ... *A Proper Job*. 'There's the number to ring about the job. I've known the Boss for years. We

152

used to get rat-arsed together at The Bee Hive. He's
expecting your call. Needs men badly. So you might stand
a chance.'

Benson had nodded glumly. 'Don't you think I'm a bit
long-in-the-tooth?'

'Probably. But more a bit work-shy.' Rob put on his
luminous jacket. 'And work-shy is just one more kind of
fear. What do I always say?'

'I own my fear so it does not own me,' Benson replied,
quoting from a Peter Gabriel song which – if he wasn't
very much mistaken – he had turned Rob onto.

'Right. So take the action, Martin. This is a program
of action. Look at Allan! Whatever you say about him
he's facing life full-square. He's got the courage to take
a bit of action.'

'I know. An example to us all. But he's scared stiff
still. He'll be better if his name's kept out of the paper.'

'Well, he'll just have to cross that bridge...' Rob said.
'Give us a kiss.' And off Rob went to judge a few more
novice motorcyclists, and save them from themselves.

On the stroke of twenty-seven minutes to ten Benson
rang the number Rob had given him. The Boss told him
– a trifle brusquely Benson thought – to come round and
collect an application and Advanced Disclosure form. If
he got them back to him that day he'd be able to join
in Training Day Thursday, which also doubled as an
extended interview during which jibs would be inspected,
the cut of...

Obedient, feeling proud of himself for taking the action,
Benson walked down the hill to the Lifeguard HQ, picked
up the forms and promised to have them back to him
in the afternoon. This, despite a lengthy interruption from
Allan, he managed to do. The Boss looked them over. '7

a.m. at the Leasowe baths. Late and it's curtains. Bring
your swimming stuff, and some sandwiches. It's going to
be a long and challenging day.'

Allan was waiting for him at home. 'The solicitor's going
to consult the police just to check I've not signed anything
that's going to cause me trouble.'

'What if you have?' Benson asked, his head full of where
his bathing-costume was. Then he wished he hadn't when
Allan's chin started to quiver.

'Busy Sandra reckons I didn't. She says they'd have had
to inform me.'

'I reckon you're worrying about nothing.'

Allan didn't look at it that way. 'You've forgotten
something,' Allan said.

'Have I?'

'Yes. Think about it, Martin. Busy Sandra is in the
police. She must have known what was happening. But
she didn't drop a hint to any of the fellows at QA.'

'You haven't heard of anyone else from QA who was
nobbled, have you?'

'Not at the moment, no. But maybe they won't bring
it up at meetings. I know I wouldn't. It's more something
you discuss with people you're close to. One to one and
that.'

Benson wasn't sure what to think. In a sense the
surveillance set up in the cottage was just an extension
of all the other types of surveillance. He'd stand in the
razor blade display at Asda, Sainsbury, Tesco *et al* in
company with other bemused men all staring at the
overpriced blades while a sign informed them that for
their own protection (Ha!) they were being watched as

they weighed price-per-blade v. number of blades v. price for four v. price for eight v. price for blades with two, three, four or five cutting surfaces v. price for a completely new razor with two blades thrown in v. going for disposables or trying for a beard to see if it was less itchy this time and didn't pile the years on. The products themselves glittered out at him from inside a plastic gaol not dissimilar, though in miniature, to the transparent prison-cells Hannibal Lecter delivered incomprehensible bits of perverse cleverness to a variety of scared-shitless cops in interminable films that Benson never quite got the hang of. Then, as you entered New Brighton, there were signs saying that surveillance cameras were in operation 'for your protection' (Ha!). He'd felt the inhibiting, self-conscious effect himself – surveillance had stopped him skipping along the pavement in time to Bach's *Goldbergs* on several occasions. And that wasn't mentioning airport security. Benson had mused once or twice that he wouldn't mind a job operating the full-body cameras he'd seen on the telly. If he wasn't very much mistaken, they showed all sorts of interesting features. Mind you, he wouldn't be able to concentrate on looking for bombs. He'd be distracted by other things.

'What a world, eh?' Benson said.

Allan said nothing.

'You'd have thought the police could have put up a notice that they'd installed surveillance cameras. They wouldn't have had to go to all the expense. Just the knowledge would have kept people away. And the police could have got on with all the other stuff they don't do anything about.'

'They're a law unto themselves.' Allan said. 'I feel such a *fool.*'

'We're all fools in one way or another,' Benson said loftily, 'Anthony de Mello says the only true position to take is, 'I'm an ass; you're an ass.''

Allan said nothing. Then, out of the blue, 'I think I'm ready to go home now. Thanks for everything, Martin.'

'You don't have to, you know. You can stay at ours as long as you like.'

'OK, then. Maybe I can be useful to you. I'll stay until Wednesday, if that's OK.'

'Why Wednesday?'

'That's when the local paper comes out.'

Benson nodded. It was obvious Allan was locked into the iffy future. He felt a sermon re. the Present Moment coming on. He couldn't resist it, but limited himself to one pithy sentence from the walls of Q.A.: *With one foot in the past, and one in the future, you piss upon the present.* And he added, *And the present is a present, and all we have.*

That shut Allan up, and Benson told him he needed peace to go and fill in the damned paperwork for the 'proper job'.

He was already dreading the interview that involved swimming kit. He'd have to turn out his drawers to find his swimming cozzy. He saw himself sucking himself in on the poolside, surrounded by fit teens wondering what a sagging old codger like him was doing in their six-packed company.

He sat down at his desk, pouring over the application form and Disclosure. Below him he could hear Allan whistling (*What's it All About) Alfie?*) as he disciplined crockery and pans. He seemed to have taken Benson's sermon to heart – while the poor, stressed preacher, an ass if ever there was one – ran through in his tape-loop head the horrific imaginary scenario of what the following Thursday would bring.

# PART 2

# B.L.O.

# 22

'Hey, you! Fuckin' Baywatch! Open the fuckin' gate!'

The roar pierced the ears of the listening beach lifeguards, pranced along the steel roof-struts, biffed the plastic roof-sheeting of the Lifeguard HQ. Its baritone echo faded at the windowless rear of the former meat-storage facility but insinuated itself into the steel-rattle kit lockers, through the mugs snoozing in a bucket of bleach in the rudimentary kitchen, round the gleaming yellow Land-Rovers and jet-skis, sixties-orange inflatable ribs, banged into the walls of blue lifebelt lanyards, tongued the polo tubes of orange lifebelts, then out to the street where it startled to the present an old lady wearing a fixed and hopeful smile, walking past in company with an empty Asda plastic bag ready for filling at the co-op round the corner. Not that she needed anything really. Her cupboard was full of pearl barley. A smile returned would work wonders, though. She smiled widely at the back of a yellow four-by-four, then paused to listen as the Boss of the beach lifeguards continued. One was never too old to learn.

'What d'you do, ay? Ay? Do you respond, 'Yes, sir! Yes, sir! Just coming, sir! I'll open the gate for you, sir! Sorry to keep you waiting, sir! I am well aware that someone in proud possession of a Freelander with don't-monkey-with-me monkey bars and a towing bar towing the top-of-the-range jet-ski with added rumpity-pumpy, bitch-pulling interior booze storage and enough horsepower to fuel the

161

Grand National would not like waiting for minimum wage, terminally aged worms like my puny forelock-tugging self to open the gates! There you are, sir! Opened squeak-free and WD 40d in anticipation of your estuarial pleasure. I hope you will not think any the worse of me, nor of the the council, for my general tardiness and lack of bravura.' (A pause) 'Have a good day!' (The old lady, taking this salutation as a sign of amiable dismissal, waved her Asda-bagged hand and, with smile still fixed on tight, lurched onward towards her fate.)

Benson was sitting in the only left-hand desk listening to the curl of low-energy snigger rise from the semi circle of participants at the Lifeguards' Training Day. For all except one knew that this part of the proceedings was not aimed at them.

This was all for the bye-law officer's (BLO's) benefit.

A week had passed. On the Tuesday of the week just gone he'd filled in the application form, started the process for his Advanced Disclosure, come up with two referees, while hoping against hope he'd fail at the first hurdle – the medical. But he'd passed. While not thus gainfully employed, he'd set to work with uncharacteristic energy on his pyrography project, hoping against hope that it would suddenly deluge him with dosh and a way out.

Benson had made copious notes in a desk diary from a year well-heeled on subjects that had arisen ... methods of rescue, resuscitation, first aid, local legalities, duty of care, the acidity of jelly fish stings versus the alkalinity of weaver fish spikes, the queer vices of tides, Youth, Risk Assessment, and the like. He had done his best to keep himself out of the limelight whenever possible. He had merged quite successfully with the yellow walls and red floor-paint of the Lifeguard H.Q.

Anyway, he was still in recovery from the early morning session in the pool, where he'd had a bit of a turn during the sixteen lengths of the timed swim. Then, bombarded by chemical odours and ear-pops, frowning at the dubious tidemark that was forever in his line of sight and sigh as he metered along the endless pool using his spectacular sidestroke, he had stopped struggling, emitted a little cry, smothered somewhat by the tsunami of his fellow swimmers, and turned over to contemplate the ceiling of the pool while the pain in his shoulder slowly abated. The seconds had ticked away as the Boss shouted that he was a big girl's blouse from the side of the pool, and he saw a summer spent rekindling the idyllic Beachboys-accompanied-summer of youth as a lifeguard patrolling the New Brighton coastline while keeping a weather eye out for people in difficulties slipping from his liver-spotted grasp.

That was when the rest of the lifeguards knew that the beach lifeguard service had procured its bye-laws officer for the season. Enforcing the bye-laws was a job that had to be done. The trouble was that nobody in his right mind wanted to do it. In previous years there had been a number of examples of failed lifeguards, or failed-at-lifers in general, taking on the bye-law officer's mantle. Most had then, feeling the weight of the mantle for a day or two, walked back to the dole, or picked up the heavy cross of supply teaching at one of the challenging schools of the area, or taken employment with S.O.B.S. – Save Our Beautiful Surroundings, whose slogan – echoing that of the Borough Council's environmental arm – was 'S.O.B.S. Inc has heard the cry of the Earth' and who answered that cry by supplying the council-tax payers with green, grey and brown wheely bins large enough to contain the body parts of three cut-up adult males of drug-taking and pushing age (one of said bins from the North End had managed this feat the previous winter – with room to spare, acquitting itself admirably, leaving plenty of room for a top-up of ripped-off wing mirrors, run-over traffic cones and domestic refuse for which there was no refuge on the pavements).

The potential candidate for bye-laws officer this year, however, showed few other signs that he was not going to complete the lifeguards' training sessions. He had managed to resuscitate adult, youth and baby manikins without mishap, run a mile along the promenade in a wetsuit – even kept going when a member of the public bayed at him that he was in reality mounting an advertising campaign by impersonating a black pudding from the Lowry Black Pudding factory (also located in the North End) whose slogan was *Lowry's meat and fish product – without taint or odour*, whose waste found its way, by way of the Dawkins River, into the eternal sea. And he had swum a few hundred yards in freezing water, albeit at his own bye-law officer pace, causing the youthful majority to shiver and gnash while they waited for his sidestroke to bring him slowly and serenely back into the shallows.

Though Benson answered to 'Martin', 'Marts' or 'Marty' from the other lifeguards, the Boss called him 'Matron'. The Boss, he was later to learn, was a master of nicknames.

'Well, Matron, what do you do?' the Boss said.

'Ah,' Benson said. 'So I'm the bye-laws officer, am I? I had rather been hoping...'

'No, that's not right,' the Boss said. 'Come on! Think on your feet, man!'

'Er...' Benson insisted on being tentative. 'Were I the bye-laws officer, I'd ask the driver if he had a permit.'

'Better than asking him his lipstick shade, I suppose. But...' The Boss made eye-contact with each and every lifeguard in the semicircle. 'What's wrong with what Matron – who is definitely the B.L.O. for the simple reason that sixteen lengths in eleven minutes might be good enough for the over-seventies' Sponsored-swim, but just isn't good enough for the beach lifeguard service official qualification – just said?'

The Boss chose Eddie who had, just prior to the Boss's commencement address, pulled open the elasticised top of his tracksuit bottoms in the manner of a befuddled pensioner opening her handbag, and was, with a profound frown, gazing down. 'Still there, is it, Eddie?'

Eddie said it was and was then asked to point out Benson's mistake which, despite an MA in Art History and Environmental Psychology from Birkenhead Metropolitan University, he could not.

'Come on, you lot!' the Boss shouted. He banged his lifeguards' manual down on the desk in front of him. 'Permits! And ... And what?'

'The permit should be prominently displayed on the vessel,' Phil Morris – aka Sparks – volunteered. A retired merchant navy radio officer who already had a bus-pass but was waiting for his pension to kick in – and worried that he would kick off before it did. Sparks had once filled in as bye-laws officer when a previous incumbent walked away in a huff to write a novel. He was now the lifeguard radio coordinator, excused P.T. and had a heated post on the prom looking out at waves and Wales, where he could consider pensions at his leisure.

'The permit should be prominently displayed on the vessel.'

'Well done, Sparks,' The Boss said. 'Pink for jet-skis. These known as PWC...' Sparks? PWC?'

'Personal Water Craft,' Sparks said, in a voice that made it clear he was probably thinking of something else ... probably Tessas.

'So...' the Boss turned to Benson. 'So...'

'So I shouldn't have to ask,' Benson said.

'Well, you can ask, Matron. But only after ascertaining whether there is a permit on the vessel. Take slow and circumspect steps in your inspection process. This will give the clients quality time to contemplate their sins. So if they've got contraband hidden – or a bomb ready and primed to blow up an oil-tanker- you might see the fear in their eyes ... or evidence of illegal substance ingestion – when you come to confront them with that fruity accent of yours. I know I'd quake if I saw you bearing down on me, backed by the mighty power of the bye-laws of the county borough. After ascertaining that there is a permit on the jet-ski, ask to see the permit badge lodged behind plastic, and containing a photograph of the culprit – I mean 'client' – and date of issue. This ascertains the eligibility of the said vehicle to proceed, with due caution, down the slip and onto the launching area for marine vehicles, the launching of.'

Benson put his hand up. 'There is another matter which occurs to me,' he said.

'Let's hear it, Matron.'

'Well, there is the matter of the rudeness to which I was subjected at the commencement of your remarks, though I realise that it was merely role-play. I would have thought that I would address the lack of cordiality in the client's manner.'

'And why would you have thought that?'

'I'm not there to take abuse, am I?'

The boss thought it over for a moment, lips pursed in concentration.

'I don't see why not,' he said at last. 'Somebody has to. You're the cow and the client's the customer. To the cow, milk might seem like good food for her beloved calf, but to the man from Tesco, it's money in the bank.'

'Er ... I don't quite...'

The Boss addressed the lifeguards. 'Matron doesn't quite ... Can any of you bright sparks enlighten him?'

Thailand Tommy, a heavily muscled lifeguard in his thirties or forties who, perhaps because of his bulk, swam about six inches below the surface of the water as a matter of routine, rather in the manner of a hardwood beam, only surfacing to breathe a couple of times every twenty-five metres; who had been a lifeguard for more years than most admitted to remembering and who disappeared to Thailand in winter where it was rumoured that he had a second family ... said that it wasn't wise to make a drama out of a crisis – or a crisis out of a drama neither. Far better to defuse situations than to take abuse too personally and end up in the hurt locker of over-active imagination.

'I couldn't have put it better myself,' the Boss said, overlooking an occasion the previous season when Thailand Tommy had not taken his own sage advice to heart and had laid out flat a trio of abusive scallies outside The Chelsea, a hostelry on the seafront. The Boss turned to Benson. 'I can see where you're coming from, Matron. I can feel your pain. But you have to understand that not all the jet-ski owners who pass your portals this summer will be well-brought-up good little boys. These are working men who've made good – founded window cleaning empires, bounced and head-butted their way to the big time on Liverpool Club entrances, and the like – they've got the dosh to buy a piece of kit that bombs about the estuary at 70 mph, doesn't have brakes and has the added advantage of being able to pick up stashes of drugs from the blind side of ships heading in from Hokey-Cokeyland without benefit of customs or any of the usual niceties. Over the years I've come up with a psychological profile for jet-ski owners. For your elevation and instruction I shall write this on the whiteboard in the form of bullet points...' The Boss turned to give the group a pregnant once-over, 'points that are appropriately named in this context.'

The Boss turned from the group and doodled a long vertical line of bullets on the board. All had learned during the course of training that the Boss had a great fondness for bullet points. As he created the latest addition to his oeuvre, Benson found himself wishing for a pound – or better still a tenner – for every bullet point The Boss had drawn on the whiteboard during the course of this long and difficult day. But financial considerations dissolved like youth away as The Boss turned from the board, eyes like bullet points, to calm the swelling hubbub with one of his meaningful looks.

As the Boss sorted through a pile of transparencies, he informed his captive audience that the following was extremely hush-hush, and was to be treated with the utmost confidence. This is what the boss displayed:

- Origin – New Brighton; Liverpool; North End; Bootle; Wrexham; Flint
- Source of income: Drugs, smuggled tobacco, stolen cars, dubious plumbing; dodgy motors, etc.

> • Morals: None
> • Social Responsibility: None
> • Awareness of Rights: Acute
> • Purpose of life: Pleasure ... i.e.: shagging, pissing, drugging, speeding, footer
> • Attitude to bye-laws: Contempt
> • Drug of preference: Alcohol, Cocaine, Weed, beating up the bye-laws officer ('Only kidding, Matron!')

The Boss turned back to the group, pushing the cap back on his marker, an action Benson noted, and approved of. In another life – a life that seemed like a halcyon dream to him now – he had used whiteboard markers. They dried out in no time. A bit like Life, Benson mused. Board markers are a potent metaphor for life. Especially if you don't put the cap back on with all due firmness. 'Any comments?'

'It does seem – I don't know – a bit *bleak*,' Benson said. 'I mean, there must be some *nice* jet-ski owners.'

''Nice' is for cake in my experience,' the Boss said. 'Cake is nice, except, of course, when it's not. But never let it be said that my thirty years' service, man and boy, as lifeguard and Head Lifeguard of all lifeguards, bye-laws officers, pool attendants, saunas, jacuzzi, fauna, flora and veruccas and slipper bath tap key operatives, has made me in any way dogmatic.' The Boss felt his stubble. 'If at the end of the season you would care to provide me with a new and updated list of character defects and virtues of jet-skiers, then I would be more than happy to incorporate it into my course and my world view. Now I can't say fairer than that, can I?'

The group agreed that was fair. They all felt deep in

their heart of hearts of hearts that that was one thing you could say about the Boss. The Boss was fair. And you couldn't say fairer than that. Mind you, he could be a bugger, and woe betide you if you rattled his cage ... but he was fair. He also had a full head of neat hair that Benson envied somewhat. True, it might have been a toupee. But how, he wondered, would a toupee stand up to the gale force winds that so urgently tempted it to flight? State-of-the-art glues, of course! Roberto of Thornton Hough was reputed to have come up with an infallible glue. It had been on *Way Up North*, though the presenter, who definitely wore a toupee, made a remark at the end of the report to the effect that he'd rather die than wear a toupee, and his normally docile fellow commentator laughed longer than she should have, and got a long, hard, on-camera look from her colleague. She'd been doing outside broadcasts since, in bleak places, while subjected to shocking weather that the BBC umbrella did little to shelter her from ... and Benson worried for her future...

The Boss said that he'd let them off early, but wouldn't put up with lateness when the season started. Everyone was then given a uniform, thrown at each in turn through a hatch. This they had to sign for, and woe betide anyone hanging around the Crabapple Shopping Precinct trying to pull wenches in it. When it came to Benson, the Boss threw everything, saying 'XL, XL, XL, XXL,' despite the fact that Benson felt he could still shimmy into L. He told them to report for duty the Saturday after next, at 9.30. Sharp. This was a new season, the Boss told them, by way of a parting shot. Easter holidays full-time. Then, apart from bank holidays and half-term, weekends until summer, when full-time duty – and total mayhem for byelaws officers and lifeguards alike – started, and sorted the men from the boys. Blame the times and the jet stream. Then in September, back to weekends before close up on the 30th and a right royal piss-up, bygones and byelaws forgotten until stand by your bunks the next year for interview-stroke-training.

'There's something to look forward to, Matron,' the Boss said to Benson.

'I don't drink,' Benson said.

The Boss sighed. 'So sober, yet so befuddled. See you, Matron,' he said.

'Righto.'

'When?'

'Saturday.'

'This Saturday or next Saturday?'

'Next Saturday.'

'What time?'

'9.15 for 9.30.'

'Right you are. I like to give you a good tongue-lashing for fifteen minutes before letting you loose on the unsuspecting public.'

'I'll be there,' Benson said.

The Boss nodded and without a word went back into the lifeguard H.Q to catch up with his office work.

# 23

By the time the Friday meeting came along, Benson's head was a mess of beach lifeguard lore, his eyes smarting from the wood-smoke of burning poems, and a fair amount of fretting over civil partnerships. Allan was silent at the meeting, but there were plenty there to take up the slack. Benson gave an inspiring account about the fear, coupled with excitement, that had pervaded his week. A new job! At his age! It was, when viewed through the correct lens, a little miracle of his sobriety. His Higher Power had intervened on his behalf – with a firm nudge from Rob – to push Benson into fighting his fear and facing the Great Outdoors of an ordinary job. But it was only when Allan came up to him after the meeting and gave a list of minor violations he had noted in the room (brown lumps in the sugar tin; brown stains in the mugs; the way people disappeared into the too-near loo and came back drying their hands on their pants...) that Benson really felt convinced Allan had accepted his situation ... and had returned to his life-enhancing Health and Safety ways.

'There but for fortune,' Benson said. 'There wasn't a fellow around the table – except Rob and Jack and the girls – who couldn't identify with your predicament. You know that Suck-it-and-see Andy was Twelve-Stepped through the glory hole at the Harrison cottage, don't you?'

Allan nodded, a bit like a hung-over drunk reminded of

the Advocaat he'd guzzled when there was nothing else left in the house. Or maybe he'd heard the story too many times. Everyone in QA knew. But he could not resist saying, 'Who you see here; What you hear here; When you leave here; Let it stay here, Martin.'

'Sorry,' Benson said. 'I'm hopeless at restraint of pen and tongue. Mind you, it is common knowledge.'

'It's common knowledge because people keep referring to Suck-it-and-see Andy's introduction to Recovery in those less-than-ideal circumstances,' Allan said righteously. Benson had been thinking that 'less-than-ideal circumstances' was pretty rich coming from Allan in his current circumstances. Allan seemed to glean what might be going through Benson's head: 'You're not going to tell anyone what's happened to me, are you?'

'No, of course I'm not,' Benson said.

'Promise?'

'Your secret is safe with me.'

'Cross your heart? You're always talking about how you love gossip.'

'It's true. I'm a martyr to it. But I promise ... cross my heart.' He crossed his heart. He hadn't done that since the days of The Rude Club.

'That's all right then,' Allan said. He turned right outside the meeting-room.

'You're going home, are you?' Benson asked. 'You're always welcome to come back to ours if you don't fancy being alone, you know.'

'I'm OK, thanks anyway. Congratulations, by the way.'

'Umm...'

'Your lifeguard job.'

The penny dropped. Benson chose not to correct Allan. Informing him he was merely a byelaws officer, and not

a lifeguard, would just complicate matters. *Keep it simple!*
'Yes. I suppose a proper job will do me good.'

'Can't do any harm, can it? For a start it will give you
a taste of what public servants have to put up with.'

'I suppose so...'

'No *suppose* about it,' asserted Allan. He waved and was
gone.

Benson waited for Rob and Jack to put in an appearance.
Bensonish thought took over. He had started waking up
with those two sides at war in his head. Funny: he'd been
retiring to bed thanking his Higher Power fulsomely for
the unexpected late vocation of venturing into life's deep
end, hand in hand with Rob. But each night, something
happened. Probably the statins he took to scrape cholesterol
from his bloodstream were prodding his liver, making it
fight back, disturbing his sleep and giving him one of
those nightmares in which he debated with himself, while
Rob snored gently, sounding a little like his well-adjusted
BMW bike. He hated the introduction of the morning
doubt after evenings of good fellowship and the feeling
that he was greatly and surprisingly blessed.

So why am I drawing back from the idea of being
faithful unto death? He knew some couples who had done
the deed. He also knew a couple more – some together
for three or four decades – who had not. He quite liked
the idea of proclaiming their relationship, at least among
friends. Trouble was, he wouldn't always be among friends.
What about the woman who officiated at the civil
partnership? What might she be thinking? She (he saw
her as a 'she') had to do it because the law told her to.
But a side of her might think it an abomination ... (*Does
a side of you think it an abomination?*) And acceptance by
the powers that be was OK too. So what was the problem?

Well, the thought that everything was tied up, done-and-dusted; that no more could he have the feeling that around some indefinite corner was The Man who would gather him up and take him away from all the mundanity of existence in New Brighton to a Shangri-La of tumescence and lifelong First Ineffable Time.

But most of him knew all that was daft. Apart from the years on his clock, experience should have banged it in – and out the other side – that it was just not like that. A one-night stand was exactly what it said on the tin. Turn it into two nights and the intensity dissolved. He used the people who used him. He had not worried about *their* souls or the death of *their* quests for Dearest Him. With Rob it was not like that. Perhaps because he had a knack for coming up with new seductive contexts, and simulating quite convincingly the atmosphere of furtive couplings - though all around, the familiar geography of home and hearth proclaimed that they were engaging in settled and domestic sexual activity. What was it then? Well, he *knew* Rob, knew him better than he had ever known anyone; had told him more about himself than he had confided to anyone else. Once he had been sick with secrets. Now there was little or nothing he could not share with Rob.

Anything else? *Stop it!* Well, Benson did own the house. Rob's money mainly went on paying the bills, alimony and hand-outs for his grown-up-but-unsettled kids. Still, Rob was not after Benson's possessions, was he? No, that could not be. Rob had saved his life, given him the best regular sex he had ever known and was pretty much everything he wanted – and needed – from a partner. Would there be a pre-civil-partnership agreement? What would that entail? No, that would be mean. Out of the question. If we do it, we go for broke. But...

175

Anyway, who would he leave what he owned to if not to Rob? He had no relations. No friend even came close. Rob was the best he had. Of course, he might want to leave some money to Oxfam or Amnesty – if there was any money that outlived him.

So, Benson thought, I am a lucky duck to be offered a commitment by Rob. That's what I am, a lucky duck. A fuckin' lucky duck – and a lucky *well-fucked* duck, at that! Not many men can expect such an offer at my age. I ought to be grateful. Well, I am. But ...


Rob came out with Jack.

'Congratulations, Martin!' Jack said. 'A proper job!'

'Yes. I'm a bit scared, but...'

'And it's great you're going to join me and Bill for our partnership.'

*Was he? Have I consented, or is he talking about the festivities, not the partnership?* 'I'm still getting over the shock.'

Jack gave Rob a punch on the arm, 'Me, too. I thought Rob would kick against it.'

'I didn't, though, did I, Jack?' Rob said.

'No, you didn't. You scraped your stubble for a minute or two and then nodded. Not exactly brimming over with enthusiasm, but that's not your way, is it?'

'So, would I be doing the right thing, Jack?' Benson asked.

'You're doing the right thing, Martin. Time to close the door on childish things.'

'How do you mean?' Benson asked, though he knew well just what Jack meant.

'Well,' Jack said, 'I think Allan is a case in point, don't you?'

'Er...'

'Cottaging at his age! If I was his buddy, I'd take him over me knee.'

Benson felt the temptation to gossip kicking in. But, having just promised Allan he would not talk about him, managed to hold it back.

Seeing his lack of response and, being Jack, probably getting it, Jack said he had a few things to say to Rob.

'See you back at the ranch,' Rob said. They wandered off towards the car park behind the church.

I won't be able to cottage if I tie the knot. Is that good or bad? Benson thought. My wings will be well and truly clipped. Trouble is, I'm used to being illegal, a bit of an outlaw! It's bred in the bone.

He considered this as he crossed the road to avoid a group of youths heading towards the clubs of New Brighton. And another side – how many did he have? – muscled in to gainsay. This side was not at all sure he quite liked all this acceptance, this council-funded tolerance and 'respect' that had come gay people's' way these last few years. What would Genet have made of it? There was something exciting about being an outlaw, and something *defining*, as well. For oh-so-many years, it had told him who he was, and helped him mind his back.

It was like some of the older set – now mainly dead – had said, 'Making it legal was the beginning of the end'. These men had remembered the war, the darker than dark streets of London and Liverpool, the randy servicemen up for anything that would calm them down and make them forget their fear.

That ineffable fear/excitement of The Hunt, risking himself in dangerous situations: it was more, much more, than simply – to use the unlovely American expression – *getting your rocks off.* Trouble was ... Stop it!

But he couldn't.

\*　\*　\*

Benson arrived home. He had boiled the kettle when Rob came in. 'Fancy a cup of tea?' Benson asked, as he poured.

'Let's go upstairs after we've had our tea,' Rob said.

'Your room or mine?'

'The attic.'

Benson knew what that meant. 'Am I the candidate or the examiner?'

'You don't have to ask, do you? You're the candidate who's failed time after time after time. This is your last chance to get it right. You'll do anything – go to any lengths – to get it right this time. But the examiner – well – he's one tough motherfucker of a bugger. You up for it?'

They drank down their tea in silence. Benson liked the silence. It had a different quality to the Quakerish ones that sometimes happened at meetings and sent him off deep into his soul. This silence was that meditative anticipation of an immediate future suffused with excitement.

At last, dregs drained, the still-stewing tea bag hitting his lips like Rob's scrotum sometimes did, they stood up.

Shaking all over, the hapless candidate for the DMV motorcycle practical test of competence mounted the stairs to the attic. The boots of his terrifying examiner banged each step behind him while the quaking neophyte hoped that his terrifying companion would not notice that the steps showed obvious evidence of a lack of low dusting.

But, deep down, he knew their game was nothing more than the truth. Rob was his last chance. And, as his friend took up the pillion seat and Benson's forehead lay against the cold milometer and he saw the brake lever an inch from his eye next to the red blur of the full-beam button, along with the pain of slow and judicious, but persistent, entry and Rob's whispered instructions, Martin Benson's racing brain stopped dead, and something at long last, when his tank had reached the last few drops of its reserve, galvanised him to race ahead into a complete and thought-free acceleration into *Yes*.

# 24

'Guess what?'

'What?' Muriel asked, sifting through Benson's stack of breadboards covered in poems as if they were samples of rare hardwoods, his wooden spoons and spatulas covered with aphorisms as if they were delicate objects, irreplaceable, pyrographed by the likes of Michelangelo or Leonardo, his copied-out poems for approval, as if newly-discovered masterpieces unearthed inside a lost Stratford Shakespeare stash, then up to Benson himself, her face a picture of amazed gratitude that he should consent to offer up the delicious fruits of his art to a humble souvenir shop attached to a humble bungalow in Loggerheads, Clwyd. Muriel certainly can make a fellow feel appreciated, Benson thought. He launched:

'Ted and I are going to have a civil partnership.'

Muriel forgot the cornucopia of pyrographed wood for a moment. 'Lovely. Will there be a reception?'

'Not sure. It's happening in Blackpool in October.'

'*Season of mist and mellow fruitiness!*' Muriel said. '*That's* great news! I'm all in favour of you gays settling down. I mean, look at the men who were caught in the toilet! It's a bit sad, isn't it?'

'Mmm,' Benson said. 'Did you read it in the paper?'

'Yes, I get the *Liverpool Echo* most days. Like to keep in touch with the old place.'

'It was in our local rag,' Benson said.

He'd remember until his dying day Allan's feverish search through the article, followed by a shuffle through every page of the paper. Names had been given, some addresses as well. But Allan's had not been amongst them.

'You're not in trouble, are you? You haven't had a mention in those particular dispatches, have you? I didn't notice your name.'

'No,' Benson said. '*The Echo* named names, did they?'

'They did. Several of the blokes were married too. I bet they're getting a roasting at home.'

'There but for fortune,' Benson said, as much to himself as Muriel.

'Let's talk about something more positive,' Muriel said. 'You'll have to do pyrographed name-plates for all your guests. Sort of wedding favours.' She stopped, thought. 'Come to think of it, they might be a seller here. Things are really moving, Martin. Keep the wooden spoons coming. And don't let me forget the cheque. These days, everything I touch that can take a burn makes me think of you.'

'Mmm,' Benson said again.

'You don't seem that over the moon, if I might be so bold.'

'I am,' Benson said. 'But I do have other news...' And he told her about his job on the beach. 'This time next week I'll be working every day! No days off right through the kids' Easter holidays!'

'But you won't mind that, will you? Out in the open air, meeting new people, keeping them safe. Right up your street, I'd say.'

'I did it for a season when I was at Uni,' Benson said. 'Funny how things come round.'

'Yes. I wonder if it's a wee bit too funny sometimes.'

'And you're anxious?'

181

'I'm a bit embarrassed, I suppose. I mean, here I am, sixtyish, doing something I did when I was a kid.'

'But you could look at it in another way, couldn't you? You could think it's pretty damned good they'll take you on. Most people our age are a bit washed up. Look at me, for instance.'

'But you've got a thriving business.'

'No partnership, though, civil or otherwise.'

Benson shuffled, lost for something to say.

'For the first year after it happened I thought he'd shacked up with a woman over there. You know what sailors are, and all that. But how would he have managed for money after all this time? Nothing's gone from his bank accounts. The company told me the ship's safe, which he kept in his cabin, was all in order. And lots of his own cash was in it. But you'd expect that, wouldn't you? I mean, if he wanted to do a runner and start a new life he wouldn't give the game away, would he? Anyway, how would he live without work?'

Benson shrugged. But a shrug didn't seem to be enough. He was not supposed to be privy to this secret. But Muriel obviously thought he was. 'Er ... so you think he might have had an accident?'

'That's one of a hundred possibilities, Martin. I don't *know,* and everything just goes around and around. I thought coming out here and making myself busy would get rid of all these stories I tell myself, but it hasn't.'

Muriel went off to make Benson some tea, but it seemed to Benson she was also moving to get the wasp-nest thoughts out of her mind. *Move a muscle; Change a thought.*

He looked around the shop, quite fancying lots of things on display. But that always happened. He seldom entered a shop and came out empty-handed. It was one of the

182

things Rob was always getting at him about. What made him buy things? Was it not just alcoholic behaviour, the need to fill himself up, change the way he felt? A quick fix?

Yes, it was exactly that. But it was also distaste at leaving a shop and leaving the owner unhappy. To buy something pleased Benson, and also pleased the shopkeeper. He'd always done it. Couldn't help himself. It was, of course, people-pleasing of the sort that flattered the ego, gave him a reward. But it was always the same – in company or alone. He could pick up litter in the street when no one was looking and still be pleasing himself, polishing his harp. It was all in the motive. And, as ever, his motives were mixed.

Today, in Muriel's shop, Benson's lust lit upon a cunning spoon. Carved from some light wood, the spoon itself was about nine inches long. Each of the three cages along the length of the shaft held in place its own single ball. The balls had been released from the wood – God knew how – to rattle in their own carved cages. At the end of the shaft a scoop about the size of a serving spoon: at the other end, twin rectangular holes formed the anchor for five twin chain links, each about an inch in length. These led to phone-box cages with eight square windows. Inside, two balls rolled free. And carved into the wooden hoops at the end of the box were two identical keys. All this had been conjured out of one piece of wood. He picked it up. Keys, chains, cells, shaft, scoop ... and he wanted it.

He wanted it because it showed two becoming one; because it had at its junction trapped balls that spoke of a conundrum, a problem of construction, yes, a cunning trick, a mystery. What did the ball represent? The constraint he feared? The open prison of partnership? The key that

183

opened a door into a new and unknown life? Perhaps there was more to it than that. Perhaps the balls were Love itself, in all its varieties. Free but in chains, hard-won, rattling – or singing – in its free-will cage. Or perhaps the ball represented the clatter of his soul, now faced with commitment, his bouncing thoughts, the conflict that this deep end brought out: Fear versus Relief; Exaltation versus Humdrum; Freedom versus Bondage. The chains were his mind-forg'd manacles, but the key to unlock those manacles swung from the end of those chains.

OK, Benson thought. OK. But out of the other end of the two sets of chain emerge one spoon. The business end of the spoon picks up food. Food is life-giving. The lovers share and feed one another. They are separate but joined. He saw the price: twenty-one pounds and ninety-nine pence. Not cheap, but a steal for the thought it provokes! And that's not even mentioning the craftsman-ship. He'd buy it. He wouldn't give it to Rob. Rather he would put it on the table and use it. For what? To spoon up honey and jam. If used carefully, if cherished, it would outlive them both. But they must use it daily. He would wash it, dry it, keep it pristine.

Muriel startled him when she came back. She saw him holding the spoon. 'Lovely, isn't it?' she said, placing his mug on the counter. 'The chap who made them lived near Corwyn, up a mountain path. He died just last week. A sad story.'

Better and better, Benson thought, then reproached himself for the thought. 'I'd like to buy this please, Muriel.'

'Would you? Well, you can't.'

'Why not?'

'Because I'd like to give it to you.'

'You can't do that.'

'I can, you know. Call it an engagement present.'

'No, really...'

'Will you *stop* all that? You're always bringing me things, but when I try to give you something back, you get all ... all *Victorian.*'

'Sorry. It's automatic.'

'Well, just stop it.'

'Thank you very much, Muriel. It's a lovely present.'

'That's more like it. Keep practising that and you'll be used to saying "Yes" in no time at all.'

'Yes...'

The shop bell rang, and an elderly couple came in. Probably in their fifties, Benson thought. 'Elderly'. He could not get his head around it. Muriel went to the door to greet them, then left them to browse. She ushered Benson over to the far counter. 'To business!' she said. 'I'll display these boards prominently. I won't volunteer any suggestions about their use. We know what occurred to us. Let's see if customers have the same idea. I'm going to put them up for sale at fifteen pounds ninety-nine.'

'Don't you think that's a bit steep?' Benson said, thinking of his love spoon.

'A pound for the breadboards. Your time for buying. An hour's work at least on the writing. Your coming out here on that motorbike. My profit. No, I don't think it's 'a bit much'. This is experimental. It's just that I have a hunch that people want to 'say' more at graves, at roadside shrines, at weddings, at all life's occasions, than they can at the moment. I may be wrong – been wrong before.'

Benson saw Muriel's face, and as she spoke, hard business dragon turned into deserted sea-captain's wife. He didn't know what to say. Instead, he ran with the risk-taking side of Muriel. 'OK. Let's try it.'

'Keep working at them. Will you do that? I know you'll be working 'blind' but we should know in a week or two whether or not they'll take off.'

'I'll do that.'

'And while you're at it, I'd like you to do twenty pieces with something I've written on them.' Muriel handed him an envelope. 'You'll understand when you open it. It's not a long piece. But make the burn really deep. Will you do that for me?'

'Righto. I was wondering...'

'What?'

'The man who made the spoon. What did he die of?'

'Old age, I suppose. I used to collect work from him. He made walking-sticks as well. Think I've still got one left. He lived miles from anywhere. A track up from the church at Bwlch-y-llys. That means 'Court in the Gap'.'

'Caught in the Gap?' Benson asked, spelling it out. That was exactly where the balls in the man's spoon were. How appropriate!

'No, C.O.U.R.T,' Muriel said. 'Some chieftain's court, I suppose.'

'Can you tell me how to get there?'

Muriel looked at him oddly. Then she wrote down directions without a word.

'You mentioned he'd done a walking-stick...'

Muriel took him over to the display-case by the door. She delved behind a soft-toy display and brought out a walking stick. She handed it to Benson.

Another couple came in.

'I'll buy it,' Benson said, reasoning that as he was getting the spoon as a gift, the walking-stick could be justified. Anyway, it was beautiful, and might soon become practical.

Muriel, suddenly busy, consented to sell him the walking-stick. She smiled enigmatically as she pushed Benson's card into the contraption. Then she wrapped the stick in newspaper, and presented it to him, along with the bag containing the love-spoon.

'I'd better be off. Thanks for everything.'

Muriel winked, then whispered in his ear: 'Bona to vada your jolly old eek.'

No answer came to him. Benson smiled, and said goodbye, waving the little bag containing his spoon and the long packet containing his walking-stick.

A mile or so of riding brought him to a garage. Though he did not need petrol, Benson stopped. He reached into his saddlebag and pulled out the envelope Muriel had given him. He opened it, and read:

**Captain John Jones**
**Please Get in Touch. It's awful not knowing.**
**As ever,**
**Muriel**

# 25

Following his visit to Muriel, he had gone straight to Poundland and relieved them of all but five of their stock of breadboards. Then he went back to his empty house, and locked himself away in his cubbyhole studio where he set about studying instructions in his pyrography book for the making of a stencil. With this he hoped to write Muriel's message to her disappeared husband in the neatest, blackest, biggest, writing he had ever attempted to pyrograph, and then painstakingly fill it in with his fire pen.

He sized everything up, with faint pencil marked up the stencil, and traced every needful letter onto tracing paper from a calligraphy book. Using his hard-to-find carbon paper, he then transferred the impression onto the stencil, and, using the little blade that had come with his pyrography pen, and a rule, cut out the impressions of each letter.

When he had finished the stencil, he placed it over one of the breadboards and, with great care, pencil-marked around each letter, first taping the stencil to the board so it would not shift and produce a wonky impression. Then he un-taped the message and sighed with satisfaction at the result. All he had to do now was turn up the knob on the pyrography pen's transformer to max, open the windows wide, and start the deepest burns he had ever attempted.

But not just yet. For, ever since reading the words next to the air-and-water machine at the garage, Muriel's obsessional thoughts about the fate of her husband had become Benson's too. He imagined a raddled burnt-out case lost in Kuching reading the burnt note. He imagined his work spread around Kuching with no one seeing it – no one who mattered. Perhaps they would all fall off the trees, shop-fronts, lamp posts, railings, to which they had been attached. Perhaps they would rot. And no John Jones would see them. But people in Kuching would see them, and perhaps be able to tell Muriel something that would cause the fragmented story to come together. Perhaps the curator of the Kuching museum would come across the bruised, moss-covered, hard-to-read, warped piece of wood and give it a place in the museum of the town. Word would spread, people murmur questions. And the story of the sad English widow would be woven into the rainforest's carpet of myth and story...

In the days that followed, Rob complained that the house smelled of burnt pine. The smoke alarm complained too, going off and ruining his concentration, forcing him to put down his red-hot pen and fan the room with an old copy of *The Radio Times* kept for that purpose.

At last he finished. No sign of Allan. This, Benson thought, was probably a good thing. If he had encountered any trouble, surely he would have been round in a trice. Mind you, he hadn't been at meetings. That wasn't typical. Benson thought he ought to ring, but the thought kept fading, and he hadn't.

Anyway, the fire was in him. It kept fears for the coming Saturday at bay while showing him his proper artistic path. All artists struggled. He saw himself at some future date, his pyrography appreciated for the Great Art it was, toasted in galleries and interviewed at length by Mark Lawson. Lynn Barber would want him too, but he wouldn't turn up for her. He set to work on one last piece before 'a proper job' robbed his time.

A poem on a rolling-pin. A poem consisting of the title, two verses, eleven lines, plus a space and the poet's name: 'Gerard Manley Hopkins'. This was the Sistine Chapel of the pyrographer's art. Pushing all thoughts from his head, he seized an old ruler. 12 inches. He thought of Allan. He dismissed Allan. Inky blots. He thought of St Bede's, of Brother Hooper. Concentrate!

He thought of Mum. What would she be thinking of him? *I have brought my life this far, Mum,* was the best he could manage. What might she have said back to him? Maybe better not to know.

With his tape-measure he pencilled in fifteen dots on the pin, ruled fifteen feint lines with the ruler along the round length of the rolling pin and thought of Allan again, checked the spaces with the tape measure, recounted the lines needed for title, spaces, attribution, and commenced writing a draft in pencil.

*He fathers-forth whose beauty is change:*

He'd forgotten '*past*'. Mum and Allan and Rob had got in the way. He erased, and prayed for a rubber to take to distraction ... And Allan was back.

*He fathers-forth whose beauty is past change:*

Nearly there. But would Muriel like the poem? *My customers*

*won't go for anything artsy-fartsy* ... and he would seek to
explain that Gerard Manley Hopkins had been a local –
sort of. He'd lived at St Beuno's and learnt his poetic
cadences from the Welsh he'd learnt there. He'd written
his greatest poem, *The Wreck of the Deutschland* at St
Beuno's ... *on a pastoral forehead of Wales, I was at rest ...
and they the prey of the gales.* This area had made Hopkins
a poet! And what was around Loggerheads but the pied
beauty of creation that Hopkins sought to nail down, and
attribute?

Yes, that'll fix her, he thought. Anyway, I am an *educator.*
I spread my enthusiasm. Not my fault if some falls on
stony ground.

> *Praise him.*
> *– Gerard Manley Hopkins*

They'd axed *Come Dancing*, Mum's favourite programme.
For decades they couldn't give a toss about its devotees,
all the women whose mums sewed on sequins, all the
men who spent a fortune on those suits. He thought of
the sad Littlewoods salesman. What had happened to
them? Those that survived saw the dumbed-down,
gimmicky, version – with amateur treading on the feet of
professional while the true professionals glowered at home
unsung – and pranced around the lounge...

Stop it.

Benson plugged in his pyrography pen like a monk
preparing his tofu. He un-kinked the wire leading from
the unit to the pen. The nibs he made himself, even
attaching them to the electrodes. He knew his way around
the pen. It was the nearest he got to being 'useful' and
'technical'. He went for 5 (moderation in all things) and

turned on. He waited until the tip of the nib glowed red.
*Pied Beau* ... he heard the sound of post flapping through
the post-box ... *ty*. Odd. Very odd. Without *ty* you had
*Beau* ... as in, 'Who was that beau I saw you with last
night, Miss O' Hara?' But take the *b* from *Beau* and you
had *eau,* which was French for water. He stuck his tongue
an inch out of his mouth:

> *Glory be to God for dappled things* – Was he expecting
>    anything in the post?
> *For skies of couple-colour as a brinded cow;* No, don't
>    think so.
> *For rose-moles all in stipple upon trout that swim;* I do
>    believe I am concentrating, living in the Now!
> *Fresh firecoal chestnut-falls; finches' wings;* A lovely
>    alliteration. Not too much; just right.
> *Landscape plotted and pieced – fold, fallow, and plough;*
>    Pu ... Pu Fu ... Fu Pu
> *And all trades, their gear and tackle and trim.* Tu ...
>    Gu ... Tu ... .Tu ... Rob's kids?
> Do they *have to* come? Rob doesn't even *like* them!
>                                But maybe he *loves* them...
> *All things counter, original, spare, strange;* What does
>    'counter' signify there? Never noticed it before.
> *Whatever is fickle, freckled (who knows how?)* 'You can't
>    look at me and not see yourself.'
> *With swift, slow; sweet, sour; adazzle, dim;* I call that
>    punctuation subtle!
> *He fathers-forth whose beauty is past change:*
>                     *Praise him.*
>                *Gerard Manley Hopkins*

I wonder if Richard Dawkins likes Hopkins? Fuck 'im.

Those Enron buggers doted on Dawkins. 'The Selfish Gene' they passed out like dolly mixtures. All the employees had to be assessed as 'fittest' every year and those who couldn't pass muster were disposed of! And that's not even mentioning Hitler. Social Darwinism rationalised shooting strangers in Australia, Africa, everywhere really. *Exterminate the brutes! Let only the fittest survive!* It would have me and Rob in the gas ovens! Poor Charles didn't know what horrors would evolve from his theory.

Benson turned the rolling pin slowly. Rob would say he'd 'gone off on one' 'gone off like a bottle of pop'. He said a prayer for Richard Dawkins, hoping it would hit him where it hurt.

## 26

The momentous morning sunrise turned into full day wearing red and yellow finery while Benson, similarly attired, saw to Rob, drank his coffee and watched the clock for his date with briny destiny. He kissed Rob goodbye, vacuumed the house from attic to cellar door, cleared and cleaned the kitchen surfaces, made himself another cup of coffee. But it was still only eight. He opened his copy of *The Beach Lifeguards' Handbook*, fingering the weighty tome open at Resuscitation, one of his many weak points, and tried to get the hang of the number of compressions for adult, child and baby casualties. His head drooped and he dozed.

Awaking at nine on the dot, after resuscitating in his dreams a team of ever-so-grateful rugby-players who had stupidly chased their stupid egg-shaped ball into the swirling estuary, he collected his things, said a prayer to his Higher Power for success to the day, and bade farewell to the house, imagining it snoozing, serene, while he scaled the heights of real life.

Benson walked down the hill towards the H.Q. A bus passed. He tested public reaction to his uniform (and his reaction to public reaction) by staring at the passengers frankly. No one stared back as far as he could tell. Only as he turned into Albinoni Road did a car pass and some lout shouted 'Baywatch' at him.

'What is this 'Baywatch'? Benson asked Reg, who was busily Swafegering his hands, in the Uriah Heep manner favoured by Rob. Benson made a quick prayer for Rob's safety. 'It's the second time I've heard the word in the last twenty-four hours.'

'Programme on the telly,' Reg said.

'Yes, I know. But what programme?'

'It's off now,' Reg said. 'Pamela Anderson had these big tits.'

'It must have passed me by,' Benson said to Reg's back, 'Maybe I was away.'

Reg had gone off and the other lifeguards slunk silently past Benson to sign in. Benson mused on 'Baywatch'. There'd been a Pamela Anderson in his class at Marymount Convent. She'd played the Virgin Mary to his Angel Gabriel at a much-applauded version of the Annunciation. Could it be? Perhaps he wasn't the only one who had strayed? Might not Pam have...? No. Far too old.

'Morning, Matron,' the Boss said. 'Sign in. Radio. You're 03. Don't forget the waterproof pouch. For radio. Protection of. Keys for hut. Pick 'em up. Want to see you performing the action. Guard them with your life. You're a public servant now. Down to beach.'

'Roger.'

The Boss paused, then stepped in front of Benson. 'What are they?' he asked, looking at his feet.

'Birkenstocks. Thought they'd be easy to step out of in a crisis. I got them in a sale.'

'Not quite the thing, Matron. Trainers with socks would be more suitable.'

Benson had socks, but did not possess a pair of trainers. He nodded, added trainers to the enigma of radio, keys and 'Baywatch', but there was no opportunity to grill Reg further as Reg was in charge of getting equipment. A second yellow Land-Rover appeared, two quad bikes and a rather fetching yellow mountain bike were cajoled through the narrow entrance to briefly block the whole of Albinoni Street. Red and yellow lifeguards milled. Then Benson signed in:

Time 9.15
Designation: Bye Laws Officer (BLO).

He removed his seriously-black radio from its place in the recharging unit – number 03 etched on it with a heat-conveying tip, or, more likely, the end of a kitchen knife, and barely readable. He locked it into the waterproof sling around his neck. Then, in company with his youthful mates, Benson played his part in manoeuvring the roll-along hut into its slot behind one of the Land-Rovers. Reg got into the Land-Rover without a trailer, followed by Emma. The back of the Land-Rover was a mess of lifebelts, a spaghetti of blue and yellow nylon rope. When offered a lift to the beach, Benson said he'd walk. Reg asked him to get some milk.

'Have you got the keys?'

'What keys?' Benson asked.

'The keys to the hut, to the gate,' Reg said, revving up.

'No. Where are they?'

'On the table.'

Benson went for the keys. They were not there. They were hanging from his hand. Adjusting his radio around his front to flatter, inform and conceal, he started for the promenade.

\* \* \*

The two landscapes again: the growing-up one that was now no more than a ghostly shadow ... and the present-day, deemed by some to mirror reality but which did not seem, to him, to be quite real. What were the inevitable changes saying to him about his own situation? Had there ever been a time in the whole history of the planet when Death and Transformation in the material world – whether tramlines, Georgian terraces, Shellac records, politeness as a given, respect for the police, button A and button B – built to last but in the end as frail and transitory as everything else – had shown poor old frail human beings the state of play – the endless dusk and doomy midnight chimes of mortality? So what kept the populace from daily awareness that they too, along with all those disappeared items, would inevitably be ploughed under? What? He gazed at the mock-Victorian shopfronts that had replaced the original; he passed the Co-op which had morphed from Somerfield which had morphed from Kwiksave which had plonked itself down on the record shop, Chester's, where he had bought his first record, *We Kiss In a Shadow*. The Trocadero cinema, now just a block of struggling shops, was haunted by three layers of ghostliness. When the Trocadero had closed as a cinema it reopened as a bargain shop. This had failed, and the site had lain empty and forlorn for a decade or more before being taken in hand by the New Brighton Development Agency – which hadn't worked – and rebuilt as shops that in the main hadn't worked either. People aren't dying the way we used to, Benson thought. We hang on. But after a certain age, an age I've reached, we get it. We get the message of all the change. Even the Internet seems more like evidence getting ready for our judgement. I wonder if the Catholic Church dreamed up Google?

Reasoning that he should support the small shops of New Brighton, Benson made for the newsagents, Lewis and Patel. Victoria Road was reassuringly empty but when he got to the newsagent's entrance he noted that some kids were going in ahead of him. He worried then, and that worry took him back four or five decades to worrying about kids when he was a kid. It sometimes seemed to him that he had spent most of his childhood avoiding other kids. They'd had a tendency to pounce, to intimidate his bus fare or his Kit-Kat off him, to barge him, and call him names. And while his outward self had filled out somewhat since, the inner fears remained, fixed in cement.

Some other kids were being thrown out of the newsagents. They fucked and cunted at the world as Benson looked in the window, marvelling at the inflated price of buckets and spades these days.

He went in, bought his *Guardian*, a large semi-skimmed milk, and a packet of Fisherman's Friend sugar-free mints.

'You're a real sign of summer,' the woman behind the counter said.

'Am I?'

'This is the first day for the lifeguards, isn't it?'

'Yes, we're on for the Easter holidays.'

'You've a nice day for it.'

'Yes,' Benson said. 'A lovely day.'

'What's that written on your top?' the woman asked.

'Byelaws Officer,' Benson said, a bit let down that the truth was out.

'Aren't you a lifeguard?'

'I'm a bit long in the tooth for that; it's on my shorts, though. I'd have to rescue you in an emergency, but I wouldn't be your preferred choice, I suspect.'

'So if I drowned, you'd save me?' As she spoke, she

looked around the shop warily. Another contingent of kids were up to no good in the five-for-ten-pence sweet display. 'You lot! I won't tell you again!'

'I'd try to stop you getting into trouble in the first place,' Benson said.

'I wish you'd been around before we bought this shop,' the woman said, still looking at the kids. 'Did you see that? That kid just popped a whole fizzy snake in his mouth. Looking straight at me, he was. Bold as brass. That's my profit on your *Guardian* gone down his filthy dirty little throat.' She turned to the group of kids, 'You lot! Out!' The kids made a bolt for the door. 'And don't come back!' She turned back to the byelaws officer, 'Now what was I saying?'

'You asked me if I'd save you from drowning, and I said...'

'You can drown behind a counter in a newsagents,' the woman said.

Benson heard the woman's cry, but did not pick it up. He sought about for something positive to say, but could only come up with something reprised from the lifeguard training session: 'There are several ways to drown in water ... there's dry drowning...'

'Have you always been a lifeguard?'

'No, I used to teach...'

'Now there's another way to drown.'

'Say no more. Say no more.'

'Do you live round here?' the woman asked.

'Yes. I've come back after seeing the world and pronouncing it 'Done'. Look I'd better go. I've got to open everything up,' Benson said.

'You came *back*?' Her eyes regarded Benson as if he too had shoved a sour worm down his throat, sans payment.

'Yes.'

He left the shop and continued his bifocal and trifocal walk down to the promenade, past the rows of new houses where there had once been rows of souvenir shops, dubious pubs and a public convenience that had been the largest in the north-west. Marble urinals stretching to the horizon. Where were they now? He'd cut his teeth on that toilet block. Gone. It waited, along with the rest of New Brighton, for resurgence – or for rigor mortis to set in when it had finally completed its three-decade death rattle.

Benson nudged himself towards the positive, stood on a fresh dog-turd, tried to reason that everything that happened to him happened for a reason – and soldiered scrappily on to the piece of prom which was to play host to the unfolding drama of his summer. He felt, deep down, distinctly autumnal. He shrugged, and shrugged, shuffling his Birkenstock soles on and on, and by the time he got to the metal hut that served as the lifeguard station, had managed to drag his soul back to the optimistic tiptoe of this day of tip-toe spring.

## 27

He had arrived at the pier area. Where the pier entrance had once been was now a sewage pumping station. Next to this was the lifeguard hut, a metal construction modelled on a buoy. And parked in front of it was the yellow Land-Rover containing Reg and Emma.

Emma, a student of marine biology at Liverpool, he had not spoken to much. But not many of the young lifeguards spoke much, even to one another. Mind you, her length underwater at the swimming pool, a length in which she had used only her legs, in the manner of a dolphin's tail, would long remain in Benson's memory as a moment of great eloquence, beauty and grace. According to the Boss, Emma was the strongest and most elegant swimmer he had ever seen. And he'd seen a lot, in thirty years of lifesaver examining, serving as Wirral's leading shoreline and poolside guardian and lech.

The pair looked at Benson as he approached. What were they thinking? Did they travel down the years ahead of them and hope against hope they wouldn't be in Benson's position when they were his age? Or did they admire his guts in coming down from his mountain-top to take up a lower-case occupation? *What other people think of me is none of my business. What I think of other people is* he told himself. This quickly followed by *Who do you think you are?* Benson beamed and determined to be cheerful. Reg got out of the Land-Rover and asked Benson for the keys to the hut while Emma looked at her nails.

As Reg wrestled the key in the lock of the metal hut, he asked, 'Where have you been?'

'I was talking to the woman in the newsagent,' he said, adding in a bruised tone, 'and I walked down, remember.'

'I'd better show you the drill for opening up,' Reg said.

'There are a lot of keys, aren't there?'

'Watch carefully,' Reg said. 'I'm only here for a bit. The Boss's sending me to Hilbre Island. I've got me bike test at the end of the month. If I get it the Boss says I can get away from this dump.'

'I'll miss you,' Benson said.

'What's in me to miss?' Reg said.

He was right, in a way. Still, Benson thought, Reg is a flailing son of Adam, same as me. He's part of the scheme. Not sure *which* part, but as sure as eggs are eggs he has a part to play.

Reg walked up the three concrete steps that led to the hut door. 'These keys,' he said, 'open the hut. This one. In the bottom. Push your bum against the door. Turn. Open. This key. Here. Push even harder against door. Turn. With luck the door will open.'

Reg tried. Then he tried harder. The door creaked, opened. It was crying out for WD40, like a man in the desert for water. They stepped into the damp dankness. Roughly circular in shape, it contained lifebelts; full-body drysuits, like hanged men, drooped from the metal steps; a power point, a pile of lanyards for lifebuoys, flagpoles, flags, a rusty toaster and a kettle, and some naked women partially clothed by damp patches seeping into them from the walls. Windows faced the sea side, though they were too sandblasted to provide much of a view. The metal ladder in the centre of the hut led up to a heavy trapdoor which lifted onto a balcony providing a 280 degree view of the area around, the other 80 blocked by the bulk of the sewage pumping station.

Reg pointed to a tangle of metal posts and chains. 'See these? You've got to set them in the holes and divide the parking between here and the slipway. They divide the public car park from the cross-hatched area for official vehicles. You put it up first thing in the morning and take it down last thing at night.'

Between them, Benson and Reg took hold of the yellow posts and chains. The chains rattled behind them like Marley's ghost as they crossed the concrete. Benson listened to their song. They pushed the posts into the waterlogged, sand-scrunched holes, then linked the chains to make a fence.

Satisfying work, Benson thought. A bit of a puzzle, though, because not all the posts matched their holes. Not all the posts had two rings for chain. Eureka! That must mean they're the end poles. Simple, but one would have to keep one's wits about one's person. Still, there was a beginning and an end to it. He liked the slotting in of the posts, the Brooklyn Bridge curve of chain. He'd have to think, but not too much. Anyway, where had thinking ever got him?

Finally, they came to the gate across the slipway. About twenty feet in width, two thick red-and-white painted steel bars were locked open in holding poles that looked like a Bauhaus duck, beaks open to receive the pole while leaving space for the serious Frankenstein shackle to go through holes in the top and bottom lip and be padlocked in place through a hole in the shackle. The padlock looked like it meant business. Made in Germany. Benson looked at them and saw serious people labouring over them with cuckoo clocks chirping the hour. But they were oblivious to the charms of the clock, intent on making a serious padlock that would be used in serious times.

Reg showed the padlock key to Benson. He said that every lock along the promenade had the same key. He opened the padlock on one half of the gate and slung the gate shut with a clatter. Then he got Benson to do the same with the other bar. They came together. Reg lifted a heavy shackle on one of the bars. This slotted over and clanged down onto the other bar, securing the whole gate.

'While you're on duty, the gate is to be kept closed all the time. When you sign off, the gate is to be locked open.'

Benson had noticed that the gates were open on one of his walks, long before he had thought of being a lifeguard/ byelaws officer. 'Why are the gates locked open at night? I'd expect the opposite.'

'A lot of people ask that,' Reg said. 'I'll go and put the kettle on.'

Benson followed Reg back to the hut in search of tea and answers.

Emma was now inside the hut, reading Benson's *Guardian*.

'Nice cup of tea?' Reg said, making no move to make such a desirable commodity.

'Where are you on?' Benson asked Emma.

'At the fort,' Emma said. The fort was three hundred yards away, at the point where estuary turned to Irish Sea.

Mention of the fort sparked Benson. 'I worked at the fort. It was the Beach Patrol then.'

'When?'

'1969,' Benson said.

'Wow!' Emma said, contemplating the mists of antiquity. 'I wasn't even born in 1969.'

'Neither was I,' Benson said, with a sigh.

'When were you born?'

'1970. That was the year I went to teach in Saudi Arabia.'

Emma and Reg exchanged looks.

'How old were you in 1970?' Reg asked.

'Twenty-four. I didn't know I was born until I went to Saudi Arabia. That's what I mean, if you get me. It was quite a fright.'

'Didn't you like it?'

'No. I gave it a chance, mind. I worked there three times.'

'But if you didn't like it, why go back?'

Benson thought about that. 'It was a job,' he said.

Perhaps it was the cold stored in the metal walls that did it. He shivered. Or was it a cold hug of regret, courtesy of the wasted years? It was a job. But there were other jobs. Jobs more useful and fulfilling. What it had been was the easiest option, a chance to save some money and retire temporarily from the treadmill.

'My folks were in Saudi Arabia,' Emma said.

'What do they do?'

'They're both dentists. They worked at a hospital in Riyadh. I was there too, but I don't remember much about it, except I had a Somali nanny called Dina. I remember her.'

'Have you kept in touch?'

'She went back to Somalia for the holidays and they circumcised her. She came back to us with a terrible infection and Mum had to take her to hospital. She was in for a month. She didn't go back to Somalia. She designs children's clothes in Milan now. Comes to see us most summers.'

'Good Lord!' Benson said.

'We left there when I was three and a half. Mum and dad bought a dental practice here.'

'You're well placed if you need fillings,' Benson said.

'Never had a filling.' Emma smiled, and the perfection of her teeth backed up the statement. Benson smiled back, keeping his lips over his teeth, a tic that had taken on muscle to become second nature.

They drank their tea. Benson worried that he ought to be by his gate, readying himself for the inundation of recalcitrant jet-skiers. But he stayed in the hut. Reg pointed out the weather boards, which had to be filled in using chalk.

'How do I get the weather?'

'Phil – he's Sparks 1 – radios it in anytime now. He's just got to check the seaweed. Then we all have to radio back to Sparks. You say, 'Sparks 1. This is zero three. Weather copied. Over.' You are zero three, aren't you?'

'Yes.'

Then Reg took out his book on The Highway Code. Emma turned the pages of Benson's *Guardian* while Benson contemplated the sea as it came in slowly but surely across the sand. All most odd, Benson thought. His own childhood. Toothache with the horrid sessions of treatment at the hands of a succession of ham-fisted dentists, who failed to deaden teeth before drilling or extraction; who hit nerves and told him to be a man – whatever that meant – when he cried out. Now, though dentists did not usually hurt – the memories of those who had hurt him then prevented him going as often as he should. One more ghost-ghastly landscape.

He rubbed down the weather board, found the chalk and carried it out, along the sea wall to his gate. He waited for Sparks to pronounce on the weather and looked out over the estuary. So here I am, he thought. Back at the same place. Like the dead landscape I came back to, the same but different but the same. What am I? Sixty, and I look it. I should be a greeter at Asda or the fellow who shows you round B & Q telling you how to install central heating, plumb and paint – except I couldn't. I've had my day – and though I don't feel any different inside and feel inferior to people a third of my age – I definitely look like my day has passed. There's no getting round it.

Benson, fed up with these thoughts, bent under the gate and started down the slipway. At the bottom of this he stood, noting the concrete roadway that crossed the sand at a left-leaning diagonal (and an adverse camber – whatever that was when it was at home) to the sea. This was the route the boats would take, pulled by their vehicles – which had then to be taken off the beach and into the car park. To the seaward of the roadway were green moss-covered rocks, which needed to be avoided by the boats. To the right of this a long wall, all that remained of what he remembered as a pool for sailing little paddle-boats. There was a hole in the wall now. In a couple of hours the sea would force its way through the hole. There had not been a hole in the pool Benson remembered. Why now? Why leave the wall? Was it not a hazard? Should he not do something about it? Health-and-safety Allan would have something to say about that! After all, come high tide it would be covered, lying in wait, a couple of feet below the surface to rip the bottoms off ten thousand pounds worth of jet-ski. Had it been left in place, this wall with a hole in it, simply to spark his desktop program named *Ghost Landscapes*?

Fearing that the weather forecast would come through on the radio before he could hoof it back to the chalk and weather board, Benson returned to the prom. He looked out over the drop. From the sand protruded a line of blunt and rusted stumps. These were all that remained of the two piers, one the pleasure pier with boardwalk, Pierrot show, prize-every-time stalls, cafes, candy floss kiosks, toffee-apple dippers, a theatre, restaurants, yacht-club clubhouse ... the other setting off into deep water to meet a floating landing stage that berthed the ferry from Liverpool and brought people to New Brighton in the old days. They too had been demolished by the tepid council in the seventies. And their foundations were a hazard too. Goodness, he thought. So many hazards. So much demolition and insensitive replacement. He frowned at the sewage pumping station, on the site where the thousands of visitors made landfall for their day of cheap thrills. It looked, he thought, like a bad example of sixties' Catholic architecture. Round, with how many? – he counted – sixteen bites taken out of the circle. These might have been chapels or stations, but were in fact provided with benches. A strange unpleasant smell arose from the vicinity of the pumping station, the queer incense of bodily functions and old dish washing water. What unloving planner had come up with that? Where was *he* now? Swanning away his lush retirement in the Dordogne? And taking infinite care with the aesthetics of his home and garden, doubtless. Visiting Romanesque remains, guidebook in hand...

He'd ship-spotted from the end of the ghost pier, using his dad's Army telescope and tripod, passing on name of vessel and city of origin to his scribe friend who kept the log. His name was Cocker, and he'd become a solicitor of no small notoriety, and found God in an open prison. Then they'd drink tea from Cocker's Thermos flask with a map of the world printed on it, and looked up their ships in *The Dumpy Book of Ships*, while seated on the hard, bled-to-white planking. The sea churning beneath them seeming always to threaten them with a drenching. A lurch when a huge wave struck and it could have been the end of them. The pier was a tiny peninsula on the end of a tiny peninsula that did not show up at all on Cocker's thermos world map. But the pier was a metaphor for life. You started out walking and then you came to the end and faced a drop and the infinite.

'*I'd rather be ashes than dust,*' Benson told the sea, 'I think.'

Benson turned his back on the sea. Behind him was a four-storey building that had once been a hotel. In recent years it had become a rock club, but that was about to end – the building was in the process of being converted into flats. There was an aura of desolation about the building. Though it was one of the few surviving landmarks of the town, Benson could not help thinking that the ravaged hotel simply served the function of some two-bit Ozymandias. The elements, ably assisted by the council, had taken the best. Might as well take the rest. Let it all go.

All summer spent by this gate in a canary outfit? What a clown he was! Doubtless, looking back, it would have passed in a flash. But time was funny; he'd never got the hang of it. The endless present moment that went on and on, as unbearable as teeth-filling, or boring the socks off him, then clicked like a spent escalator stair, into the past and becoming formless – one of a great crowd that it was pointless to remember – until it came back to carry you down. Life as an escalator...

'There used to be a pier here...'

Benson was about to say, 'Do you have a permit?' He turned and saw an elderly man with a Honda 50, which he was in the act of pulling onto its stand. Benson had not heard the man on the Honda approach. He must have wheeled it. And here he was parking it on the section of the car park reserved for Authorised Vehicles! Shall I mention it? No, I don't think so. Anyway, I've a great attachment to Honda 50s. I had them in Arabia. And Iran. And Argentina. And Kalimantan. But in Kalimantan it was a Yamaha 50. Not a patch on the Honda. Two-stroke.

'Did there?' Benson asked, as if he didn't know.

'Well, two would be more accurate.'

'Mmm,' Benson said.

'Gone now, of course.'

'Things pass,' Benson said.

'So you're the new byelaws officer, are you?'

'Yes.' He almost added, 'Sorry,' because the man looked disappointed.

'I got very friendly with the fellow last year.'

'Was he the one who wrote the novel?' Benson asked.

'Did he finish it? Good for him!' The man said. 'Needed to get it out of his system. Maybe it'll get it out of the way, like. He'd curl your hair with his stories.'

'Out of the way?'

'He couldn't stop talking about all the abuse he had. Had some of the women in tears, he did.' The man's chin quivered, and he held onto the saddle of the Honda for support. Then he brightened up. 'The name's Steve. Steve Dowd. Is Reg on again?'

'Yes, he is, Steve. He's in the hut.'

'Byelaws officers are more useful than lifeguards,' Steve said. Then he gestured, 'Don't tell them I said that.'

'Do you think so?' Benson asked.

'I do. The boats need policing.'

My name's Martin Benson,' Benson said.

'I expect you prefer Marts, do you?'

Benson didn't, but said he did. 'I like your bike,' he said.

'Do you? They're great little bikes.'

'I used to have one. Yours looks like it's straight out of the shop.'

'How old you think it is?' Steve asked.

He might as well have asked me how old he is, Benson thought. I don't know, do I? Whatever I say will be wrong and will disappoint. 'Five years?' he asked.

'Add another twenty and you'd be close,' Steve said, pride in his voice. 'I got it when I worked on the floating crane, *The E.D. Morel.* I was Chief Engineer. We never knew where she'd dock, so it was useful to have a bike. They get through the tunnels for free. Did you know that?'

'All stations, this is Sparks 1 with the weather...'

'Excuse me,' Benson said. 'Duty calls.'

'Has Sparks lasted another year?' Steve said. 'Wonders will never cease!'

But Benson was too busy writing to respond.

'Winds north-westerly, Force 4 or 5, becoming westerly, force 3 or 4...'

'I don't have room on the board for all that,' Benson told Steve.

211

'Just say, 'W. force 3–5,'' Steve said.

Benson did so.

*Weather: mists, sunny periods, showers and possibility of thunder.*

Steve must have seen Benson looking bewildered, faced with too many words for too short a box. 'Just say 'sunny and showers. Let's keep the thunder as a surprise.'

'Thanks.'

*High water: 15.04 Height 9.1. metres.*

Benson wrote this word for word. He managed Low water, and Sea State: Smooth to Slight. Then he filled in the information on the second board before turning to Steve to thank him.

Steve then told Benson where to put the weather boards. One was to lean against the seawall, just next to the gate. The other clipped on the lifeguard flagpost, a hundred yards away, past the sewage pumping station. Benson placed them in position, stepping back to admire each in turn.

Reg shouted from the hut: 'Radio, Matron!'

Benson, blaming Steve mentally, picked up the radio, pressed the button and said: 'This is Sparks 1 to Zero Three. No, it isn't. This is Zero three to Sparks 1. Weather copied. Over'

A silence, then a tired-sounding Sparks. 'Cheers, Zero three.'

The other lifeguards up and down the coastline acknowledged receipt of the weather forecast. Finally, the Boss acknowledged, adding 'for Zero Three's benefit' that the rubric was to state the name of the recipient first, followed by one's own name. 'Now, for Matron's benefit, let's do it again. Chronologically.'

Benson knew his blunder was being aired all around

the coast. He repeated his acknowledgement, then distracted himself by getting back to Steve, who was polishing the spokes on the front wheel of the Honda.

'Thanks for that,' Benson said.

'All part of the service,' Steve said.

'Would you like a cup of tea?'

'Milk two sugars,' Steve said.

Benson went back to the hut. It was empty, the lifeguards having gone off on patrol.

Benson put on the kettle and watched it taking its time to boil. He made Steve's tea. It was good to make friends. It made up for a lot, a friend did.

# 28

Benson got back to the gate with his pot of tea. He laid the pot down on the parapet of the railings, looking round for Steve – and hoping that Steve didn't take sugar, because the sugar was in the hut. Steve appeared, and did take sugar. Benson trotted back and forth. As he was scissoring over the railings a red BMW four-wheel drive, towing a red jet-ski, approached his gate at speed, squealed to a halt.

'Permit please,' Benson said, but not loud enough to penetrate the window glass and the Scouse-House music blaring inside.

The driver looked at him. Then, without apparently moving a muscle (though he seemed to have plenty that might move), lowered the window. The volume of the Scouse House decreased until only a too-fast fart beat could be heard. Benson repeated his request for a permit.

'Dog et it, mate,' the man replied.

The driver furrowed his brow and made his right cheek smile widely. He was, Benson judged, a badly-worn thirty-something. Bald, too. A pity, for a generous quiff might have covered the amateurish-looking tattoo on his forehead, which asserted, 'Deadly Weapon'.

Benson, though made a bit shaky by this spectre of pumped-up maleness in all its overblown prime, responded, 'Did the dog also eat the permit that's supposed to be prominently displayed on the front of the jet-ski?' He swallowed. 'Did he?'

'She, arct-yu-all-y,' the man replied, cruelly sending up Benson's quick-rinsed-in-Mersey received pronunciation, and turning it into Princess Margaret-with-a-skinful, while taking the time to look into the back of the vehicle, where his mate was twisting a ring about in his nostril. The two friends tittered in brasso-scoufundo.

'**She** didn't eat the vehicle permit, did she?' Benson asked.

'Yarss,' the muscular driver replied. 'See, mate. I don' like t' keep the permit on the ski 'cause i' migh' ge' nick't.'

'So where do you keep it?

'In the walle' tha' go' et.'

Benson was not quite sure how to proceed. 'I can't let you launch without seeing a permit,' he said.

'Go an' check wi' Safe water,' the muscular man said. 'They'll 'ave our names, an' the car number like.'

That was what the boss had told Benson to do. Yes, that is what he would do. 'Wait here,' he told the men.

Benson checked the licence number. He even made sure to note down the car's make and model, and paced off sternly to Safe Water Training, located in a shop a few yards up Victoria road. He showed the licence number to Tracey behind the counter, who was swathed in red Goretex. Tracey looked through her computer records and said that they had no record of that number.

'I'd better go and deal with it,' Benson said. What happens now?, he thought. I am being tested.

Rounding the corner, Benson saw with some relief that there was no sign of the car. Perhaps the driver, fearing discovery and reprimand, had decided that discretion was ... whatever discretion was. In a way, though, he was sorry not to be able to test the effectiveness of his controlled ire. Still, he decided to place the car number in his little black book for future reference.

Steve was back standing by his Honda, a mug of tea in his hand. 'I minded your bag for you. You shouldn't leave it. Not round here.'

'Thanks,' Benson said. 'It looks like the jet-skiers've left. As I thought, they hadn't done the necessary.'

By way of reply, Steve thumbed over his shoulder to the concrete slip and the glittering estuary. And there, on the very end of the concrete, Matron saw a red car launching a red jet-ski into the waves. 'I told them you'd be angry,' Steve said.

'And what did they say?'

'What do they all say?' Steve said. 'Fuck off, granddad.'

'Typical,' Benson said.

'I'd mind your bag again while you go and deal with it, but I've got to be off. Meeting me mates at twelve.'

'Thanks, Steve,' Benson said. 'See you again soon, I hope.'

'Spend most of me life down here. Amazing what you can learn. It's holy ground,' Steve said.

Benson picked up the bag and hefted the loops over one shoulder manfully, then started down the slipway toward the car, and the illegal pair.

As he walked he wondered about Steve's last remark. Holy ground. Well, he'd have to ask Steve what he meant. If he survived the next five minutes. Here he was about to take his life in his hands – for minimum wage plus fifty p. Holy ground? Perhaps I've made a terrible error in judgement, Benson mused, as the bulgy muscular man loomed in his wet suit, like a novelty easter bunny moulded by Michelangelo. His top half was muscle, but went to fatty seed the further down you looked. Mind you, wouldn't say no. Yes, I would.

Benson opened his lips to speak. 'Excuse me! Excuse me!' he said.

'Wa'?' The man said.

The BMW winked its doors shut, and the man turned and trotted towards the sea. He got on the jet-ski behind his companion while Benson chased after him, shouting Look Here! until he noticed what he was saying, and stopped. Then, before Benson could protest about flagrant breaches of the byelaws and threaten punishment by the Borough Council, the jet-ski noisily thwacked the agitated water and its passenger made unflattering gestures with his right arm, aimed at the byelaws officer.

Benson watched unhappily as the jet-ski nosed out into the estuary. The ski was showing its feathering on its underside. This, Benson had been told, indicated it was doing more than the bye-laws-stipulated speed of five knots. He's going to be in trouble, he thought, as he made his way back toward the promenade.

He could see Reg between himself and the fort. It was amazing how lifeguards stood out in their yellow and red uniforms. That was the point of them really. Reg was walking at some speed towards some kids on the rocks close to the fort. That was admirable. The Boss had intimated that Reg was an admirable lifeguard. He had nicknamed him Duracell Bunny because he had a lot of energy. He went on and on while, the Boss said, other lifeguards surrendered to sunbathing and other disreputable pursuits. A finger of water glistened, showing that the tide was inching round the rocks. Reg would warn the kid away.

Some things did not change. It was there Benson had saved a kid forty years ago. The kid was being swept away after going in to save his beach ball. It was as clear as yesterday. He could see it still, and feel the fear of it too. The beach ball pushed out by the wind. The boy running after it, despite Benson's frantic shouting and whistles from an Acme Thunderer. The beach ball being caught by the out-surging current, the boy refusing to surrender it, and being caught himself. Running, heart pounding, as he discarded his clothes and slammed into the water, wading and then swimming after the boy. Himself taken by the tide and swimming harder until he had hold of him.

But there was no getting back with the panicky boy. They were locked together, being spewed out by the power of the tide. They had passed the Brazil buoy that marked the edge of the shipping channel, a buoy that the older lifeguards said they'd swum around in their younger days. The boy cried and Benson told him not to worry. But he was worried. He was very worried. He looked about him, to the sea, to the fort, and past it to his town where people were listening to *Morning Story* while he was being washed out to sea. He changed his hold on the boy to make it easier to swim with him, and then started side-stroking across the impossible current in the direction of the fort. They passed the lighthouse, and then Benson knew it was treacherous sea. But he kept up his steady, break-no-records stroke in the Wirral direction. They passed an island of floating sewage and condoms. Some were knotted; some not. Mersey goldfish, they called them. At last he called a halt, as much to calm the boy as to rest, though he needed rest too. Benson, treading water, felt his tipped toe rub on sand. 'I'm in my depth,' he told the boy. 'Hang on.' Twenty more strokes and he could stand comfortably. He held the boy, and struggled towards the shore. As they did so, the lifeboat headed up from the sea side of them. Benson stood up to show he was out of danger. The crew saluted him and, after waiting for the pair to reach the shore, turned and went back to its moorings by the pier.

The Boss – not this boss, but a boss long gone – had been there at the shoreline with a small crowd and a man from *The Echo*. 'I'll carry you,' Benson told the boy. The boy said he didn't want to be carried, but Benson lifted him up and carried him anyway. And the camera flashed.

But in Benson's eyes the rescue had been a failure. He had developed a philosophy of lifeguarding which dictated that 99.999% of the job consisted of warning. He should, he felt, have been on the boy's tail before the beach ball went into the water. He should have been in a position to restrain the boy from following it, saying, 'Say goodbye to your ball, kid,' as the water took it to God Knew Where. The rescue – all its exertion and fear and drama – had come about as a result of not warning. Of course, there was precious little heroism in warning. One always sounded like a maiden aunt, a spoilsport. But it was what the job was about. You couldn't tell the public often enough. Constant repetition was the *sine qua non* of the job.

But now, years on, here he was beside the same treacherous water. The tide was coming in. There was no red jet-ski in sight. Only a spanking new BMW sitting on the launching site with the incoming tide approaching its tyres.

The three Ws of Lifesaving: Wait. Watch. Warn. Yes, that's good, he thought. He eyed the BMW. 'Now what?' he told it.

# 29

Benson got back from his fruitless errand to find the Boss waiting for him. No flash bulbs, no saved child. All that was past and forgotten.

'Oh dearie, dearie, me,' the Boss said, after alighting from his Land-Rover, glancing over the sea wall, and imbibing, along with the strong westerly wind, the full enormity of the situation.

'I've failed,' Benson said. 'I'm not cut out for this job.'

To shut Benson up – the Boss was busy composing in his head a succinct message to Sparks 1 prior to transmitting it fluently – the Boss told Benson to keep his hair on ... after all there was fucking precious little left of it. Then he pressed the transmit button on the radio. 'Sparks 1. Sparks 1. This is Lifeguard 1. Over.'

Phil came in.

'Sparks 1. Lifeguard 1. We have a vehicle on the Pier jet-ski launchway which will shortly be inundated by the incoming tide. ETA of tide at BMW's vital parts: one hour. Alert the lifeboat and coastguard. Inform both that there are no lives at risk. Merely resale value of 10 Reg, BMW X5 Security ... Over.'

'I'll note it in the book,' Sparks said, and outed.

'I ...' Benson said.

'I me no Is, Matron,' the Boss said. He stretched through the window of his Land-Rover, found a pipe, pulled it back through the window and lit it with a blue Bic.

'Proceed,' he said from behind a blue cloud.

Benson proceeded to tell the Boss what had happened
... 'then I shouted at the driver that he had performed
an illegal operation and should return behind the barrier
forthwith...'

'And what did he ascertain in his response?'

'He was already in the process of hopping onto the jet-
ski, travelling off into the river.'

'No verbal abuse, then?'

'Not in so many words. No. Some pithy hand/arm
movements, though.'

'What sort of arm movements?'

'The one for 'fuck off' and the one for 'wanker'.'

'Well, he got one right,' the Boss said.

'I ...'

'Only joking, Matron.'

'I see.'

'Any threats against your person?

'Nothing one could put one's finger on. I don't suppose
he can help his intimidating build. And his unfortunate
manner. Do you know what he had tattooed on his forehead?'

The Boss ignored this. 'Did you warn him that the tide
was inward bound?'

'Well, no. I didn't get a chance what with one thing
and another. I'd put the weather board up in a prominent
position next to the gate, though.'

'And he should know where the tides stand. If he'd
taken the course. Which he hadn't. And he opened the
gate himself, did he?'

'Well, I wasn't here, but he must have because I didn't.'

Benson looked at the car, with the waves licking hungrily
a few yards from its back axle. 'I hope the lifeboat hurries
up,' he said.

'The lifeboat won't come, Matron.'

'Won't come? But if it doesn't come the car will be ruined!'

The Boss nodded, and considered his pipe. 'Insurance won't cover it, neither. Not seeing as he's got no permit. But the lifeboat won't come because there are no lives in danger. I know what they'll tell Sparks. 'Call a towing company,' they'll tell him.'

'And will we?'

'Will we buggery!' the Boss said. 'There are, Matron, some small satisfactions in this job ... saving people from a watery grave, dabbing Dettol on cut knees, vinegar on jelly-fish stings ... directing the public to public conveniences ... finding lost kiddies ... aiming hurt looks at dog-owners who don't pick up their pet's poo ... but none compares with watching some scalliwag's BMW – bought with ill-gotten gains I wouldn't be surprised – slowly sinking beneath the salty brine.'

'But ...' Benson said.

'But me no buts, Matron.'

'No.'

Benson was silent. He watched the waves breaking. Each one was bringing doom closer to the car. Odd, he thought. The Rule of Twelfths states that in the first hour of incoming, the tide moves one-twelfth of volume, in the second hour, two-twelfths. Then there is a speed up. Third hour and fourth hour it approaches at three-twelfths each hour. Then the fifth hour is back to two-twelfths and the sixth hour one-twelfth again. He'd only realised that during training. For sixty years *sixty years!* he'd assumed that tides came in at the same speed for the six-odd hours. What obvious-else in life had passed him by? He pushed that one aside. Back on the Rule of Twelfths he wondered where this tide was on that sequence? He looked at his own high-tide time on the blackboard. This is the beginning of the fourth hour, he thought. 'There's no time to lose!' he announced to deaf ears.

'This seat taken?' the Boss asked, gesturing to one of the collapsible stools Benson had brought out of the hut. He sat himself down while Benson thought. 'Don't even think about it,' the Boss said, relighting his pipe.

'Maybe we really should call a towing company. We could charge him, of course. The Rule of Twelfths states that...'

'It's beyond our remit and our duty of care.'

'But we can't just let...'

'We can, you know. Those scallies...' and the Boss wagged his pipe in the direction of the estuary, 'have enough dosh to shell out on a great big car and then drop another ten grand on a jet-ski. Yet they can't be arsed to pay a hundred to do the course, learn about this treacherous stretch of water – and check the tides. If they'd done the course they'd know that they can't leave a vehicle in the launching area – nor the beach when the tide's coming in – but must put it in the parking area provided. The launching pad might be needed by the RNLI. They know that, if they play their part, we'd go through hell and high water to see them back on terra firma safe and sound...' the Boss took a deep draw on his pipe. Then he turned and surveyed the soon-to-be-inundated car and sighed an exhalation of smoke and satisfaction.

'But...' Benson began, knowing that he wouldn't finish.

'I've told you once. You were going to ask, if I'm not very much mistaken, what happens when the naughty jet-skiers land their jet-ski, and find that their car is covered in water, weren't you?'

'I had been wondering. I mean, they looked really rough.'

'Once again, it's beyond our remit, Matron. We've done the best we could. Did you open the gates to let them through?'

'No.'

'No. Did you warn them that cars should not be left on the foreshore?'

'Yes, but only at the end. He might not have heard me. He was...' Then Benson thought. He was lying. He hadn't. He was in a crisis and doing what came naturally. 'Correction,' he said. 'I didn't tell them that. There wasn't time. I left him waiting behind the gate – closed – while I went to check.'

The Boss gave Benson a sideways look through pipe smoke.

'Did you see me call Sparks to alert coastguard and lifeboat?'

'Yes.'

'Yes.' The Boss knocked out his pipe on the railing. 'You've done as much as could reasonably be expected. Now go and make me a nice fresh cup of tea, Matron. I'm parched.'

Benson, having restrained himself from saluting, scuttled off. The water had to be brought from the tap by the sewage pumping station in a plastic water container and emptied incrementally into the kettle. It was nice to be away from the gate. There was a moment of complete peace as the water flowed into the plastic container. He looked about and saw bands of sunlight on the river towards Liverpool. Oyster-catchers wheeling at the tideline, using the walls of the ruined paddling pool to take their rest. A seagull standing on the break in the wall where water gushed in. As he watched, the seagull spread its wings and pecked at the flow. A flatfish appeared in its bill. The gull pecked at the flatfish. Everything seemed to stop. Worry about red BMWs and fat/muscular men dropped away. Just for a moment. Then the plastic container was full to overflowing and hard to carry. He dragged it back to the hut, wondering about the moment.

Nothing much to it. What was it? Peace? Happiness? It was what it was. It had felt good, though he had not been able to realise its goodness until it had faded.

Then he saw that a small group of people had gathered on the sea side of the sewage pumping station. They were watching the red car, and the approaching tide. He could not be sure about what the people were thinking, but could infer from his past knowledge of his fellow citizens that they were wondering why the byelaws officer was making tea while a rather nice car was about to drown only yards away. For a moment he wanted to climb up to the balcony atop the lifeguard hut and address them. 'Fellow citizens and council taxpayers!' he'd say. 'We have done all we can for the vehicle that is about to be ruined! The fate of said vehicle is out of our hands. We are powerless over time and tide. And both are against the vehicle, the owners of which were deaf to my protestations. Let this be a lesson to you all. Go thence from here and tell your fellows what happens to those who dare to flout the quiet might of the byelaws of the Borough Council!'

Yes, he thought. That might have done nicely. That might have gone some way to satisfying the disquiet of the citizenry. But he hadn't done it. He could've, but he hadn't.

He plugged the kettle in, and switched on.

And suddenly a strange thing happened. It was as if

the flicking of a switch made people thirsty, got their legs moving in the direction of the byelaws officer's domain. Reg appeared from nowhere, asking for milk and two sugars – and while he was at it, three extra, plus milk, but no sugar for Lynn, Pat and Irene, whoever they were. That was six mugs, including Benson's. He wondered if the pot would stretch to it without another walk back to the hut. So he put a tea bag in each mug, made the tea, and ferried it out to the people using as a tray an old wooden 'No Bathing' sign. He was greeted and introduced all round, but then attention turned to the plight of the red car. Waves were breaking against it now. He looked at his watch. He couldn't stand looking at the slow drowning anymore and withdrew to the hut. He refilled the kettle and plugged it in.

Tea was obviously going to be a leitmotif to his job. But the present incremental way of fetching it was surely not the best way. Perhaps, thought Benson, I could find a really big flask. Then, with just one trip to the hut, I could make a milky brew of tea, sufficient for everyone, and then – not forgetting the sugar and teaspoons – manage the whole procedure on one trip! But it would have to be a really big flask. And not a glass vacuum compartment, either. Stainless steel. A pump-action stainless steel Thermos, like we've got at the Friday meetings! Eureka! But where shall I find one that doesn't cost big bucks?

Then a man came to the door of the hut. 'You Matron?' he asked.

The man was wearing a stained mack, and his wispy hair was drawn craftily over the dome of his head, thereby drawing attention to his baldness.

'Yes,' Benson said, providing a *nihil obstat* to his name.

'I've bought you some biscuits,' the man said. 'I'm Jerry.'

Benson took receipt of a heavy cardboard box. When he opened them, a library boxed set of nude Penguins, layer on layer of them, confronted him.

'Naughty but nice,' Jerry said. 'They're seconds. Good as the ones that cost a bomb. Get them from the factory gate.'

'You shouldn't have ...'

'And why not? I can't count the number of cups of tea I've had from you lot over the years.'

'Milk and sugar?' Benson asked.

'Both please.'

Jerry excused himself to watch the car get what was coming to it. Benson made tea, added the milk to the pot, filled a plate with Penguins, and went out to pleasure his unexpected, but very welcome, visitors. This is more like it, he thought. This makes perfect sense. I suit this. I could become good at it.

\*　\*　\*

The Boss, Eric, the three women and their dogs wandered off, leaving Reg and Benson alone at the gate. High tide had come. Though not the highest of the cycle, it had managed to half submerge the vehicle. Perhaps, Benson thought, then communicated to Reg, the BMW is such a quality car that its seals will stop the water from entering the interior. Perhaps the engine will forgive one wetting in salt water. A quick wash-down, perhaps a jet-wash, will have it right as rain.'

'What will be, will be,' Reg said.

'Yes, I suppose so.'

Then Sparks was calling the Boss on the radio. The

Boss had gone away for a meeting, but answered. Sparks told the Boss that complaints had been passed on to him from the ranger on Hilbre Island. A red jet-ski had approached the colony of seals on Hilbre. It seemed intent on terrifying the creatures. Could something be done?

A silence, and Benson knew the Boss was composing a fluent reply. 'Sparks 1. This is Lifeguard 1. I believe we know the culprit. If it is who we think it is, he is also the owner of the aforementioned BMW. (Break) Make a note in the log. I'll get back to you on further developments. I'll be returning to the standby point precipitously. Be sure of this: that jet-ski will not launch on our stretch of coast in the foreseeable future.'

Having pronounced Bell, Book and Candle, the Boss signed off. 'Out.'


Time passed. The tide retreated, leaving the BMW – seen from a distance – much as it had been. Benson badly needed the toilet and, having been informed by Reg that an overhang of the prom with the sand offered a safe place, he radioed off-station and made for it.

A row of concrete columns, very like a cloister, in that one could walk through it under cover from end to end. It had been built out over the promenade wall, which formed the blank side of the passage. But each pair of columns framed the turn of the estuary to the sea. All one had to do was angle oneself out of sight of any passing people, and relish relief.

It took Benson a while. Though dying to go for more than an hour, the flow was not his usual gushy tinkle. It was intermittent and slow. Perhaps his bladder was too full, or he'd caught a chill on his kidneys. Was it something to worry about? No, it wasn't.

He rearranged the layers of uniform and noticed the BMW. He walked to it and peered through the windows, while trying to seem casual. Everything looked dry inside. Perhaps the seals had prevented water seeping in. If that were the case, then it was a good advert for the car. Maybe he should suggest it to the BMW people.

But something wasn't quite right. He walked back to the gate slowly, wondering what it might be. Was he afflicted by 'H.A.L.T.'? Was he Hungry, Angry, Lonely, Tired? No, he wasn't. He heard the gate clang open. A jet-ski towed by a white van came through it. A red jet-ski. Suddenly Benson knew exactly what was worrying him.

'Sorry I missed it,' Benson told the Boss, thinking of the return of the wicked jet-skier and the news he would have to impart.

'Nothing to be sorry about, Matron,' the Boss said. 'You were answering a completely natural call of nature. Seeing as the toilets have shut due to lewd behaviour and have been pronounced a crime scene your options are somewhat circumscribed.'

'Yes.'

'They were caught on CCTV,' the Boss said.

'Who?'

'The people indulging in lewd behaviour, Matron.'

'Mmmm.'

'I know what you're thinking. So, if it's an open and shut case, why close the facilities, especially when the Easter hols are heading up.'

'Well, they would come in handy...'

'They would. But they can't be reopened until the court case is finished. And you know what The Law's like.'

229

'Er,' said Benson. 'I was wondering what I should do when the jet-ski returns. Should I lock the gate and refuse them exit?'

'No,' the Boss said. 'We can stop them launching but it is no part of our remit to prevent them making landfall. Law of the Sea.'

'I see. So what do I do?'

'The sea has done it for us. The sea's good at that. You can give them one of your looks if you like. And note down and remember any verbal abuse they may aim at you. We won't let them back. They've driven a train – well a BMW and jet-ski – through the byelaws. We've got to start strict.'


The rest of the day dragged. In late afternoon clouds billowed up from the north-west, threatening – but not delivering – rain. Two more jet-skis – their owners permitted and pleasant – availed themselves of Benson's services. The rest of the time, he stood gazing out to sea. Once a man with an Australian accent approached him and asked if he was dreaming.

'I was a bit,' Benson said.

'No,' the man said. 'I was wondering if I had been dreaming. Is this really New Brighton?'

'Yes.'

'But wasn't there a pier over there?'

'There used to be.'

'And up there, wasn't there a funfair and a huge building?'

'There used to be.'

'Is that Victoria Road?'

'It used to be.'

'The only thing I recognise is the fort. I was looking for the pool. I used to swim the summer away in the pool.'

'Gone,' Benson said.

'But wasn't it the biggest in Europe?'

'It used to be.'

'I emigrated to Australia in the fifties. First time back,' the man said.

'You can never go home again,' Benson said enigmatically, before the thought came to him that he'd have to think about that. He rather hoped it wasn't true.

'I never understood that, but I'm beginning to,' the man said. 'I went to the cemetery...'

'I know what you mean. Still, the sea's still here. It's cleaner than it was. You used to have to breaststroke the rubbish out of the way. It's not like that now. Lovely light. Did you know Turner wanted to live here. For the light?'

'But it's not the same.'

'No such thing as progress,' Benson said. 'Fancy a cup of tea?'

'That'd be nice,' the man said.


Though Benson had scanned the horizon for the jet-ski, as a dying man might scan the covers of his bed for the Angel of Death, there was no sign of it. At four the Boss told his lifeguards to make ready for stand-down. A frenzied ten minutes of cup-clearing, gate-opening, fence-dismantling, followed ... followed by the Boss coming back on the radio: 'Stand down and return to base.'

Benson plodded away from his stage. Then he stopped, looked back on it and smiled benevolently at the cross-hatch yellow, the red steel gate and promenade wall ... with the infinite – still in retreat – behind it all.

# 30

Benson signed out, said goodbye to the other lifeguards – refusing to be more than somewhat miffed when some did not respond – and started up the hill home, feeling tired and happy. There was the question of the forlorn BMW drying out on the beach; that might make him worry about the morrow, but he consigned that to its proper place. The weather was bright, but cold – an easterly wind blowing that the weather people never seemed to mention, though it made all the difference. I don't see why...

'Matron! Radio! Keys!'

Benson turned back, looking down the hill at the way he had come. The Boss stood on the corner of Albinoni Street in his red and yellow. Even at that distance Benson could see that he was not best pleased.

Struggling to get the radio out of its waterproof case, searching round frantically for the bunch of keys, Benson trotted back. How could he have forgotten? He'd spent a few minutes watching other lifeguards handing in their radios, placing keys on hooks, putting everything back in its place. As he'd walked up from the beach, he'd reminded himself not to forget to hand the items in...

But other things had taken their place: whether or not to say goodbye, or be like Reg who just walked away to the car of a blonde, got in and sped off as if the Lifeguard Service no longer existed; whether he should help push the trailer back into the hut or help wash down the sand-splattered quad bike. And in the midst of all this indecision he had forgotten the basic thing. I'm losing it, he thought. I'm over the top. *Why should old men NOT be mad?*

He turned the corner, and found the Boss standing all alone at the door of the vacated H.Q.

'Sorry,' Benson said, breathless and penitent.

'The radios need to recharge overnight,' the Boss said.

'Yes, of course they do.'

'And the keys. Well, you might get a duplicate and use the hut at night to drag a wench back for some rumpy-pumpy.'

'I wouldn't do that.'

The Boss gave his new employee a knowing look. 'No, you probably wouldn't. Anyway, hand them over, Matron.'

Benson did so. The Boss disappeared with the radio and keys, then re-emerged to lock the sliding door of the HQ with a pair of those serious padlocks Benson was getting to know so well from his gate. The Council must buy them by the tonne.

The Boss turned and seemed shocked to see Benson still in the vicinity.

'Don't you have a home to go to?'

'Yes.'

'See you tomorrow, Matron.'

That sounded conciliatory. Sort of. But he badly wanted more. What? An inquiry as to what he planned to do with the evening? The Boss's best regards to Rob? Still, it was the best he was going to get.

'Righto,' Benson said. He turned – still feeling there was something missing – and climbed the hill again, thinking of heterosexual men in general and the Boss in particular.

The Boss had something that Benson really rather

233

admired. There he was, year in year out, taking on a succession of seasonal ne'er-do-wells like himself. At the training sessions he had commanded complete obedience and – doubtless grudging – respect from each and everyone, even Reg and Thailand Tommy. They might moan at the Boss behind his back, but they were people-pleasing omega males in his presence. The Boss's 'technique', if technique it was, was something that intrigued Benson. Rob had it, too – and so did Jack. What was it? A Sergeant-Major gene? A Headmaster gene? Or was it just growing into a role so that it became bred in the bone?

Benson had tried to put on an appearance of being an authority figure, but had never managed to carry it off convincingly. His Saudi firemen – *Where were they now?* – had shown up for class only when it suited them, which was seldom. He'd tried a Benson version of stern, even looking up quotations from the Koran that insisted on respect for teachers and the Islamic duty to acquire knowledge. These he aimed at them in hesitant Arabic – having been taught the tags by a Bangladeshi friend. But it had done no good. Nothing in Benson seemed capable of inspiring obedience. He'd had to get the boss in – a fearsome Iraqi – to read the riot act. And then, with the aid of a BBC Betamax language course full of leggy and busty women – he had managed to get near-perfect attendance. His Saudi boss was carved from the same hard wood as the Boss, with gold-plated knobs on.

Benson reached his house, trudged up the drive, and opened the front door. He smelled chips. Surely not!

'I've made your tea,' Rob said. 'How was it?'

'You shouldn't have!' Benson said. (He never had before! What's going on?) He looked around. The kitchen table had a cloth on it, though not laid down tidily: two white plates, probably cold, sat next to one another. A knife and fork lay across the plates rather than in the Benson-preferred position, left and right. Still, these were carping details. The stove was full of boiling pans and he could feel the heat from the oven.

'Get your kit off,' Rob said. 'I'll need some help serving it up.'

'You shouldn't have,' Benson said again. It just slipped out. He'd always said that when Auntie Phyl gave him socks or hankies for birthday and Christmas. Mum had taught him 'You shouldn't have'. Where had she got it? Where did all this self-effacing stuff come from? Still, it fitted neatly into other situations and rang bells from his past: *You shouldn't have* ... but you did. *You should have* ... but you didn't. Those sad little modal auxiliaries provided the sad little props for his Steps Four and Five.

'And why not? I was home first.'

'How many did you pass?'

'None.'

'None? Was it a full day?

'Very.'

'Why?'

'The usual. You go and get changed. The chips are done. The fish is, too. I'm just waiting for the peas to soften up.'

Obediently, Benson trotted upstairs.


'So how was it?'

Benson told Rob about the BMW, and Rob laughed fit to bust. 'That must've made the Boss's day. He loves it when an erring member of the public gets his come-uppance.'

'He certainly does,' Benson said. 'I don't though.'

Rob turned serious. 'No. You don't. You'd've paid for a towing company to come and save the day for the fellow, I suppose.'

'Well, I wouldn't have gone *that* far. I might have got a towing company in, but I'd have made sure the driver paid for it.'

'And how would you have done that? The bloke's rude to you, tells you lies, shows no respect – just bombs off onto the most dangerous river estuary in Britain without a by-your-leave, with no notion of the consequences of his actions, and you, bleeding heart that you are, wanted to welcome him back with a nice dry car and a letter of commendation from Drug Pushers Anonymous ... 'Oh, and by the way, there's the little matter of the towing bill which I, saver of the day that I am, paid for out of my own pocket!' You're still a people-pleaser, Martin. Right the way down to your fingertips. The Boss did the exact right thing. The man pushes his way onto the beach – shame on him. You make it easy for him to gain from his sins – shame on you.'

Benson had heard this before. 'You're right but...' he tried.

'Can't you see that you are *not* being a good person by giving way in situations like this? Can't you *see* that? All you're doing is making yourself feel like Mother Theresa – and I'd say Mother Theresa was a pretty tough cookie. You wouldn't find Mother Theresa enabling bad behaviour to make herself feel better. But that's what you want to do. All the fuckin' time.'

'You're right but...'

'I haven't passed anyone today. You know why. They weren't ready. They have to learn by their mistakes. If

236

they think I'm a shit and slag me off all over the shop,
well let them.'

'You're right. I know you are. But – well I find it hard.'

'At least you're aware of the problem. You can see it
for what it is.'

'It's not easy...'

'Nothing about this is *easy*.

'*No...*'

'I'm off to a men's meeting in Liverpool with Jack
tonight. Fancy coming?'

'I think I'll go here.'

'Fine,' Rob said.

'Of course, if you want me to I could join...'

'What have I just been saying?'

'Right.'

'We've got a bit of time. Is there anything you fancy doing?'

Benson reared up. 'I'll have a shower, and get myself
fixed up. Then I'll go to bed. You can come in and startle
me just as I'm getting off to sleep.'

'I'll be up in ten.' Rob made to clear the table.

'Don't do that. I'll do it later.'

'Suit yourself. By the way, has Health-and-safety Allan
got a buddy?'

'A Q.A. buddy? I don't think so.'

'Maybe you should suggest he gets one. He needs
someone to take him through The Steps. Sharpish.'

'Hasn't he done them?'

'Not sure. But my gut instinct tells me he's flailing.
And I heard something at work today. About Allan, and
all the other idiots in the cottage. He might be needing
all the help he can get.'

Benson tried to get more details, but Rob was closed
to inquiry.

'I'll find out tonight,' Benson said. He left Rob causing mayhem in the kitchen and ran upstairs to buff himself into a Rob-preferred condition.

# 31

Benson arrived at the QA meeting with only a minute to spare. It was not that Rob had made him late. No, Rob had been his brisk and determined self, rolling off His Intended at 7 on the dot, shimmying himself into his clothes in no time at all, and squirting something intolerable by Gillette about his person, emitting a peremptory 'Ta-ra' at wrecked Benson, then setting off to collect Jack for their sober tryst on the wilder shores of Liverpool.

It would be nice, Benson had thought, to just loll and drift off. But lolling and drifting off would mean missing the chance to share the triumphs and anxieties of the day with his fellow drunks. What would he say? *The work is more than the job.* Yes, that would be the gist of it. He might expand byelaw officers to include binmen and traffic wardens, checkout staff and street cleaners. After all, these jobs were demotic and disgustingly underrated. He, Benson, after his day of experiencing life in the incorrectly-perceived loser lane could speak from personal experience of the skills, unseen and unappreciated, that went into such work.


The meeting was crowded. He had to find himself a chair from the next room, and squeeze it in next to Busy Sandra and her Zimmer – which now sported a teddy roped to one of the verticals, a teddy with a policeman's hat and a bandage on its arm, the arm that was not holding onto a truncheon – in order to sit at the table. He looked around. A few people he did not know. Maybe they were new, or maybe they'd come over from Liverpool or Southport. It was not unusual for members of QA to travel great distances in order to find fresh meetings, and, unfortunately perhaps (and who was *he* to judge?), the chance of a quick seduction. Once they'd had an American in who was making a holiday of going to all the meetings he could in Britain and Ireland. Now that he was retired, he had time, he'd said. His name was Roy and he'd had a really rackety life, but all that was behind him. Benson and Rob had let him bed down with them. Roy taught them things that night he and Rob had never thought of, and promised he'd recommend the meeting to his chums back home in the States. But so far Roy had been their only American source of enlightenment.

Benson thought of Roy – and used him as the subject of his quiet meditation during the silence – before Banker Pete started on his script.

Banker Pete had been chairing the Saturday meeting for years. He should have known the process by heart, liver and kidneys, but he still read everything from a script. 'This is the Saturday night meeting of Queer Alcoholics at the New Brighton crypt. Our meeting is in two parts: first, I will speak a bit about a topic, then the meeting will be open for shares. Keep in mind that this is a crowded meeting and I'd ask you to limit your shares to five minutes maximum. If you feel you need to talk longer, find someone after the meeting.'

Banker Pete chose spiritual experiences as the topic. He quoted from book after book ... William James, Bill Wilson, Anthony De Mello, Buddha, Jesus, Mohammed and Delia Smith. When he'd finished he informed the group that his spiritual experiences at QA were of the educational variety. He'd come to QA morally and spiritually bankrupt. Alcoholism was a disease – a 'disease' – that had affected him physically, mentally and spiritually. We get better in reverse order. The body mends itself, our mental faculties return ... but unless we experience a real moral upheaval that, day-by-difficult-day, brings us insight into ourselves and our powerlessness and dependence upon a Higher Power as we understand that concept we shall not be able to build up our defences against the first drink.

Very true. Very true, Benson thought. He wondered if his 'My work is more than my job' could be levered into a share on spiritual experience. Hmm...

But he was too late. One of the strangers at the meeting came in. Benson sensed from long experience that he was feeling a bit on the desperate side, and might try to go on for some time.

'My name's Gary. I'm a queer alchy. My home group is the YMCA in Speke. I'm at the end of me tether. Full of fear, I am. I did a spot of cottaging down Hatter's Castle on the prom. The police filmed me at it in that sting they had. I was hauled in and went to court. I pleaded guilty and was fined three hundred quid, which I paid. Now today me name and address are in the paper. Not only that: the article says I'm married with two kids. They don't mention the number of me house. But they don't need to. It's a dead end street with six houses on each side. Me house is the only one with two kids. And, of course, me name's in the fuckin' paper as well. Think about it. There I am a year without a drink, trying to figure out what the right thing to do about me partner, me kids and meself. I mean, I knew it was daft going to

241

that place, but I couldn't help meself. I was powerless to resist it – the excitement, the thrill, the possibility that I'd get what I want...' Gary paused, then continued, weighing out the words, 'Get what I want. And not only do I get hauled up in front of the beak, but the fuckin' paper outs me with the family, and sure as eggs is eggs the kids'll get bullied at school. I've been landed right in it, I can tell you. You can tell me – because I tell meself every day – that something like this had to happen if I continued living a lie, playing the straight family man. Well, I don't know what happened. I mean, I knew what I was from way back. I should never've got married. But me mum and dad were pestering me for grandchildren. All me friends were settling down. So I caved in, even though I knew I just wasn't made for marriage. I was rat-arsed when I got married, rat-arsed when I got the wife pregnant. The odd bit of cottaging managed to keep the lid on things. But that's all gone now. On the way here I stopped off at Bargain Booze. I went in and asked the woman for a flatty of vodka. But as she was getting it, I saw the booze on the display and in a flash I saw what the future held if I necked any. So I told the woman I'd changed me mind and bought a great big slab of Cadbury's instead. Me sobriety means everything to me. Without it I'd be completely lost. But I feel very lost today, I can tell you. Me name's in the fuckin' shithouse. I want to murder the reporters who took me details. I want to murder the busies who put cameras in the cottage like this was fuckin' Romania. Thanks for listening to me.'

The meeting went silent. This usually happened after a powerful share. People were so busy digesting the meaning and import of what they had heard that no one felt they could follow it with something that would sound petty. Benson moved his 'the work is more than the job' share to a later date. And then he realised that Health-and-safety-Allan was absent.

A woman in her forties called Daisy broke the silence. Daisy lived with a woman in her thirties called Miriam. Miriam was a proctologist at Clatterbridge hospital, while Daisy worked nights cleaning the carriages of Merseyrail undergound trains. Not facing up to one's orientation, Daisy said, was similar to her own inability to admit to her problem drinking. For years it had not been a problem for herself ... she loved booze to bits; loved the taste, the smell, even the empty bottles that grew like forests around her bed, her easy chair, her car. She could not part with them. But everyone else suffered. Her boss had suffered. Her family too. But so insane had she been throughout the years of drinking that she hadn't seen the effect she was having. She could sympathise with Gary's situation. It had been different for her. There was just no hiding her masculine genes: the rough games she'd loved at school, the hangdog way she'd followed the girls about. She knew. Too fuckin' right she knew. Everyone knew. But the powerlessness of the alcoholic over booze is mirrored in most other areas of life. Sexual instincts are natural, but when society tells us that ours are not, it takes a certain defiance and guts to trust those instincts. No one here made a choice to be gay. It's simply the way God made us. We know that, and many societies – including our own – appreciate that. But full acceptance is some way off still. And even here it's not universal. To this add those people who never came to terms with it ... people who grew up when it was illegal, Thatcher's children hearing stories of AIDS and not being able to approach teachers or hear the topic discussed in class ...

what happened to them? We can be as addicted to the way the world sees us as much as we can to booze. I know how the world sees my surfaces. I've got 'bull dyke' written all over me. Nothing I can do about it. Now, Gary, some sleazy free rag has written something on you. You've been outed. I can't tell you how to proceed. It's not my place. But I can tell you to stick like a limpet to the fellowship of QA. This is an honest programme of action. As such it involves a lot of pain. But I know I have often been surprised when I've made an amend to find that the person I make the amend to is far more understanding than I gave her credit for. I'll finish on this: *Don't worry about what people think of you; worry about what you think of other people.* And that includes dodgy reporters and bent busies. Thank you.'

Busy Sandra shuffled. Benson was hoping against hope that she wouldn't share. At QA it was not the custom for shares to turn into arguments. 'Crosstalk', it was called, and crosstalk led to controversy and splits. It was as lethal to fellowship as gossip.

Lionel shared next. Lionel lived with Henry and together they operated an 'everything for 99 pence' shop in Birkenhead next to what had been a Woolworths. But Poundland had opened up and his business was on the skids. His partner, he said, wanted their shop to diversify into lines that Poundland didn't stock. He was having a shocking time trying to persuade Henry – who drank, but not alcoholically – from stocking a 'gay' range of items. He was especially against the 'room odorisers' that Henry had bought off his own bat from a bankruptcy sale in Blackpool. He'd bought boxes of them and reckoned they'd be a big earner at 99 p. But he knew what Poppers were for. He'd used them himself. They were a drug, pure and simple. They took away inhibitions and got people into all sorts of irrational behaviour in bed they'd live to regret. And that's not mentioning what kids use them for at clubs and such. And using them along with Viagra could kill. Don't mention *that* on the bottles, do they? And Henry wanted to sell them, along with all sorts of other items that would frighten away the old ladies who were his main customers. But, above all, he was feeling a fierce resentment against Poundland for coming in and throttling the small trader. Pound shops were a life-saver for the small businessman, but even they weren't safe from the fat cats.

Then Condenser Jane – who installed and maintained central heating – came in to share. Condenser Jane spoke very quietly, and Benson always had to cup a hand behind his ear to hear her. He cupped his hand for two reasons: to help him get the gist of what Condenser Jane was saying, and to point out – though it had no effect – that she could only be heard by the lucky few sitting close to her.

Condenser Jane had got her name because she always increased her volume when she asserted: *I told her: bin the one you've got and get a CONDENSER boiler!* It seemed to be her cross to advise the change, but no one seemed to listen. She was forever labouring away at trying to make uneconomic, gas-guzzling, clapped-out boilers work for one more year.

On and on went Condenser Jane. Not a word about spiritual experiences. Benson, were he to give Condenser Jane a piece of advice – which he wasn't – would have told her to accept the things she couldn't change. His own experience of condenser boilers was that they were forever going wrong. He rued the day he had allowed his 'Glow-worm' to be ripped out and replaced with a condenser boiler. For a start it took the water ages to make its way from boiler to tap and...

Benson stopped himself. He was letting his stupid head take over. Stinking thinking, criticism, judgement, were leaking into what should be a time of spiritual awareness and growth. Rob kept telling him that the very worst meeting might be a test of tolerance, but perhaps that was what he needed to exercise. After all, a meeting was a practice court for life. All sorts of things were aired at meetings and many of those things might make a fellow angry, fearful, bored or judgemental. If he was disturbed by meetings, what did that say about himself and his own view of people? And if he was able to still his racing brain, lance the boil of stinking thinking at a meeting, then his chances of behaving becomingly (Rob's word) in the outside world were increased.

So Benson let Condenser Jane flow over him. He tried to empty his mind, but was soon thinking about Gary's situation. It could so easily have been his – or that of many others around this table in the Unitarian Church meeting-room. And what about Health-and-safety Allan? He'd accepted a caution, so hadn't been hauled up in court like Gary. Things looked better for Allan, didn't they? But why wasn't he here? He seldom if ever missed a Saturday meeting. Maybe, he thought, I should collar Busy Sandra when the meeting finishes and ask her straight.

Not-sure Shirley came in after Condenser Jane's share subsided into silence. Not-sure Shirley was not sure about her orientation, not sure that she was a Real Alcoholic, not sure that she belonged at the meetings. Still, she was sure – she thought – that she wanted to stay off alcohol because every time she had drunk she landed up in the police cells or covered in dew – or worse – on a park bench without an inkling of what had happened to her. Both her two boys, Seth and Noah, whom she loved the bones of, had been conceived in blackouts. She had not an inkling as to who the fathers were. Still she wouldn't change anything for the world, but was looking for a lady-friend who would help her with their upbringing and be a loving partner.

Every time Not-sure Shirley shared, everyone in a recovery meeting – be it gay, straight, women-only, whatever – were convinced to a man or woman that Not-sure Shirley belonged in the rooms. While the only qualification for membership was 'a desire to stop drinking'; while it was never stated exactly what the alcoholic state consisted of – that was up to the individual to decide – everyone who had ever heard Shirley expound on her war stories was convinced that Shirley was an alcoholic of the most extreme type. She'd been offered buddy after buddy to help her through the simple Twelve Steps of the programme, but at each one she had pronounced herself Not Sure. Not Sure about her powerlessness over alcohol, her life being unmanageable; not sure about whether a Higher Power could restore her to sanity; Not Sure that she wanted to be restored to sanity or to dredge through her past life – what she could recall of it – and tell her Higher Power, herself, and another human being the exact nature of her faults; completely Not Sure that she wanted to make direct amends to the people she had harmed. Still, for all her uncertainty, Not-sure Shirley had been sober for twelve years. Her younger son – a beautiful mixed-race boy (Seth) was doing well at Caldy Academy and was sports-mad. 'So I must have done something right. Not sure what, but *something*. Thanks.'

A silence followed. Benson could hear it. He knew that

every last one of those who knew Not-sure Shirley was knocking on heaven's door, pleading to whoever or whatever they considered their Higher Power to be to intervene, to show Shirley that she had already tapped into the power of the fellowship and was just not sure what He, She, It, was. Perhaps it was the group of people sitting round a table trying to be honest, to live a day at a time, to realise that, whatever the Higher Power might be, it was not *me*. No, it was *us*.

A man whose name Benson did not catch said he'd been caught cottaging too. His name wasn't in the paper, which didn't seem fair. But they'd caught a fuckin' busy at it as well and the report said he'd been fined three weeks' salary, but he wasn't named and shamed. And what was *that* all about? Well, we all know the answer to that, don't we? Still, he couldn't complain. He knew cottaging was wrong, but he'd cottaged since he was knee-high to a grass-hopper. He was genetically programmed to cottage. He'd taken his punishment like the proud queen he was and would be more careful in future. At least, he said, when sober, he had his wits about him.

This promoted laughter and a smattering of applause. Banker Pete made signs that he was about to bang the wooden collection box on the table to restore order, but was interrupted by the door to the room opening with a shocking suddenness.

Into the room lurched Health-and-safety Allan. He was holding a three-quarter-empty bottle of Asda No-Frills whisky in his hand. No cap on. He made to swig from it, but a restraining hand – the hand of Irish Tommy – stopped him. Tommy whispered into Allan's ear.

But Allan wasn't listening. 'Giz it!' he said to Tommy. 'Giz it! It's all I've fuckin' got left!'

'Sit down and shut up,' Banker Pete told Allan sternly. 'You've had a slip. We can see that. But you came back. That's good. But you're drunk, Allan. Very drunk. If you want to stay for the rest of the meeting you must be quiet.'

'Fuck off!' Allan shouted.

'I won't tell you again,' said Banker Allan.

Irish Tommy whispered some more into Allan's ear, and Allan slumped down.

There was silence in the room for a long time. Normally, Benson enjoyed silences, thinking them Quakerish and affording him an opportunity to stroll around the fragrant garden of his soul and smell the flowers and consider the weeds. But not this silence. This silence eloquently stated that people's hearts and minds were full of disappointment for Allan, fear that he would go off again like a bottle of pop and have to be thrown out, worry that each of them at some point in the future might come back to QA in such a state of dis-grace and, above all, above all else, the exquisitely painful feeling that is that perfect blending of fear and pride: Embarrassment. All were the captain of their thoughts and feelings, but the wind that blew them came from the distressed deposed king of all things healthful and safe, all things lighthouse and foghorn and street-sign, Health-and-safety Allan.

Into this mayhem Benson ruddered his way: 'My name's Martin. I'm a queer alcoholic,' he said.

Several in the group greeted him. 'Hello, Martin!' they said in a tone that came to him as one of relief. 'This meeting has been an especially helpful one to me. As fellows have shared, I've been constantly reminded of my own vulnerabilities, doubts and thought patterns. I've found identification with everyone who's shared. With

some, it's been in the 'But For The Grace of God Go I'
sort. Only a very small number – I suspect – of the males
here have not done the things that two people shared. I
started cottaging when I was fourteen, loaded down with
a heavy sense of sin but an obsession and compulsion to
find what I was looking for. What was I looking for?
Another man's cock. Why? Why when I have a perfectly
OK one about my own person I do not know. But that
obsession and compulsion has stayed with me from
childhood to where I now find myself in early middle
age...' Benson waited for the laughter, but only Irish
Tommy got it. 'OK. Late middle-age. I also find myself
sober after many years of attending these meetings and,
like Sheila, I'm not sure why. Drink for me is no longer
a problem, but it could become a problem again in no
time at all if I don't follow the simple programme that
is the Twelve Steps. There's not a lot new in those Steps.
They're a spiritual guide that suit people of all religions
and none. But my sobriety I believe is dependent on my
following those steps to the best of my ability. The most
consoling passage in our Big Book is, to my way of
thinking: 'Do not be discouraged. No one among us has
been able to maintain anything like perfect adherence to
these principles. We are not saints. The point is that we
are willing to grow along spiritual lines.' At every meeting
we hear our fellows admitting to their daily failures and
successes. That's part of the beauty of these meetings.
Every day, we fail. But as each day closes, hopefully we
fail a little bit better. For those of you who don't have a
buddy in the fellowship to guide you through the steps,
I'd recommend that you find one pronto. Thanks.'

And Benson lapsed into silence, wondering if his share
had been honest, wondering if he'd been up on a pulpit

preaching instead of down at ground level – where he belonged – with his fellows. Honesty was a ticklish concept, especially when discovered in middle-age, after half a lifetime or more of cover-ups and a head that made Janus seem straightforward. But that was part of the smile that he usually had on his face after each meeting. Buddha was always seen smiling. Not that he was comparing himself with Buddha. Rather the comparison – and the smile – applied to the oddly comic conundrum of all the conflicting programs playing on the Random Accessed Memory of his head. It was either smile or despair. Take your pick.

Benson's share signalled a couple of others to console the silent presence of poor slipped Allan. Banker Pete came in and read from his sheet that it was the end of the meeting; that they were self-supporting from their own contributions. The pot went round. People were thanked for making tea, putting out chairs and emptying ashtrays (though smoking had been banished from the rooms for the last three years). But it was written down, and Banker Pete never seemed to notice the little laughs when ash-trays got a mention.

The Serenity Prayer was recited, each fellow hand-in-hand with neighbours. A group gathered around Gary, some more around the man whose name Benson had not caught. Benson looked around for Allan. And Allan was looking straight back at Benson.

# 32

While the group dispersed and the rump of fellows who had their jobs to do in returning the room to the condition they had found it got to work: moving chairs into neat stacks, washing up the mugs, emptying the sugar-bowls into its airtight tin, putting the uneaten biscuits back in their box, counting the collection, removing the big scroll that had the Twelve Steps of QA printed on it, going over the floor with a past-its-prime Ewbank: Benson sat with drunk-as-a-skunk Allan.

Not that Allan seemed to notice Benson's presence. He sat curled over, looking at the floor. His time sitting quietly had brought about a change in him. Though still in the middle of inebriation, just coming to the meeting had leached out all pleasure and vitality from his state.

Benson knew what had happened. People who 'slipped' – though that word did not seem to do justice to what happened when sober recovering alcoholics drank – soon discovered that sober time put in at the Fellowship completely ruined a drinking bout. After all, every meeting banged in the message of all that. *The First Drink*, followed inevitably by the second, third, then the necking from the bottle and the wild search for more, fulfilled all the pessimistic forebodings of those who told of the experience. To start boozing again you did not start out as a neophyte, drinking like a gentleman or lady, drinking like most 'civilians' drank. No, alchies of the type who belonged in QA started where they had left off.

For Benson, the hard disk of his burnt-out Catholicism still running beneath everything, a 'slip' seen in others was best compared to the misery of committing what he had then thought of as a Mortal Sin. Those acts, almost always sexual in nature, had left him in a God-gone state of high anxiety, only healed by a humiliating and humbling trip to confession.

In the case of a slip – and Benson had not had a slip, and prayed daily to his Higher Power that he never would – the important thing was for the drinking alcoholic to get back to meetings, stop drinking – perhaps with the aid of prescription drugs, for alcohol withdrawal, in the chronically addicted, could be dangerous, even deadly – and learn from the experience. Learn what? Well, learn again the truth of Step One of the programme: that he was powerless over alcohol and his life had become unmanageable. That first step came first for a reason. It led seamlessly to all the others and had to be accepted completely, so that the taking of each would be built on rock-hard foundations of the ones already worked on.

But, as everyone said, alcohol is cunning, baffling and powerful, most of all for alcoholics. It will seize upon a crisis – something Benson intimated from the meeting poor drunk Allan was in the middle of. Had he been named in the newspaper? Had he been quietly worrying himself sick with a feeling of impending doom? Whatever had happened, it seemed clear to Benson that something had gone wrong. Allan knew the tools of QA very well. He had always been pretty good at pointing out those tools to Benson when Benson failed to pick them up. But in the middle of his crisis, though armed with telephone numbers of fellows who would help, a neat and comprehensive shelf of recovery literature, a twenty-four-hour network that would swing into action to help a recovering alchy on the edge ... he had bought that bottle of Asda whisky, cracked open the sealed screw-top, and necked perdition.

As Allan stared at the carpet, and Banker Pete made ominous sounds with his keys, Benson looked at Allan and wondered. He wondered about Allan's predicament and how he had got there. Had he, Benson, done enough to help him? Now, in the corner of the empty room he remembered what Rob had said. He had never asked Allan whether he had a buddy who would take him through the steps. Allan had never mentioned a buddy. Benson, of course, had Rob. Without Rob he did not know where he would be. Without Rob to explain things and help him through each day ... it might have been his hand, clasping that bottle of perdition.

'I've got to close up now,' Banker Pete said.

Allan looked up, but did not move.

'Come on, Allan. You can come back to ours and have some coffee. Rob should be back.'

Allan just shook his head.

With some help from Benson and Pete, Allan was manoeuvred out of the room, along the corridor and into the street. Pete offered Allan a lift home. Allan shook his head. Pete said he had to go. Benson wished he'd stay, but told him he could manage, though he wasn't sure he could.

Allan found the gate of the Unitarian church, and leaned against it. He then announced that he was going to be sick, and duly did the deed.

Benson looked around, aware that they were back in the

254

busy world of Saturday night New Brighton, with cars zooming past making for the pubs and clubs. Pedestrians passed as well, taking in the scene, giving them a wide berth. Benson was determined to remove himself from the scarlet letter of the smelly mess that Allan – so contrary to his Health and safety persona – had left outside the Unitarian church. What, Benson wondered, would the parishioners think as they assembled for their Sunday worship? Would they blame the QA meeting and wonder if their kindness in giving them the rooms for such a low rent was misplaced? Or would they think the vomit at their gate was the result of late-night revellers and see it as a common sign of the times? Yes, drunken youth might get it in the teeth. But it was important that he and Allan remove themselves from the scene of the crime.

'What do you want to do, Allan? Will you come home with me?'

'No.'

'Shall I take you home and put you to bed?'

'No. I can manage.'

'You won't go to Bargain Booze, will you? You've had a skinful already, you know.'

'I'm going home.'

'Don't you want to talk things over? Rob's...'

'No.'

Benson watched as Allan disengaged himself from the gate, dodged his own vomit with the same sort of fluke fluency that made silent cinema clowns escape open manholes, and lurched down the hill towards...

Home? Bargain Booze? Some pub? The sea? Benson watched him go, feeling that he shouldn't just watch. He knew what Rob would say when he came in. He waited until Allan took himself around the corner.

He turned and made his way up the hill home.

An idea came to him. He dismissed it, but it came back. Again he dismissed it, but the idea insisted. Benson sought about in the pantry for his water container. He filled it with the slow flow of hot water yielded by the condenser boiler, added some disinfectant and screwed the cap on the container. He took a brush from behind the side door, and walked back to the pavement outside the church. He upended the container uphill from the pool of vomit and attacked it with his brush. He kept at it until the pavement was clean, the residue consigned to the gutter. Then he brushed it doggedly to a nearby grid, replaced the cap on the container, and walked nonchalantly back home.

It was only when he got home that he remembered reading about his namesake in The Brothers, another Brother Joachim, who had taught at Brothers' schools in America. At the time he had been very impressed by one act of that Brother Joachim – whose obituary was probably what he had read. That dead Brother Joachim had been in charge of a class of First Communion boys. One of these boys, having received the Host, got back to his pew where he promptly vomited onto the pew in front. He was led away.

When the service was over Brother Joachim was seen down on his hands and knees, his tongue reclaiming the Host of his God from the vomit.

# 33

'What you doing with them?'

Rob came out of the garage just as Benson was about to put the key in the lock of the front door.

'Nothing.'

'What's that mean?'

'There was a mess in the road. I cleared it up.'

'How was the meeting?'

Benson told Rob everything that had happened, right the way down to Allan's departure for who knew where.

'You did the right thing. Can't help an alcoholic until he's good and ready.'

'You helped me.'

'You were ripe for it.'

'S'pose so, but isn't Allan ripe? He came back to the meeting, didn't he?'

Rob conceded that he had. 'But you asked him to come back to ours, didn't you? He declined all that. He chose to go off and do what alcoholics do.'

'Drink?'

'Maybe he hasn't had enough.'

'Allan didn't say anything about it, but I think the outing of the people from Liverpool got to him.'

'Well, that's fair enough. It would get to me too. But he's been in The Fellowship long enough to know what to do when the shit hits the fan. I mean – Christ! – that's why we go there. Anyone can swear off drinking for a while, but if we're going to stay off for good a day at a time we need the tools of the programme. Did you find out whether he's got a buddy, by the way?'

'No.'

'Bet he hasn't. Bet he hasn't been taken through the steps. Have you taken anyone through the steps?'

Benson knew Rob already knew the answer to that. 'No.'

'Why's that, I wonder?'

'I don't know. No one's asked.'

'What's wrong with you going up to someone and telling him you'll be his buddy? That's what they did at the start of the fellowship. They'd take people through the Steps while they were still in hospital, still rattling from the booze. At the bottom. All they reckoned they needed was for the alchy to be able to take it in.'

'But I'm not sure how to do it.'

'You just tell them how you did it. You know how you did it, don't you?'

'I listened to you.'

'Yes?'

'Went to meetings.'

'Yes?'

'Made tea.'

'Right. Any tea on the go?'

Benson boiled the kettle, slung tea bags into mugs, put milk and sugar on the table. 'How was your meeting?'

'Packed. You'd've loved it. A dozen hairy bikers up from Leicestershire for the weekend. They're camping in a farmer's field outside Ormskirk. Rough as fuck on the outside – Jack was creaming his pants. But there was some rock-solid sobriety there. No pity-pot crap. No therapy. Just bread and butter QA and no frills.'

'Camping! But it isn't even Easter!'

'I'd say that crew have ways of keeping warm.'

Benson nodded. 'You're a bit like the Boss,' he said.

'How d'you mean?'

'*Je ne sais quoi* ... You lead and people follow.'

'*Wa?*'

'*Je ne sais quoi.* A certain something.'

Rob seized his mug. 'It's funny, but I don't see meself like that. I'm probably like that with you, mind. You like to be led by the nose. Fits you like a glove.'

'You're right.'

'I mean, stands to reason. I get it from the job, from bringing up the boys. Not that they take any notice. I definitely get it from being a buddy to drunks.'

'Tough love.'

'It's a two-way street, mind,' Rob said. 'Jack doesn't take any nonsense from me, you know.'

'I was wondering...' Benson said.

'Wa?'

'Have you mentioned our plan to your family?'

'Yeah.'

'What was their reaction?'

'The boys didn't take to it. I asked them if they'd come to the do, but they didn't seem keen. Yvette was fine. But she'll be away on a cruise with Andy. She's just glad to be out from under. She's really blossomed, I must say. I'm happy about that. I took that woman to hell. Anyway, I just have to take all that on the chin. I've made me amends. I do what I can for them. But I can't force them to do things they don't want to. I may have a certain *je ne* ... what-you-said, but they saw me when I was self-will run riot, they remember the drunken rages, the beatings. There's a price to be paid for all that. I've just got to accept it, make me amends and move on.'

'Do you think I'll ever get to meet your family?'

'Stranger things have happened. But...'

'It all comes down to the Serenity Prayer in the end, doesn't it?'

'Too right. That prayer is a cunning little sentence. It's the positive side of the notion that alcohol is cunning, baffling and powerful. I still don't think I've really got to the bottom of it.'

'More tea?'

'No, ta. Time for bed for you. I can lie in, but you've got work. Why not drop a note in to Allan? Ask him if he wants a buddy to take him through the programme. Offer yourself.'

'Are you sure?'

'It can't do any harm, can it?' Rob pinched Benson seductively, and propelled him towards the stairs. 'And telling him your own experience, strength and hope might save his bacon. All you've got is your story.'

# 34

The following morning, having pushed a note through Health-and-safety Allan's door, together with one of the praying-hand serenity prayer wallets he'd bought in Holywell, Benson was spooning out sand from holes in the promenade, much in the manner that his fellow residents might well have been extracting the innards out of eggs.

As soon as he'd arrived on the promenade, he looked over the wall, half-expecting to see the BMW on the concrete, but it had gone.

Overnight the wind had blown spitefully from the south-east up the sweep of estuary from Runcorn. It managed to stir up sheets of sand on the shoreline and deposit it all over the area where Benson worked, effectively filling in all the square holes into which he slotted the metal posts of his fence. Behind these, miniature banks of fine wind-blown sand were forming. They had covered the 'NO PARKING EMERGENCY VEHICLES ONLY' sign. They had soon filled his shoes, gritted his mug of tea. He pondered what to do about the invasion, but got down to cleaning out the fence holes.

This work, which entailed Benson getting down on hands and knees with his spoon, did not bother him. He had decided that he was going to view the task as a humble but necessary one. True, passing members of the public, not that there were any about at this hour on a

Sunday, might mistakenly be of the opinion that the task was as low as it got ... but that was not how he chose to see it.

No, the 'work' was greater than the 'job'. It was time he put into practice a notion he had often thought (in theory) – and when seriously pissed off – at checkouts: ('You're not just endlessly bleeping product through to customers. No! You might be the only person the customer will speak to all day. You can make that day – or leave him or her lonely'). All sorts were included in this world-changing notion: binmen ('Thank you for keeping our homes clean; for helping to prevent disease; for sorting recyclables out to save the planet ... and for doing it all without unnecessary noise.'); Traffic wardens ('You're knights of the road. You *do* know that, don't you? Without you the whole country would be snarled up in no time'). Benson's 'vision' operated for all the lowly jobs he saw people performing. Why not get rid of the Queen's Official Birthday – what on earth did she want with *two*? – and devote it to binmen instead ... the day to hug a binman and show him that you cared. Lots of days could be devoted to the (so-called) ordinary and unappreciated. Fill diaries with their days! Have rituals that celebrated them. Who would fill all those Letts diaries? Why, everyone who contributed, but who got not an ounce of recognition ('Look at that loser!') And now he was beginning to realise that as a humble byelaws officer he was – if only he were in charge of how things worked – first in line for a day all to himself...

*What shall we do today?*

*What do we always do on Byelaws Officer Day? Go and hug a Byelaws Officer and tell him he's useful and appreciated.*

*Yes. Let's!*

The wet sand from his spoon (for it had also pelted rain through the night) Benson deposited on the tarmac, where it grew into little piles like those dogs laid without a moment's hesitation – or a backward glance. Still, there was also a certain satisfaction in watching the piles grow as he went from hole to hole. If the sand were a tad wetter he could wow the populace with one of his dribble castles, whereby wet sand fell incrementally onto a small circle that served as the castle site. Then, dribble by dribble, a fairy castle like those on The Rhine – only made of cheap-as-chips damp sand and not pricey marble, granite and ormolu – grew and grew. It was a precarious business, of course. He could not count the times he'd had crowds around him ... kids, mothers, men, – in Saudi Arabia, Oman, Argentina, Ghana, holding their breath as he dribbled the pinnacle of a tall tower; the sigh of collective disappointment as his sandcastle of truly Dubaian dimensions and unreason, collapsed to the ground. Ah, Glory Days!

When he had completed the last hole, Benson stuck in the first two posts. He was pleased at the way they fell into place like the strike of a Swan Vesta. He went back to the hut for another pair of posts, carrying out the weather boards and a piece of red chalk – he'd used yellow the previous day and was determined to add a novel touch – together with a yellow-stained J-cloth of dead yesterday's climactic weather headlines.

He was all alone. Reg had gone off to check lifesaving equipment along the promenade between the Birkenhead docks and New Brighton. Emma had just wandered off towards the fort without a by-your-leave or an offer of a cup of tea.

Benson fretted briefly about where Emma would find

a toilet around the fort. He was all right when the tide was out. He could go down in the beach, secrete himself in the place he had decided to christen 'The Cloisters'. In this hallowed space Benson was able to find a place out of sight and relieve himself (Number 1 only of course), while looking at the happenings on the beach and, beyond that, to the great world.

The second set of two posts glided in. He connected the chain and once again thought of the Brooklyn Bridge. The bridge linked him to his times in New York, his generous friends there, the good times ... Then he went back for the other one. He took his time. God knew, he had time.

This he was carrying toward the hole, remembering that he had forgotten to fill the kettle and switch it on, when he looked towards The Chelsea. Then he looked again, pushing his glasses up his nose. Surely not, he thought.

He dropped the metal posts and ran to the railings next to the main entrance. He peered, pushing his glasses farther up his nose. Oh, surely not, he thought again.

'Are you all right?' Benson asked the dog impaled on the railings. But the dog plainly was not all right. The railings it was splayed on were rust-red with its blood. More was flowing into pools in the gutter below. Two spikes stuck out clean through its body, on each side of its spine.

Benson turned away and heaved a nauseous burp. The dog – had it fallen from the building? Had it died – or been killed elsewhere and then impaled like that, as if it were an empty Coke or Fosters can?

'All Stations. This is Sparks 1 with the weather forecast.'

The message reminded Benson of his duty. He had to

radio in the incident. It was urgent. People would soon be walking up and down the promenade. He turned again to look at the body, felt his gorge rise, turned back towards the sea, then looked right and left to see if anyone was coming. No one was. But if someone were, what would he do? He couldn't let a kid see this. No one should see this.

'Winds north-easterly. Force four to six...'

No, I must radio in. But how can I do that when Spark is giving out the weather. I can't just butt in, can I?

'Weather: blustery with sunny intervals and showers...'

I can wait for the message to finish. The dog's dead. There's no hurry. I know what...

Benson ran back to the hut and looked around the bleak interior. His Yves Saint Laurent bath-towel, bought at a sale in Colchester thirty years (half his lifetime!) ago – and still good as new ... no, he couldn't use that. It meant a lot to him. He could not use it as a shroud and cover it with memories of this. The towel did not deserve it. Its story contained dryings-off on three continents, serving as insulation for many an exciting escapade...

'High tide...'

Benson's eyes lit on two No Bathing flags – red cotton and, above all, handy, and not his. He seized them and ran back to the corpse. Reverently, he reached up and laid the flags over the body of the dog.

'Hoist No Bathing flags...'

'Oh...' Benson retched again, and bits of Grape-Nut and fat-free milk came up as far as his epiglottis. He pushed them back down.

Finally, the weather forecast finished. Benson moved away from the red-bedecked corpse and tried composing in his mind what he would say.

'Sparks 1. This is Zero 3. I haven't copied the weather. There is a dead dog impaled on the railings of The Chelsea. A large dog of indeterminate breed. Maybe part Alsatian but with the pampas-grass tail of a golden retriever. No collar that I can see. A lot of blood. Can the authorities be contacted? Over.'

'Zero 3. This is Sparks 1. I'll think what to do and note it in the book. Out.'

Then the Boss came on the radio and Benson knew everything would be all right. 'All that's been copied Phil. Talk through to Zero 3 ... Break ... Zero 3, this is Chief Lifeguard. I'll be there in a couple of minutes. You OK? Over.'

'I'm OK. I've covered the body with No Bathing flags. Over.'

'Roger. Out.'

So OK was Benson after his exertions that he managed to insert the last post in the hole – just as Sunday morning's snoozing population managed to listen to the radio as they slotted bread into toasters – although the sight of the little piles of sand spooned from the holes was making his stomach churn again.

Then he tried to fill in the weather on his board. Winds? What are the winds going to do? What direction? What force? What's the sea state? Who could have done this? Who did the dog belong to?

He dropped the board and paced the lines between the authorised parking area and the gate. Back and forth he went, resolutely keeping his gaze averted from the railings of The Chelsea.

'How are you today?'

Benson turned and saw one of the women from yesterday. She had a plastic bag, to collect her dog's doings. He placed himself between the woman and The Chelsea, trying to corral her away. 'Come this way,' he said.

'I want to go that way. The girls...'

'Just do as I say.' He searched about for the woman's name, but it didn't come. 'Please. Walk with me along the prom a bit.'

'Have you seen Pat?' the woman said, as Benson took her arm and frogmarched her out of sight of the flag-covered corpse.

'No,' Benson said, trying to remember which of the women with dogs was Pat. 'I'm sorry to be so odd. Tell you the truth, I feel a bit odd.'

'What's the matter?' the woman said.

'I'll tell you in a mo. Let's just keep walking.'

She looked at him. She had a lovely face, he thought. A lovely way about her too. Not that he knew her or anything but ... the sight of her made him want to cry. And he did. Was he crying for the dog? Maybe, though dogs had never figured on his list of lusts. Maybe it was the manner of its passing, or looking into the eyes of this woman and her well-beloved pet, sporting a pink collar and matching lead. She was quiet, took her time about everything, looked at you with soulful eyes. Seemed to know things you didn't. But ... *Give not your heart for a dog to tear.*

The woman stopped. 'What's the matter, love?' she asked again.

'Nothing. Let's keep walking.'

Obediently, the woman continued beside him, giving the dog a tug whenever a section of prom railing tempted her. 'Come on, Betty,' she said.

The Boss's yellow Land-Rover came into sight down Tollemache Street. It swerved around the corner and stopped next to Benson, the woman and Betty.

'Where is it?' the Boss called out, leaning across from his driving seat.

'Over there. To the left of the front entrance. Under the flags,' Benson replied.

The woman made to look back. Benson tried to block her view. 'The fort. Look at all the flags!' he said.

'What's happened?'

A police car appeared, lights flashing. Benson turned and saw that The Boss's Land-Rover had been positioned between them and the dead dog.

'There's been an accident,' Benson said. 'There's a dog over there.'

'Outside The Chelsea?'

'Yes. I was putting up the posts, and I saw it.

'Is it dead?'

'I think so. Look – I've forgotten your name – I'd better go and well ... be around. See you in a bit.'

The woman nodded, throttling Betty's lead. 'I'm Irene.'

'Irene...'

The Boss beckoned him over. 'When did you find the dog?'

'Just before Sparks called in the weather forecast. I'd been putting in the posts, and I looked. I must have passed it earlier, but just didn't see it.'

'Odd the things you find, Matron. Just when you think you've seen everything...'

A policeman came over and he and the Boss went into a confab. They consulted for a while, then the policeman moved his car in front of the railings, and the Boss moved his Land-Rover next to it. The flag-covered scene was blocked to prying eyes. The Boss came back. 'There are some fellows on their way. They'll remove the corpse, we'll hose the area down and be able to present a respectable face to visitors. Lucky you spotted it when you did. Any time now people will be down to organise the finishing line for the Liverpool to Wallasey 10 k. run. It'll be bedlam here in a couple of hours. We'll be twatted, and a dead dog impaled on the railings will not do our reputation as a reawakening holiday resort any good at all.'

'No, I expect not,' Benson opined. 'I missed the weather. I need to write it on the boards.'

'I've got a copy I can give you. Where's Reg?'

'He's checking lifebelts and lanyards.'

'Good. They need to be in good order for the race. It doesn't really concern us, unless one of the runners slips off the prom and into the water. You never know round here.'

'Will there be lots of runners?'

'Should think so. Everyone who finishes gets a medal'

'Everyone?'

'Prizes for all. Wouldn't do to disappoint anyone.'

The Boss handed over the weather forecast, written on an old lottery ticket. Benson made off to fill in his boards. He then positioned them by his gate and took the other one to place on the Lifeguard pole – which displayed a 'Bathing' flag – not that anyone would at this time of year. Only then did he realise that he'd forgotten to close the gates.

# 35

A van drew up next to the Boss's Land-Rover. Two men in serious-looking white jumpsuits got out and, carrying much plastic sheeting, disappeared behind the cars. A few minutes later they emerged, the plastic enfolding the corpse of the dog. They drove away after talking to the Boss, and were shortly followed by the police car.

The Boss moved his Land-Rover back across the road. He beckoned Benson over. 'Could you do me a favour?' Benson nodded enthusiastically. 'Get a few buckets of water and pour them over this area. Brush it down. Doesn't have to be pristine. Nothing round here's pristine. Just enough to get rid of the blood.'

A task! Benson thought happily, and he trotted over to the hut and carried the tap to the water board hole in the road, covered by its square metal cap. This he removed, then screwed the stand-pipe onto the thread. He knelt down over another metal-covered hole, the cap of which was on a hinge, and turned the water on. Bucket after bucket he filled to the brim, then carried them twenty yards across the road to the stained railings and area around. When six buckets had sluiced it all down, he returned with a brush and energetically scrubbed the water down the grid. He looked at the scene. How quickly everything had returned to normal! Who would guess that this place had been the centre of a miserable happening just a few minutes before? Still, the whole world – every square yard of it – had probably seen blood and pain at one time or another. Was there one innocent patch of earth anywhere?

The death of a dog. How interesting was it? Well, that depended. Depended on what? On your attitude to dogs, he supposed. He wondered about his own attitude to dogs. Well, he admired their innocence. The worst dog was more innocent than the best human being. Perhaps if he had kept one as a pet, he would know what all the dog-walkers in New Brighton knew. Still, he could make the leap. Dogs were much easier to love than people. Much. But was it reciprocal? Did the dog love its master? Well, that depended what you meant by 'love'. But it seemed to Benson that there was a misapprehension in the relationship. The dog owner, when the dog looked at her with soft eyes and nuzzled, was thinking: 'She loves me!' But was that what the dog was thinking? Maybe the dog was thinking that her owner was a fridge door which, if you rubbed it up the right way, would open up its cornucopia of delights. And how was that different from the more unscrupulous footballer's wife? Or Benson himself, for that matter? How many times had Benson whispered 'I love you' when he actually meant, 'I love your dick, cock, penis, prick'? Many times. *The lineaments of gratified desire.* And what about the faithful hound, Gelert? That story had unfolded only an hour or two from where he was standing! Llewelyn had this faithful hound called Gelert. But one day he arrived home to find Gelert covered in blood. He searched around frantically for his child, but could not find her. Thinking Gelert had eaten the child, Llewelyn stabbed the dog with his sword. Only then did he move some blankets and find his child, alive and smiling. And beside the child; a dead wolf which Gelert had slain, its blood soaking his fur in the process.

Hmm, thought Benson as he watched the tide heading in, and the people in yellow jackets setting up their bunting and tables for the end of the race. Llewelyn should have waited, should have searched harder. He made a false inference about Gelert, that's what. But ... But ... had Gelert been hungry and the baby the only food to hand, what then? Mind you, what about *Alive!* where the rugby players had eaten their dead friends. And them Catholics! But their team mates were dead when they ate them. But sailors in lifeboats killed their comrades in order to eat and survive. But can a dog love – selflessly? Can we?

Benson switched back to Kipling: *Brothers and Sisters I bid you beware/ of giving your heart for a dog to tear.* Well, the poet could bid dog owners beware as much as he liked, it never stopped them. And Edward Albee in *Zoo Story* had had Jerry say: 'Start by loving a dog.' – or words to that effect. It was – like pretty much everything in life – extremely complicated, and mysterious.

But the mystery of the morning was: who had pinioned the dog to the railings? What was going on there? Some nasty piece of work? Well, certainly that. But why? Rage against dog dirt? But animals were innocent. Why pick on man's best friend, even when the friend fails to care?

A jet-ski approached the gate. Benson made for the driver door, noting a permit badge on the vehicle. The driver – as pleasant as you please – showed him his car permit, and even his certificate of competence. 'Have a good day!' Benson said, opening the gate at speed, and reminding the nice man to wear his life jacket, not to park on the concrete – the RNLI might need it – and to bring his car back to the promenade because of the tide.

Reg came back and asked where the dog was.

'It's been taken away,' Benson said. 'Fancy a tea? I'll get it if you mind the gate for me.'

Reg agreed.

The promenade close to the finishing line was filling up with people. It wouldn't be too long before all those exhausted runners reached it, and went around all puffed and covered up with aluminium blankets – pleased with themselves – parading their medals.

He made the tea and allowed himself to contemplate the arrival of his bronze medallion for lifesaving. He'd managed that, though it had cost him dear – and the Boss had promised him a medal, seeing as the lifeguard qualifications had been denied him. Where would he put it? With his Ethiopian Cross? On the chain – the one Emerson had brought back for him? Or would he have it as a lapel badge? The former, he thought. Should I remind the Boss? No, maybe not. Not just now.

He was taking Reg his tea when it started raining. This was not advertised in the weather forecast. The hut beckoned, but there were sights to be seen, people to be directed towards public conveniences. (He thought of Health-and-safety Allan. He'd give him another hour and then ring him). Anyway, what was he other than a waiter, a watcher and a warner? A WWW. Yes, that is what he was. WWW. He would face the rain, get wet through if necessary, and make the shower at home when the clock ticked to that impossible land of Future even more ecstatic and consoling than usual.

He gave Reg his tea. Reg drank it down, and then went off to check the beach, without washing his mug. It stopped raining. Two permitted jet-skis came. No trouble at all, though he still dreaded their arrival and his need to inspect and appear officious. Why was that? What was it in him that hated enforcing byelaws? People-pleasing, hating not to please. Makes me feel like a shit.

Benson got his Asda binoculars out. Runners were arriving at the finish line. Their names were ticked off by an official while another delved into a huge cardboard box and placed a big golden medal, the size of a small chocolate bar, around the neck of the triumphant participant. Lucky ducks!

'Awful about the dog.'

It was Irene. 'Yes. Very sad. Very nasty.'

'Do you think it fell out of the Chelsea?'

Both of them looked at the building. All the windows were shut. It was a building waiting for something to happen. And this being New Brighton, that wait could be protracted. 'I don't think so,' Benson said.

'You don't think someone put it on the railings, do you?'

'I hope no one did that, but I can't think of any other way it could have happened.'

'Who would have done anything like that?'

Benson looked down at Betty. She was watching the road intently. A motorcycle passed, and Betty let out a stream of growls and barks, straining on her pink leash. The bike passed and Betty settled back to her serene self.

'What brought that on?

'She doesn't like motorbikes,' Irene said.

'Did you find Pat?'

'No. Me and Betty just walked up to the boating lake. There are twenty swans on it. It's lovely to see.'

'I bet the people sailing their boats don't like the swans.'

Irene thought. 'I don't think they mind. I think they rub along OK.'

'Well, that's good, isn't it?'

Irene looked around. Three women with dogs were heading towards her through the crowd of runner and watchers. 'I'm in trouble now,' Irene said.

But she was not in trouble. One of the women – was it Pat? – with a fat mongrel stoic on the end of a frayed leather lead – came straight up to Irene and whipped out a medal from her bag. This she put around Irene's neck. Irene looked hard at it. 'What's this?' she asked.

'What's it say on it?' the woman asked.

'Mersey Tunnel 10K,' Irene said. 'But I haven't done the 10K run, have I?'

'They've got lots left over. No good for next year.' The woman looked at Benson, 'Would you like one, dear?'

Benson wanted one very much indeed. It was yellow, like his sweatshirt. It was on a yellow and black ribbon. Yellow and black always brought to mind the Dawes drop-handlebar bike he had lusted after as a kid, but never got. 'I don't know. Have you enough?' The woman opened her everlasting Asda jute bag and he looked at the haul of medals inside.

'The bloke was desperate to be shot of them. All the runners are in and they overestimated the number they'd need. Go on, take one.'

'Thank you very much,' Benson said, meaning it. He placed it over his head and let it hang down between his radio and his whistle. It was becoming quite an eventful tangle down there. He asked the group if he could make them a cup of tea. All four declined. He asked them their names and they answered in turn: Pat, with old mutt on leather lead; Fran, with black devilish dog who was obsessed with balls; Lynn (with hairy mixed breed dog on a glittery collar) ... 'And I'm Irene,' Irene said.

275

'I'm Martin,' Benson said.

'What happened to the car?' Lynn asked. 'It's vanished.'

'Don't know. I was hoping you'd be able to tell me.'

'Lovely car. Such a shame.'

'The driver should have removed his vehicle from the shore – not that he should have been there in the first place. No permit. He just opened my gate without a by-you-leave. My first customer, too. Not a promising start.'

The women all agreed that it was not. They wandered off, with Benson's profuse thanks for his medal ringing in their ears.

Benson, alone again at last, commenced waiting by his gate, like the soldier in *Faithful Unto Death*. The wind buffeted him, and he let it. A gust took the heavy medal and banged it into the right lens of his spectacles. He took it off, folded the ribbon around it, and put it in his pocket. He contemplated the incoming tide.

Reg appeared, holding a mug of tea he had made himself, for himself. He said nothing to Benson, just opened his *Highway Code* and started studying.

Time passed. The rain started in earnest. A man with a brolly, taking a break from the sandwich shop he'd opened next to Safewater Training, gave Benson shelter and a long moan about how bad business was. He left, and left Benson – now in oilskins – to face the wind and steady, chilly, rain. This he did, feeling the sensations of standing there watching the swelling silver river and the misty presence of cranes and wind turbines across the river, the slow tug-nudged entry of a vast container ship into a dock entrance that seemed way too small for it but managed to take it, the walkers – many completely unprepared for cold and wet – scuttling along the prom towards home, the flash of red, blue and yellow jet-skis on the river.

The Boss came back and invited Benson to sit with him in his Land-Rover.

It was a whole different world. Warm, clean and tidy. The radio played chatter between ships and then, at a touch of a button, coastguard announcements.

'How old are you, Matron?' the Boss asked.

'Fifty-nine.'

'Not long before you'll get a bus pass.' Perhaps he saw Benson's face fall. 'I'm not far behind you,' he said. 'A few years.'

'I'm learning to accept it,' Benson said. 'Each birthday ending in a zero has been a bit traumatic. But I've found I grow into each decade. Thirty, forty, fifty ... I think fifty was hardest. But I'm ready for this one. I think.'

'I've got six years to go. A side of me thinks it can't come fast enough. Retirement and all that. But another side...'

It came as a relief to Benson to hear the Boss talking about 'sides'. Despite his years at QA listening to people's complicated stories, he still could not quite believe the consolation that everyone else was as complicated as he was. And the Boss presented himself very successfully as an integrated person who knew exactly where he stood. But Benson knew a lot about masks.

'Rob's been a great help to me,' Benson said. 'Since I've been living with him, I've learnt an awful lot about what makes me tick. Not that the learning has been a particularly comfortable experience. Not that I am able to change myself off my own bat, but the knowledge, the awareness, that I'd been wrong for so long in lots of ways at least helps me recognise my behaviour when it comes at me.'

'Not sure I get you.'

'Well,' Benson said, 'thinking of ageing, King Lear – a play I studied at school without getting – now means the world to me. Here's this old King giving away his land and property to the two daughters who flatter him while banishing the one who deserves to be cherished. His Fool tells him, 'Thou shouldst not have been old, till thou hadst been wise.' Those words hit me daily now. I am getting old. Time to get wise. But it is a slow daily struggle. An impossible dream, because most days I feel such a fool.'

'Rob used to be a shocking drinker. You met him because of that, didn't you?'

'He tripped over me on the prom. I was out for the count. That was my last drink. He took me home, put me to bed and told me there was a way out.'

'A Good Samaritan, then?'

'Exactly.'

'And he moved in?'

Benson was uncomfortable at that. 'Not at once.'

'Anyway, you've never looked back?'

'I look back all the time. If I forget where I came from I'm finished. My past – rackety and foolish and full of faults – is the bedrock of my recovery.'

'Interesting,' the Boss said. 'I'm going to have to chuck you out now. Got to patrol to make sure the others are keeping a look-out.'

Obediently, Benson opened the snug door of the Land-Rover, feeling a trifle miffed. He smiled, and as the Land-Rover drew away, thought of how strange the few minutes in the vehicle with the Boss had been – and how typical of him to feel the sudden withdrawal of big-boy conversation. But that was informative too. He'd have to stack that up for washing along with the rest of the empties. And he'd have to laugh at himself while doing it.

# 36

After signing out, but before going home, Benson decided to retrace his steps and see if he could get Allan to answer his door. He'd got the answerphone each time he rang during the day. Plodding back down the main street of New Brighton, noting the number of parked cars – on double yellow – outside Bargain Booze, he tried not to be judgemental. He failed. He tried again, failed again. But then Bargain Booze had passed seamlessly into the past and Benson concentrated on Allan.

Saying a quick prayer, Benson rang Allan's bell. It was the only one in the skyscraper set of bells that had a name on it. Also, Benson noted, Allan had managed to print in tiny letters below his name: NO HAWKERS, NO CIRCULARS. Well, Benson told himself, I am a hawker of sobriety. I have the circulars of QA literature in my head. I am making a Twelve-Step call on a poor slipped mate.

He rang again, presenting what he thought just might possibly be his better side to the snoopy surveillance camera that might or might not be connected to Allan's flat; that might or might not work. A long moment of nothing. An elderly BMW passed, farting Scouse House from its open windows. He turned his back on it, banning it from the beach of his mind, and waited.

A rattle came from the speaker. 'Hello,' said Allan, in a fragile and uncertain voice.

'Allan, it's Martin. I've been calling you all day.'

'I'll buzz you in. Wipe your feet.'

Benson did as instructed, thinking dark thoughts. Allan sounded distinctly the worse for wear. Good. He might have learnt something. He might be ready to hear the message. He might be ripe. But he might have spared me the 'Wipe your feet' remark. I always wipe my feet.

Benson had to ring another bell outside Allan's flat. After what seemed like an age, Allan answered, his head peering around the door while the rest of him was hidden by the white PVC of the door frame.

'It's you,' he said.

'Yes. Can I come in? Are you OK for visitors?'

'You'll have to take me as you find me. You woke me up.'

'Don't worry about that,' Benson said as the door opened. He stepped inside. 'I...'

Allan did not have a stitch on.

'...I just came round to see...' Benson stared determinedly into Allan's pale face. He took in every broken vein, every red line in his eyes, every wrinkle. He would not look down. He would not. He was here on serious business. This was what the Twelfth Step of QA was all about. He was here to give away what he knew about sobriety. He was here to give it away in order to keep it.

Benson looked down, and Allan noticed. Benson looked up. 'Have you had a drink today, Allan?'

'Not yet.'

'Well, that's a step in the right direction. Did you get my note?'

'Yes.'

'Do you have a buddy?

281

'No, I used to.'

'It's just that Rob and me were thinking that maybe you needed to be helped to have a ... a bit of a refresher on the Twelve Steps. Meetings and service on their own won't keep us sober. Not when a crisis hits.'

'Come and sit down,' Allan said.

'I'll do that,' Benson said. 'But I'd like you to er ... to put some clothes on, if you would. The sight of you in the nude – well, it's distracting.'

'You like a big one, don't you?'

'You know I do,' Benson replied. 'The thing is that I won't be able to talk about my experience, strength and hope coherently if I can see you in all your glory. It's a real distraction and I'm a bit nervous about being a buddy.'

'You're tempted, aren't you?'

'Course, I am! We've been through this before. But I am promised to another.'

'You were promised to another last time.'

'But I'm even more promised now, and I'm here on a very different sort of errand.'

'I had a buddy when I first came in. Won't name names, but he couldn't keep his hands off me.'

'Ah,' Benson said, understanding all too well.

'And then, when he had used me 'til he used me up he said as how he did not feel he was the one to pass the message to me. I've been doing it meself since.'

'Mmm,' Benson said.

It had occasionally seemed to Benson to be an Achilles heel of QA to have gay men buddying gay men. The logical thing would have been to have men buddy women and vice versa. At straight meetings, men stuck with men, and women with women, because then the problem of sex did not arise. The trouble was that QA had brought this straight version of buddying into their gay context. And problems arose, problems now manifest in all their power, glory and magnificence, before Allan's Buddy-in-waiting. But, of course, gay women were often at a loss when confronted with the complex psychology of gay men – and, in Busy Sandra's case – totally at sea. Relationships between the sexes were no simpler for the gay than for the straight – perhaps even more complicated.

'So, Allan,' Benson said – taking in Allan from every angle as he tried to explain why such a sight was beyond the pale – 'that's why – if I'm here to buddy you – it's important that we keep it all above board. You don't need a suit and a tie. A dressing gown will do. Even a pair of jim-jams.'

'Oh, all right,' Allan said. He stood up, stretched and his dangling penis strobed a foot from Benson's face.

'Your flat is really tastefully done,' Benson said. 'And tidy as well. A pity about that door.'

'What door?' Allan asked, looking round, giving Benson a chance for one more look at his nether regions. 'Yes, it is a bit of a mess. It was like that when I moved in. I've been in touch with the landlord, but you know what they're like.'

Allan turned away from the door, just in time to see what Benson was up to. Benson noticed and returned his attention to the door. 'Looks like someone has been hitting it with something sharp. I'd keep on at your landlord if I were you. Or you could cover it with a nice cloth. I do a lot of that. I've got these lovely cloths from Isfahan. That's in Iran. You could have one if you want. I've got lots.'

Allan flopped his arms to his sides and, without

283

acknowledging Benson's offer, he lurched into the bathroom, returning in a white dressing gown.

'Will this do?'

'That's fine,' Benson said, and got down to business.

He told Allan that there was no reason why he should need to take another drink if he was prepared to take certain steps. But he had to have the *want*. He needed to want to recover with all his heart. Benson was willing to do whatever it took, spend any amount of time with Allan. But all he had to offer was his own experience, strength and hope, and the last two were in the changes that had come about by doing the Twelve Steps to the best of his ability. Not that he'd done them perfectly. He wasn't a saint. He added that for him alcohol was no longer the problem. No, his problem was the Old Benson, the Benson that ran on self-will, selfishness, resentment, fear, and all the other things he had learnt about himself since Rob fell over him on the prom.

'I remember you then,' Allan said.

'I don't remember you. Not then. But you've been a great help to me over the years, and I was sad to see you'd had a slip. Still, a slip is just that. You need to get back to meetings as soon as you can – like tonight – and really get going on the Steps.'

'I'm scared of them. Especially Steps Four and Five.'

'Piece of cake. I was scared too. Who wants to make 'a searching and fearless moral inventory of themselves, as we do in Step Four? Who wants to admit to our Higher Power, to ourselves, and to another human being the exact nature of our wrongs? But Rob, when he'd heard my Step Five – and it took a whole day – said I was really boring compared to some of the others he'd buddied. And, of course, along the way, he pretty much told me everything there was to know about himself. We do all this by exercising as much honesty as we are capable of. You'll learn as much about me, as I will about you – if you decide you want me for your buddy. But I'm going to be strict with you – because Rob was strict with me. If you're not prepared to go to any lengths then I don't want to be your buddy. Are you prepared to go to any lengths?'

Silence from Allan.

'If you're not, just say so.'

Silence.

Then, just as Benson had started thinking of a way to leave without slamming all doors, Allan said, 'Yes.'

'Good. Where's your Big Book? Let's look at Step One. *We admitted we were powerless over alcohol; that our lives had become unmanageable.*'

# 37

'So you went to see Allan, did you?' Rob asked.

Having found Benson absent, Rob had set about making tea from what he'd managed to find in the packed fridge. Rob prided himself on being hopeless in the kitchen, but had produced a very dry and somewhat burnt Spanish omelette that both showed his willingness to try culinary daring, while illustrating that Benson should be home to make the tea if he wanted to eat something edible.

'I passed on what I was taught,' Benson said succinctly. He was relishing the omelette, enjoying as he did anything crisp and a bit burnt. The dryness of the concoction he compromised with liberal squirts of HP and tomato sauce, until it looked like an African flag.

'How's the omelette?'

'Just the job,' Benson replied. He knew that Rob wanted to hear more about his time with Allan. Well, he wasn't going to get it. Before leaving Allan, saying he'd see him at the meeting later, Allan had reminded his buddy of his tendency to gossip. And Benson had promised to keep things between themselves.

'How were things down at the beach?' Rob asked.

'I found a dog impaled on the railings outside The Chelsea,' Benson said.

Rob tutted. 'How did it get there?'

'No idea. It couldn't have done it itself.'

'What happened?'

'It was taken away. There was the 10 k. run from Liverpool. It ended just up the road from us. I got a medal.'

'Did you now?'

'There were lots left over. One of the dog-walkers had been given stacks of them. She gave me one.'

'What'll you do with it?'

'Not sure.'

'What about the BMW on the beach?'

'It wasn't there. Either the fellows came back and drove it off, or they got a towing company in. There wasn't much business on the gate, and what there was played by the book.'

'That's good. So do you think you'll take to the work?'

'It's not bad. I'd prefer to be a lifeguard. Reg can walk about while I'm stuck to the gate.'

'Reg?'

'He's with me at New Brighton, but he wants to go to Hilbre.'

'Who wouldn't? All on your own, in the middle of Dee Estuary, with only birds and seals for company? So what caused Allan to slip, do you think?'

Here it comes, Benson thought. 'He's an alchy. Alchies – if left to their own devices – drink. And he's been under stress, as you know.'

'He's his own worst enemy,' Rob said.

Benson moved swifly on. 'Are we swapping rings at the ceremony?'

'Hadn't planned on it. Why?'

'I was just wondering.'

'Let's keep it simple.'

'Right-o.'

'You wash and I'll dry.'

'The dishes?'

'What else is there?'

This was progress. 'OK,' Benson said.

He washed each dish with care, making sure to rinse. He always rinsed assiduously because he had read somewhere that the residue on dishes was responsible for emasculating modern men. Then he laid them out reverently on the draining board for Rob to pick up and swish the soda bread recipe tea towel over them. He watched, rating his work as Rob was forever rating his motorcycle-riding technique. Not perfect. Still, it's best to do without the hygiene than offend the washer-upper. Or was it?

'That dish could do with another go, Rob,' he said, feeling guilty, mean, bossy.

Rob picked up the dish and dried it again without a word, then placed it back in the stack.

'You just need practice,' Benson said.

# 38

'I want to apologise for my behaviour the other night at the meeting. I'd had a slip. 'Slip' doesn't really cover what I had, though. I can blame all sorts of things: fears, frustration, stinking thinking. On and on. But I thought a drink would make me better. I really did. This in spite of everything I've heard in these rooms over the years about how it's the first drink that gets us drunk. I'd really believed that one drink would fix me. Of course, it hasn't been like that. In no time, and without a thought, I went from pouring an inch of whisky into a glass to necking great gulps from the bottle. I can find many excuses for my behaviour: I'm scared of things that have happened recently. It's made me feel insecure and unsafe. My reputation is threatened, and so is my livelihood. They're looking at me oddly at work, and I know my boss is looking for anything he can get on me. But I'd slipped long before I had that first drink. I was back to old patterns of risky behaviour. I'd stopped saying my prayers. I haven't looked for help from people in the rooms. Rather I thought that all the usual stuff: sex, porn, Mars bars, work, would fix me. Well, they didn't. I now have a buddy and I've started back on the Steps with him. I've only been pretending that I did the Steps. I really didn't. I held all sorts of things back from my Step Four and Five. This time, with the help of my Higher Power and all of you here, things are going to be different. Thanks.'

A short silence followed Allan's share. Benson wondered whether he ought to come in with his 'The Job is more than the Work' share, well-rehearsed and ready for the oven. No. He had been about to launch into one more apt. It centred on Stinking Thinking, or Rationalisations, and was very close to his heart, to the nub of him and – perhaps – to Allan's situation ... but Busy Sandra broke the silence:

'My name's Sandra and I'm a queer alchy. I've really been hitting the meetings since my work-related injury. In spite of painkillers and physio I'm in agony and I'd be lying if I said I hadn't stopped as I hobbled past the booze display in Asda and romanced the drink by thinking it could fix me. I've imagined myself at home with a really good single malt, watching my favourite movies on the telly, forgetting the pain and relaxing. It would probably work, too. For a bit. But alcohol is great for making promises and then not keeping them, isn't it? Not that it doesn't give us plenty of warning of how it's going to be: we wake up in strange beds with strange women and wonder how we got there. Alcohol says, this is a blackout. I got you here. Have another drink. We get up of a morning feeling like shit. We act like shit through the day as our poor livers try to process the poisons from the last night's binge. And alcohol says, 'I'm the poison, but come this evening you'll feel right as rain. I'll meet you at that dive in Liverpool at nine. I can fix you.' Alcohol is the great deceiver, the Great Liar. It will tell us that we're not alcoholic – even after years of hearing all the symptoms of alcoholism in these rooms it will tell us: You're Not a *real* Alcoholic. This despite the fact that the drug alcohol has been costing us a lot more than a lot of money, year in and year out. It cost this alcoholic relationships, respect, financial security, sanity. I'm only that first drink away from a drunk. What do I do to keep my sobriety? Well, I say a prayer in the morning that I'll have a sober day. I say another in the evening to thank my Higher Power for the sober day just past. And She's never let me down.'

'Now it looks as if my whole life will change as a result of this injury. The lawyer from the Police Federation seems to think I might get pensioned off. Of course, I'll be devastated to no longer be able to serve the public in my capacity as a law-enforcement officer, but with the help of this programme, I know I'll be able to survive whatever life throws at me without taking a drink. Thanks.'

Another silence. Benson noticed that Allan was shooting daggers at Busy Sandra while she stroked the fur on the bandaged arm of her Zimmer-attached teddy. To forget the sight, he closed his eyes and plunged in:

'My name's Martin, and I'm a queer alchy. There's a Jewish story about evil. The first time we commit an evil deed, said the Rabbi, it feels like evil. But the third time, it feels like virtue. 'What does it feel like the second time?' the student asked. The Rabbi looked hard at the student and said, 'We're working on it.'

'Stinking thinking is what is happening between the first and third time. It's also called rationalisation. I'd define 'rationalisation' as reasoning with our moral compass bashed to smithereens with a hammer and locked away in a drawer. I'm an expert on Rationalisation. Most of us, I'd say, are. Rationalisation is easy-virtue reasoning. It allows us to bring the facts around until they fit us like a glove. It takes away the sting of facing up to the hard facts of the case. Drinking is what brought us to QA, but I've discovered that what QA says is right, 'Alcohol is but a symptom'. The real disease has multiple symptoms, and they all involve human nature ... instincts that are good in themselves, but which get out of hand: sex, gluttony, sloth, pride ... all the usual suspects. The thing is, that if we don't root out the grosser symptoms of our human disease – and the problem is recognising what they are – we will drink again. However, this is not a religious programme. It is a spiritual programme. We all have somewhat different notions of what is right and wrong. But these notions must be thought through rationally, not through the three-step suit-yourself programme of rationalisation. I know whereof I speak, believe me. It is so tempting to rationalise every area of my life, and make things that don't fit, fit me like a glove. I think this is what the poet William Blake meant when he wrote of 'mind-forg'd manacles'. I want something. How can I get it without feeling like a complete shit? I want it. I need it. I deserve it. I'm worth it. Everyone else does it. I won't be happy unless I have it. If I don't have it I'll go crazy. Well, that's the behaviour of the alcoholic without a programme. The programme is the Twelve Steps of recovery. We've got something wonderful here. A bunch of queer drunks being honest with other queer drunks. A few simple steps, honestly undertaken. And giving it away to other alchies so that we can keep the great gift we've been freely given. Those steps provide us with a simple template for living. We'll never master them. We're not saints. And if we were, we'd probably be appalling people. But we are prepared to attempt to live differently. That is all that is required of us. An honest attempt. We fail every day, but are granted insight into the failures. And we are happy. Abraham Lincoln said, 'Most men are as happy as they make up their minds to be.' Happiness

is being as far as we can get away from that first drink
– that pivotal daily action that eventually brought us to
our knees and to this room where, a day at a time, we
are shown that no matter what happens to us in life, it
is never going to be anything like as bad as the best day
under the tyranny of King Alcohol.'

A silence – longer than any of the others – followed.
Yes, Benson thought, that was pretty damned good. That
was a damned good share, even if I do say so myself.
He then, as ever, realised what he had just thought. Had
he been completely honest? Mainly. He believed what he
had said. But, as always, as fucking always, there was
Benson with GCEs and Benson with a 2:2 honours degree
from UCW Aberystwyth, and Benson with a world of
travel under his belt, and much reading – did they get
the references? Had they been impressed? He'd forgotten
to bring in The Bard: *Nothing is but thinking makes it so.*
Nothing about 'The Work is more than the Job'. But he
laughed at himself as he went back through his compromised
share. Even as I share the message, I'm learning more of
the deep roots of my egotism. How nice it would be to
be 100% *honest!* Without all those added ingredients of
self-aggrandisement, holier-than-thou. But he still had a
long road to travel to such a selfless place. Would he
make it? Probably not: and probably just as well. If it ever
happened that in the quiet following a share he felt 100%
pleased with himself...

After the meeting, Benson accompanied Allan home.

'I know what you want!' Allan said as he turned the
key in his flat door.

'You're talking to your buddy, Allan!' Benson responded

righteously. 'I'm here to go through Step Two and Three
– and get you preparing for your Step Four. I could be
at home getting myself ready for work, doing little jobs,
or lying in front of the telly with Rob.'

'Sorry.'

Benson, as if he owned Allan's flat, gestured him to
sit down on the sofa. He took an easy chair, Allan's
coffee-table acting as a chastity belt.

'Right, Allan, where do you stand on God?'

Allan shuffled. 'Dunno.'

'Well, that's a start. I was told by my buddy that the
most important thing to remember is that I am not God.
It sounds daft, on the surface. I mean, the idea that I
could be God! The thing is, though, that we have a strong
tendency to *think* we're God. If only the world operated
according to our opinions and our moral compass! We
seek to *control*. We resent when things are out of our
control; when people, places, things and institutions do
not behave in the way we *demand* they should. Does this
ring a bell with you, Allan?'

'I have a job to do,' Allan said.

'Hmm,' Benson said. 'I know Health and Safety is your
vocation. And I know you are very committed to it. But
when people refuse to obey what you believe to be right,
do you not sometimes feel resentful?'

'I suppose so.'

'You want to change people's behaviour to fit in with
what you know is right?'

'Yes.'

'I know what you mean, believe me. I go around the
town wishing people would be polite, not litter, not play
music so damned loud in their cars … a million and one
things irritate me. The television irks me as well. Did you

know I have a real resentment against Kirsty Wark? No? Well, I do. She interrupts people all the time. I miss things she says, even though she almost shouts a lot of the time. But as an alchy, I can't afford to have all these resentments. I acknowledge them as things I cannot change. So I have to pray for Kirsty. It's like pulling teeth, but it's part of my routine now. And it works! It really does, Allan. Don't know how or why, but I no longer give a toss about How and Why. Did you know there are tribes in the Congo without a word for 'Why'? I used to think that was crackers, but now I know different. I mean, Allan, here I am, unable to understand how most of the things that surround me *work*. Why I am as I am. Why I've only got an average dick while you have that mighty one; why I'm gay and others aren't. Why we're here. But it's generally a waste of time to ask. Think of those Congolese surrounded by rainforest and mists, wild animals, birds and trees of the most amazing variety! Why would they bother to ask why? It just is. The miracle of it all is the spirit that is ineffable and inaccessible to meaningful enquiry. Anyway, when I resent someone – let him or her live rent-free in my head – it will undermine my serenity and sobriety. Resentments don't give pleasure. It's like stabbing someone and dying oneself. I have to hand all my shit over to my Higher Power in order to keep sane and sober.'

'But who *is* your Higher Power?' Allan asked.

'My Higher Power is the people in Q.A., mystery, the perfect moments that sometimes come – sunsets and cloudscapes, listening to music, reading a book, poetry. And *Something* behind all that. He, She or It is an acknowledgement that I am not running the show. I surrender to that Power, believing that He can help me live contented and booze-free. I refer my problems to Him. I've been doing that ever since I came to QA. *I came to believe that a Power greater than myself could restore me to sanity.* I've surrendered to that Power, and He has removed from me the need for a drink.'

'Mmmm,' Allan said.

'I don't think too much about all this. I say my prayers. I try to do the right thing. The rest is Mystery, and not really my business. My business is to live a day at a time and every day, like Samuel Beckett said, 'Failing better'.'

'Mmmm,' Allan said.

'You've heard all this for years at meetings, and you've read the literature. Are you ready to take this Step?'

Silence from Allan.

'Are you willing to acknowledge that you, Allan, are not God; that you can't stop drinking on your own – if you could have you would have ... and that you need a Higher Power?' Benson was pleading as he spoke with his amorphous Higher Power, who sometimes impinged as the God of Catholics, sometimes the God of Quakers, sometimes as the Gods and Goddesses of Pagans, but usually as the spirit he found in QA, to show Allan the way out of his addiction. 'None of us knows who God is. All we have are intimations. Thomas Aquinas at the end of his life lapsed into silence on the subject, saying that for him God was the Great Unknown. We are on a journey, Allan. Are you willing to take a step?'

'Yes,' Allan said.

'Righto,' Benson said, relieved. 'So that's Step two. Step three follows that: *Made a decision to turn our will and our lives over to the care of God as we understood Him.* You have embarked on a lifelong journey of discovery in Step two. Willingness is all. The rest will come – and I'm still on

296

the nursery slopes – with daily practice of the steps and a daily willingness to dethrone self – ego – as God and replace that ogre with something outside. You are no longer running the show. You're no longer in charge, Allan. If you can't make people do as you say in the Health and Safety department despite all your best efforts, then you need to hand it to your Higher Power to complete the job.' He could see Allan's discomfort at this thought, but soldiered on, 'Why surrender? To win, Allan. To hold onto your sobriety and not get yourself in the position that will pull you back to the drink. We're alchies. We can't be at war with the world. That's why we change the things we can, but accept the things we can't.'

'But how do I tell which I should change and which not change?'

Benson was ready for that. 'Wisdom. To know the difference.' He showed Allan the pages in the Big Book to read. Allan said he'd read them often before, but Benson countered that perhaps they might go in this time. He asked him if he was prepared to go to any lengths to hold on to his sobriety. Allan said he was and Benson looked at him Rob-like and reminded him that this was a simple programme but required honesty. He showed him a prayer to say every morning and every night. Preferably on his knees. Why on his knees? Well, to show himself that he was no longer God, that's why. 'At night it's a good idea to throw your shoes under the bed. That'll get you on your knees come the morning.'

'Thank you,' Allan said.

'No thanks necessary. You are helping me by being my buddy. You know that. Just do the work. I'll come back in a few days and we'll talk about Step four.'

He thought he saw Allan flinch but chose not to pursue

it. Refusing a cup of tea, saying that he had to get ready for work in the morning – and liking the feeling that gave him – he left Allan alone with his *Big Book* and a plan for action.

Walking back up the hill towards home, Benson felt a lightness of spirit that brought tears to his eyes. Before surrendering himself to Rob fifteen minutes later, he knelt down by the bed to thank his Higher Power for making him a drunk. He prayed for Allan and all the fellows ... and signed off by wishing Kirsty Wark all the best.

# 39

'Seen Irene?'

Benson was busy spooning sand out of holes the following morning. The fierce winds overnight had once again blown fine sand across the promenade and filled his five holes to the brim. The only way he was going to get his posts down them was to clear them out again.

He frowned, but took Lynn's interruption of his essential job as part of his duties. Anyway, Lynn had given him a medal. She was holding a leash in scarlet that ended at the glittery collar which had no business being round the neck of the plain mongrel, whose rear end was squatting a foot from his face and letting go of a stream of dark urine making its way straight for the hole he had just emptied. 'No,' Benson replied.

'Suit yourself,' Lynn said, and pulled her dog away in mid-gush as if a foot from Benson's face was far too close to risk the dog infection from his unfriendliness.

'Isn't it a bit early for Irene?' he asked, trying to pull back the icicle he'd stabbed into Lynn's bosom, scooping away to show her how very busy he was with essential tasks, trying wordlessly to make amends.

'She said she'd meet me here at a quarter past. I can't hang about.'

'I'll tell her if I see her...' He forgot Lynn's name. *I have wasted time and now doth time waste me.* '...Lynn.'

'That's me,' Lynn said.

'Righto. I'll tell her. 'Where are you walking ... your dog?'

'Her name's Dolores.'

He'd remember that name. 'Where are you walking Dolores?'

'Thought we'd go up to the fort and back, but I wanted to go with Irene. I've got news.'

'OK,' Benson said, 'I'll tell her when I see her. If I see her.'

'Tell her it's about the Tanzanite,' Lynn said.

'Tanzanite?'

'She'll understand.'

'Righto,' Benson said. He shifted his crouch with an agile little hop to the next hole, slightly spoilt when he tipped over, landing on his left buttock. He adjusted his position and scooped at the sand.

'What are you doing?' Lynn asked.

'Digging to Australia.'

'Aren't you a bit long in the tooth to be digging to Australia?'

'Don't see why,' Benson said. 'I've never been and I thought this might be as good a way as any. I mean, I don't want to fly: That would play havoc with the ozone layer.'

'I don't believe in the ozone layer. You'll never fit down the hole,' Lynn said.

Those, if Benson was not very much mistaken, were two unconnected responses. He decided to follow the second, as it promised less of a brick wall. 'Well, I'm digging five holes. Then I'll start digging properly.'

'You'll have a trench, then.'

'Yes,' Benson said.

'You won't be able to take much luggage with you in a narrow trench.'

'I've been wondering,' Benson said, standing up with a creak from his uncomfortable crouch. 'What is this Tanzanite?'

'Irene will understand,' Lynn said, her tone cryptic, almost coquettish. She looked up and down the prom – perhaps for sign of Irene, perhaps to make sure no one had overheard. She walked off, with Dolores fighting to hang about.

After considering his attack of bad manners when dealing with Lynn, and resolving not to give way to such behaviour in future, Benson continued with his work. Tanzanite, he thought as he scooped. Something to do with Tanzania ... perhaps a native of that country? I'd say they're Tanzanians, but might there not be an alternative as in Yemeni, Yemenite?

'What are you doing?' Irene asked.

Benson ignored the question. 'Tanzanite,' he said.

'Lynn's been, has she?'

Benson nodded.

'That woman is obsessed with Tanzanite. She's been buying it whenever it comes up on the Shopping Channels. And she's trying to rope me in. Says it's the best investment I can make. Says supplies are shrinking fast.'

'All Units. All Units. This is Sparks 1 with the weather forecast.'

'Everyone's early today. Why is everyone so early?' Benson said, making a rush to his board, searching for chalk in his tracksuit bottoms as he went.

He filled in the boards to Sparks's dictation and acknowledged receipt. He stood up creakily – he'd been crouching again – to place the boards where the public could read them. He hung them up.

Irene and Betty waited for him stoically. 'It's all happening this morning,' Benson said.

'Anyway,' Irene said, 'Tanzanite is a precious stone. It all comes from just one mine in Tanzania, close to the Arusha game reserve – though if this goes on it'll all have transferred to a tiny house on the Barrett's estate. If you want to see some, you look no farther than Lynn's neck, ears or fingers. She drips it most days. She says she's building up a stash to leave to her family. They're not going to get any money, she says. Just Tanzanite. I don't know what they'll make of that.'

'And she wants you to join in?'

'Yes. But I'm not going to.'

'I'd better finish these holes, Irene. Any news about the dog?'

'No. But all the dog-owners are being dead careful. I won't let Betty off her lead.'

'No.'

They stood together for a moment, saying nothing.

Are you new to New Brighton?' Irene asked.

'No. I was born here, went away and came back. I live in that house up there.' He pointed.

'Are you married?'

'Not yet.' Shall I? he thought. Shall I?

'I'm a widow,' Irene said.

'I've got a friend. Rob.'

'Oh,' she said. 'And you and Rob live together, do you?'

'Yes.' *That didn't hurt, did it? I'm as sick as my secrets.* 'Fancy a cup of tea? I put the kettle on – well about half an hour ago.'

'I should go and see Lynn.'

'I should put the barrier up. I've finished scooping the sand out.'

'A cup of tea would be nice though.'

Reg was in the hut, reading his *Highway Code*. 'Making a cup, are you?'

'Two sugars?' Benson asked.

'Heaped,' Reg said, returning to his book.

'I've brought down some of my bran loaf. Fancy some?'

'No, ta. Maybe later.'

Benson fixed the tea, glad he'd had the presence of mind to wash the mugs at the tap the night before. The kettle was taking its own sweet time. Watched kettles. But then he realised that even slow-coach watched kettles might benefit from being turned on.

He removed some odd bugs from the inside of the mugs. The boiling water would take care of any germs, he thought.

'You know Rob Sullivan?' Reg asked.

'Yes. Very well,' Benson said.

'He's failed me three times,' Reg said.

'You can't have been ready,' Benson said.

'I was ready.'

'Have you passed your theory?'

'You can't take the practical if you haven't. I'm hoping I get the other fellow for the test.'

'Bert.'

'Yes, Bert.' Reg shuffled. 'If I get Rob – not that I'll know until I go – could you put in a good word for me?'

'No,' Benson said. 'Here's your tea, Reg.'

Reg did not acknowledge receipt of his carefully-crafted cup of tea. Benson was about to say, *You're welcome. You're welcome,* following the lack of *Thank you* had become one of the teaching tools in his armoury when check-out people failed in basic courtesy. Not that it worked. Benson had learned not to look for positive results. After all, if someone didn't have *Thank you* in his or her daily armoury, it was unlikely they'd have a bloodhound-scenting mechanism for mildly ironic *You're welcomes.* He'd been lecturing Allan

303

about accepting things he couldn't change. But Benson knew he did the opposite all the time.

He took Irene her tea, wondering how Reg knew about him and Rob.

'Lynn,' Irene said, 'thinks she's the reincarnation of one of Henry VIII's wives.'

'Does she? Which one?'

'She didn't say.'

'Anne of Cleves, I'd say.'

'Why Anne of Cleves?'

'She got away. Lived to fight another day. Henry sent her back to Cleves.'

'She had a lucky escape.'

'He died of syphilis,' Benson said.

'Not surprised.'

'When he died they put him into his coffin, but he leaked.'

'He didn't.'

'He did. Then they put another coffin around the one he was leaking out of...'

'And what happened?'

'That leaked as well. They hummed and hawed for a while, then they put him into a lead coffin.'

'And what happened?'

'That did the trick.'

'Funny,' Irene said. 'I think I'd heard about that before. I mean, it rang bells.'

'Who told you?'

'The nuns at Maris Stella.'

'The Brothers at St Bede's told me.'

'You think it's true?'

'Should think so. Did you see the state of him in that Holbein picture? Big fat thing. Anyway, it's what the

Catholics say. I don't suppose Protestants are aware of the coffin story.'

'Probably got covered up.'

'Probably. But you should ask Lynn which wife she thinks she is the reincarnation of.'

'Anne Bolyn would be more like it.'

Irene drank her tea. A pleasant man – maybe retired – came down with his jet-ski. His permit was in order. The licence plate on his vehicle matched the permit. He had a life jacket and knew the state of the tide. Benson reminded him to keep below five knots to the landward of the yellow buoy and wished him a great day.

'Any sign of the man with the car that got drowned?' Irene asked.

'No, thank God.'

'He'll be really angry, I expect,' Irene said.

A dull ache of anxiety pushed into Benson. 'Yes,' he said. 'But he shouldn't have been on the beach in the first place.'

'But he probably won't see it like that.'

'My instinct was to get him towed off. But The Boss said we couldn't.'

'Why not?'

'No lives at risk.' *Except mine.*

Irene looked down the promenade towards the fort. 'Here's Lynn now,' she said. 'She's running! What's she running for? She never runs.'

# 40

Rob farted noisily beneath the duvet. As he did so, he asked, 'So why was Lynn running?'

Benson had long since realised that Rob's farts – along with many another character trait – were a thing he could not change. Not by words, anyway. Instead he postponed gratification as a point made and punishment administered by not telling him what happened next.

The silence continued.

'Better out than in,' Rob said, turning over a page of *Motorcycles and Mechanics*. He then hefted the duvet on his side of the bed and agitated the fringe to release the fug.

It was a gesture, Benson thought. Not ideal, but something.

'Well,' Benson said. 'I noticed at once that Dolores wasn't with Lynn...'

'Where was she?'

'I'm coming to that. Lynn comes up to us all puffed. We sat her down on one of the stools and I gave her my cup of tea while she recovered. She couldn't get a word out. At her age she really shouldn't have run all that way from the lighthouse and...'

'Cut to the chase,' Rob said. 'You drag everything out.'

Again, Benson was irritated. But he soldiered on. 'She told us that she'd let Dolores off her lead on the beach. Dolores ran off and had a poo. Lynn searched about for a bag to pick up the dog-dirt and was heading towards it. Dolores ran off behind the riprap groyne – the one that lies parallel to the tide between there and the fort. She thought nothing about it, picked up the mess and walked up the beach a bit, expecting Dolores to follow her. Well, she didn't. Still not worried, she went behind the groyne. The tide was coming in and there was only a narrow strip of sand for her to walk along. No sign of the dog. Then she saw Dolores...'

Benson stopped, as much for effect as anything.

'Was she dead?'

'How did you know?'

'Stands to reason.'

'It could have been stuck, had a fishing hook in its mouth, have been having sex with a Staffordshire bull terrier...'

'But that's not going to make Lynn run all that way, is it?'

Benson thought about that. 'A hook in its mouth might have.'

'Yes, but she'd have carried Dolores then, wouldn't she? It's so obvious,' Rob said. 'Remember last week?'

'Of course I remember last week.'

'Well, Marts, I've no time for dogs meself, as you well know. When you told me about the dog on the railings a mean side of me thought, 'A few million still to go.' Seeing Benson's shocked expression, he continued, 'Don't get me wrong. It was only a side. But I reckon you've got someone in New Brighton who has it in for dogs. Thought that when the other dog copped it.'

Rob saw Benson looking at him strangely, looked away, and turned over a page of the magazine.

Benson paused. He looked over at the advert for half-priced leathers.

'How did Dolores meet her end?' Rob asked at last, as it was clear Benson had shut up shop.

'An arrow.'

'An arrow?'

'Straight through the poor thing's neck.'

'Nasty!' Rob said.

'Very,' Benson said. 'Of course, Lynn fled when she saw what had happened. She reasoned that whoever had done it – shot the arrow – was probably still hiding among the concrete blocks of the groyne.'

'So what did you do?'

'I got on the radio and reported the incident.'

'Didn't you go and check?'

'I can't just 'go and check'! I have to consult. I'm married to the gate. I can't just walk away, much as I'd like to. Anyway, a risk assessment has to be made.'

'So what happened then?'

'Reg was sent to check. But by then the tide was well up the groyne. He waded along the whole length but couldn't find Dolores.'

'What about the police?'

'They were called, but didn't come for ages.'

'That figures,' Rob said.

'But we found the body later. It was brought in with the tide.' This was not the way he had planned to tell his story. There was much more to tell about Lynn's anguish, and Irene's intervention. 'The police came about an hour after we found the body. Irene took Lynn home. And that's all I know. Watch this space.'

'That's two dogs killed in a week. It's all happening down your way.'

Benson nodded. 'A fellow from *The Wirral Murmurer* came down.'

'You mark my words,' Rob said, 'there'll be more.'

He closed his magazine. This was usually the signal either for lights-out or sex. Benson placed his bookmark into *Berlin Alexanderplatz* and put it on top of his bedside cupboard.

'Changing the subject, like,' Rob said.

'Yes?'

'Blackpool,' Rob said.

'Blackpool?'

'Yes, Blackpool. There's that weekend conference of QA in Blackpool on the first weekend in September. That's D-Day.'

'Thought it was October. I'll still be on the beach.'

'But the Boss will give it you off, won't he?'

'Not sure. He's a stickler about people being available.'

'What if you told him that you were tying the knot there as well? I thought it'd be good to have our civil partnership then. We'd be with our own kind. The hotel's cheap and all we'd need to do is pay for a really slap-up meal after.'

'Let me think about it,' Benson said.

'OK,' Rob said. 'Night-night. Don't forget your prayers.' He turned his light out, and Benson did the same. A motorcycle – sans-silencer – roared up Malcolm Lowry Street. It faded. Silence.

Benson waited. Usually at this point there would be a hiatus. Then he would feel Rob's hand or a restless movement from his side of the bed. He waited. Nothing.

He thanked his Higher Power for the day. He looked at the things he had not done that he should have; the things he should not have done that he had. He wished all the people he had met that day well. He said a prayer for Lynn. He thought about a civil partnership ceremony in Blackpool. He prayed for Kirsty Wark.

Silence from Rob next to him in bed. Rob Next To Him In Bed! He thanked God for Rob. He thought about it. He stopped his endless sides of indecision in their tracks, and made a leap:

'Are you still awake?

'Yea.'

'Sounds just the ticket. Let's do it, Rob,' Benson said.

A silence. Then before Benson knew quite what was happening, Rob reached under the bed for his crash helmet, put it on, and mounted him.

# 41

The following day it was sunny. Not take-off-your-layers-O-blithe-Byelaws-Officer sunny, but at least bright. The estuary was blue and silver beneath a blue and cumulus sky. The wind had abated to a tiny knot in the corner of a handkerchief reminder of the snotty behaviour it was capable of.

Business was brisk and Benson had little or no time to think.

It was not really until late afternoon that he noticed something strange: he'd never seen more dogs on the beach than today. He took time to take a sample of dogs he could see from his post and came up with fifty-six.

There'd been no sign of Lynn. None of Irene, either. Perhaps they had locked themselves away, in mourning for Dolores. Or perhaps they were demanding that the police did something, were besieging the Cop Shop in Manor Road and laying down the law.

Two dogs killed under suspicious circumstances. Maybe the two deaths were unconnected: one performed by some nasty drunk, the other by a kid playing with his latest lethal toy. Reg thought Dolores must have been shot with a crossbow.

As if thinking about Reg conjured him up, Reg appeared on the slipway.

'I've got a date for my motorbike test,' he said.

'That's good. When is it?'

'Week Friday. There's been a cancellation. Some poor bloke just couldn't face your chum.'

Benson said nothing. What should he say?

'Well,' Benson said, 'you just need to get in as much practice as you can. Make a special effort with observation, and don't forget those lifesaver glances.'

'Hope I don't get your mate.'

'Rob's fair, you know. He's got a sixth sense for people who aren't ready. Just be ready and you'll be all right.'

Reg didn't seem convinced. 'I might get Bert.'

'You might,' Benson agreed, 'but Bert's no pushover.'

'Maybe not. But he's not a fuckin' Hitler like your Rob.'

'That's my friend you're talking about,' Benson said. 'Yesterday you wanted me to put a good word in for you. Today you're attacking someone I value more than any other person in my life. You're not logical, and you're not going the right way towards making friends and influencing people.'

Reg said nothing.

Benson did the same.

'Any tea on the go?' Reg asked at last .

'I'm not making any, if that's what you mean.'

Reg walked off. Five minutes later Benson saw him standing at the door of the hut with a mug of tea in his hand.

A feeling of something not quite right – or fair – pushed into the byelaws officer then. But it didn't last long. He'd been the tea-maker, and hadn't minded at all. What he did mind was Reg's attitude. If being around difficult people was the best education a chap could have, Benson felt he was in for a good dose being around Reg. A side of him ached to get Rob to pass him so that he'd be moved on. The thought took shape as the promenade

emptied and the minutes slowed down waiting for the
Boss to announce Make Ready. Return to Base. If he
explained the circumstances to Rob, might he not give
the nod to Reg and let him pass? It really would be
wonderful not to have Reg around. But that was not on.
Any hint from Benson that life might be a mite easier
without the presence of testing Reg would undoubtedly
make Rob yet more strict with him. And Benson would
get a lecture about accepting life on life's terms, facing
his fears. For just as Rob would be strict but fair with
Reg, so he would be strict and fair with Benson. He
laughed at the thought then. The idea of Rob saying,
'Righto. If he can stay upright I'll pass him just to get
him out of your hair.' This followed by Benson's fulsome
thanks and a final riposte from Rob: 'What are friends
for?' Well, it was completely beyond the wilder shores of
possibility. It would blow off the whole of the fulcrum
upon which the relationship was based. It was, quite
simply, Not On.

Why were difficult people so useful, so educational?
*You can't look at me and not see yourself.* Benson wanted to
please people, to be liked, to get on. It was hard-wired
into him. Mum *Eternal rest grant unto her!* insisted on
politeness from him. When she'd held him up on street
corners talking to acquaintances with far too much to say,
his tugs on the hem of her coat only served to make her
talk – or listen – longer. When Benson voiced a negative
opinion on people, she would intervene with an account
of his own faults. And Mum had been backed up by the
nuns, the Brothers, everyone really. They had *insisted* on
the imperative that he be a gentleman. She yanked him
to the road side of the pavement so that he'd get the
splash if a carriage spattered up mud. Not that there were

carriages even then, but the Victorian notions had been communicated to his Edwardian mum and thence down to him. What had happened? In the Seventies people had stopped surrendering seats on buses and trains. They went through swing doors and let them swing in the face of the next person. When you said 'Sorry' to someone you'd bumped into on the street, the recipient said nothing, or 'You *are* sorry.' What was going on? The old ways were dying. Get out of the new world if you can't take the cold...

But it had been more than just a mechanical act. Brother O' Toole had insisted that manners should exhibit courtesy. And courtesy was an acknowledgement of the other person's humanity. It was warm etiquette. He should aim to be a Gentleman. And a gentleman did not hurt others. What had Newman said? Newman had said: 'Hence it is that it is almost a definition of a gentleman to say he is one who never inflicts pain. This description is both refined and, as far as it goes, accurate. He is mainly occupied in merely removing the obstacles which hinder the free and unembarrassed action of those about him; and he concurs with their movements rather than takes the initiative himself. His benefits may be considered as parallel to what are called comforts or conveniences in arrangements of a personal nature: like an easy chair or a good fire, which do their part in dispelling cold and fatigue, though nature provides both means of rest and animal heat without them. The true gentleman in like manner carefully avoids whatever may cause a jar or a jolt in the minds of those with whom he is cast; – all clashing of opinion, or collision of feeling, all restraint, or suspicion, or gloom, or resentment; his great concern being to make everyone at their ease and at home. He has his eyes on all his company; he is tender towards the bashful, gentle towards the distant, and merciful towards the absurd; he can recollect to whom he is speaking; he guards against unseasonable allusions, or topics which may irritate; he is seldom prominent in conversation, and never wearisome. He makes light of favours while he does them, and seems to be receiving when he is conferring. He never speaks of himself except when compelled, never defends himself by a mere retort, he has no ears for slander or gossip, is scrupulous in imputing motives to those who interfere with him, and interprets everything for the best. He is never mean or little in his disputes, never takes unfair advantage, never mistakes personalities or sharp sayings for arguments, or insinuates evil which he dare not say out. From a long-sighted prudence, he observes the maxim of the ancient sage, that we should ever conduct ourselves towards our enemy as if he were one day to be our friend. He has too much good sense to be affronted at insults, he is too well employed to remember injuries, and too indolent to bear malice. He is patient, forbearing, and resigned, on philosophical principles; he submits to pain, because it is inevitable, to bereavement, because it is irreparable, and to death, because it is his destiny. If he engages in controversy of any kind, his disciplined intellect preserves him from the blundering discourtesy of better, perhaps, but less educated minds; who, like blunt weapons, tear and hack instead of cutting clean, who mistake the point in argument, waste their strength on trifles, misconceive their adversary, and leave the question more involved than they find it. He may be right or wrong in his opinion, but he is too clear-headed to be unjust; he is as simple as he is forcible, and as brief as he is decisive. Nowhere shall we find greater candour, consideration, indulgence:

he throws himself into the minds of his opponents, he accounts for their mistakes. He knows the weakness of human reason as well as its strength, its province and its limits. If he be an unbeliever, he will be too profound and large-minded to ridicule religion or to act against it; he is too wise to be a dogmatist or fanatic in his infidelity. He respects piety and devotion; he even supports institutions as venerable, beautiful, or useful, to which he does not assent; he honours the ministers of religion, and it contents him to decline its mysteries without assailing or denouncing them. He is a friend of religious toleration, and that, not only because his philosophy has taught him to look on all forms of faith with an impartial eye, but also from the gentleness and effeminacy of feeling, which is the attendant on civilisation.'

Newman who was on his way to becoming a saint; Newman who had started out as a Protestant, then turned Catholic. Odd, that. Benson, centuries after the rest of England, had come round to the idea that the Reformation was a pretty good idea. QA, though not a religious fellowship, took its spirituality mainly from Quakerish, William Jamesian and Ralph Waldo Emersonian notions. The meetings, though seldom silent, were open to anything. Things happened during meetings. People were moved and changed, experienced moments of spiritual awakening that they could not quantify or explain. It had something to do with the flailing attempts at honesty, but it was so different from the priest-dominated aura of Catholicism. Confession was in QA, but it was ordinary people confessing to ordinary people. Priests had never in Benson's experience confessed to the laity. A pity, it might have stopped the scandals which had come about ... all those nails in the coffin of Catholicism.

316

But all these thoughts went out of the window when a woman came running up and told him there was a dead dog on the tideline.

Benson radioed the message in. Sparks said he'd note it in the book. Then the Boss came on and told Reg to go and see. Reg responded. Benson watched as Reg ambled across the beach towards the incoming tide.

'Matron,' the Boss said, watching Reg at the tideline with a small knot of people, 'I think it's about time you warned all dog-owners who pass the gate to watch themselves. I reckon we've got a serial dog-killer on our hands. I've seen most things down here over the years, but I've not seen anything like this. Well, not *quite* like this. We've had a few poisoning cases over the years. Did you know you can kill a cat by boiling up starfish and leaving it out? Can't resist starfish, so they do say. And it does for them. Had a bad case of that once. But never a crossbow. Takes too much skill. Vandals round here prefer the scattergun approach. Mind you, I can understand it.'

'Understand it?' Benson asked.

'Yeah. Can't you?'

'People love them.'

'Yeah. They're dead easy to love. But if you think of the tonnes of piss and shite a dog produces in the course of its lifetime, multiply that shite by a few million dogs; then subtract the shite that isn't picked up by decent dog-owners; add to that the dangerous dogs used as weapons plus the dogs that bark all day and all night alone in houses or back gardens; then multiply that with the dogs jumping up and soiling clothing, the dogs on sofas, the dogs scaring children, the dogs tripping up people with those great long leads, the dogs who can't do anything

317

wrong because the owners love the bones of them, the dogs that go berserk and bite and kill both adults and babies and infect kids with the worms from their shite ... and then take the silent – and generally dead tolerant – majority who do not own dogs, but on a daily basis have their lives affected by the fuckers: their shite trampled over carpet, their kids afraid or hurt or killed, themselves intimidated by weapon-dogs ... this damned sharing of a cramped little island with a vast population of beasts that the majority don't particularly like, but have to appear to like or at least tolerate ... well it all adds up to a situation where I at any rate can sort of understand the odd incident of the kind we are witnessing. Tell you the truth, Matron, I'm surprised it's taken so long.'

'I quite like dogs,' Benson said.

'I don't hate them or anything,' the Boss said. 'I like them like I like lamb. Good in stew. Those Koreans have the right idea. Wouldn't fancy the dish meself, but...'

A council van approached Benson's gate. The Boss went over to the driver's door and talked with the Community Patrol officer. After about a minute of this, the Boss nodded and Benson opened the gate. The van took off down the slipway and across the beach, making for the red and yellow shape of Reg at the tideline.

'He shouldn't go that that way,' the Boss said. 'I tell him but he never listens.'

Benson had been about to ask why when he saw the van stop. Then it started again, throwing up sand from its rear wheels, lodging it deeper into the sand. The driver got out and made wild signals in Benson and the Boss's direction.

Shaking his head, the Boss said, 'Open your gate again, Matron,' got into his Land-Rover and gunned it down the slipway. He did not follow the route of the van, but skirted to the right, coming to a halt at an angle to the front of the van and about ten yards away from it. The Boss got out, opened the rear door and removed a tow rope. This he attached to the front of the van, returned to his Landrover and disappeared inside. The Land-Rover engine whined. It moved forward. The rope went taut. The van moved out of the hole its wheels had dug for it and sat four square and Bristol fashion on the hard sand to the seaward of the soft sand. The Boss got out, detached the rope from the Land-Rover and the van. He then engaged the driver of the van in conversation. Benson wasn't there, but he didn't need to be. He got the gist.

At last the Boss returned up the slipway. The van containing the dead dog disappeared. Benson closed the gate behind him. A minute or two later the Boss radioed: Stand Down.

# 42

That evening, Benson wrapped up his pyrography work for Muriel, strapped it to the back of his motor-bike and set off – leaving a note for absent Rob – for Loggerheads. He did not ring Muriel. She would probably be in, and even if she wasn't, it didn't matter. He wanted to show he'd put in the work for her.

He considered the neat parcel of breadboards, lashed to the back of the bike, each covered with a deep burn. What was Muriel planning for them? To post them off to Kuching and have some acquaintance nail them up around the place? To go out to Kuching again to have a look? No, surely she wouldn't go, leaving the shop just as the season was about to get going, would she?

He wondered if he should ask. No, he wouldn't. It was not really his business. Maybe Muriel would tell him. But with so much time having passed, it seemed like a hopeless enterprise. People disappeared, and stayed disappeared. At some of his own lowest points in drink, Benson had thought of doing just that. Maybe Muriel just felt the need to make one last attempt. Yes, that was probably it.

But he badly wanted to get away for a few hours, to leave the sea, the job, the meetings, behind him for a night. A few minutes on the bike humming along the motorway at 60 lifted his mood, made him realise how relative the queer squiggle of geography that had enveloped him was. Maybe Captain Jones had felt a similar need:

to walk away from his ship and his captain's cabin and embrace something new, strange and unknown. After all, his ship, though constantly on the move in foreign seas, contained all the complications of any landlubber's life: a bickering crew, the same routines and watches, the anxiety over pirates in the Malacca Strait and breakdowns, schedules and owners' demands. The ship itself, as much as Benson's gate on the beach or his house at the top of New Brighton, would anchor the seafarer. *The sailor who fell from grace with the sea.* Where had he heard that? Was it the title of a poem, a novel? How would a sailor 'fall from grace' with an endless succession of water-drops ... a rosary, each bead of which was attached to every other bead to girdle the globe? Perhaps by insulting it with pollution, by underestimating its power to destroy, misjudging its myriad moods? Or by turning his back on it, as Benson was doing now?

He'd started to hear the sea even when he was not near it. Each night he took home its buzzing breaking sound. But maybe it was a sign of age. He missed things people said when the roar of the full tide competed. There it was behind his guarded gate, like a wild animal. He was the zoo keeper. Those with permits were the customers who had enough knowledge of what lay quietly snoozing, or battling and roaring at the bottom of the slipway waiting for the suckers to be allowed to hazard their lives by petting the beast. The sea got to you. It was wild and wasteful; seductive and betraying. It didn't care: not about precious beach balls or 150,000 tonne container ships.

The sea, though, had its own Higher Power. It might play at being God, but was really totally dependent on winds, the magnetism of moon and sun, currents and geography.

It had basic natural laws to obey. It could do no other. But there was a pecking order of powerlessness. Fish could be thirsty, though surrounded by billions upon billions of gallons – more numbers than a National Debt – of the stuff. It could toss an iceberg carelessly into the path of a titanic passenger liner, discarding hopeful emigrants into icy depths, burying in barnacles bullion and fur coats kept in refrigerators, forcing tearful farewells from puny lovers, ditching dreams, showing itself for what it was: a cruel acolyte of other Higher Powers who tossed one thing after another, carelessly, at all and sundry.

But, left to itself, it mirrored serenity, communicated serenity to those who were privileged to approach close. And people loved it. *All along the strand The people look at the sea ... They cannot look out far; They cannot look down deep. But when was that ever a bar To any watch they keep?* But to be married to the sea? To be forever dependent on it? Well, it showed who was master there. It demanded humility from puny people, that was for sure.


Though distracted for much of his trip, Benson made it to Loggerheads. It was getting dark and, despite the many layers of clothes on him, he was shivering. He looked forward to tapping on Muriel's door, being ushered in and given tea, sympathy and congratulations.

He parked the bike outside the shop, unpacked the parcel of breadboards, and made for Muriel's bungalow. How would he be when she oohed and ahhed about his product? Bashful, proud of achievement, humble ... listen to yourself! *The peacock spreads his fan.*

He was halfway up the path when he saw the shadow of a motorbike parked round the side of the house. He stopped, looked at it. He veered from the path to get a closer look. He read the number plate, noted the model, the luminous yellow strips, the serious lock around the rear wheel.

Quietly, feeling like a burglar, Benson walked around the bungalow. The curtains were drawn, the blinds in the kitchen closed, and showing no light. Back at the front step, he placed his heavy parcel down. He looked down at it, wondering if the wood would be all right were it to rain. Even if it wasn't, did he care?

Returning to his bike, Benson zipped up his layers, put on his gloves, tightened the strap of his helmet under his chin and wheeled the bike away from the car park in front of Muriel's shop. He got on. The engine started first time and he headed back the way he had come only a few minutes before, his head a wasps' nest of stuff he was unable to sort through or dismiss. The wheels of the bike turned and turned – how many revolutions in twenty miles? What should he do? Too late to go to a meeting. He'd pop in on Allan. *The night is dark and I am far from home*, he sang into his crash helmet.

# PART 3

# H.A.L.T.

# 43

'Righto, Allan,' Benson said, 'you've read all the literature on Step Four. You've made a thorough and fearless moral inventory of yourself. Hopefully, Allan, you've learnt a bit about what makes you tick, what makes you unhappy, what makes you feel uncomfortable, what makes you feel worthless, what makes you want to reach for the bottle. I've told you a lot about the things that swamped my boat: resentments against people, places, things and institutions; fear in many of its guises out of control; hurts done to others ... I've told you what I found lay at the back of them; the universal human traits and instincts, which had got out of hand: our needs for security, social acceptance, sexual satisfaction. Perhaps you've seen how these problem areas blend together. For example, when my pride is hurt, fear kicks in. And anger. That in turn might make me give up an enterprise and result in sloth. I used to seek to change myself by moving jobs and countries. Leave the ungrateful place where I wasn't appreciated and go somewhere that would see me for the Real Me in all My Glory. Off I'd pop and end up still stuck inside the old shell of Martin Benson because I hadn't changed from the inside. Running on self-will, I was – thinking that I'd be able to change in the fairyland of future. The evidence of the past should have told me that it wasn't going to happen but I endlessly rationalised and idealised the future. It wasn't until I came into QA that I came to believe that I was powerless not only to stop drinking but also to change all those things that caused me to drink. I had to dethrone myself, stop running the show, and seek out a Higher Power of my understanding who would help. That is what you've started doing in Steps Two and Three. We're no longer in charge, Allan. We've started on the road of acceptance of the way we are, the way the world is, the way – infuriating, I know – that we can't change the vast majority of what's happening in the world. We can't even change ourselves without a huge spiritual shift in our ideas. Here in Step Four you have been striving to push aside the undergrowth, blow away the heavy clouds that stand between you, a relationship with your Higher Power and the people, places and things on the planet. You'll become willing to accept life on life's terms, not just Allan's.

When I was working on my Step Four, I wrote screeds and screeds. I was looking round for all sorts of things that I couldn't remember but which I felt must be there. Days passed into weeks. At last Rob said that perhaps I was being attacked by scruples. The noun, he said, was bad. The adjective good. It was good to be scrupulous – to admit to everything that came to mind and made me feel like a shit. But not to delve too deeply into the maybes of scruples. He also told me that he didn't want to hear every sordid example of bad behaviour on my part from the year dot. What he wanted was for me to connect my behaviour with the old-as-the-planet vices that lay behind them. These vices, he explained, were simply human instincts – in moderation good in themselves – but out of hand through the influence of self-will. So, he asked, what actions in the past and up to the present make me feel like a shit? What actions by others sink my boat, causing me to resent? When I resent, what is at the back of it? What part of my ego is threatened? I filled in the columns of all the people, places, institutions that I resented. I went on to consider what these people had done to me, what aspect of my character had been affected and then, hard this, *what part I had played in bringing about these resentments*. And then on to the people I had harmed by my self-will, by my sex instinct out of control, by my fears.

'And what is the point of all this? Awareness, Allan. Self-knowledge. The sunlit uplands of being a lover and beloved on the earth. Awareness is a great teacher. When I am tempted to be abrupt with the person at checkout in a supermarket, I find that I have a moment of reprieve. I can see what's happening. There is a moment between the hammer and the anvil during which I can make a conscious decision to pull back and not act on my self-righteous feelings. Sometimes I do just that; other times I launch in bitchily and tell the hapless person what I think of the service. The thing is, whatever I do, I know what is going on. I am no longer deluded.

These Steps are a lifelong pursuit. I'm taking you through them now, and everything I tell you comes back to me and deepens my awareness of what they involve. In steps Six and Seven we ask our Higher Power to remove from us every single defect of character that stands in the way of our usefulness to Him, Her, It, and our fellows in QA and in the Greater World. We'll write down the names of people we've harmed – those people who have come up in Step Four – and, when appropriate, make direct amends to them all. Then, in Steps Ten, Eleven and Twelve, we'll 'work' the steps on a daily basis. We'll discover all sorts of new things about ourselves – both positive and negative. We'll pray and meditate to approach closer to that Wisdom and Spirit of the universe that is our Higher Power ... and we'll give away what we have learned to other struggling alchies ... and, by right living, to all the people we come into contact with. Sorry to go on.'

Allan fanned the pages of a large hardback ledger. The draught from it, Benson saw, was messing up his combover. Why, Oh, why, did Allan not present himself at O'Toole's the barber and in exchange for four quid subject himself to ten minutes on the goings-on in Dublin while Mr O'Toole shaved away the shaggy sidelines and revealed a new Allan sporting a severe Number 2 haircut? That combover really needed to go. With it gone, Benson was sure that a new craggy Allan would emerge. 'I'm not sure I'm quite ready for Step Five,' Allan said.

Benson's heart sank. The hammer was raised to strike the anvil of Allan's procrastination. He smiled instead. 'Is it the tendencies behind the behaviour? Are they causing the problem?'

The problem was that Benson thought he knew pretty much exactly what ought to be in Allan's Step Five. He was probably not unique in that insight: every fellow in QA knew, every uneven paving-stone knew, every 'Do Not Cross This Line' tape knew, every 'Danger! Deep Mud!' sign knew, every 'The Council cannot accept any responsibility for people who park in this car park' notice knew. Trouble was, Allan did not know. In all their meetings since starting on the Steps Allan had not given his spectacular obsession with Health and Safety even a glancing blow.

Benson had heard much of how Allan had followed where his spectacular dick led. His accounts of orgies, assignations, photo shoots, his time with a combo called

'The Cucumbers' back in the eighties, together with Benson's own experiences with Allan's sexuality, convinced him that Allan followed his cock around in the manner of a stage-struck mother shadowing her spectacularly talented offspring. Allan the man went along because it was demanded. What he had between his legs was what was wanted. All manner of men, and a few women, had been willing to buy off the person attached to the object of desire. They danced attention on the 'mother' in order to use the 'offspring'.

QA was fairly indulgent about sex. They asserted that there was probably no human being on earth without problems in that area. *You can say that again.* The point was to attain balance. Not to use. Not to be selfish. Not to let it rule.

'Allan, we've looked at sex. We've looked quite a bit into your resentments. Is there anything else in that department that we've not covered?'

'I don't like to say.'

'Why?'

'It concerns someone in QA.'

'And is it eating at you?'

'Yes.'

'Spit it out, Allan!'

'Busy Sandra.'

In truth, Benson had been entertaining a certain amount of resentment against Busy Sandra himself. His gossipy side ached to hear Allan's take on Sandra. He delved, hoping to find common ground between his and Allan's feelings. Was Allan pissed off that Busy Sandra might be in line for medical retirement and a pension – and she only just into her forties?

'Busy Sandra must have known about the cameras in

the cottage for months, but she didn't warn us!' Allan said.

'No,' Benson said.

'I hate her! Can't help it.'

'But nothing's come of it, has it, Allan? You've not been named and shamed in the papers. You're not on the Sex Offenders' Register, are you?'

'Not so far. But it's a blot on my copybook, isn't it? Who knows where the information goes and what excuse they need to bring it out and hang me with it? It's a stain on my character that won't go away. Busy Sandra could have quietly said to any of us at meetings, 'Keep away from that cottage. They've got cameras in it.' But she didn't.'

'You're right, Allan. Of course, you are. I can't condone Busy Sandra's action. But as I've said before, we're not here to take other people's inventories; we're dealing with our own shit. You have a resentment against Busy Sandra. The trouble with resentments, Allan, is that we suffer and die because of them. The people who bring them out in us skip merrily along, and in Sandra's case, have medical retirement to look forward to. You clean your side of the street and leave Busy Sandra to clean hers. The important thing is that you be rid of the resentment you feel. You won't be able to live serenely if you don't. And you'll drink.'

'I've tried, but I can't.'

'You can't. Your Higher Power can. Time can. Prayer – wishing Busy Sandra well – can.'

'You mean, I should *pray* for the bitch?'

'That's exactly what I mean. You are up against a brick wall of resentment. It's an example of the sort of negative emotion that kills alchies. We just can't afford this stuff.

It's robbing you of the open-handed sobriety we're after at QA. I know it's counter-intuitive. But so much at QA is exactly that: 'Surrender to Win', 'Give a Sucker an Even Break', '99% of what happens in not my business' ... all these things challenge our deeply-held assumptions about being in charge, in control, being God.'

'I'll have a go,' Allan said.

'That's all that is required, Allan. We're never going to reach the end of this. The important thing is to give it our best shot. Now, before we finish, are there any other areas in your life you think might be in need of some housecleaning, something...' and Benson thought for a long moment as if he was searching round frantically for what else might, just possibly, maybe, be a problem that had not been covered. '...work-related perhaps?' he asked, his tone rising sharply, like a graph depicting the results of a survey on the unpopularity of bankers.

'Don't think so,' Allan said. 'But mind that second stair on the third flight down. The carpet's riding up. I've taped it, but it could still be a hazard.'

'See you at the meeting tomorrow, Allan,' Benson said.

# 44

The Easter holiday stint on the beach was over, leaving Benson with weekdays free to wrestle the house back to Rob-preferred condition, to explore the shops, restocking his freezer and larder, to keep Health-and-safety-Allan on the steps and off the booze. He put in time on his pyrography, burning poem after poem on breadboard after breadboard ... but Muriel's absence and the resulting lack of a market for his product was disheartening.

Rob, probably after tripping over his breadboards on his way out of Muriel's and adding two and two, had confessed to Benson that he had been having it off (Rob's term) with Muriel for quite some time. He and Muriel went way back. A bit of slap and tickle came naturally to both of them and he knew it helped Muriel cope. Sorry for not mentioning it before, but he was mentioning it now.

Benson had been accepting of Rob's confession. He even mentioned a sample of his own slips in the sexual department, honing in (totally) on the man in the garden centre and his optical infidelities with Allan. The two of them, after all, had always kept a hinterland of playmates.

Still, Benson thought, that's the way some men are. Rob is queer, but not queer in the same way I am. *You can say that again!* He'd left it at that. On the back burner – with the heat off and the gas supply disconnected.

But Rob had also been bidding farewell to Muriel. She

was going off to have one more search for Captain Jones in Kuching and the surrounding area. She had an open return ticket. She was not sure when she would return, was really sorry to be going away, but knew that – with or without Captain Jones – she definitely would. The issue had continued to nag her and she knew that she needed to go and see for herself where her husband had met his end – or started his new beginning. The plans she had for Benson and his wonderful fire-writing would have to cease for the time being.

Benson's only problem with the whole thing came with the feeling that Muriel could have told him herself. Perhaps she would have, if he'd come with his package at a more appropriate time. Still, he persisted with the work, purchasing more breadboards from Poundland, finding more poems to write.


Reg had failed his motorcycle test. When Benson heard him radio in to inform Sparks that he had an appointment to attend and would be off station for the rest of the day; when he saw him walking away without a backward glance for Benson to use to wish him luck, he had started a barrage of mixed-motive prayers for Reg's success.

There was something about the man that made him uneasy. All his conscientiousness as a lifeguard could not cancel out the fact that Reg had a litany of qualities that grated on Benson: he was rude to the public when he considered they were erring; he seemed to have a complete gap where 'Thank you' should be; he was – whenever Benson mentioned something to do with safety – quick to inform him that he was a byelaws officer and not a lifeguard. He'd told him, for instance, to take off his hat, which had 'Lifeguard' on the front, adding to the hurt by asserting Benson wasn't entitled to it ... this despite the fact that the Boss had given it to him. Benson did not follow this instruction and Reg would stare at the cap malevolently whenever he wore it.

By the time the test-day came, a silence had descended between the two of them. No more did Benson offer tea, though he made tea for anyone else who came along. Neither did he speak to Rob about his difficulties with Reg – or that there might be a way out of it. He knew what Rob would say.

So Benson came to the conclusion that he would just have to take the freeze between them as a daily reality. For what was Reg after all? A human being, with a programme running in his head: it might be incompatible with Benson's own programme, but that was not something that he could change. It was a bit like the war for attention that went on in his computer between RealPlayer and Microsoft Media Player. Benson preferred the former, but always got the latter. In the end RealPlayer had just disappeared from his computer in a huff – Lord knew how – refusing to reinstall, leaving the screen to its incompatible competitor.

Things got worse when Reg failed. He put in for another test straight away, but was told by the Boss in no uncertain terms that he would have to stay at New Brighton.

'There's a positive side to all this, Matron,' the Boss told Benson on the Sunday before the end of Easter duties.

'Is there?' Benson asked, thinking the Boss might be about to bring up the vexed state of play between himself and Reg.

'Word has got out that dogs are in danger, so people are keeping them on the lead.'

'And they're picking up the poo,' Benson said, though he would have preferred to be told that the Boss understood that Reg could be a rude bugger but had redeeming features.

'Yeah. I suppose it's harder to ignore it when they're laying a great steaming turd only a length of rope away. Hard to do a Nelson.'

Benson agreed that that must be the case.

'When I was a kid,' the Boss went on, 'dog turds were not so – how shall I put it? – substantial. People fed them anything that was left at the side of the plate. Scraps. These days the big boys have got their mitts in, dogs get fed 'properly' and their turds would do credit to your average adult human male. They're somehow more disgusting than they used to be.'

'You're right. And you don't see any of the dog-food manufacturers pitching in to help clear it up, do you?'

'You don't.'

'Have you ever seen a 1,000 pound puppy?' Benson asked.

'Is this a joke?'

'No. I think it was probably an insult aimed at a minimum-waged byelaws officer. That plumber with the white Nissan and the big white fishing boat showed me his. It was nice enough. But not a thousand pounds nice.'

'Nothing in the dog department is a thousand pounds nice.'

"Will they catch the fellow who's doing it?'

'I should think so. I hear they're under a lot of pressure. The complaints have been huge. Almost as many as they get about dog-fouling and naughty kids.'

\* \* \*

By the Wednesday of his second free week, Benson had
tired of pyrography. He kept bumping into the word-burn
smell in the most unexpected parts of the house. Not
that it was particularly unpleasant, but it might work its
way into everything. He looked and sniffed about the
kitchen, deciding to give it a good going over. *Move a
muscle! Change a thought!* He took down everything from
shelves, dusted the herb and spice jars, sprayed and cleaned
the surfaces, scrubbed the tiles, polished the sink ...

He kept the cluttered pine table for the end. Half was
taken up with papers and paperwork. Around the middle,
a rattan mat island provided a safe and sacrosanct haven
for cruet, sauce and honey. It was as he removed this
that he saw the Celtic love spoon Muriel had given him.

The spoon had lived unused, perhaps unseen, since
he'd placed it there. Why was that? He held it up and
fell in love with it again. So why had ne not shown it to
Rob? *Why, oh why, had Rob not noticed it?* Why had he
not paraded it about the table with honey on its end to
make Rob ooh and ahh? He decided he'd been distracted.
Well, that was his usual state of disgrace. He was a martyr
to it. How often had he bought a CD, played it and
forgotten it? And ditto endless entrancing purchases?
*Distracted from distraction by distraction, men and bits of paper*
... There were certainly enough bits of paper, but he did
not feel in the mood to deal with the stacks. Instead he
sat and considered the spoon.

And, as often happened, he went from that thought to
others. Perhaps he should take up spoon carving! It might
be a new departure for his craft. Instead of seeing wood
as a blank canvas, he would be like Michelangelo and
consider every piece of wood he encountered as containing
the humble cherub of a trapped Celtic love spoon. Instead

of violating wood with burns, he would emancipate the love spoon that snoozed beneath the rough – or smooth – exterior of every piece of wood.

Then he considered the route his craftwork had taken. As a child he'd been hopeless at anything practical. Mum had put this down to his being left-handed, and so not quite getting any instructions given. Scissors never cut straight for him; nuts tightened when he thought they were loosening; tin openers left tins grazed but undamaged...

But when he had stopped drinking, he'd found himself aching to make things. St Bridget Crosses out of pipe cleaners, which had led to his discovery that a Legs of Man could be wrought from the same design and a wondering as to whether the Celtic tradition of design had also included the Legs of Man. Was there a PhD in it? Probably, but perhaps he could make the shapes from different, more precious, material. This hit the buffers when he found that pliers still would not work for him, that silver wire pierced his fingers, and the shape he produced was never quite right. He'd also made bird houses from lollipop sticks.

Assembling the double bed he'd bought from Ikea for him and Rob to use (replacing a rather suspect futon that had seen too many nights) he found his greatest challenge. It was one of the first fruits of his sobriety to find that he could take all the time he needed to decipher the Herculean task of assembling that bed from the opaque instructions given; to realise that – with no effort on his part – he did not rant and stamp, but could methodically labour until the project was complete and no 'spare' nuts and bolts remained.

The bed creaked a bit, but it had a lot to creak about – especially in those early days. But all the things he had

339

made were not *like* Benson. They were a tangible sign of a change taking place. Working on a task centred him. Maybe carving love spoons was the next best thing. He had more than enough pyrography items to wow Muriel with on her return. But perhaps he should seek out the home of the creator of the love spoon that had inspired him. It would get him out of the house, give the Honda a bit of exercise and maybe – just maybe – fire him up with inspiration. For with Muriel absent, the kindly hand on the tiller of his creativity had been removed.

And a good walk in the country might get the vexed relationship with Reg out of his head.

# 45

'Anything else?' Benson asked Health-and-safety Allan.

Allan shook his head.

'Are you *sure*, Allan? Is there *nothing* that you can recall that you ought to get out, and tell to yourself, me, and your Higher Power?'

'No. Think that's everything,' Allan said.

A hesitation. 'Well, if you're *sure...*'

There had still been no mention of Health-and-safety Allan's obsession with all things healthy and safe. Though, God knew, Benson had given him hints: 'Nothing that comes from your job, is there, Allan? I know I used to really get steamed up at work. Still do. They kept changing the curriculum for teaching. All sorts of fly-by-night methods that I didn't believe worked with learners, but which we had to follow. They brought up massive resentments. Nothing of that sort? I often find that I accept the things I can't change, but can't move a muscle to change the things I CAN CHANGE. I've told you that we alchies can't afford anger. Acceptance of the world *just as it is* is at the nub of the sober life. Do you ever seek to change things that cannot be changed, Allan?' And so on. But Allan could not see.

He decided not to pursue it farther. After all, the important thing was that Allan should complete the Steps. He could then, a day at a time, put them into practice for the rest of his life. Other things – including the Big

One that was as clear to Benson and to anyone in the QA meetings who had an ounce of grey matter, but invisible to Allan – might become clear with the passing of time. But it was not for Benson to take Allan's inventory, to decide for him what were his faults and assets. The Higher Power knew that he had dropped as many little hints from his own experience as he could.

'Righto, Allan. We've completed Step Five. Now for Step Six you need to become entirely ready for your Higher Power to remove all your defects of character. It's willingness again, Allan. Willingness is at the nub of this programme. You've brought your grosser defects of character out into the light of day. No longer can they bite you on the bum and maybe cause you to give up on yourself and start drinking. They're out in full daylight for you to work on. I've told you a lot about myself as I've tried to make you aware of your own defects of character. I've mentioned my life full of lusts, fears, resentments, sloth, fuzzy thinking, self-will. You've played your part by dredging through the mucky bottom of your own character. And you've shared them with yourself, with your Higher Power, with me, and learned a lot about yourself. But we are powerless to change without Help. So from now on, every day and many times during each day, we need to hand over our will and our lives to our Higher Power in order to be the best version of ourselves that we can be. Are you ready for your Higher Power to remove your faults and failings?'

'Yes.'

'Good. But if my experience is anything to go by, it isn't going to happen just like that. If you're anything like me, there'll be endless stumblings, endless failures. These are the experiences of everyone at QA. They are expected.

They are also a blessing. What do I mean? Well, simply put, every time we stumble and fall into old behaviour – and *know* what is happening – we are increasing our awareness of our tendencies. I've picked up a bugger of a resentment at work. It's causing me a lot of suffering. But, as I suffer, the object of my resentment goes through his days oblivious. I've got to stop him living rent-free in my head. But how? I'm powerless on my own. I have to hand it over, and pray for the bastard. At least I know what's going on. Our self-knowledge grows in every direction through a daily practice of this programme. I don't want a drink to get me through it. So are you entirely ready to have your Higher Power remove from you all these defects of character?'

'Yes.'

'Right. That's Step Six. Step Seven is simple. We get on our knees and pray. You don't have to kneel, but I find that kneeling is a visible manifestation of me being one more creature. We are humble when kneeling. We know our right size. Our strengths and our weaknesses. Our ignorance about the big picture.'

They knelt down and prayed for the removal of their defects. Allan stood up before Benson, who'd had a mind to have a moment of Quakerish silence. Allan stood, his front a few inches from Benson's praying lips. And Benson ached to reach across, open Allan's flies and let loose. But, as so often happened, a moment of reprieve came. The hammer was raised and would fall, breaking up everything. But for a moment, he had time to stop the hammer's trajectory. Benson stood up. 'That prayer is on page 76 of *The Book*. I say it every night and morning,' Benson said. 'Read those chapters I've mentioned, and start thinking about Step Eight, which is 'Made a list of

343

all persons we had harmed, and became willing to make amends to them all.' We'll meet again in a few days to discuss that.'

'Will you give me a hug?' Allan asked.

'Of course I will, Allan. Of course I will,' Benson said, seeing himself as St Francis and Allan as The Leper, then pushing the picture away before he got quite lost.

They hugged in the manner of stout-hearted Americans at the arrivals point at Kennedy airport.

'How's the job?' Allan asked.

Benson thought about drowned BMWs, youths with too much money but no inclination to do the necessary to make them competent on the water, dead dogs, Reg ... Then he thought of how good it was to have a job to go to, a job that showed him to himself on a daily basis. 'A job is often more than the work,' he said.

'You'll have to explain that,' Allan said.

'I'd be glad to,' Benson said.

# 46

It took Benson a day of intermittent searching to find the address of the spoon-carver and decipher the fuzzy directions Muriel had given him. He told Rob he was going for a run on his bike. Rob approved, merely reminding him to keep remembering the lifesaver glance at every opportunity.

'We'll have to start doing some planning,' Benson told him.

'What for?'

'For the civil partnership,' Benson said.

'Not much to plan for,' Rob said, while eating porridge, and not chewing. 'Jack's booked the rooms. They're part of the fee for the convention. We have to pop up for a meeting with the registrar ahead of time, but we can do that in a day. On the day itself we've only got to add our names to the booking Jack's made with the registrar. What else is there?'

'How about the reception?'

'Thought you and me, Jack and Bill, could go out for an Indian.'

Muriel's mention of pyrographed place names came to mind. 'So no guest list?'

'Let's keep it between ourselves, eh? Nice and simple.'


Benson set out for Corwen under dark clouds. He thought of Rob's plans for the simplest occasion possible. It was a bit like one of those Las Vegas weddings, but in Blackpool. At least he'd be spared all the Elvis-impersonating vicars, all the trouble and fuss. Rob had consented to him baking and icing a cake to be brought to the New Brighton meeting and that was about all.

He found the village, but after going up several roads into the hills came to dead ends or rutted tracks that showed no evidence of a 'really rundown cottage'. Plenty of lambs running about the spring fields, but they were losing their lamby cuteness and piling on the pounds. Were I a sheep, Benson told himself, I'd warn the lambs to go easy on all that grass. The more they eat the sooner the farmer will dispatch them. But, not being a sheep, he dismissed the thought. The lambs were living fully in their present moment. The future was unknown to them. He turned his attention to other things: plenty of trees in fresh early leaf. All those shades of green! A lovely time of year, and so fleeting! Soon it would all settle into the unchanging green of summer.

He went back to the village. He parked the bike, locked his crash helmet on it and went off in search of someone to ask.

On his second hundred-yard-scan of the scant village, Benson saw an elderly woman holding a trowel. She was making her way slowly up the path at the side of her house, frowning at the flower beds.

'Hello,' Benson said.

The woman squinted at him and said something in Welsh.

'I don't speak Welsh,' Benson said. 'Sorry.'

She came up to the fence, smiling at him. 'There's a pity,' she said. 'I'm better in Welsh. Lovely day.'

'Yes. Really lovely.'

'Everything's growing. Hard to keep up with it.'

'Your garden's beautiful. All those white flowers.'

'They're weeds. Shocking smell of onion. Can you smell it?'

Benson sniffed. 'A bit.'

'Well, I didn't plant them. They just arrived. Blew in, shouldn't wonder. And they've taken over. I pull them up. But the roots burrow underground and keep on coming.'

'They're like white bluebells.'

'If you say so.'

'I was wondering...'

'Yes...'

'A friend of mine in Loggerheads told me a man lived in your village. He used to make spoons, Welsh Love Spoons. He made walking sticks as well.'

'Aled.'

'Yes.'

'He's dead.'

'Yes. I'm an admirer of his work, and I was wondering where his cottage was. I got directions but I can't find it.'

'There's not much to it. It was always a bit of a ruin, and Aled didn't do much to improve it.'

'No. I've been up all the roads leading off to the right into the hills. But there's no sign of a place that answers Muriel's – she's my friend – description.'

'Try the track on the left. By the war memorial,' the woman said.

'Ah. The left.'

'It's the only house on that road. There's a big farm at the end, but the place you want is halfway up. Surrounded by trees. But why do you want to see Aled's house?'

347

'I'm not sure,' Benson said. 'I bought one of his spoons and really admired his work. It's a sort of pilgrimage.'

The woman looked at him.

'I might go back home by way of Holywell,' Benson said.

'Why? Is there something wrong with you?'

Benson had to think about that. 'Just the usual. Resentment about weeds – but in the head and heart; worries about growing older. Sadness about where my life has gone. You know.'

'Yes, I do. Don't get me started.'


Benson left her there and walked back to the bike. He decided to leave it where it was after checking he had locked it – he hadn't – and walked up the track. The sunbeams were soon speckled, then blocked, by the trees. The incline grew steeper. After five minutes, the strain on his calf muscles was beginning to get to him, but he pushed himself forward. He was on top of the cottage before he saw it. The little front gate had 'Bwlch-y-llys' carved onto a rough piece of wood. Beautifully done. Every incision in the wood perfect, and contrasting with the splintery surface. He opened the gate and walked into the overgrown garden. Lots of flowers, including the white bluebells the woman had thought of as weeds. Well, weeds were a point of view.

He looked at the tiny place. In need of maintenance, had been in need of maintenance for quite some time. One up and one down. He looked through a window, but apart from a stone spiral staircase close to the window he could not make out much. He didn't try the door.

Feeling illegal, Benson started walking around the cottage

to the back. A lean-to shelter supported by stout wooden columns but without walls. It was full of wood. Wood for fires. Wood for craftwork. Wood gathered from the area around, he supposed. He was in the middle of saying a prayer for the dead craftsman when he caught sight of a large basket of kindling close to the back door. It was full to the brim with pine. He went closer and stopped: wooden spoons, mallet handles, a mallet end axed in two, and 'Souvenir of Loggerheads' pyrographed everywhere. 'A shard of 'If', *And all men blaming it on you ... when all men doubt you ... you'll be a ... my son.* the first four lines of Sonnet 30, *When to the sessions of sweet silent thought...*

Benson rummaged in the basket. The kindling went on and on ... *No man is an island ... It tolls for thee ... took the road less travelled ... great difference ... the falcon cannot hear the ... I was much too far out all my ... a robin redbreast in a cage puts all of heaven in a ... And did you get from this life what you wanted e'en so? ... Because I could not stop for death he kindly...*

Benson walked back to his bike and made his way to Merseyside by a route that avoided Loggerheads but included Holywell.

# 47

An hour later Benson was floating in the pool where the waters at St Winefride's Well passed after bubbling up from the ground on the start of its short journey to the sea. While trying to forget the icy temperature and making sure the vent in his boxer shorts was not showing anything immodest to the looming lifesized statue of St Winefride holding its lily of purity while red-holder nightlights winked tiny prayers, he tried to stop considering the implications of what he had seen at Aled's cottage.

But his head would not let go of the short story of those chopped-up-for-kindling shards of his pyrography output. So much of it! And all ending up waiting for the fire inside to warm the poor man who made such wonderful things. All his own work. He had been amazed at himself that he'd managed to make a red-hot nib obey him to form letters on wood. It was so unlike him. Then, surprise on surprise, he had been amazed when Muriel took to them and asked if she could put them up for sale in her shop. And flabbergasted that they had shifted! And cocky unto death that she had requested, nay, *demanded* more.

Well, they hadn't shifted. Muriel, stuck with them, had decided to have a clear-out. She knew, perhaps, that Aled lived from hand to mouth and passed them onto him to light his fires with. How much had gone up in smoke? Maybe he'd only seen a small fraction of the stock that Muriel had given to Aled. Anyway, they hadn't sold. And

Muriel, generous to a fault, could not tell him the truth of it. Instead she had kept enthusing about his work, opening up the possibility of new markets, inspiring him to greater and greater efforts. And all the time she had been passing on his labour to Aled to keep him warm!

Benson swam a couple of lengths of the small pool. He allowed his head to go under the freezing water and then brought it up, trying to gasp the pain of cold out. Would he ever get used to it? Was it doing him any good?

He lay on his back and looked at the sky. Clouds. St Winefride watched him like a lifeguard.

St Winefride had had a hard time too. Having your head chopped off, watching the blur from inside – like a horrific funfair ride – as it bounced down the hill of Holywell to form the well that fourteen centuries later was now freezing him. Then, just as consciousness was finally going out, to feel Bishop Beuno lifting up that bruised and bloody head, saying, 'Don't you worry, my dear Virgin and Martyr, I'll have you to rights in no time at all. God willing.' And God had willed. But that unsightly scar on her neck! What else to do but keep it hidden with a wimple and stay away from the sight of men and her growing reputation for almost dying, then returning in the odour of sanctity? I mean, bad enough to go through the pain of beheading only to return to life and in the fullness of time have to go through the whole thing again in whatever way Death snuck up.

Yes, Winefride had had a hard time of it. And now to end up as guardian spirit of *The Lourdes of North Wales*, forced to minister to sick souls like Benson instead of enjoying carefree pleasures in paradise! They'd built an oratory around her spring. It had survived the wicked iconoclasts of the Reformation because it was in a remote place. But not so remote that poor lost souls like Benson could not locate it with their urgent Sat Nav of need.

The names of the cured and curious were everywhere around, carved or scrawled into the stonework above the burbling spring. When Benson was little there'd been vast displays of crutches and crude prosthetic devices and walking sticks – all redundant to the cured pilgrims skipping their way home to a new life, spreading the news that St Winefride was busy working miracles from beyond the grave.

So here he was, freezing in the unaesthetic rectangular pool built to cater to the sick. Benson had never seen anyone partaking of the pool, and he'd been coming to the well for fifty years, man and boy. Until today he'd never considered partaking himself. But here he was, humbled, head full of gremlins, sick as his secrets and his pretentions to artistic endeavours and entrepreneurship, lying in the underused pool and seeking to sort out his hurt feelings.

Benson kicked the water hard. He kept it up, churning the pool into a minor storm of whiteness. A wave bounced against the side, swept back on him and over his face. He swallowed a generous mouthful. He swallowed again to bring what had come back up down again. He stilled, grunting, and watched the looming clouds.

Of course, looked at in another way, perhaps he was surrounded by blessings. Was it so bad for one's work to end up warming a craftsman in a draughty cottage? Who knows but his spoons, spatulas and mallets had allowed Aled to produce a few more exquisite pieces before Death knocked at the door and commanded him to follow him into the cold of an unknown night? Perhaps he had even produced the love spoon that had set Benson on fire while burning Benson's pyrography output! Was there consolation there? He thought for a moment there might be, then decided that though there might be a few drops of it, it did not go anywhere near to putting out the flame of his resentment. What could have been going on in Muriel's head – to buy from him over and over again, and then pass on his work to someone else? *Maybe you can find a use for this. I've not been able to shift it.* Should he be so surprised, after all? He had been surprised that Muriel wanted more, that demand for his work outstripped his ability to supply it. Well – and not for the first time – he'd been wrong. Muriel, for reasons best known to herself, had kept reordering despite all the evidence in her shop that should have made her call a halt.

Rob. Rob had been in on it. That must be it. Rob had asked her to buck up Benson, to show him that he could do something that would make him some useful dosh. Not to worry if it didn't sell. He'd pay her back in money or in kind...

But then that thought, simply by thinking of everything he knew about Rob, dissolved away. No, that was just not the Rob he knew. It would have gone contrary to everything Rob had been trying to instil into Benson with his buddying. He insisted on facing up to life, living life on life's terms, accepting the good with the bad – all those Christmas card mottos that seemed trite but were in fact the bedrock of a life well lived.

So maybe it was Muriel – Muriel with her partiality for gay men ... *Why?* Her fondness for eccentricity and for whatever it was in Benson that floated her boat? What to do? Nothing to be done.

Raindrops kept falling on his head. They plopped about on the pool surface, making tiny explosions like fairy bombs all about him. Gulliver in Lilliput. Gulliver had been one of Benson's childhood fantasies. He'd imagined being chief Lilliputian of the gang who'd tied up Gulliver with an endless succession of tiny ropes. It had taken hundreds of lengths to stop Gulliver from getting up but once Benson, as chief Lilliputian, had made sure Gulliver was powerless, he'd climbed up Gulliver's legs – telling the other Lilliputians to be off about their business as he was in charge of guarding this giant and wished to have time alone with him in order to start a detailed interrogation – and having scaled the massif of Gulliver's flies, achieved the pinnacle of one of his trouser buttons and managing to insert himself under the flap to see what was what down there. Then he'd climbed up Gulliver's enormous memory-foam member and made a bed for himself in the soft crinkly flower of his foreskin. Then the flower parted and Benson had found himself grasping on to a purple upland that reared up. And in the centre was a huge hole with sides like lips and ... *I'll see you all right, Mr Gulliver! We can be special friends!*

'You all right in there?'

It was the woman from the shop, who'd rented him a towel, who'd said she was glad to see that not everyone was scared of a bit of cold water. She stood above him as he floated, startled back to consciousness with an awareness of rain everywhere and an erection beneath the thin skin of his boxer shorts, an erection that – thankfully – had not poked out of the flap and turned him into *persona non grata* at St Winefride's Well.

'Fine, thanks. I was meditating.' *Liar!*

'Well, don't catch cold.'

'No. I'm used to it now.'

Perhaps, Benson thought, I should volunteer to be a

lifeguard at this pool. But that was no good; not if nobody used it. Anyway, it's only about four feet deep. He swam to the end of the pool where the water entered straight from the spring. *The Holy Lifeguard of Holywell!* It had a definite ring. He placed his hot groin in the middle of the fast current to cool himself down. So what do I do? he asked it, and the saint who was behind it.

And Rob said, 'Chalk it up to experience. Acceptance is the key.'

Yes, Benson thought. That is what I'll do. I'm powerless over this. I should be grateful. I earned money for the work. What have I lost, apart from my pride?

He put his clothes on and went to the shop to return his towel. There he bought another four Serenity Prayers in their own plastic cases, along with a tiny statue of St Winefride. Then he made his way home – a still point of serenity inside his goldfish bowl of a stern helmet – through the driving rain.

# 48

Benson arrived home wondering if he should summon Rob to an urgent meeting. The happenings of the day needed to be aired; the implications for his craftwork and its future discussed. He'd planned it out on the trip home: he'd just lay out on the table what he had discovered and leave it to Rob to tell him what he knew. Maybe he'd come clean if he were in any way involved – which Benson doubted.

If Rob had gone for advice from Jack – and he was forever doing that – then he couldn't imagine Jack giving Rob any encouragement to allow the wool to be pulled over Benson's eyes. Nor would Jack have allowed Rob to go along with Muriel's desire not to show Benson that his pyrography enterprise had bitten the dust. It just wouldn't have been honest.

But all that dissolved when Benson found a message from Health-and-safety Allan on his answerphone. Allan wanted a meeting as soon as possible. Could Benson get back to him, on his mobile?

Benson did not like phoning mobiles. Phoning mobiles cost an arm and a leg. It was one more way in which the wretched plutocrats at the phone companies drew everyone – even innocent landline users – into their web of exorbitant charges. Bastards!

Saying a prayer for the mobile phone plutocrats in order to lessen the negative effects of his sudden attack of anger, Benson listened to Allan's message again and wrote down the last digits of the mobile phone number he could not commit to memory. He rang. As it was Allan.

To make matters worse, he was answered by a message from Allan. This informed him that he welcomed the message but hoped that the caller was holding the headset at least three centimetres from his/her ear in order to lessen the dose of microwaves which might or might not cause long-term damage. He could leave a short message now.

'It's Martin, Allan. I'm home. Hope all is well.'

He rang off. After fifteen seconds or so, the phone rang and Benson answered. He listened.

'Come round right away,' Benson said. 'I'll put the kettle on.'


Benson used the waiting time to scour a couple of mugs to Allan-preferred condition inside and out. He put the kettle on and inspected the biscuit barrel to make sure none of the biscuits inside had gone soft. He helped himself to a couple of Nice, though he didn't think they lived up to their name. Then he drank a glass of water to get some saliva back into his mouth.

Allan knocked at the door.

'That was quick,' Benson said.

Allan nodded. 'Is Rob in?'

'No. Too early.'

Allan was holding a parcel in his hand. It was large, and fairly flat. It seemed to have been packed out of a big blue IKEA bag of the sort one carried around the shop looking for the exit. But most of the blue had been covered by many rounds of rough gaffer tape. 'What's that?' Benson asked.

I want you to keep it for me. I don't want it in the house.'

'It isn't booze, is it, Allan? You haven't...'

'No, it isn't booze. I just want it out of the house. I don't trust myself with it. And what if I was burgled?'

'You burgled! With all those locks and alarms! I don't think that's likely.'

Allan thought about that. 'You never know. Anyway, I just don't want to be tempted.'

'What is it?'

'I'd rather not say.'

'It's a secret, is it?'

Allan walked straight into his buddy's trap. 'Yes,' he said.

'But you know as well as I do that we're as sick as our secrets. Do you have a secret concerning this package?'

'Yes, I do.'

'So what is it?'

'I'd rather not say.'

Benson poured Allan his tea, taking time to consider the situation. He was feeling really curious about the parcel, already imagining Allan leaving it with him and – much relieved – disappearing down the drive and back to his secure flat and when the coast was well and truly clear giving the parcel a good feel to see if he could braille its contents through the layers of gaffer tape and IKEA bag. But instead he said, 'I'm not sure I can keep it for you if you don't tell me what's inside.'

'Can't you trust me on this?'

'Can't *you* trust *me* on this?'

'No.'

'No?'

'No.'

'Then I can't keep the parcel for you, Allan.'

'I'll drink on this.'

'I can't stop you from drinking if that's what you have decided to do,' Benson said, feeling like Rob, and a long way from his own comfort zone. 'But it seems to me, Allan, that there's something in this parcel that is robbing you of sobriety. I've been trying to explain to you that there are lots of triggers for drinking for real alchies. It's part of the reason why we do the Steps and then live them each and every day: to be aware of the patterns of behaviour that bring us to the first drink.'

'But I only want you to keep it until the heat's off,' Allan said.

*Until the heat's off!* 'What do you mean by that?'

'I can't tell you.'

'Allan,' Benson said, 'though we are friends – and I find there is much to admire in you – you asked me to buddy you. A buddy is a bit different from a friend. A buddy is a guide. Now the only qualification I have is my own experience, strength and hope. This I have been trying to pass on to you. Believe me, as your buddy there is nothing I want more than for 'the heat' – whatever it is – to be off you. It seems to me that the presence of this parcel on the table between us is a sign that something has not been quite right with our Step work thus far. Step Four and Five demand rigorous honesty. I've just had the feeling that you're holding something back. Something crucial. Now it's not for me to point out what this holding back consists of. But this parcel might be at the nub of it. Do you get me?'

'I can't see why you won't do me this favour. Don't you trust me?'

359

Benson thought about that. He didn't trust Allan. Not at this moment. *So say it!* 'No, I don't. You're a week away from being drunk and off your head. What's to trust?'

'I see,' Allan said. And he picked up the parcel. He stood up.

Benson was stuck for something to say. He badly wanted to tell Allan that his obsession with Health and Safety was standing between him and sobriety like a great high brick wall. He would have to surrender to his powerlessness in that area of his life if he were ever to attain sobriety. But, if Allan couldn't see what was evident to everyone else in QA, then it was not for Benson to take Allan's inventory for him. That was just not on. Or was it?

'Let's say the Serenity Prayer together,' Benson said, thinking that that prayer contained everything that, if Allan had ears to hear, he needed to hear.

'Fuck the Serenity Prayer! Fuck you too! You were only ever after my big dick! All the rest was just so much crap.' And Allan turned and left the house, carrying his parcel.

It was now Benson's turn to recite the Serenity Prayer. This he did, again and again. Such a lot in those few words! Serenity to accept what cannot be changed; courage to change things that can be changed; wisdom to know the difference. The nuances of the prayer kept coming to him, and then leaving him. Like Allan, Benson constantly wanted to change the things that could not be changed but to leave those that could be changed snoozing under the rug. What an interesting day! he thought. I've learned all sorts of stuff. I've been humbled. Can't shift my pyrography. Can't help a buddy. And, of course, Allan was right in a way: I do look at him and think of his cock. Can't help myself. Funny me thinking of Gulliver in the pool. And with St Winefride looking down at me, polluting her holy waters with my thoughts. Daft! I could so easily dethrone my notions of a Higher Power – Fellowship, Rob, Mists, Tides, Winds, Mountains, the vastness of space, the imponderables of expanding or contracting universes, the time before Big Bangs, the mystery of it all – and place Allan's dick up on a plinth to become the object of my devotion! And I wouldn't be unique. The Romans put phalluses on street corners where we put post boxes – which are also phallic, come to think of it – the Thais have phalluses all over the place and cover them in gold leaf. For me, there's nothing more ineffable and adorable than a big dick. Face it. One more thing I am powerless over. The easiest of Higher Powers.

Benson heard the sound of Rob's motorcycle. The front door opened. Rob stood there.

'What's up?' Rob said.

'I think I've lost my buddy,' Benson said. And that wasn't mentioning the rest. In the next half hour it all came out.

'Time for a visit to the attic. What do you think?' Rob said when Benson had unburdened himself.

'Yes, I think so. I'll be down on my hands and knees inspecting the slow puncture...'

'That'll do for starters,' Rob said.

'Go easy on the pressure gauge. You know how you get carried away.'

And Benson, banishing all else, aimed a prayer for Success to Trade at the stippled kitchen ceiling.

361

# 49

Benson didn't want to go to the QA meeting that night for fear of meeting Allan. But Rob said that Jack was coming over to do the Chair. He would be disappointed not to see Martin, and they might be able to get together afterwards to plan Blackpool.

With Rob and Jack at his side, Benson felt he could face anything. But when he saw Allan enter the room, clearly drunk, his first reaction was to bolt for the door.

Instead, he twiddled his thumbs, looking at them hard and trying to keep in mind what Rob had told him. It wasn't his fault that Allan had drunk. That's what alchies do. Benson had done his best to buddy Allan in the only way he knew: by telling Allan his own story; telling him how it had been for Benson; telling him his only story of experience, strength and hope. 'We all fail at buddying,' Rob had said. 'We pass the message of QA in order to keep it. And when we do that, we don't drink.'

Tentatively, with some sober trepidation, Benson looked up. Allan was looking straight at him, and, if looks could kill, Benson felt he would have dropped dead on the spot. But looks could not kill. He was surrounded by friends. He had the quiet might of QA about him. Then the door was held open and in zimmered Busy Sandra, a lady-policeman Teddy ribboned on to her Zimmer to keep the other one company. A quick check of Allan's ray-gun eyes and he noted with feelings of some relief that the look of malevolent attention had shifted to Busy Sandra.

Jack gave his usual chair about Step-work. He included each of the first nine in turn, along with short accounts of how he had approached each one. But when he turned to the last three steps he expanded upon them, saying that those last three were simply the way he used to keep up his practice of the first nine. He examined his conscience each night to find the failures of the day. He prayed to be released from his defects of character. Throughout each day he recalled to mind his Higher Power, meditated on his life, on the world, and on what his Higher Power might want of him. 'Thy will, not mine, be done.' And when he prayed that prayer he was simply expressing the idea that he should fit in with the rhythm, the breath, of life and in no way seek to stunt the great world into which he had been born. And he tried to communicate the message of the Twelve Steps of Recovery: by his attendance at meetings, by never refusing to buddy a fellow alchy, and by being the best version of Jack, the recovered alcoholic, that he could be. He then said he hoped as many people as possible would share with him.

Allan had a drunken go to come in, but Busy Sandra got in first. She said that she was still in pain and confined to work at the cop shop. She missed contact with the general public and the daily conversations she had with people about their everyday problems. For was she not, first and foremost, a people person?

Sandra went on. And on. Benson tried to retreat into the garden of his soul in order to tune her out. But there were gremlins in the garden. All his resentments against the police force in general for their complete invisibility, their failure to turn up when needed, their undeserved high wages and ridiculous pensions, their actions during the miners' strike, the G7, and, above all, their covert surveillance of the public toilets, whipped away all serenity. He found himself agreeing with Allan. Why could she not have dropped a word to the wise about the sting operation? Why couldn't the so-called 'gay-friendly' busies – what a sick joke that was! – have put up a sign, as they put up signs elsewhere regarding surveillance. Sat Navs in cars were allowed to warn those motorists who could afford one that traffic cameras were heading up; signs in city streets broadcast the use of surveillance cameras; the cameras themselves were impossible to miss – they stared down at everyone. They stared down at Benson as he argued with people giving him grief at his gate. But not once in all the time he'd been there – not long, though it felt like a lifetime – had a cop car stopped to ask him if he had any problems. So why, in the case of gay men behaving badly in a public place, could not some hint have been given? Benson's interior garden withered. He came back to the room just in time to catch Sandra speak of the opinion of police doctors that she should seek early medical retirement. Fortunately, the terms were excellent and she was young enough to find herself another job, perhaps part-time. Yes, that might be a good outcome and she owed it all to the fellowship of Queer Alchies.

There was much shuffling in the room at that point. It was clear to everyone except Busy Sandra that many did not think she was the recipient of much grace from the fellowship. She was as she had always been: self-will run riot. She might be a 'dry' alchy, perhaps she had never really been a fully-fledged alchy at all, but did she by her actions show that she had 'got' the programme and made it the centre of her life? Well, – though everyone felt guilty about making such a judgement – *hardly*.

Benson looked at his watch. Though he had not consulted his Timex when Busy Sandra started he could compute that her marathon had begun around five past. It was now twenty-seven minutes past. Over twenty minutes! Why, oh why, was not the group leader – a quiet chap called Kevin – intervening, pointing out that it was a crowded meeting, and that everyone should get the chance to say what was on their minds, in their hearts?

But meetings, Benson had decided a long time ago, were like practice courts for life. One sat and 'took' whatever happened. The quality of a chap's sobriety could be gauged by his or her acceptance of that reality. Looked at in this light, Benson felt he was not particularly sober tonight. True, he did not want to drink. But sobriety could be as short as a little finger or as long as the M1.

At last even Jack tired. Busy Sandra was going into all the possibilities as to the nature of her rosy second life after the police: small shop, emigration to Canada or New Zealand, security consultant ... when Jack came in and said, 'This is a crowded meeting, Sandra. I think we'd better move on.'

Sandra, holding her hand up, said, 'I'll finish on this.' And she launched into an account of her grasp of the Twelve Steps. Three fellows stood up, two going out for a smoke, one heading for the toilet. When they came back Sandra was still talking. Then she paused for breath and before she had time to let go her exhalation, Allan said, 'My name's Allan. I'm a queer alchy.'

The room of queer alchies went from supine and bored to tense and alert. The frisson was palpable. Benson was full of fear. He felt that Allan would start on him; tell the room what a crap buddy he was; tell them Benson only liked him for his prodigious dick; tell them he had come to the rooms to stop drinking but had had the misfortune to come slap bang wallop against the brick wall that was Benson, who didn't know anything about how to take someone through the Steps because he hadn't done the work on his lousy self...

That would, of course, have been unforgiveable on Allan's part. Though nothing was 'forbidden' in the meetings, crosstalk was strongly discouraged. Shares should, like medical interventions, *do no harm.* But Allan crosstalked. He voiced his resentment against Busy Sandra in no uncertain terms. These followed very much from Benson's own dark meditations.

At first, Busy Sandra sat looking stoically ahead, Patience on a monument smiling at the folly of outrageous unfortunates below her on the pavement. Her gaze focussed on the banner of the Twelve Steps on the wall. But as the drunken diatribe behind her continued, Benson saw her lips tightening, a deep plaque of frown between her eyes form and darken. Jack tried to intervene, but Allan would not stop. Had Busy Sandra not gossiped to Leila about the goings on in the cottage? Was she not someone who ran with the fox and hunted with the hounds? He, Allan, might not be sober, but he'd rather be drunk than have Busy Sandra's version of sobriety ... Then he stopped, or maybe paused for the next *in vino veritas* pronouncement. Jack said, 'Now then, Allan. We'll talk after the meeting.' And Allan nodded and slumped.

Silence. Then Busy Sandra manoeuvred herself, with the aid of her Zimmer, to a standing position. She turned the Zimmer towards the door and, slowly – and Benson had to hand it to her – with some dignity, made for it.

Condenser Jane opened it for her from a sitting position, and Busy Sandra exited.

A couple of women left the meeting – doubtless to see to Busy Sandra. A silence. Then Rob came in. He said that he hoped none of the newer members of QA had been put off by the behaviour at the meeting. A drinking fellow was welcome to attend a meeting but should never, ever, share. For what did he have to share, apart from his own failure to stay sober? Resentment was the number one killer of alcoholics and in the share just past it was plain why the founding members of the fellowship had come to that conclusion, for had resentment not been written on every word just spoken? At QA everyone came to meetings to learn how to steady themselves, to avoid all that emotional claptrap and mind-games that played tricks on the alchy. The first share had been of a ridiculous length for such a crowded meeting. Still, whatever happens at meetings and in life should provide an educational experience for those of us who have ears to hear. He thanked everyone and stopped.

Silence. Benson wondered about 'The work is more than the job' share. No. 'My day in Corwen and Holywell'? No.

Instead, a man whom Benson recognised but could not exactly place, came in and said that his wife was divorcing him. Yes, Benson thought, he's the chap who shared about being exposed in the papers. The fruit of surveillance? The wages of sin? The start of an honest life? Hard to tell. The man said he'd miss his wife and kids. He'd got himself a buddy who was helping him through the programme. His life was in tatters, but he was sober.

The chastened group told him to keep coming. Benson wondered how the kids were managing at school. Had the mean exposure impacted on them? Well, clearly it had, partly through the antics of their dad, partly because of the paper's nasty gossip. He said a prayer for those kids, and for the wife, whose life had also been turned upside down by events.

And Busy Sandra? Would she ever come back?

Well, if she had really 'got' the programme of QA she'd be examining her part in all this, praying for silly Allan. It didn't seem likely, but unlikelier things kept happening in QA.


That night, Benson, his hand clenched around Rob's cock, considered the day. What had he done right? What wrong? A bit of both, he decided. But all very interesting, especially Gulliver and Benson, the Lilliputian boss of prisoner restraint. Where does all that stuff come from? Then, giving Rob a goodnight squeeze, he dropped off into dreamless sleep.

# 50

On the beach things seemed to have calmed down. There were no further reports, nor any bloody sightings of dead dogs. Perhaps the culprit had made the point – whatever that was – that had been at the back of it. Perhaps the articles in the paper, headlined AN ATTACK ON OUR BEST FRIENDS had done the trick. Anyway, from the viewpoint of the Boss and his byelaws officer a noticeable discipline from dog-owners had come upon the beach. They no longer let their pets go free to wander and maraud. The Boss even hazarded the controversial opinion that maybe the dog-killer had performed a useful function that all the years of stickers, notices, free plastic bags, appeals to common sense ... had failed to manage.

In the area of Benson's area of influence, most of the boat-owners and jet-skiers had decided that it made life easier to avoid the ire of the bye-laws officer. They did their sea-safety courses, paid their fee and – on the whole – obeyed the bye-laws. True, he had had to stand stubbornly at the gate refusing gangs admittance to the beach in company with one jet-ski and determined to 'play swapsies' with it, despite the fact that not a one had done a course. But he managed this. Anyway, once he went off duty – and throughout those days and nights when the beach lifeguard service was not on duty – they had free access to the river. Gates had to be locked open. It was a rule of the sea that no vessel should be stuck on the sea side of it, unable to reach a safe haven. And, of course, this worked to allow launching by the unscrupulous.

The bye-laws did not seem to exist in written form – or if they did the Boss was keeping them very close to his chest. So Benson learned by listening to the Boss's observations as he leaned against the promenade wall watching the jet-skis zoom through the water, go round and round, churning it white all about them, or proceeded in a seventy-mile-an-hour straight trajectory, resembling Donald Campbell on Coniston Water, prior to making a turn of the steering wheel that produced a radical 120 degree turn and a plume of water in the shape of a wing not unlike Hockney's 'Bigger Splash'. 'That bugger's in the bathing area,' the Boss'd say. And Benson would enquire – not having seen anyone bathe – of what the bathing beach consisted. The Boss would say, 'Too fast! Too fuckin' fast!' And Benson would enquire about the speed to be recommended for vessels to the landward of the yellow buoys. '5 knots', the Boss said. The jet-skis didn't have an speedometer. Benson passed on 'five knots' to jet-skiers entering his domain and they would ask him what fuckin' five knots looked like. 'What does five knots look like?' Benson asked the Boss. 'The vehicle should remain four square in the water. No planing. Any planing and it's more than five knots.'

On crowded days there wasn't enough parking to be had along the promenade, and the Boss said that, as a special treat and because the tides were 'right', the permit holders could be permitted to leave their trailers and vehicles on the beach, 'close to the wall'. But on no account, not ever, were they to park on the concrete launching area that swept from the bottom of the slipway to the sea. 'Why not?' Benson had enquired. 'Because the lifeboats might need it, and they get totally pissed off if they've got to skirt the concrete and get sunbathers out of the way.'

Benson noted it all down and added it to his stock of bye-laws and wise safety suggestions. Among the latter, lifejackets were first and foremost. Most of the jet-skiers took his advice; most of the fishermen did not. They seemed to think that an oily, holey Aran would do the job. There was no law against not wearing a lifebelt – though in Ireland there was. He also recommended ship-to-shore VHF communication, which the fishermen usually had, but the jet-skiers didn't. The jet-skiers were more the mobile phone types, but the Boss did not approve of mobile phones. There were 'dead' spots in the estuary. The Boss also encouraged Benson to discourage jet-skiers from surfing the wakes of fast ferries, pilot boats and tugs. This was not in the bye-laws, but it offended The Boss greatly. The jet-skiers found it hugely exhilarating, of course, and were hopelessly addicted to the practice. Also, as this practice generally occurred at some distance from the shore, it was something that Benson could show his Nelson Eye to, and consign it to the drawer of things he couldn't change.

The Boss was also a stickler on the weather. The No Bathing flag went up most days. Not that bad weather stopped either fishermen or jet-skiers – the former accepted it while the latter adored it. But Benson often had his heart in his mouth when vessels launched or beached with rollers breaking in and a stiff inward current surfing up the river. Vessels tugged themselves out of the hands of those left to guard them. They came to semi-grief on the flat sandstone rocks to the south of the launching area. They drifted out to sea empty and lost and had to be rescued by fellow boat-users or, as a last resort, by the lifeboat.

Other hazards entered Benson's lexicon. One he re-remembered from his time on the beach patrol. Any ship passing up or down the estuary would create a wake. The trouble with this was that you could forget about it. The culprit might be heading for the horizon, the water showing no evidence of disturbance. Then, all of a sudden, large waves in quick succession would break on the shore, and cause mayhem to toddlers and people trying to launch or retrieve their boats.

Yachts and boats with no engine or an engine under five horsepower did not need a permit, though their cars needed one on the beach, which was, according to the Boss, owned by The Council, who had bought it from The Queen. No, he did not know how much she had made on the deal.

Anything inflatable was banned from the beach. This went from inflatable kayaks and dinghies to beach balls. Beach balls were watched like a hawk.

'I always get uneasy when I see a beach ball,' the Boss said.

'Kids chase them,' Benson said.

'They certainly do, Matron,' the Boss agreed. 'It was a beach ball that nearly did for me when I was a kid. So I know whereof I speak.'

'What happened?'

'You remember those beach balls that were flat at both ends? You don't see them now. When you threw them you never knew where they'd go. They bounced funny. Anyway they were the rage at the time. Well, I was swimming...'

He pointed with his pipe and Benson thought of *The Childhood of Raleigh*, a painting that showed an Old Salt telling stories by the sea, gesturing across the salty brine while two kids listened. He'd also seen an updating of that picture in the form of a cartoon showing a modern seafarer telling tales of the world away, and the two kids shivering and shaking at the horrors he was recounting. 'I was swimming and the beach ball got away from me. Being a kid who couldn't imagine life without his new beachball, I swam after it. But it had been picked up by the current. The tide was on its way out. A bit like now. Anyway, then I was caught by the current. If it hadn't been for a beach patrolman, I'd have been a gonner. He ran in and got to me, but he'd been taken by the current and we couldn't get back. We passed the Brazil buoy and were then swept between the lighthouse and the shore in a bugger of a ten-knot current with all sorts of eddies and whirlpools. All the time the chap held onto me and said everything would be all right. I just had to hang onto him.'

'And did you?'

'Course I fuckin' did. What sort of a wanker do you take me for, Matron? He was a well-built fellow. He seemed old to me, but he was probably only around twenty.'

'So what happened?'

'Somebody had called the lifeboat, but by the time he came the chap had swum us into shallow water and dragged me ashore. He just waved at the lifeboat crew and walked me back to me mates.'

'Lucky,' Benson said.

'But you know wha'? I was bellowing for me ball! There I was all safe and sound, my life returned to me, and all I could think of was the fuckin' ball bobbing away from me! Mad or wa? Course I was probably in shock. Anyway, the fellow took me back to me mates, gave me a hot drink and collected his kit – you could leave your kit on the beach in those days – and you know what he did? He gave me a half-crown and said, 'Get yourself another ball. Woolworths is open until half-five. But don't let me ever catch you playing with it close to the water. You may not be so lucky next time.'

'Wow,' Benson said, moved. 'Did you ever meet the beach patrolman again?'

'No, it was the end of the season. I looked the next season, but he wasn't on.'

'You've remembered it. though.'

'It's not something you forget. I think it got me where I am today. I started doing Lifesaving at school, and that led to a pool job when I left school and...' the Boss sighed, 'so on. So fuckin' on.'

'I know what you mean. It just goes, doesn't it?'

'You're telling me. That was a lifetime ago!'

'Time picks up speed as you get older.'

'Too right.'

'We've heard the chimes at midnight.'

'Come again?

'Remember you were telling us about the Rule of Twelfths on training day? It struck me that that's what happens with people too. Everything speeds up at the third and fourth hour of the tide – middle age. I'm just wondering if it'll slow down again for the last two 'hours' of the tide of my life.'

The Boss didn't say anything for a long moment. 'It doesn't look like it, does it? I mean, you're pretty much there ... the tide of your life is pretty much in – or out. You're into your sixth hour.'

'Am I?'

'I'd say so. Sixty is the start of the end, isn't it – no offence like?' Then, seeing Benson's gloomy face, The Boss pulled back a bit, 'Not that I'm far behind you.'

'There's not a lot we can do about it.'

'No.'

The Boss had gone off on Bossy business. He didn't leave Benson depressed, though. For he was thinking of the long-dead day when he had saved the boy who was to become his boss from a watery grave. Should he tell him? A side of him ached to. No. The fact that he had saved a life – and been blessed by meeting the life again after all those years – was consolation enough. To remind The Boss of the fact might embarrass him. And anyway, Benson had only been doing his job. And a side of him still felt that if he'd warned the kid sooner he wouldn't have had to save him.

Then, just as the pump of his virtue had filled the tyre of his virtuous sobriety past bursting, Benson saw himself revealing the secret if and when the Boss got at him for something. Typical, he thought. And he made a resolution not to give his ego the pleasure. Not to tell a single soul. Not even to tell Rob.

His thoughts turned to Allan. He had no idea what to do about him. Should he call in after work? Or should he have another good talk with Rob first? In the meantime he looked out to sea, admired the silver and blackness, the surge of fourth-hour incoming tide, the seagull taking up position by the hole in the ex paddle-boat pool waiting for its dinner to try and sneak by ... and said a prayer for Allan...


He was startled to hear his gate clang open. Two loud bangs. And there was Reg standing next to them, aiming daggers at Benson. 'The lifeboat's coming,' he shouted.

The lifeboat came, passed through and launched from the beach.

'Sorry about that,' Benson said. 'I lost attention.'

'Fuckin' faggot!' Reg shouted. He came at Benson, as if about to hit him. Then he drew back, contenting himself by placing both of his fists an inch from his eyes and shaking them at him. 'Fuckin' faggot!' he said again, quiet and malevolent. Then he walked off down to the beach to chat with the driver of the lifeboat tractor, leaving Benson to consider what had happened.

# 51

Benson considered.

A minute or two passed. He could hear his heart thumping in his head. Should he accept what Reg had done? No, it was unacceptable. I am not going to tolerate the intolerable. I'm fucking not! Time for action.

He raised his radio to his head, pressed the button and informed Sparks 1 and The Boss that the Senior Lifeguard had just called him a fucking faggot – and added injury to insult by using threatening behaviour. The Boss came on, and told his shaky bye-laws officer that he'd be coming soonest.

'Roger. Out,' Benson said.

He looked out at the sea. The lifeboat had launched. Reg was standing close to the tractor, his back to the sea, staring up at him. He would have heard the message, as would the rest of the lifeguards. Was he worried? Well, yes. But he could not see what else he could have done. His heart was no longer racing. He was calming. Reg could think what he liked about him, but he had no right to insult and threaten. No fucking right.

'You shouldn't've sworn on the radio,' the Boss told him.

'I was passing on what was said to me. Verbatim.'

'The radio is listened to by all and sundry. I told you about that during the course.'

'You're turning on me when you should be disciplining Reg.'

377

'I'll bring you together to talk it through.'

'There's nothing to talk about.'

The Boss walked down to the beach. He approached Reg and they talked for some minutes, facing out to sea.

I could put in a complaint. I could get Reg sacked. How am I going to be able to continue working with that man after what he's just said and done? No way. No fuckin' way.

He stopped himself. I'm using 'fucking' a lot. Way too much. I never used to swear. Am I becoming coarse?

He took time to think about 'coarse'. Life had most definitely coarsened him, and life back in New Brighton simply brought it out linguistically. There was, perhaps, some truth in what Reg had said. But that was between Benson and his conscience and his Higher Power. How dare he! How *dare* he!

At last the Boss, accompanied by Reg, approached.

'Reg has something to say to you,' the Boss said.

Benson looked at the Boss, then at Reg, who was squirming. Reg looked back at Benson then looked away. He paced up and down in front of him, a circumscribed version of his Duracell Bunny patrols up and down the beach. Lord, Benson thought, he's going to apologise.

And that is what Reg did. 'I'm sorry I called you a fuckin' faggot,' he said.

Benson did not believe Reg for a minute. He knew exactly what was going on; knew by the spitting way 'fuckin' faggot' had come out; the pulling-teeth body language of a man forced by the Boss and current council policy to eat his words.

'Right,' The Boss said. 'Reg has apologised. Are you willing to accept that and let the incident pass?'

'No,' Benson said.

378

'So what do you want?' the Boss asked, while Reg fumed up and down, striking the bar on the prom with his fist, perhaps wishing he had not let himself be persuaded to come out with the humiliating mouth-burning formula of words.

'I want it noted,' Benson said. 'I know I could put in a formal complaint. I don't accept the apology because it's as clear as the nose on your face that Reg doesn't mean it. He's eaten up with resentment that I wouldn't put in a word for him with Rob about his motorbike test. Apologies can wait until he's ready to give one that is sincere. But I want his behaviour noted in case such a thing happens again. I don't give a toss what he thinks of me – well I do, but I can't control that. But I do care about how he behaves towards me at work.'

'He's apologised!' the Boss said.

'That so-called apology was just one more insult,' Benson said. 'But let's leave that aside. An apology can't be forced, but appropriate behaviour from a Senior Lifeguard can be enforced.' *Yes! That was good!*

The Boss took Reg aside. He walked with him toward the hut. Then, as Reg continued on, passing the hut and walking off toward the fort, he returned to Benson.

'So you don't want to put in a complaint?' he asked.

'No. I just want you to note it.'

'Don't you think you're being a bit oversensitive and precious about this? I mean, people make remarks all the time. You know, manly banter and all that.'

'I know the difference between 'manly banter' and what Reg said and did to me,' Benson said. And he looked at the Boss, thinking about 'oversensitive and precious'. 'Maybe I am oversensitive and precious. I'll have to give some thought to that. But I can recognise a bully when he's

379

baying in my face. And I'm not willing to put up with it.'

'All right, Matron ... am I still allowed to call you 'Matron'?'

'I'm growing into the name,' Benson said. 'I'd miss it if you stopped. But you calling me Matron and Reg calling me a 'Fucking Faggot' are not the same thing.

'No.'

'I'm sorry this had to happen,' Benson said.

# 52

Benson, despite his best intentions, only made it as far as Allan's answerphone at the door of his flat. Allan answered, sounding grumpy and told Benson that he didn't want to see anyone. Benson – holding back the fact that he was not just *anyone* – responded that in his experience the time for seeing people was exactly when he didn't want to, when the pain of living in isolation with only his own thoughts for company was the easy option, when he was as sick as his thinking, critical of everything, not moving muscles, not changing thoughts, not in fellowship. 'Move a muscle; change a thought,' he repeated to Allan, but without much hope.

As often happened when he thought up sage advice to spread over others, the advice came back to stab Benson. Didn't he need someone to talk to as much as Allan? The confrontation with Reg and its aftermath had planted a wasp's nest of conflict in his head. Now the season on the beach no longer unrolled seamlessly a day at a time, but appeared to be a daily battle. Perhaps he should not have radioed in like that. He'd outed himself with the whole coast. At sign-out the lack of civility was worse than usual. Only Emma had given him a smile. Sparks hadn't said anything to him. And how would he face the coming weeks and months in company with wicked Reg?

'I'm sorry, Martin. I want to be alone,' Allan said.

Benson did not pursue it. For a start everything Allan

said was amplified hugely – doubtless at Allan's well-intentioned desire to assist the hard-of-hearing – but it inhibited Benson. The stream of people on their way in and out of Bargain Booze, were giving him looks. He tried, and mainly succeeded, in not being thrown off by this. But what if Allan – perhaps pissed – launched into Benson's fascination with his endowments! He'd never live it down ... weren't things already bad enough? And him still in his yellow and red lifeguard uniform!

'OK, Allan. You know where I am. We'll need to look at some things again. But have you thought that your obsession with all things Health and Safety might be getting between you and the sunlight of the spirit? And have you thought that speaking with your buddy might help your buddy as much as you?'

There, it was out.

"The Simpsons' is coming on,' Allan said. 'I'll be in touch.'

'Righto,' Benson informed the microphone. As he spoke, the sound of receiver being rattled onto cradle came through loud and clear and rude. Benson looked at the contraption, shook his head and made off up the hill.

He tried to wish Reg well. This was reckoned to defuse resentments. But in a trice he was thinking that he should have lodged a complaint with the council, made an issue of it. Bullying was frowned upon, wasn't it? No, I did the right thing. But that right thing means sharing a beach with Reg. He saw himself not sleeping that night. How could things ever be the same?

The trouble with Allan and his Health and Safety obsession is that it gets him into the habit of propelling his stinking thinking into the future, Benson thought. *What if* ... I do it. We all do it. I'm doing it now. But

Allan has a particularly bad case of it. We've only got today. That's it. The here and now. The past is sorted, done, and – if Step Four to Nine has been completed – dusted. The future is complete guesswork, or, in Allan's case – and often my own – an endless fantasy horror movie. Allan has a Sword of Damocles above his head the whole time: Will I be outed for my cottaging? Will someone see the video clip of me, pissed and rampant, parading my endowments in the lounge of a dismal terraced house in Seacombe? Will someone trip, fall, drown, collide, come to harm, suffer trauma, because of something I did or did not do? Some of these things might happen, but they were out of Allan's – and Benson's – hands. Why could he not see that? Why could he not *see?* It made such good sense to hand everything over to the Higher Power. The bottom line was that you couldn't sue Him/Her or It. It wouldn't suit the lawyers, but it would contribute immeasurably to Allan's quality of sobriety. He prayed that Allan would see. *O wad some Pow'r the giftie gie us To see oursels as others see us! It wad frae mony a blunder free us, And foolish notion: What airs in dress an' gait wad lea'e us, And ev'n devotion!*

Well, Benson had given Allan a hint as to what others might see lying at the nub of his trouble. Should he have done it? It wouldn't do any harm, would it? Allan could either accept or reject Benson's opinion. Mind you, it was not the usual thing to do in QA. It was generally left for fellows to come to their own conclusions about what was wrong with them. To decide for them was a kind of crosstalk.

Rob was home, but hadn't made a move to get the meal ready. Men!

Benson set about doing the necessary, and as Rob

passed through with a bike tyre draped across his shoulder, he asked him if they could have one of their heart-to-hearts. Rob said he'd been lent a DVD of vintage TT races. Benson said it shouldn't take long. He really needed a bit of a chat to help him make sense of one or two things. They hadn't had a chat in yonks...

'It's Allan, isn't it?'

'A bit. I'm not sure I'm doing a good job. The evidence isn't exactly encouraging, is it?'

'Hand it over. You're doing what you can. Anyway, I've always thought Allan was a bit of a tyre-kicker. Beneath all that Health and Safety stuff is a scared and selfish little boy – same as the rest of us. But he's not willing to take the action. He drinks when life doesn't go his way. A classic case. You're there for him, aren't you?'

'Yes. I popped round to see him just before, but he wouldn't let me in.'

'Remember I asked you if you were willing to go to any lengths when we met?'

'Of course, I do.'

'Well, tell Allan that. Read him the riot act.'

'I'll have a go.'

'You know from your own experience that a complete change of outlook is needed to stay sober. That's what Dr Jung told our founder. Where have you got him in The Steps?'

'Six and Seven,' Benson said.

'How was Allan's Step Five?'

'Pretty comprehensive. But he didn't bring up Health and Safety. Actually, I mentioned that to him over his answerphone today.'

'It's so obvious. But he won't let go of it, will he?'

'No.'

384

'What about that big dick of his?'

'He'd be lost without it.'

'But he doesn't see it as a problem?'

'He does and he doesn't.'

Rob sighed. 'All you can do is wait, Martin. Perhaps he hasn't suffered enough. When he's ready, he'll be back.'

'What'll happen if he doesn't come back?'

Rob shrugged. 'He'll die.'

'We all die,' Benson said.

'Not like alchies die.'

'No.'

'I met the Boss,' Rob said.

'Did you?'

'Just said I did. Anyway, he says you're pretty good at the job. You don't let those jet-skiers get away with anything, he says. He says you're pretty strict. He's not sure which planet you're from, but he's happy with the job you're putting in.

'How do you mean, 'Which planet'?'

'He thinks you're eccentric. No surprise there. I think you're eccentric. It's not a bad thing to be. I find it loveable.'

'How am I eccentric?'

'Let me count the ways...' Rob stopped. 'No, I'm not going to do that. Let's just say you don't come across as from round here. It's like living with a foreigner.' Seeing Benson about to protest, Rob continued. 'I like it. Wouldn't have you any other way. Anything else?'

'You know I went on a ride to Wales yesterday?'

'Yes?'

'Well, I went to see the cottage of this dead carver of Celtic love spoons.'

Rob twinkled and nodded. 'You did?'

'A sort of pilgrimage.'

'Yes?'

'Well, I found the place and wandered round. I'd hoped that some of the chap's skill would rub off on me. I was there to pay respect to his skill and craftsmanship. And do you know what I found?'

Rob was smiling. What was he smiling at?

He pushed on with the nub of his tragedy: 'I found a hoard of my pyrography work in a basket ... wooden spoons with 'Souvenir of Loggerheads' and lots of my poetry breadboards, axed into kindling.'

'Things you'd taken to Muriel to sell?'

'Yes.'

'That's fuckin' odd,' Rob said.

'You're telling me! I've been thinking that Muriel's been lying to me. Maybe she'd never been able to shift the stuff. Maybe she took it as a favour to make me feel good. And maybe you put her up to it, out of kindness.'

Rob shook his head. 'No, I wouldn't do that.'

Benson believed him.

'So what did Muriel do? Why did she keep encouraging me?'

'Don't know. Maybe she'd taken a shine to you, and wanted to help you. Muriel's eccentric too.'

'What does that *mean*?'

'It was a joke.'

'I don't find it funny. I was trying to help Muriel with her business as well, you know! I thought we were business partners.'

'Every time I went into her shop,' Rob said, 'I thought, 'Who buys this stuff?' I told her I thought a cafe for bikers would be a much better bet, but she wouldn't have it.'

'I bought one of the Celtic spoons. It's been on the table for a while.'

'Where?'

Benson pointed at the island mat. 'There.'

Rob picked it up. 'Not very practical,' he said. 'Nice carving. But you're not going to be able to get to the bottom of the honey jar with it. Say you got honey in that cage thing? It'd gum up the ball. And why are there two handles and one spoon? Anyway, I thought you said you'd stopped buying things. Haven't you got enough?'

'Forget it.' And Benson took the spoon out of Rob's hand and placed it back on the mat. 'It's symbolic, but it's obviously lost on you. Anyway, I only tried to buy it. Muriel gave it to me. As a Civil Partnership present.'

Rob nodded. 'How's it symbolic?'

'If you don't know, I'm not going to tell you.'

Rob smiled infuriatingly. 'Look at it this way, Martin,' he said. 'When you sell something, it is no longer yours. If Muriel decided your stock wasn't shifting and would be better warming an old man then it's her decision. It might be eccentric. It might be dishonest. But maybe there's love there. A bit for you in trying to get business for you and to flatter your ego. A bit for the old fellow. Who knows, maybe she gave some of his love spoons to some other old fellow to keep him warm? I don't know. But I do know that once you part with something you have no right to it. You've surrendered ownership and sent it on its way to continue its own story. There was this woman in hell. An angel came down to hell and said that God had decided to allow any of the damned who could come up with a good deed done during their lifetime to enter heaven. The woman rushed up to the angel and said, "I once gave an onion to a tramp." "Very good," said the angel. "Let's see if the onion will lift you into heaven." So the onion was put on the end of a piece of rope and the rope lowered from heaven into hell. The woman hung onto the onion and the angels pulled it up. But as it was rising above the pit, all the people in hell tried to grab hold of the rope that the woman was grasping hold of to lift her up. The woman shouted to all the damned, "Let go! It's MY onion!" The rope broke and everyone was back in hell. The woman hadn't really given away the onion in the first place.'

'Who told you that?' Benson asked.

'Jack. When my eldest crashed his car and couldn't afford the insurance on a new banger, I bought him a bike. Felt really good about it – amends and all that. But he left the bike out in the rain, didn't care for it. I complained to Jack. And that's what I got. And it's true. I think of it quite often. If I give a bit to charity and then, when I see starving people on the box, I think of my 'good' act and reassure myself that I am a good person, then I'm taking back the gift to make me ego grow.'

'But this isn't like that!' Benson said.

'No. Not quite. But there are similarities. You don't know the whole story, though. Accept what you know. Accept what you don't know. It's not your business.'

'I'll have to have a straight talk with Muriel when she gets back...' Benson said, thinking that he probably would not.

'If you insist,' Rob said, 'but don't let it weigh you down in the meantime. Let it go.'

Rob reached over and picked up the spoon. He turned it over and over in his hand. 'It's growing on me,' he said. 'Let's go upstairs.'

'The attic?'

'No. Fancy a bit of horizontal.'

'Righto.' He paused. there were other things to discuss
... 'I thought you wanted to watch that DVD.'

But bed and balm beckoned. Rob pushed him towards
the stairs and Benson, though Reg was back on his mind
aching for an airing, hadn't mentioned it to Rob. He
would, but just talking with him about other things, things
outside himself, had sent the scratchy thoughts away.

# 53

The following Saturday, The Boss addressed the lifeguards before sending them off to the beaches. He informed them that, while they had been using their time hanging out at Talula's Tavern and around the Crabapple Centre he, as a full-time servant of The Council, had been run ragged getting the relevant authorities to take away dead dogs. Doubtless all knew that New Brighton had seen a spate of dog-killing. This, after a short pause for breath by the assailant, had now spread to other locations around the coastline. Four more dearly-beloved pets had bitten the dust. All lifeguards were to be on the look-out. Dog-lovers were up in arms. The council switchboards were glowing red-hot with all the people ringing in about the massacre of pets. The murderer's weapon, it could be revealed, was probably a crossbow. Whoever he or she might be, he was a subtle bugger, using the myriad of groynes laid across the beaches to take his aim and fire, then somehow melting away to join the decent council-taxpayers on the beach. He had during the week used the sandhills that backed some areas of the coast to perform his wicked acts. Clearly, there was a knobhead on the loose. But he was a clever knobhead, who had a thing against canines. Lifeguards should keep eyes peeled and radio in any suspicious occurrences at once.

He also informed the assembled that Reg was being sent to Hilbre in charge of a pedal cycle with which, having failed to pass his motorcycle test, he would patrol the treacherous sands and banks.

Benson wandered down to his gate, thanking his Higher Power fulsomely for relieving him of Reg's presence. True, he was no longer going to have the daily educational experience of being around someone who was, to say the least, *difficult*. All his spiritual reading told Benson that people like Reg should open up pages on his own character that remained shut while surrounded by easy people. Still, he'd had a taste of that, hadn't he? His Higher Power knew he was, to say the least, a weak vessel – oversensitive and on the odd occasion a teeny bit precious. The bye-laws job gave him, he reckoned, more than enough of the types of people who did not operate according to Benson's own preferred program. Maybe that was enough for now. Maybe his Higher Power was giving him a break. He thanked Him, Her, It, for that.

As to the dog-killer, what did he hope to achieve? Had a dog bitten him? Had a loved one been blinded by the worms in dog dirt getting into his eyes? Had he been savaged in his childhood? Or was it just killing for its own sake – one more piece of social madness?

He spent the day, in company with a young lifeguard called Stu who'd been seduced back from Hilbre with the promise that he'd be the controller of the lifeguards' jet-ski. Stu was easy to be around, and seemed to know all Bob Dylan's songs by heart. They developed a game based on these. Benson would sing the first word of his arsenal of songs and see if Stu could continue. He could. But, as he played this most satisfactory game, Benson was looking at everyone who passed, wondering if their shopping bags or knapsacks might contain a weapon.

Then, in mid-afternoon, a car drove up and parked on

Benson's cross-hatch markings. Stu was off patrolling, The Boss off on bossy business. The cross-hatch, as big yellow letters proclaimed, were for emergency vehicles only. Benson approached the passenger window. The window went down. A man in a suit asked if he was the bye-laws officer.

'Yes.'

'Then you're the man I want to see.'

The man got out of the car and showed Benson his badge. This asserted that the man was called Derek Clitherow and that he was an inspector in Special Branch.

'I suppose you can park here then,' Benson said. 'Still, be prepared to move if the lifeboat or any launching boats approach.'

'Fine,' the man said. 'This shouldn't take long. I'm only here to fill you in on a few things. You control access to the estuary from here, don't you?'

Benson nodded as his chest swelled at the elevated job description. *Ego, get down!*

'Right. Well, I've got two things to talk to you about ... We've done a risk assessment and...'

A large red four-by-four, towing a large white fishing boat, approached the gate. 'Sorry to interrupt,' Benson said. 'I've got to see to this. And your vehicle...'

'I'll move it.'

'That would be better. There are parking places on the far side of the railings.'

While the man moved his car, Benson checked the driver's ID. He took the plastic card and compared it with the registration number on the vehicle. Then he noted that the number on the boat backed up the fact that it belonged to the insured vehicle. Then, to fill in time and wait for the man to move his vehicle out of the way, he asked about lifebelts, two-way radios, notification of the Coastguard. He told the driver – who looked really bored – that the tide was on its way in. It was a big one. Strong currents. Extra care needed to be taken in launching. Soft sand was becoming a hazard on the seaward side of the launching area. Please bring the vehicle back to the promenade. There was plenty of parking.

He then opened the gate and wished the boat-owners a pleasant day. They passed through. He closed the gate, and saw the man from Special Branch was back, leaning against the railings next to his tea-making equipment.

'Thanks for moving your car,' Benson said.

The man nodded. 'This won't take long. I can see you're making checks. We have two concerns about boats – and especially personal water craft – on the Estuary. One is that they're a great means for illegal drugs and contraband to enter the country. All it takes is for a stash to be dropped off the side of a ship, then straight up your slipway and on sale the same day. The other is that a jet-ski is a perfect vehicle for the delivery of a bomb. As you probably know, oil tankers and gas liquid ships come up and down the estuary on a daily basis. There's nothing to stop a bomber from using a jet-ski to slam into the hull of a ship carrying an inflammable cargo. And if that happened...'

'But...' Benson said.

'I know you're not a policeman. All I want you to do is keep a weather-eye out. Do you keep a log of the boats that pass through the gate?'

'Yes. It's a bit rough, though. Sometimes, if I'm busy, I miss some. I generally remember the permit numbers, but the vehicle numbers sometimes escape me.'

'That's fair enough. But if you could keep a note from

now on, it would be useful. I'll come down from time to time and take a copy to run checks.'

'You think this is a real threat, do you?'

'I don't know that. But we've got to think outside the box to stay ahead of smugglers and terrorists. This is a risky area because of the ocean-going vessels. Your gate is the only place on this side that can be used for launching. The other slipways are all locked shut ... am I right?'

'We've got keys, and so has the RNLI. I think the council beach cleaners have as well.'

'What I'd like you to look out for are any vessels that are new to you. The ones who come down frequently are probably less of a risk – though they might be smugglers. I've been to the permit issuers and asked them to inform me of any new people who might ask for permits. This isn't fail-safe. The permits could easily be forged.'

'But I can't stop anyone with a permit from getting past the gate, can I?'

'That depends on the risk you think they pose.'

'What are the signs?'

'Nervousness. Foreign appearance ... I'll talk to your boss about all that. I'm actually on my way to see him at the HQ.'

'Right,' Benson said. 'But you know we're only on duty when the kids are off, don't you? And in the evenings we leave the gate locked open. Wouldn't it make more sense for smugglers and terrorists to wait to launch until then?'

'It might, yes. But we have the responsibility to police those times. The cameras over there, and other methods I won't bore you with, are in place. All I'm asking is that when you're here you keep a weather-eye out.'

'Right-o,' Benson said.

The man refused Benson's offer of a cup of tea, and left, leaving the bye-laws officer with plenty to think about. 'The work is more than the job,' he thought, mentally adding to the share he knew he would edify his fellows with at some meeting of QA in the near future. A dog-killer to watch out for. Smugglers to spot. Terrorists to refuse entry! Beach balls to track. Notes to keep. Tea to make. First Aid to give. Lost children to mind. Public to chat to about the old days. Talk about a front-line service! I'm indispensable! I'm a fucking big useful bugger, that's what I am! But I won't be able to mention the hush-hush aspects of the job. No, I won't. I must exercise restraint in pen and tongue, that's what I must do. He looked at the card. 'Derek Clitherow', that's the man's name. I wonder if he's any relation to Laurence Clitherow. Probably not, but. That detective could be the son – no grandson – of Clitherow from school. He must ask him, if they ever met again. A side of him hoped they wouldn't.

Clitherow. He'd gone to Oxford. They'd met a few times during the vacs, but it hadn't been the same. Before he'd finished at Aberystwyth, they'd lost touch completely. For a start Clitherow had a steady girlfriend. Benson had phoned and written, but seldom got a reply. When they did meet up the girlfriend was usually in tow, and this closed the door on both reminiscence of their time in the sixth form – at least the good bits – and Benson opening up about his adventures since. Clitherow had never said in so many words that he had put away such childish things. After his initial degree, he hoped to study medicine. His girlfriend – what was her name? – was already doing so.

So they had grown apart. Benson, with his dithery uncertainty about his future apart from the fact that he wanted Dearest Him and some spectacular sex – and hoping that lifelong commitment after a short search would bring him both in one neat package – was not particularly career-oriented. None of the jobs on offer to Arts graduates enthused him: Teacher, Probation Officer ... not quite him.

He'd met Clitherow last when he'd come home – late – from his summer in New York. His job there – nurses' aid – had suited him. He'd felt a freedom there that he could not feel in England. But a phone call from Dad had been sufficient to make him pack his bags and return home to finish his degree. Was that the moment of life that had dictated his trajectory? An uncertainty, a willingness to cave in and please, a worm of cowardice and people-pleasing (for not to please people made him feel lousy about himself) that had sent him flying, and flying about the world, looking for a place where he would be happy and not himself, find a new self in a new geography, a new cross-hatch of longitude and latitude?

And now, on this cross-hatch entrance to a council gate, he was back where he had started, but convinced that the adventure had been here all the time. The real travel was within. *And you – if you have no foot – choose to journey into yourself.*

On the positive side, he knew, he was a lucky bugger. Buggers can't be choosers. Not that he was much of a bugger. An aged catamite is what he was. Dictionary Definition: A sodomite's minion. In the days when he'd tiptoed about the free videos on porn sites – before Rob found him at it and told him what a corrosive pastime it was, and backed up his lesson by getting Lecky Leonard to come in and place strong, Benson-foxing child-protection on the computer – he had seen what catamites got. In that porn world, they got little in the way of respect – putting it mildly. They were used and abused and passed round. And that use and abuse and passing round thrilled him as he peered into the desktop. The buggers had big dicks, insatiable appetites and shocking manners. They were real men, whatever that meant. But, according to that world, the sucker and sodomite's minion was of little value. He got his rocks off in his head, while his cock – a pale reflection of the thrusting male – lolled on his front, a waste of space. They took the most prodigious cocks, the sort of thing that would have required of Benson a week's notice in writing and the sort of careful docking required by space capsules at the edges of space.

But, sitting in the ray-glow of the screen, Benson had always envied the passive member of the team, the bitch being ruined by the fearsome butch. Were these butches really gay? Hard to say. Straight porn was pretty similar, women appearing to love the attentions of rough, hugely-endowed fuckers, and as many as possible.

'They cry afterwards,' Rob had said. 'Every one of them is worth more than that.'

Rob had said a lot more than that, too. And Benson had agreed with him. Rob said that he'd watched porn, but it always made him feel wretched, hollowed out. Until the next time. He'd prayed about it, he said. And one night he watched a gay orgy and the distress of the man taking a gang of probably-drugged men. It brought him excitement until there was a split-second look by the fellow – his mouth full of cock, his body stained with semen, a cock up his arse – looking at the camera. Just a pair of eyes which said that he'd got into something that was too much for him, that he was being subjected to torture.

He wanted everything to be over and all right. He wanted to amend his life but didn't know how. He needed the money. He...

'I saw the sad story,' Rob said. And I saw my part in it. Through that damned machine I was creating the market for his pain. I spoke to Jack, who hit the roof. And I stopped.'

These days Benson prayed for the people in porn films, and wished them a happy outcome. But he reserved his most fervent prayers for the catamites, for they threw themselves through the screen at him and told him what he had been but, with Rob, no longer was. He had been stumbled over at a low point in his life, and lifted up. Not that life was easy. No, but he had been stumbled over, and then stumbled into recovery in all sorts of areas. He looked back at his old self as that foreign country, where the inhabitants did things differently, went with the flow, drowned the voice of conscience with drink, and endless Rubik's cubes of rationalisation.

All changed. A terrible – and terribly difficult – beauty was born.

On Monday he rang Derek Clitherow to ask him if by any chance he was related to his old friend Laurence. He was. And Laurence – his grandfather – still lived in Warren Drive, but was bedridden following a stroke. The death of his wife, everyone agreed, had brought it on.

'I went to school with your grandfather, but we lost touch,' Benson said. 'Do you think he'd like me to visit?'

'I'm sure he would,' Peter Clitherow said. 'Apart from the family and an endless succession of carers he doesn't see many people. A visit from an old chum might do him the world of good.'

# 54

That night, after the meeting, Condenser Jane came up to Benson and asked for a word. He walked a few yards down the street and away from the chatting QAers with her, wondering if he should bring up his own concerns about his condenser boiler at home and its failure to heat water without a hell of a wait, the clunking noises it made when under the slightest stress, its total inability to step into the shoes of the ancient Glow-Worm he had inherited when he bought the house.

'Have you heard about Allan?' Condenser Jane asked.

'Heard what?'

'He's under arrest.'

'He isn't.'

'He is. Busy Sandra told me.'

Benson considered this. Busy Sandra had been sitting next to him at the meeting. They had talked about her future, but no mention had been made of Allan. 'Did she indeed?'

'She's devastated.'

'Well...' Benson stopped himself. He had been about to boil over about Busy Sandra, to cast doubt of her 'devastated' state; to imitate Busy Sandra's voice, to show his true opinion of Busy Sandra. But the hammer paused a fraction above the anvil. '...I expect Allan is pretty devastated too. Did Sandra say why he's been arrested? Has it something to do with the unfortuate toilet incident?'

'No. Allan went to the police station and confessed.'

'Confessed to what?'

Condenser Jane did not reply. She looked around uneasily.

'Confessed to what?'

'I'm not supposed to say,' Condenser Jane said.

'Busy Sandra told you, but you're not supposed to say?'

'She made me promise to keep schtum.'

'So did Busy Sandra say, 'I'm telling you about Allan's arrest but don't tell anyone why?' Is that what she said? Well...' The hammer raised high in the air and slammed down hard on the anvil like the Solti version of *Siegfried* Act 1. 'Well, that's pretty rich! She told Allan he'd be OK if he accepted a caution. If he's been arrested we can safely make the assumption that it wasn't the end of the matter. As it is, Allan's not been the same since then. I'm not surprised Busy Sandra doesn't want us to know.'

Condenser Jane shuffled about.

'So why tell me, but not tell me?'

'You're his buddy.'

'So why didn't Busy Sandra tell me?'

Condenser Jane shrugged. He could see that shrug serving to condemn many a perfectly serviceable Glow-Worm to the scrapheap.

Benson made to walk away.

'He confessed to killing dogs,' Condenser Jane said.

Benson stopped. Not knowing how, he rewound his movements of the five seconds just gone into the lost-forever past and was startled to find himself back staring into Condenser Jane's brown eyes. 'He confessed to killing dogs?'

Condenser Jane nodded glumly. 'Don't tell Sandra I told you.'

Benson ignored this. 'Allan confessed to killing dogs?' he repeated.

And as Jane reiterated that that was what Allan had done, and looked round for a way of escape from Benson's gimlet glare, Benson was thinking how it made sense in a way. During all his ruminations about the motivation of the dog-killer, his thoughts had kept coming back to his own resentment of their shit all over the place, the inconsiderate dog-owners who did not pick up, did not heed council notices about the health risks of dog dirt, the danger of unmuzzled, unleashed dogs to innocent people, the talk he heard on the beach about 'dogs owning the fuckin' place', about 'love me; love my dog.' The damned *entitlement* of the dog-owners. *We need a cull...*

Hadn't the Boss said that the councillors were afraid of losing the votes of the barmy army of dog-owners if they tackled the issue head-on? Moves to close beaches to canines during the summer months had been dropped. He'd heard murmurs from people startled by growling dogs that the culprits needed 'putting down'.

And Allan, devoted as he was to all things healthful and safe, had found that he was incapable of changing this. Knowing a bit about how he worried about his job, how he saw Health and Safety as the core of his belief system, he could see how an obsession had grown in his mind, robbing him of all serenity, until he'd started on his mad enterprise ... if that was indeed the case. And where had that led? Back to the bottle. Or had the bottle come first, uncorking the madness of his serial killing?

'I'd better be going,' Condenser Jane was saying. 'I'm dead busy in the morning.'

Benson was startled back.

'So is Allan still in the police station?'

401

'I should think so. They wouldn't just let him go, would they? Not after confessing to something like that. Anyway,' she added, 'people would want to lynch him. Busy Sandra said they'd probably have to keep him in gaol for his own protection.'

Benson nodded. 'Thanks for telling me, Jane.'

'How's the boiler?'

He told Jane – politely but firmly and with the merest touch of ambiguity – that he couldn't get his head around the boiler at present. 'Thanks for asking, though,' he said, making up the hill toward home and hoping Rob would be back.

# 55

'The daft fuckin' bugger!' Rob said after Benson had recounted the news an hour later. 'Talk about self-will run riot!'

'I should have...' Benson said.

'Don't start,' Rob said. 'You buddied Allan to the best of your ability. The dog-killing started around the time when you started on the beach, so all the time you've been buddying Allan he's been at it. It's like he'd plotted to do the best he could to really give his buddy grief. None of it came up in his Step Five, did it? He never once hinted what he was up to, did he? The one bit of craziness that was bound to make him drink. You'd've thought that the caution would have reined him in, but not a bit of it! Allan had been planning to take potshots at dogs for yonks. He'd bought the crossbow – God knows where – and turned himself into the William Tell of New Brighton. And he told you bugger all about what was eating him. If an alchy doesn't tell you the whole truth, you can't be expected to know. This is an honest programme. Take away honesty and there's no programme.'

'I think he's leapt ahead of himself,' Benson said charitably. 'He's decided to go and make amends to the people he's harmed.'

That's Step nine,' Rob said. 'You remember how I told you that Step Nine – *made direct amends to all the people we had harmed except when to do so would injure them or others* – takes a deal of thought and sobriety to finish. You don't just apologise and admit to everybody without thinking it through and talking about it with your buddy. Remember how long it took you to make amends to your old headmaster?'

Benson nodded glumly. 'Years,' he said.

'Yes. You had to be sure that approaching that person would not cause that person harm. You had to realise what cleaning your side of the street actually *meant*. If you'd known that Allan had been doing what he's been doing, you would have made him give the matter a lot of thought before he turned himself over to the busies. First the harmful behaviours would have to stop. Next he'd have to consider the harm caused and change his attitude to dogs and dog owners, and third he'd have to consider the implications for himself. But Allan, probably drunk, decides to turn himself into a martyr by going to the cop shop and ruining his whole life. Daft fuckin' bugger!'

'So what should I do?'

'Nothing,' Rob said. 'Let him stew.'

This was not a totally unexpected response from Rob. But Benson could not help himself. 'But...' he said.

'But fuckin' wa?' Rob said. 'But fuckin' nothin'! If Allan's ever goin' to be picked up, he's going to be picked up by his Higher Power. He's going to be picked up by a complete revolution within. He's got to realise – not know, *realise* – that he's hit bottom. Him being an alchy is just a symptom of a much larger disease. And maybe all this: the caution, his slavery to his own big cock, his obsession with Health and Safety – when was this world *ever* a healthy and safe place to be? – will have to be tackled. Maybe he knows now if he's in the cop shop lock-up that he has well and truly hit bottom. Maybe he's where you were when you passed out pissed on the prom, when Jack found himself at Shannon Airport when he should have been at work at Vauxhall's, when...'

'I didn't know that.'

'Well, you know now. He started on this Sunday night binge in Liverpool and still doesn't remember how he came to in the meditation room at the airport the following Thursday. Almost a whole lost working week. Lucky for him an alchy cleaner found him there and Twelve-Stepped him. Anyhow, we're not taking Jack's inventory. The thing is that Allan has got to wake up to himself. We can assist, but only when he realises he needs help to get through the whole programme. Do I make myself clear?'

'Yes,' Benson said. 'I know you're right.'

'Too right I'm right. Wait for Allan to get in touch.'

'OK,' Benson said.

'Your chum Reg had his second go at a test today...'

'Did you fail him?'

'No. He passed with flying colours. Just a couple of things. He was within an inch of putting his foot down during the 180-degree turn, but he managed not to.'

'He'll be pleased. He doesn't like patrolling on a bike.'

'He mentioned you. Said you made him really take the exam seriously.'

'Mmm,' Benson said. 'What did you say?'

'I said he should think about taking the advanced courses.'

'I should too.'

'Yes,' Rob said,' you should.'

'I should send Reg a card.'

'Might be a good idea . I fancy a bath after all this,' Rob said.

405

'Is there room for a little one? I need a bit of relaxation after tonight, as well,' Benson said.

'OK,' Rob said. 'But how about you taking the role of the bossy slipper-bath superintendent? You can do me if you like.'

'Righto,' Benson said, chuffed as anything.

'You were too posh for slipper baths, I suppose. Had a bath in the house when you were a nipper, eh?'

'Yes.'

'I'd be sent to the corpy baths every week for one. There was a fellow there who cleaned the baths, gave us towels, ran the water. He had this big brass spanner – they didn't trust the public with the taps – and he'd run the bath. Deep as you wanted. Anyway this fellow was queer as a threepenny-bit. He'd often give us a gobble when he came in to add some hot with his spanner.'

'You've never told me that. Not very professional. How old were you?'

'Never thought much about it. Just a bit of a bonus come bath night. Anyroad, there's a lot I haven't told you. Tonight I'd like a nice slow screw from you, like the sort of thing I usually do for you. Think you're up for it?'

'I thought you'd never ask.'

'Well, I'm asking. Not that I think it's going to become a routine. I wouldn't like you to start expecting it every time. Don't think I'm built for it. Not like you.'

'You reckon I'm built for it, do you?'

'Oh, yeah,' Rob said. 'Defo. Fuckin' defo.'

They mounted the stairs.

# 56

'O Wisdom and Spirit of the Universe,' Benson prayed
– contentedly sleepless beside a snoring Rob – 'Thank
you for another sober day. Sorry about all the things
undone I should have done; all the things done I should
not have done. Thanks for the meeting and all the people
there. Bless Kirsty Wark and Condenser Jane and Busy
Sandra. Bless Reg. Thanks for getting him through his
bike test. Help Health- and-safety Allan, all the fellows
suffering because of the unfortunate cottaging incident,
and make us satisfied to worship the pinnacle of your
creative achievements in a setting that is becoming. As
you probably know, Allan is spending the night in a prison
cell. I feel bad about this even though Rob says it's not
my fault. It's probably my ego that wants me to be a
successful buddy. In fact, it might be good for my humility
if the enterprise turns to shit. And, of course, Rob may
well be right in asserting that Allan might need to touch
bottom in order to gain sobriety and happiness in the
fellowship of QA. What he did – allegedly – was wrong.
I saw the effect it had on Lynn and other dog owners.
They were, as they said themselves, completely devastated.
A dog is a fine example of your creativity, but I can
sympathise with Allan's attitude in a way. There are far
too many of them – and far too many owners who let
their dogs run riot. Not the dogs' fault. I should have
realised something was amiss when Allan brought me that

parcel. I thought it might be porn, but I suppose it could have been a crossbow. Had I taken it and kept it that would have stopped Allan from using it. But he said nothing to me. I thought I was doing the right thing. Then there was the shocking state of the door, Lord. It really stood out in an otherwise pristine flat. And I had to hand it to Allan then that even though he'd been drinking he had managed not to let his standards slip – except for the door. But I accepted his explanation that they had been there when he'd moved in. Now, though no DIYer myself, Jesus, I know that it's dead easy to get a panel cut to size at B & Q to place over an unsightly door. A bit of wood glue – which is apparently stronger than the wood itself, though that does stretch credibility rather – and everything's shipshape in no time. So why hadn't he gone to that small trouble? Well, he was using it for target practice. Thinking about the layout of that door, there's a clear run from one end of the flat to the other. So, if Allan had sat on the settee by the sea-facing window he could have aimed a crossbow at the door and had a ten yard – at least – range to perfect his aim. It all makes sense to me now, but I didn't get it then. What's going to become of Allan? What? He'll probably lose his job, go to gaol. And what might happen to him in gaol? It doesn't bear thinking about. Still, he might find a QA meeting in gaol and be able to get some sobriety in. He might learn a trade that he could use when he comes out. Health and Safety won't be open to him anymore, that's for sure. He'd be too much of a risk factor to be allowed near it. What happens to his pension? What happens to his sobriety – assuming he's able to get some time between himself and a drink? I place under your kindly feathers all of us poor souls born to die. All those men I used shabbily or shallowly. All my brothers who have died – and my sisters too. Simple Wisdom of the Universe, show me the way. Amen.'

'P.S. I've been thinking of looking up Laurence Clitherow. But I'm embarrassed. Don't know what I'll find. Don't know what he will think. So much time has passed. Guide my steps.'

Then, remembering a trifle late in the prayer, that Rob thought silence from a still and thought-free heart was the best kind of prayer – for did not the Higher Power know everything anyway? – Benson lapsed into silence and deep breathing which, as was usually the case, merged seamlessly, like a babbling brook and the serene ocean, into sleep.

# 57

'So. How was it for you, Martin?'

Benson had to lean close to Clitherow to hear.

'This and that. Teaching abroad. Wandering. Looking about.'

'That's a precis.' Clitherow said. He said it three times before Benson got it.

'I was never much use at Precis,' Benson said, 'Always thought I'd miss something important out. But the full story left a lot out, too. I'm sorry we lost touch. You know what Yeats says, don't you?'

'What?'

'*Be not unkind or proud, But think of old friends the most; Time's bitter flood will rise. Your beauty vanish and be lost For all eyes but these eyes.*'

'I didn't know you at first.'

'I knew you. All these people in your life! Children, grandchildren, great-grandchildren. You a consultant and everything. You've had a big life.'

'It happened. I had Mary. Met her at Oxford. She did it all. I just went along for the ride.'

'You ploughed some really deep furrows. I just scratched about. I never really got the hang of things.'

'Dearest Him?'

'You remember that? Funny you should mention that. Not until I came back here. I flitted from flower to flower. Quite outrageously sometimes. But now I think I have

410

found a friend. The Friend. Not what I'd expected.'

'That's good, isn't it. *See the place for the very first time...*'

'Yes.' *Yes!*

'How did we lose touch?'

'A day at a time. Mind-forg'd manacles.'

'Don't understand.'

'Time passing. Embarrassment. *What would Clitherow think if I just turned up after all this time?* Pride. You going from strength to strength. Me a cabin-class Flying Dutchman.'

' "Mind-forg'd manacles". A good phrase.'

'Blake,' Benson said. 'Our minds chain us into patterns of behaviour. But think about the double meaning of 'forged'. It means to make something of metal using heat. But it also means to counterfeit. I have let my mind tell me a good many lies in my time.'

'Lies?'

'About people, places, things, situations. My mind's stopped me from doing things I should have done and retreating from things I should have embraced. You, for instance.'

'But you got here today?'

'I did, didn't I? Well, you see, Laurence, I'm trying to change. Not fast. Worn-out tools and that. I suppose I'll shuffle off much as I am. Thing is, these days I have better insights into myself. I no longer look at the manacles and think they are pretty bangles.'

'What happened?'

As Benson was considering how to reply, the door of Laurence's bedroom opened and two women came in. They were wearing maroon uniforms. Benson greeted them, but he did not get a reply. They went straight to a table in one corner of the room and started looking for something.

411

'OK, are we, Laurence?' one said. Then she disappeared into the bathroom while Laurence was framing his response.

'I'll go shall I, Laurence?' Benson asked.

'Maybe better,' Laurence whispered back. 'I don't want you to see me on the cross.'

Benson squeezed his hand, got up and left the room, noting that the two women were talking to one another, not seeming, Benson thought, to be aware who they were there for.

He stood still in the old hall, wondering which door to open. It was forty years since he'd been in this house. Much came back: the stained-glass window on the sweep of stairs, the heavy wood panels ... but more than anything else, the remembrance of how he'd felt back then in this house. Mrs Clitherow was there. And Doctor Clitherow, liberal and risque. He'd come alive here, imagined a future of surprise and possibility. This hall, with Clitherow now being seen to by a couple of carers who did not seem that caring, had flashed in front of his mind's eye times past computation. Meeting Clitherow and his family had changed things, and then he'd left them behind as the possibilities they'd suggested might exist took over.

Benson considered the doors. He knocked on one. A woman's voice said 'Come in' and Benson opened it.

A woman with a baby on her knee sat facing him inside the room. Benson had not seen her before.

'I'm Sarah,' she said, 'Derek's wife. And this is Martin.' *Martin!*

'Hello,' Benson said. 'I left Laurence because the carers have come.'

'They won't be long. Cup of tea?'

'No, thanks. I'm fine.'

'Laurence doesn't get on with the carers. It'll do him

412

the world of good to see you. You will come again, won't you?'

'I will. Of course.'

'He's made great strides since the stroke. He can move. His speech is better, but what he needs is stimulation. A speech therapist comes in. He's got all sort of exercises to do, but it's daily conversation and practice and motivation that he needs.'

'I can have a go at that. I'd like to.'

'Would you?'

'Yes.'

The carers knocked at the door. Sarah signed a form they presented to her. They left without saying anything to Benson.

Sarah looked at Benson and Benson looked back. 'They don't seem very chirpy,' Benson observed.

'I don't think they're treated very well. Some of them are wonderful. Some...'

'TLC,' Benson said.

'Yes. Those that have it shine. Those that don't...' Sarah paused, 'don't.'

'The work is more than the job,' Benson said.

'Exactly,' Sarah said.

'Shall I go and see Laurence now?'

'That would be great. It's his nap time, though. If he drops off, just leave.'

'You must tell me the best times for me to come.'

'Every day's different, but I'll have a go,' Sarah said. 'A lot of his friends from the hospital have visited, but they don't come back as regularly as Laurence would like. I think they find themselves at a loss.'

Benson was tempted to tell Sarah that he would not be like that. He was busy promising his Higher Power that he would commit even at this late stage to proving himself to be a good friend, a friend in deed, to Laurence. After all, so much of his Step Four had been about things not done that he should have done. How could he make amends for these things not done other than by action? And it would be a pleasure. He might be able to play some small part in bringing Laurence back, just as Rob and all the fellows at QA had played their parts in bringing Benson back.

But he didn't make any promises. 'I'll go and see how he is,' Benson said.

He was back in the hall and in a trice it brought back those momentous visits. He stumbled over himself when young as he opened the door of Laurence's room. 'I'm free! Are you free?' he asked.

# 58

The summer – together with the kids' summer holidays – came. They brought for Benson a seven-day-week work schedule on the beach that was nothing short of gruelling. It was not that the days worked him off his feet; the weather turned poor as soon as the kids were off. But the long hours at the top of his slipway with wind blowing and tides advancing and retreating passed slowly and drained him.

The end of July brought him to his sixtieth birthday, which Rob forgot. He received only one card, from the mother of Emerson – who never forgot Benson from the sad mists of eighties antiquity. But this card, handed to him on the day fresh from the doorstep by Rob, did not remind Rob of birthdays past. Benson acknowledged the day, but decided he did not want attention drawn to it. Let it pass like any normal day.

Anyway, he'd seen the cards people sent for the sixtieth. Jokes about memory loss, penile dysfunction, baldness, even the approach of the Grim Reaper, seemed to predominate, and had replaced the racing cars, pipes, stags-at-bay of middle years. Benson acknowledged the day by thinking it was probably time he grew up and put aside childish things.


He rode out to the open prison in deepest Cheshire to

visit Allan, as he did every Thursday evening. The first time he'd gone, he was full of fear as to what might be in store. But in that case, as often happened, his imaginings were much worse than the real thing: a bit like his whole life. The prison seemed more like a disciplined holiday camp than the prison of his imaginings. He'd come to reception, been searched and waited in a pleasant room with a view of fields for Allan to make an appearance. When he came in, his hair cut short, the navy and white uniform hugging his slim body and the thin trousers showing Allan's endowments off to advantage, Benson thought that if only Allan could keep up the sartorial and tonsorial insights pushed on him by the prison service, he would do very well on the outside.

Allan had no complaints. He was not drinking – not that any was on offer. He attended meetings in prison and was going through the Steps with the input of Benson, a fellow prisoner called Bert and a warder called Archie.

'Today's my sixtieth birthday,' Benson told Allan that day.

'Happy birthday,' Allan said.

'I don't feel sixty.'

'You look it, though.'

'Do I? Thanks.'

'Honesty is the best policy,' Allan said.

'I suppose so.'

'No 'suppose' about it!'

'I suppose not. However, as in so much else, I find that what we call 'honesty' can often contain other less desirable qualities.'

'Like what for instance?'

'Lack of sensitivity, self-righteousness, showing off. I

know my version of 'honesty' often does. I think I'm being honest, but don't notice that I'm putting the boot in. I'm thinking of a person in the room who does not come up to the high standards I fancy I have for myself.'

'Don't get you.'

'Let's take an example: I tell people how much I love the sound of my own voice and am tempted to make my share go on and on because it pleasures me to hear all the wisdom overflowing out of me and into the rooms to instruct the people.'

'Fair enough.'

'Ah,' said Benson, like Archimedes straight out of the bath, 'but in the room there is someone who has just bored us rigid for half an hour about the illness, death, burial and mourning for her dead cat. What was the motivation behind my confession about long shares? Why, to stick the knife into the cat-lover is what. Sometimes silence is the only true honesty.'

'Any news?' Allan asked.

Benson was silent, though he could have given a potent and lengthy honest share about Distraction. At last he replied, 'I've bought a big pot of latex.'

'What's that?'

'It's liquid rubber.'

'What are you going to do with it?'

'Well, I thought I'd make garden statuary with it. What you do is paint the latex on, say, the marble faces of statues. You've got to keep putting layers on, coat after coat, until you have a mould of the face. Then you peel it off and pour cement into the mould, wait a few hours and pull the mould off: Bob's your uncle, you've got a copy of the face. Then – and this is the best bit – you can make as many copies as you like in no time at all.'

'Why?'

'Well, Muriel says that people are always looking for statues for their gardens. Of course, the idea is still in its early stages.'

'Who's Muriel?'

'She owns this craft shop in Loggerheads,' Benson said. 'Didn't I ever mention Muriel to you? She used to be my main outlet for the pyrography work I did. I must have mentioned Muriel. She went off to Kuching – that's in Borneo – for one last look to see if her hubby was still alive. No sign of him. She's come back and started proceedings to pronounce him dead.'

'Doesn't ring a bell,' Allan said. Then he saw Benson about to put his coffee mug down on the table. 'There's a coaster there, Martin,' Allan said.

'Thanks for that. Wouldn't want to make any rings on the table.'

'I've made great strides with my comrades here,' Allan said. 'But you've got to keep at it.'

'A day at a time...'

'Exactly.'

'So what happened to the pyrography?'

'Juvenilia,' Benson said. 'I've moved on. I want an art form that will outlast me. Pyrography fades so quickly. Cement on the other hand...'

'You think cement doesn't rot? Have you seen those flats on the front?'

'Which flats?'

'The Colonnades.'

'What's wrong with them? They're really pricy.'

'They're coming down.'

'Really? Well, it just goes to show...'

'It does.'

'I know. Still, I thought I'd give it a go. I tried going back to pyrography but the inspiration had gone somehow, then the heat regulator broke and I reckoned my Higher Power was trying to tell me something.'

'So what statues are you going to copy?'

'There are some lovely ones in the cemetery.'

Allan looked at Benson oddly. 'So you're going to paint latex on people's memorial statues?'

'Just the faces. First things first. My book says that latex moulds have to be reinforced to accept depth without deformation. I thought painting faces around the cemetery would give a focus to a nice evening walk.'

'Have you got permission?'

'No.'

'Don't you think you should?'

'Don't see why. The latex won't damage the statues.'

'But that's hardly the point, is it?' Allan said. 'What are loved ones going to say when they see rubber all over the faces of angels and stuff?'

'Anyway, Allan, how are you?'

'Are you trying to get off the hook, Martin?'

'I mean, you're well in yourself?'

'Let me be an example to you,' Allan said.

'I take your point,' Benson said. 'But when you think of all the statues in the cemetery missing wings, heads, arms and legs, covered in spray paint, etc., then my latex copying is an enhancement rather than a subtraction. I am carving a plus where people have scrawled a minus...' He saw Allan's reaction to that, did not like it, and added, 'At least I think so.'

'But it's not *legal*, Martin! It was you who taught me what rationalisation meant. I wish I'd listened. But it looks as if the preacher is not obeying his own teachings.'

419

'I suppose that's true,' Benson said. Then, not meaning it at all, he added, 'Thank you for that.'

'Ah,' said Allan. 'But will you put it into your life a day at a time?'

'I'll have a go,' Benson lied. 'I suppose I could try reproducing my Buddha head. I bought it in Bangkok. A lovely face, and it is my property.'

'There you are!' Allan said. 'When The Lord closes a door, somewhere he opens a window.' Use your own stuff! God knows your house is cluttered with all kinds of things that are begging to be *used.* All those African heads, Indonesian puppets...'

' "Cluttered" is not the word I'd use,' Benson said, 'You're probably right, though.'

'I think I am.'

'You are.'

Moving swiftly on, Benson turned to Allan's life in prison. 'Any adventures?' he asked lasciviously.

'I don't go short,' Allan said.

'No?'

'No.'

A silence. Benson waited, in vain, for details. But Allan was closed to all enquiry.

'Any thoughts about Step Nine?' Benson asked.

'Don't!' Allan said.

Rather pleased by Allan's discomfiture, and displeased with himself for being pleased, Benson said, 'It has to be faced. I mean, now you've made a list of all the persons you've harmed and become willing to make amends to them all. You have become willing, haven't you?'

'In theory.'

'In theory?'

'I'm praying for all the dog-owners. I did apologise in

court, didn't I? I did give every dog-owner a thousand quid, didn't I? That's cleaned me out. And I'm taking my punishment like a man, aren't I? What else can I do?'

'Busy Sandra...' Benson said, half-hoping that mentioning the name of the one person Allan could not abide being reminded of would both get back at him and get him back onto a more exciting topic.

'How is she?' Allan asked, sweet as a nut.

'She's got early medical retirement. Don't see how. She hardly uses her Zimmer. It's covered in cards, soft toys and similar kitsch, but it's not as if she uses it for support. It's more of a fashion statement. I reckon she's as fit as a flea.'

'But you and I both know that the face we present to the world can be very deceiving. Look at me, for instance. The best thing we can do is pray for Busy Sandra.'

'Yes, of course,' Benson said.

'But I can't imagine myself going up to each and every dog-owner and apologising. Remember how they were when I was taken away in the paddy wagon?'

Benson did. It had not been an edifying sight. The stone-and-dog-turd-throwing crowd had made no secret of the fact that they'd like to see Health-and-safety Allan hanging from the nearest lamp post.

He'd provided a character reference for Allan and been a witness for the defence. Not that he defended his actions, but he had been able to hint at the problems Allan had, and the dangers of ever-festering resentments. He'd been hauled across the coals in cross-examination but had held up quite well, he thought, listing example after example of the festering power of resentment and self-righteousness in the world...'

'I won't be able to go back to New Brighton,' Allan said.

421

'No. Might be better if you made a new start. If I were you, I'd retrain. Do something as far away from Health and Safety as you can. I'm thinking of becoming a carer. Home visits and that.'

'Are you?'

'Yes.'

\* \* \*

Benson left Allan, wondering about it all. Allan had changed, but the change had brought out more of the old Allan. He was busy transforming his old Health and Safety obsessions into himself as teacher by example. Self-righteousness was rearing up. Was he, Benson, like that as well? Was he in the middle of his honesty becoming burdened with an enormous dose of self-righteousness? He could see it in Allan clear as day, but often he could not see it in himself. At times, though, he could.

He'd done a recce of the cemetery, looking out for likely faces to brush with his latex, while tutting at the broken statuary, the dog-dirt, the laid-down corpses with their health and safety notices. Not My Business. But the QA experience also contained the words that had given him consolation at the start and continued so to do. *No one among us has been able to maintain perfect adherence to this programme. We are not saints. The point is that we are prepared to grow along spiritual lines.* Perhaps it was just as well that he, Rob, and Allan showed forth this total inability to be perfect. Think where feeling perfect led! He'd be a complete and utter prat. He *was* a complete and utter prat, even on his better days. His life sat behind him, a chronicle of wasted time, a boring bun with an occasional bit of mean dried fruit to keep it from total inedibility. But ... He Knew. He knew himself well enough to be able to see what Whitman had seen.

> *I too knitted the old knot of contrariety,*
> *Blabb'd, blush'd, resented, lied, stole, grudg'd,*
> *Had guile, anger, lust, hot wishes I dared not speak,*
> *Was wayward, vain, greedy, shallow, sly, cowardly,*
>     *malignant,*
> *The wolf, the snake, the hog, not wanting in me,*
> *The cheating look, the frivolous word, the adulterous wish,*
>     *not wanting,*
> *Refusals, hates, postponements, meanness, laziness, none of*
>     *these wanting,*
> *Was one with the rest, the days and haps of the rest,*

These words in 'Crossing Brooklyn Ferry' gave the lie to William James's theory that Whitman had lauded Evil along with Good in his poetry. Benson had been shocked to hear Walt so calumnied and would have, had James still lived, pyrographed the lines from *Brooklyn Ferry* and sent them to him. He thought of those lines most days. They consoled him, for they ended by placing him in the centre of the conundrum of what it meant to be human.

On his way out, Benson saw a prisoner mopping up the reception area. The man was bald and had a tattoo on his forehead, and Benson knew who it was straight away.

Without pausing for thought, Benson approached the man. 'Hello,' he said. 'Remember me?'

The man stared back at him. Then he smiled. 'You 'ere too?'

'No,' Benson said. 'Just visiting. Mind you, there but for fortune, and all that.'

The man nodded. He looked around. 'Come regular, do you?'

'Yes,' Benson said. 'I expected to see you again on the beach. But you never showed up.'

'Busies nicked me ski,' the man said. 'Banged me up as well.'

'Sorry,' Benson said, looking at *Lethal Weapon* on the convict's forehead.

The warder at Reception was giving Benson looks. 'If you come back, could you bring me some Dairy Milk?' the man asked.

'What if I don't see you?'

'Give it to the man at the desk. Say it's for Rod – me name's Roger Norrington. Chocolate stops me rattlin'.'

'Rattlin'?'

'Yeah. Rattlin'.'

'I'll do that,' Benson said. 'Sorry for the misunderstanding on the beach.'

'*You're* sorry! It got me banged up. Sort of.'

'But it wasn't me that barged through the gate!'

'No.'

'I'll bring you chocolate, Rod.'

'Ta,' Rod said. He got back to his mopping as the man at the desk stood, preparing to come over.

'All the best, Rod,' Benson said.

He made for the door. The warder buzzed him through it, giving Benson a stern look.


As he rode back to Rob, Benson repeated 'Roger Norrington'. He'd heard the name before. *Dairy Milk!*

*Remember Dairy Milk!* Then he thought of Allan striving after virtue in gaol. Those baby steps that were one forward and nine-tenths of a step (if he was lucky) back. But no reason for him to think any the less of Allan. For, as Allan had pointed out, Benson had his own share of darkness. He was, like pretty much every soul on the planet, an eternal early dawn or late twilight.

It was so different from Benson's experience of spiritual things as a Catholic kid. The image of the soul of man as a white sheet spotted by sin, blackened and festering through mortal sin, had been replaced by an indefinite power greater than self to whom he could turn for help. What that was, Benson had little idea. He intimated it only.

He turned his thoughts back to Muriel. Rob had told him a couple of weeks before that she was back, and in good form. He might ring to welcome her. No need to mention the fate of his pyrography, unless she did.

Shaking a bit, Benson lifted the receiver, dialled the number and found Muriel pleased as Punch to imagine his jolly old eek on the end of the line. She'd loved Kuching and, though the search for Captain Jones had yielded no results – this after many trips up wonderful rivers, and up to mountain peaks- she had found amazing craft to bring back and sell at her shop. She had contacts and felt confident that the tribal rattan and carvings of Borneo, together with the most wonderful batiks, would go down a bomb at the shop in Loggerheads.

'I've been a bit busy. I haven't done much in the way of pyrography,' Benson said. 'Poundland stopped stocking wooden breadboards. They're all plastic now. And the transformer on the pen is playing up.'

It was then that Muriel suggested garden statuary as a way forward.

As soon as she said it, he saw his production ending up ground down into potholes, being disposed of in all sorts of utilitarian ways ... anything to stop them deflowering a garden ... but he'd said nothing.

'I'm sorry you didn't find Captain Jones,' he said.

'I'm not really surprised,' Muriel said. 'I had to give it one last go, though. If I'd found him lying on a hammock in the midst of a pretty family with a pretty brown wife fanning his fat stomach, I'd probably have killed him. I didn't. Absolutely no news about him. I met the owner of the guesthouse he'd stayed at. She returned a knapsack of clothes he'd left there on the day he disappeared. But, despite all your pyrographed notices – which received many compliments, I have to say – nothing but a big fat zilch.'

She now could declare to the powers-that-be, the family, and to herself, that Captain Jones was lost for good. Perhaps he was dead in the literal sense: perhaps he still drew breath, but was no longer Captain Jones. Either way, he was, at long last, dead to her. Benson wondered if that finality brought Muriel grief, relief (and with it, guilt), or simple resignation. Benson got home, saw to Rob, and decided to pop in on Laurence Clitherow, armed with *Under the Volcano*.

'My name's Martin, and I'm a grateful member of the fellowship of Queer Alchies ... and a recovered alcoholic,' Benson said.

He had not been asked in advance to open the proceedings. Banker Pete approached him five minutes before the start of the meeting, and asked him to step into the breach as the scheduled fellow hadn't shown up. Benson didn't say no, though he'd have liked to just sit quietly and retire into the garden of his soul – replete with his statuary of course – and sip the insipid tea.

But, as soon as he was asked, the topic that had been going through his head for some time came seamlessly to the surface:

'I've been thinking about work recently. I've got a summer job in the beach lifeguards as a bye-laws officer. I check permits, give advice about state of the tides, safety equipment. That sort of thing. But there's a lot more to the job than that. There are people to be told how to find a public toilet, litter to be picked up, lonely people to be talked to ... an endless flow of little tasks that surround the job but which are not on the job description. I can choose to do these extras or look away, and out to sea. So the work is more than the job. Lots of jobs seem 'small'. 'You'll end up as a binman!' You've heard it. I've heard it. But what more useful job than a binman! Same goes for working on a checkout. There's a world

427

of difference between the ones who 'just do the job' and those who make each and every person who they come into contact with feel better. A smile. A kind word. A bit of human contact and interaction lifts the lowly and mechanical job into the realms of the spiritual. This is what I have learned from my humble job. I wish I had realised the truth of it many decades before I did.

'I didn't need an excuse to drink. Looking back at the Step-work I've put in, I drank on resentment. Drink blunted the pain of life when I was under the influence. Hangovers were a different story. And I spent much of my adult life hung over and jaded. For the alchy, alcohol gives with one hand and takes with the other. It says, when you're in the middle of withdrawal and fighting a beat-up liver, 'I'll make you better. I can fix you!' So day after day, week after week, month after month, year after year, decade after decade, the daily ritual of the first drink leading to the tenth, the passing out, the waking up to a world that pisses the drunk off something shocking, that sends him to his work – if he has any – feeling the job is only the fucking job; wasting his precious time with hopeless negatives that frighten all spirituality away and anchor the poor drunk in past injury. For me, it was a Catholic childhood that obsessed me. I hated a lot of what had been seared into me, while I let its indoctrination hold its power. These days I no longer feel resentment against the Church. It simply fell away as I got a hold on what had made me tick throughout my life. If I was powerless over my alcoholism, and so much else, then all the unhappy teachers I'd had, all the celibate old men who had pushed the notion of hell and damnation into the nub of me, had felt the same things. They had handed on their misery to me because they'd had misery handed on to them. It is breaking the cycle – throwing away the bathwater, but cherishing the baby – that this fellowship is about. Alcohol is but a symptom of the disease of humanity. Many aspects of my personality could have brought me to my knees: lust, envy, sloth, pride, fear … but it was the disease of my alcoholism that finally managed it. I at last realised my powerlessness to change. After thousands of hungover mornings of 'never again' – you all know the way of it – I finally realised I was washed up as a human being so long as I drank. I was told by the man who brought me into QA that I need never drink again. And, a day at a time, I have not. He did not tell me then, though he never stops telling me these days, that my sobriety is conditional on my willingness to surrender to Something Outside Myself, and do the work. And what does this work consist of? Why, acquiring self-knowledge, finding out what makes Martin tick, and ridding myself of my grosser handicaps. Then passing it on to others. What an order!'

'Well, yes and no. It is a challenge, but it is also very sweet and deeply rewarding to follow a path that inclines ever so gently in an upwards direction. These days, I have a handle on myself. I can often see where I'm going wrong. And where right. There is no place for pride, or even the wank of a pat on my own back, in all this. I have – some of the time – an awareness of who I am, why I act as I do, or don't act as I ought … and I have the tools to mend things, if I choose to pick them up and trudge with them.

'I heard it said once that we at QA are seeking to obtain slowly the spiritual insights that alcohol gave us speedily. I can't argue with that. I feel different because every day contains surprises and insights, as long as I am open to them. There is a joy now in a few things done well.

'Recently, I met – as a result of a chance meeting at work – an old friend from my late teenage years. His name is Laurence and he and I were best friends when I was in the sixth form at St Bede's. We lost touch when he went to Oxford and studied medicine. Both his parents were doctors, so I suppose it was bred in the bone. Anyway, back then, Laurence and I were blood brothers. We fought a war against Catholicism at St Bede's. We were revolting together. We had a bit of adolescent sex together, too, though I always had the feeling he wasn't really gay. At least not in the way I was.

'But we lost touch. I thought of him. I thought of getting in touch. What stopped me? Fear, embarrassment, the feeling that he'd have a better job ... on and on.

'We met a couple of weeks ago. Laurence became a doctor. He specialised in diseases of the ear, nose and throat and became a consultant. He married and had a family. And he went back to The Church. Two years ago his wife died, and he retired. A year ago he had a stroke that has left him pretty much bed-ridden at home. Carers come in twice a day and his family do what they can. So Laurence is physically incapacitated. Luckily, he is regaining the power of speech and his mind is sharp.

'I go to see him every day. When I'm with him the years drop away and I am back in that small nub of time when my spirit was at its liveliest, when the old Martin Benson seemed to be dropping away for good and life was full of possibilities and boundless energy for the search for Dearest Him. I thought then that the whole of my life would be as fresh as those late teenage years. It didn't happen like that.

'Laurence has given me a spiritual experience. In 1967, before most of you were born, I worked as a nurses' assistant in New York. I felt then that the job suited me. It was more than the work. Emptying bedpans, irrigating stomas, giving bed baths, ministering to the sick in all those hands-on ways, lifted me. There was skill in managing these tasks without causing embarrassment to the patient. There was a feeling that here was a reason for living. But I believed the wisdom of the world. What was that sort of job for a fellow studying for a B.A. Hons?

'Laurence puts up with his carers. I've watched them, and often been tempted to tell them that they are seeing the job only as a job, and have swallowed the world's view that it is lowly. It is not. Done well, done with every bit of brain and heart power we can bring to it, it is a job that in a world without illusion and snobbery would be seen as the highest vocation. To do it well, and with love, is to heal the world a person at a time, and heal oneself.

'I don't know if this makes any sense to you. I think it probably does. Anyway, I've decided when the season on the beach is over to enrol in a caring course. Perhaps in a few months you'll see me dressed up in a uniform and marching from one New Brighton house or flat to another en route to my next 'client'. Or maybe I'll become Laurence's carer. That is my preference, I have to say, because the friend I lost for all those years ago when I was too lost to be found will be there and we'll have great laughs together. He'll puncture my delusions when I come over all St Francis-ish and, while I make myself useful, I'll be able to keep the radio on Radio Three ... the carers he's got insist on Kiss FM.

'We are not saints. I saw Allan a couple of days ago.

431

He's sober and trying to get his fellow inmates to observe elementary rules of health, safety and personal hygiene. He asks to be remembered to you all.

'Thanks. And I mean that.'

# 60

The time for Blackpool came. A weekend of QA meetings and get-togethers: bingo, quizzes, a quarter marathon that took in all the landmarks of Blackpool and St Anne's, all meals provided, and this to be followed on Monday by Jack and Bill, Rob and Martin, slipping off to the Town Hall to enter into civil partnership – this to be rounded off by a trip to the funfair, an Indian meal, a sober bike-ride home.

The weekend was just what Benson needed, the hotel filled to the gunnels with queer alchies, the pool and sauna a place of some excitement. Of course, Benson – readying himself to be the blushing civil partner – did not partake of what he felt was definitely on offer, but he took hold of the atmosphere and squeezed it tight.

To be surrounded by people like himself for two whole days! Queers who were recovered alcoholics with roughly the same take on life gave him an inkling of what heteros took as their birthright. He had gone through life seeing everything through a different lens. He didn't get the nuances of male to female attraction and all the things that went with it: the fashions, ads, art, jokes, needs. It was wearing sometimes, not to fit in, not to be a part of the great worldwide dance of attraction and reproduction which led – sometimes – into an ordered routine of work, rest and play, worry about kids, and so on down to their kids and on and on.

But here in their little enclave, the fellows of QA could be themselves and relax. They could talk about the straight world for what it was: a queer world where, as in a foreign country, they did things differently. They could share their pains, worries and incomprehensions about that world, while exercising in the common ground of their own. It made a big difference, this tiny forty-eight hours in a ghetto of like-mindedness and common purpose.

There were speakers at the meetings. Some of them had travelled great distances to be with them. They had been asked to come – unpaid – because of their wit and their ability to pass on the message of QA in the manner of the after-dinner speaker. The laughter in the great auditorium, he thought, could be heard all along the promenade, might cause the donkeys to bolt, the waves in the brown sea to fall back on themselves in surprise, the Tower to detumesce in order to bend and listen.

In smaller meetings – and meetings went on all day and all night – people shared their experience, strength and hope with strangers. They tried to be honest and, if they were honest, to find a friend.

Benson came out about his forthcoming civil partnership and how afraid he felt sometimes. People came in and said how afraid they'd felt, but how glad they were to have taken the step.

The weekend ended with a great ball. Benson danced with all and sundry, throwing his pelvic thrust at anyone in the vicinity for their amazement and admiration until his lower back went funny. Then he had a snogging session with Rob on the sidelines and told Rob that he loved him. Rob said he'd see him upstairs in half an hour. He'd come in and find Benson rifling through his panniers. Well, that couldn't be allowed to go without comment.

Benson fell asleep on the bed, and woke up to find Rob's alarm-clock cock pushing itself between his lips.

They were second in line for civil partnership, behind Jack and Bill. But they knew the other two couples by sight from the weekend, and accompanied them into the room. A Lord Mayor looked down on them from the wall.

A young woman presided, and she did not seem in the least fazed. She put everyone at their ease.

They made their vows, and Rob – despite his previous rejection of the idea – slipped a Hopi silver ring onto Benson's finger, and produced an identical one for Benson to put onto his. They signed all the papers, then walked out of the building where a sun dodged white clouds rolling in like groups of wandering friends from Ireland.

With Jack standing behind Bill's wheelchair and watching from a safe distance, The Big One, Blackpool's legendary roller-coaster, set off up the steep ascent with Rob and Benson sitting hand in hand at the front. 'I'm not sure about this,' Benson said.

'Relax and fuckin' enjoy it,' Rob replied.

Well, Benson thought. There's nothing to complain about thus far. I'll just stay in the miracle of the present moment. Surely I can manage this if I anchor myself in each trice of time. I am powerless to change things. As soon as I stepped aboard The Big One I surrendered control of my life for the length of the ride. True, the thing is going higher than I'd like, but at a snail's pace. It – and therefore I – definitely feel in control. This ride, like everything else, is in the hands of my Higher Power.

Now I know that once it reaches the top it's going to speed up a bit, but I can cope with that, can't I? I've coped – sort of – for sixty years after all…

The slow climb, like the steps and the decisions he had taken, the slow turning of the gummed-up cogs of his brain, reached the top. There was sea, with its own rule of Twelve Parts, its drops beads that banded the world with the Ariel wind as overseer. But in the immediate future of the ride, there was no reassuring rail to contemplate. That reassuring rail with its serious bolts and, he was almost certain, daily maintenance and rigorous health and safety checks by people for whom the work was more than the job – had disappeared. He thought of Allan, banged up and facing God knew what in his future. He wished him well, promised him ongoing succour. *And Laurence! And Dairy Milk for Rod!*

Where was he? There was nothing but a sea view and Rob beside him. *Rob beside him.* He tightened his hand grip and the car came to the drop. He saw what was coming, did not like the approaching kink in the rail one little bit and wanted out. But thought stopped and prayer started then as they were into it and past it and his stomach had shifted, the candy floss coming back in a sweet deep-pint-slurped-back burp and the car kept accelerating. Beyond his control.

Jiggle and jar, nausea and G-force. So that is what the poor astronauts felt! They were supposed to be made of The Right Stuff. Well, he wasn't ever going to be made of whatever was in that recipe for right stuff. When would it end? When? Judder and lurch. Shudder and strain. Twist and cramp. This was most unpleasant! And people paid good money for this, did they? He saw the people below looking up at him and Rob on their cross.

But the worst was over. After the fall, the car used its own momentum to cruise back to earth, with its occupants vowing never again, or let's join the queue to do it again, or, swank their achievement about, to show the photograph of themselves off to prove they'd dared. He'd buy one of himself and Rob together on the ride. He'd buy a frame, too – something very Blackpool and camp – and pyrograph a pithy sentence onto it. He'd put it up on the wall in the kitchen.

Condenser Jane, who had recommended the ride to them, said that they took the photo when the car went into a tunnel close to the end. Time to compose himself and show a bright, post-civil-partnership, face to the world. But a sudden series of jolts and jiggles that set fear off once again distracted Benson, and the tunnel was on him in the middle of a panic. He saw a flash. That must have been it. How had he looked? Would he come out posed and composed? He'd been fine until the inconsiderate jiggle. Had his photo-friendly face survived that?

Rob helped Benson off the ride. The boardwalk moved. He took a step forward, but it turned to a sideways lurch. 'That was good, wasn't it?' Rob said.

'Not bad,' Benson said.

'Suppose you'll want a snap, won't you?'

Rob and Martin waited about for the photos to be developed. At last they came down a slide and Benson saw the one intended for him. Rob looked like Rob. No fear. Just Rob on a ride. Benson on the other hand had been caught in mid-pose between assumed serenity and abject panic. Behind his snap came those of the noisy revellers. Arms in the air, ecstatic faces. Clearly posed,

437

Benson thought. They knew exactly where the camera was. They'd had time to prepare their plastic smiles, their macho 'look-no-hands' poses. Someone had warned them about the jiggle. Condenser Jane hadn't warned him about the jiggle ... just as she never warned clients about the draw-backs of changing boilers. Or maybe his fellows had been serene throughout.

'I'll buy it for you,' Rob said. 'They certainly know how to charge, though.'

Benson looked at the photo again. 'No, let's leave it.'

Rob shrugged. 'That's not like you,' he said.

'No,' Benson said, as Rob walked behind him with both hands on Martin's shoulders, guiding him down the exit ramp to stop him veering drunkenly against the side rail and the pleased crowd.

Rob was right. The panicked picture was just not a good likeness. He did not know himself. Rob asked him why he hadn't bought it.

'Don't need it.'

'It wasn't bad of me.'

'No. Are you happy with the way things turned out?'

'Yeah. You?'

'Very,' Benson said, meaning it, way down to his nub. He saw Jack and Bill, all smiles and pithy comments re. the ride ready for sharing. And off they would go – if spared – for the meeting of QA at the Quaker Meeting House, only the effort of an easy chatty mile from The Big One.